FALLEN

FALLEN

A novel of Noreela

TIM LEBBON

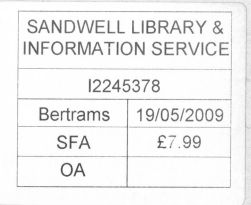

Allison & Busby Limited
13 Charlotte Mews
London W1T 4EJ
www.allisonandbusby.com

Hardcover published in Great Britain in 2008.
This paperback edition published in 2009.

A CIP catalogue record for this book is available from
the British Library.

10 9 8 7 6 5 4 3 2 1

ISBN 978-0-7490-7998-7

The paper used for this Allison & Busby publication
has been produced from trees that have been legally sourced
from well-managed and credibly certified forests.

Printed in the UK by CPI Bookmarque, Croydon, CR0 4TD

Born in London, TIM LEBBON has lived in South Wales since he was nine. He has always been interested in imaginary worlds, folklore and myth, and the supernatural. He started writing at an early age, and since the publication of his first novel, *Mesmer*, in 1997, Tim has gone on to have a dozen further novels published, as well as many novellas, and several collections of his stories. Now a full-time writer, Tim's work has won the British Fantasy Award three times – twice for Best Short Fiction and, in 2007, for Best Novel – as well as several other awards. He is a *New York Times* bestseller, and he has several novels and novellas under option with film companies on both sides of the Atlantic. He now lives in Monmouthshire with his wife and two children.

www.noreela.com

www.timlebbon.net

*With huge thanks to Howard,
Caspian and Danny, and to everyone at
Allison & Busby.*

Part One

The Final Voyage
Ten – Into the Wild – Betrayals

———————

'Humans crave knowledge, and when that craving ends,
we are no longer human.'

Sordon Perlenni, the First Voyager

CHAPTER ONE

Ramus Rheel hated the moment between sleeping and waking. It was a strange place, haunted by recent dreams and the ghosts of those long since passed, and he loathed it even more when one of the fading dreams was a good one. This latest had been about a voyage, though one he had not yet made. Dreams about voyages he *had* made were more usually nightmares.

He sat up and held his head as the dizziness filtered away and real life forced itself in. He was forty-four years old. He could recall a dream he'd had when he was six – sailing west from the shores of Noreela and finding the edge of the world – but he had already forgotten the one he'd just had. He wondered whether this was peculiar to him.

Yet what had woken him? It was not yet dawn, and the streets were still quiet. A dog whimpered somewhere and surreptitious footsteps echoed, but Long Marrakash was largely still asleep. And so should he be, if he knew what was best for him.

Something banged in the room next door. It was the main

room in his home and contained the only door onto the street.

He froze, listening hard. Another knock, wood against wood. *That was my chair being nudged into the table,* Ramus thought. He stood quickly, wincing as his knees popped, and reached back across his bed. He kept his leather weapon roll on a shelf above where he slept, but it had not been used for a while. He grabbed one trailing strap, pulled, and the roll unravelled onto the bed.

Something scraped across the floor, and he heard a muttered curse.

Ramus's heart was thumping. He'd had occasion to fight several times on his voyages, but he had never thought himself a fighting man. He had no grace of movement and his reaction speed was slow, and he had scars that bore testament to that.

He drew a short knife from the roll and knelt beside the bed, losing himself in deeper shadows.

'Ramus?' The voice was low and uncertain.

Ramus half-stood, then thought better of it. *Just because they know my name doesn't mean they're here for anything good.*

'Ramus, are you—?' Whoever had broken into his home tripped as they reached for his sleeproom door. They grunted, fell into the door and knocked it open.

Ramus pressed his knife to the invader's throat.

'Ramus, by all the gods, it's me!'

'Nomi?' Ramus fell back and dropped his knife, appalled. *Was I really going to slice her throat?* Maybe, maybe not. Like his dreams, his true intentions already seemed to be fading away, and for that he was glad.

'I think I've broken my wrist.'

'You scared the shit out of me, Nomi!'

'Can we have some light in here? I need to see if the bone's sticking out.'

'If the bone was sticking out you'd be doing more than whimpering about it.' Ramus stood and went to the window. He drew the curtain aside to let in death-moonlight, its pale yellow glow revealing more of the room's shape and depth.

Nomi was still sitting on the floor by the open door, nursing her left arm. 'Don't you have a lamp?'

'Running low on oil.'

'I'll give you some money for oil, Ramus.'

Ramus sparked his lamp and turned it up. He sheathed the knife and retied the weapon roll. Nomi mumbled something and Ramus looked at the back of her head. She seemed bedraggled and flustered, which was rare for her. Not good for her image.

'What are you doing here?' he asked.

'Came to see you.' Nomi held her hand up, flexed her fingers and sighed, seemingly happy that her wrist was not shattered.

'I doubt it'll even bruise,' Ramus said. 'Nomi, it's obvious that you've come to see me. But why break in? And why sneak around in my rooms like a thief?'

She stood and brushed herself down, smiling contritely. 'I suppose I look like a fool. But I came to tell you something. *Ask* you something.' She sighed, sitting on the bed and brushing loose hair back from her face.

'Spit it out,' Ramus said. Nomi had been to his home a hundred times before, but this was the first time she had been in his sleeproom. It made him uncomfortable.

'I'm not thinking straight,' she said. 'Give me a beat. Something like this doesn't happen every night.'

'You got humped!' Ramus said, mock-elated. He threw his hands in the air and reached for a bottle of wine on a shelf.

'Ramus, this is *important*!'

He popped the cork with his teeth and sat on a chair. 'Fine,' he said, taking a swig of wine. It was good – a gift from Nomi following her latest importation of Ventgorian grapes – but the first taste always made him cringe. He offered her the bottle and she accepted, taking a long draught herself. 'So tell me.'

'I met someone,' she said. 'Last night, just before midnight in the First Heart Wine Rooms. He looked exhausted, like he'd been walking forever. I knew he was a wanderer – there was a distance in his eyes, as though he'd seen things no one else could imagine. He looked around, then approached the bar and asked if they had root wine.'

'So, a wanderer ordered a drink. Are you going to get to the point?'

'Ramus, you have to meet him!' She stood and paced the small room, nervous and excited. 'I've arranged to meet for breakfast, down by the river. He has something he wants to sell, and I think we need to buy.'

'"We"? You know I don't have two pieces to rub together.'

Nomi waved at the air and shook her head, as though impatient. 'No, no, I'll pay. But you and I need to enter into this together.'

'Enter into what?'

'An agreement.' She sat again, never taking her eyes from Ramus. *I could get lost in that gaze,* he thought. He shoved the notion aside. He and Nomi had met ten years ago, and they were the most friendly enemies he had ever known. Competitors, jealous Voyagers, and so dissimilar that he sometimes wondered how they even spoke the same language. Yet he harboured emotions for her, keeping them so deep that even he was not certain of them, and sometimes he saw confused thoughts in *her* eyes. But he feared that they were merely reflections of his own.

'You're a mess,' he said. 'Look at you. Your trousers don't even match your jacket.'

'I got dressed quickly. Went home, couldn't sleep, then knew I had to come to see you.'

'Why? What has this wanderer got?'

Nomi's eyes burnt, her cheeks flushed and her lips pursed. A smile burst across her face. 'I won't tell you,' she said at last, the words bursting from her. 'But we need to agree—'

'Nothing, until I know what this is all about. How much money is involved?'

She shook her head and swigged from the wine bottle again. 'That's not important.'

Ramus pretended to collapse against the wall. 'Now you *truly* have me worried!'

'You'll see.' She stood and clunked the bottle back onto its shelf. 'You'll see, Ramus. Meet me at Naru May's for breakfast. You must hear what this wanderer has to say, and see what he has to show.'

'I do?'

'If you want to change your life, yes.' She glanced around the room, and for a second Ramus hated her; the look of disgust was bad enough, but the vague contempt in her voice was cutting.

Nomi left without another word, and Ramus was glad to see her go.

✳   ✳   ✳

Ramus had never thought of Nomi Hyden as a real Voyager. To him voyaging was a way of life, not a means to an end, and the wealth Nomi had gathered during and after her two voyages to Ventgoria had bought off whatever spirit she'd had to begin with. She was rich in coin but poor in heart, and that had always been a barrier between them. Ramus had little but knew much, and he strove to know more.

It had been over a year since he returned from his last voyage, bringing back maps, charts, plant samples, three books and a collection of myths from the Widow in the mountains. The mountains had no name, and neither did the woman, but she claimed to be adept at magichala – rich in the knowledge of the plants, animals and seasons of her land – and he was beginning to believe her claim. He had made three voyages into her mountains, and each time she showed him more.

He craved to go further. He had voyaged across the north of Noreela: the Cantrassan coast, Pengulfin Woods, and two sea journeys out to some of the unnamed islands of The Spine. And though his *real* vision took him past the mountains, past the Pavissia Steppes and into the uncharted areas to the south, he had no money to hire Serians to guard his way, and the Guild of Voyagers would not aid him. Most of them thought he was a minor Voyager given to mad dreams.

He simply wanted to be the best.

With Ramus filled with thwarted desires, Nomi angered him. Her money could take her anywhere, yet she had only ever been to Ventgoria: the first time, he still believed, with a true sense of discovery; the second, simply to establish a continuing exportation of finest Ventgorian fruits, which now flavoured the wine that had made her name. She lived well on the proceeds.

And now, this. He was intrigued. He would not be able to sleep again that night, so he made himself some red root tea, took out some books – his own treasures – and began to read.

It was a mile down to the river. Ramus gave himself plenty of time.

He always enjoyed watching the city come awake. As the sun peered around the shoulders of the mountains to the east it seemed to cast life upon Long Marrakash, sending away the night things – and there were some, though most people did their best to ignore them – and giving the city back to the day. There was always a sense of enthusiasm about daybreak. Most people attributed this to the potential in the time to come, though some claimed it was thanks for the days gone by. A few, if questioned in one of the wine rooms after a few cups of root wine, would claim that it was gratitude for surviving the night.

She came to me in the night, he thought. That troubled him. *Whatever it is that's excited her, she came through the dangerous dark to invite me down here.* There were night blights that lived in shadows, and grew and shrank with them. There were the Stalkers, who slept by the day and made the darkness *their* time; normal people with abnormal desires, though many sought to make monsters of them. And there were other things: the wraiths of those long gone, and truer shadows that had a semblance of life. Long Marrakash was the heart of Marrakash, and Marrakash was the heart of Noreela, yet even here people vanished into the darkness and were never seen again.

But day was good, and dawn was the hour of worship, especially for those who worshipped commerce: traders and dealers rushing this way and that to reach their shops, Cantrassan street vendors shouting at their slaves as they pushed loaded wagons to market, egg sellers shrilling at their flocks as they wheeled extravagant perches through the crowds, wholesalers flitting from one shop to another as they muttered orders under their breath, and people sitting along the streets taking breakfast before a full day of buying and selling, trading and dealing, loaning and hiring.

There were also those who chose to give dawn's hour to their own particular gods. Ramus passed by several groups chanting and running their fingers over runes carved into the foundations of ancient buildings. Some claimed to understand what the runes meant, but Ramus knew that they were all but unreadable, the forgotten language of a vanished civilisation. Perhaps if the giant stones had been brought here in order and assembled in the correct sequence, they may have retained their meaning. But all across Long Marrakash, similar blocks were incorporated into buildings upside down and back to front. Most were badly weathered, and Ramus could not help looking down on those who worshipped them. The runes were the history of a long-dead people, their story spread across the city like crumbs from broken bread. Paying homage to such a tale was like worshipping dust.

Others crowded into temples built to the moon gods, or gathered around shamans in the street. Some of these shamans could read, and they held books as examples of their power. A few used such knowledge to twist the histories they read, telling stories to give themselves honoured backgrounds or imaginary ancestors, and Ramus despised such perversions of knowledge.

But he reserved greater hatred for those taken in by it.

Halfway to the river he passed a relatively new building – perhaps only five generations old – that housed a shrine to the Sleeping Gods. It was a simple stone structure without windows, a variety of symbols carved on the outside, a glow emanating through the door from the hundreds of candles burning inside, and once again Ramus felt its draw. *I have my own beliefs,* he would tell himself and anyone interested enough to listen. *The God of Knowledge, and the power of the land. Nobody tells me what to think.*

Still, sometimes he considered going inside. The Sleeping Gods had long been a fascination for the Voyagers, ever since the first Voyager, Sordon Perlenni, had set out to discover their legend one hundred and forty-three years before. He had returned again and again, from different parts of Noreela, but all he had ever brought back were more scraps of campfire myth. Some said those benevolent gods were Noreela's First, its founders and shapers, and that they had gone down to sleep – and left Noreela open and available – when the humans arrived.

Perlenni had vanished over a century before, and some believed he had found what he was seeking. Others suspected he had simply been swallowed into the distant parts of Noreela like so many Voyagers since.

A distant bell rang, and Ramus realised he would be late for his meeting with Nomi.

Naru May's was an expensive eatery built on a heavy timber deck over the River Kash, and Ramus only ever ate here with Nomi. He much preferred the food from street vendors back in the Heights – it was fresher, cooked better, and a tenth of

the price – but in the valley was where the wealth
congregated. He didn't mind venturing down here on
occasion, so long as Nomi paid.

He paused a hundred steps from the wooden bridge leading
out to the deck, taking in the scenery.

The riverside was bustling. Fishing sloops bobbed on the
waves, nets cast, and a few had already offloaded their
morning's catch. The scent of fresh fish filled the air, and a few
impromptu auctions had started.

Along the riverfront, traders had set up stalls, and the
largest was run by a dozen heavily tattooed Cantrass Angels
selling fine woven cloth: silk so sheer it was almost weightless,
rugs, and decorative hangings. Some of the women were
naked – clothed only in the complex and mystical tattoos –
and their stall was busy. Ramus had never trusted their kind.
There was far more going on with them than anyone ever saw,
and he believed that one day they would be revealed as
something more than simple weavers and traders. And indeed,
buying and selling was not the only exchange occurring at
their stall. While ten women displayed, two stood back in the
shadows, examining the crowd with dark eyes and making
cryptic marks on their bodies. Black ink, traced there using
the claws of mountain wolves.

Ramus was certain their tattoos changed day by day.

Further along the riverside a couple of transport boats
nudged against the stone quay, their decks dark with piled
cages of differing types and sizes. Ramus could smell the
animals from here, and not all of the smells were familiar.
Sheebok was the strongest – the rich, pungent stench of shit
and fear from a species that seemed to know it was bred only
for eating. But there were other, wilder scents, and he debated

whether or not to investigate. The trade in exotic food was increasing as the Age of Expansion pushed the borders of civilisation ever-southward, and he had often commented to Nomi that some people were too greedy to consider the dangers of what they were bringing back. She had laughed at him, of course. *A goat from here is the same as a goat from there,* she'd said. But he had reminded her of her own voyages to Ventgoria, and what she had seen there, and her expression had clouded for a few beats before she waved his concerns away.

He had heard of ravens existing far to the south that stole dreams. Pecked holes in skulls while their victims were asleep. Bring a few mating pairs of those things to Long Marrakash and—

'Ramus!'

He blinked, looked at the wooden bridge and saw Nomi standing there. A tall, slender man stood behind her, head bowed. She beckoned Ramus over.

'Ramus, this is Ten.'

Ramus nodded at the tall man. 'First name, last, or one in between?'

'Only name,' Ten said.

Ramus held out his hands and, after a brief pause, the man grasped them in his own. 'Good travels,' Ramus said.

Ten smiled, a hint of mockery behind the leathery mask of his face.

'Let's eat!' Nomi said. 'I'm starving. I hear they caught a cloud of river plumes last night. Shall we?'

Nomi went first and, after an awkward moment, Ten followed. Ramus came last, using the time it took them to reach Naru May's to examine the man.

He really was a wanderer. Ramus had been doubtful last night, but the man's true nature was obvious. The mix of clothes, skin leathered by the sun and elements, neutral accent – although Ramus thought he'd detected a twang of the Pavissia Steppes somewhere in there. Ten also exuded the vague superiority projected by every wanderer when they visited a settlement, especially one as large as Long Marrakash. The feeling was often well earned; the average wanderer had seen more than most Noreelans.

It was also rare that they lived into old age. The dangers of Noreela would take them – the harsh elements, clashes with other wanderers, nomadic tribes or marauders, or falling prey to some of Noreela's deadlier wildlife. This man looked ten years Ramus's senior, which Ramus could respect. He carried a long bow over his left shoulder, a quiver of arrows across his back and a short, wide sword in a scabbard strapped to his leg. Ramus could hear the clinks of other weapons secreted beneath his cloak.

They took a table close to the edge of the deck and a server hurried across, ignoring the outstretched hands of several other patrons.

'Savi,' Nomi said, 'it's a good morning, and we have a guest. I want a bowl of sautéed river plumes, a selection of bread, a bottle of cydrax...' She looked at Ramus, eyebrows raised.

'Sheebok testicles?' Ramus asked. The girl nodded, then looked at Ten.

The tall man said nothing.

'And a bowl of plumes for my guest,' Nomi said. 'And Savi? The good plumes. Make sure they haven't dried out.'

'Of course, Mam Hyden.' The girl hurried away to the

covered kitchen at the corner of the deck.

'You might as well own this place,' Ramus said.

Nomi shrugged. 'Ten, this is the man I was telling you about.'

'The Voyager?' Ten looked at Ramus, appraising him for the first time. 'Where have you been?'

For a heartbeat Ramus was ready to curse him. But he sensed Nomi's tension, her simmering excitement, and he was intrigued. Piss, he was more than intrigued, he was *interested*.

'My main interest is the unnamed mountains, bordering Ventgoria and—'

'I know where they are,' Ten said. 'Where else?'

'Pengulfin Woods,' Ramus said. 'The Cantrassan coast. Some of the islands of The Spine.'

Ten nodded thoughtfully. 'I've been to the Divide.'

The table fell silent. Ramus held his breath, waiting for Ten's expression to break into a mocking smile, but it did not. His eyes were cool, his mouth downturned.

Nomi's eyes glittered.

'No one has been there and returned,' Ramus said.

Ten snorted and rolled his eyes. 'You believe that?'

'Of course. I know that. I'm a Voyager, of the Guild of Voyagers. I know three Voyagers who went south for the Great Divide over the space of ten years. No one has seen them again.'

'Haven't they?'

'Stop answering me with pissing questions!'

'Why?' Ten smiled, and Ramus realised he was playing the wanderer's game.

'What's it like there?' Nomi asked.

The wanderer looked past Ramus at the kitchen, lifting his

head and sniffing the scent of food on the air. 'That's part of my story,' he said.

'Is that where you found what you showed me last night?' Nomi asked.

'What *did* he show you?' Ramus was becoming frustrated that the stranger seemed to have taken control of the conversation. He likely spent nine-tenths of his life on his own, yet in company he had quickly and easily gained the advantage.

Nomi looked across the table at Ramus, jaw clenching as if ready to speak. But then she shook her head. 'It's for him to show and tell,' she said. 'But Ramus, you know I wouldn't have come to you with something trivial.'

'Not friends?' Ten asked, glancing from one to the other.

'We're Voyagers,' Ramus said.

'Ah. And voyaging doesn't allow friendships.' Ten took a spiced nut from the bowl on the table and chewed slowly.

That's right, Ramus thought. *He knows us well.* He glanced at Nomi and she looked quickly away.

Savi came with a bottle of cydrax and three mugs, and three plates balanced on her right hand and arm. She placed them on the table with a flourish. 'Anything else, Mam Nomi?'

Nomi indicated the two empty tables next to them. 'Some privacy would be good. Keep those tables free, if you will.'

Savi nodded, glanced at Ten and walked quickly away.

'Sweet.' Ten said.

'She's thirteen.'

The tall man shrugged.

'Why are you called Ten?' Ramus asked.

'I was my mother's tenth child.'

Ramus nodded thoughtfully and pushed the roasted

testicles around his plate. The sauce looked perfect, the meat tender and delicious. 'It's an unlucky number for some.'

'It was for my mother. She died having me.'

'I'm sorry.'

Ten chewed a huge spoonful of river plumes and sighed with delight. 'I never knew her,' he said through a full mouth. 'But she had a good life for a wanderer, and long, and I'm told she loved her children well.'

Ramus looked across at Nomi. She was spooning her food around the plate, frowning, tense and expectant. He could see the excitement there that had been so apparent last night, but this morning it was tempered by something else. Caution, perhaps? Or concern that this wanderer could take them for fools?

'Many people have seen the Great Divide,' Ten continued, his voice dropping slightly. He finished his mouthful and put his spoon down. 'Truly, I have seen it. But few who see it choose to talk about it. It's...frightful.'

'Huge?'

'Massive. Immense. But not only that. It bears its own awful gravity, that tears the wonder from you and replaces it with fear. It's the end of the world. At least, that's what legend says. But...there's more. Truly.' Ten frowned and shook his head, as if to loosen a memory. He poured a generous mug of cydrax, hesitated, then poured for Nomi and Ramus as well.

'Surely some who have seen it could talk about it? You are.'

'I have better reason than most.'

'And that is...?'

'The parchments,' Nomi said. 'You found them there.'

Ten nodded and took a deep swig of cydrax. He belched lightly and drank some more.

'Parchments?' Ramus asked. He hated being led along, but there was something behind this story and Ten's telling of it that rang true. Maybe it was Nomi's fascination and excitement. Or more likely, it was Ten's obvious discomfort.

'You read?' the wanderer asked.

'Of course. I'm a Voyager, and the mind is the greatest place to explore. The minds of others, too, when they choose to record what they think and know.'

Ten looked across at Nomi. She nodded. 'That's why I told him. Perhaps he can read the parchments.'

'Then they're worth something?' the wanderer asked.

And it all comes down to this, Ramus thought. *Money. Well, I'm glad Nomi is here.*

'Let me see them,' Ramus said, 'and—'

'You'll hear my tale first,' Ten said.

Ramus finished his food and leant back in his chair. The world went on around them. People ate and chatted, boats and sloops drifted along and across the river, traders traded and fishermen fished. But he suddenly felt more removed than usual.

He always felt like a visitor to Long Marrakash. He was driven to travel and explore – scratchy feet, his mother had called it – and whenever he lived in the city, even for two or three years at a time, it always felt temporary. Just somewhere to rest and plan his next voyage.

Nomi waved Savi over and ordered two more bottles of cydrax, and the three of them fell silent. Then Ten started talking, and Ramus experienced an instant of intense emotion: excitement, exhilaration, and the taste of a fresh voyage ahead.

❊   ❊   ❊

'I've spent a long time walking back and forth before the Divide,' Ten began. 'It draws you. I know I said earlier that it's...terrifying, but there's an attraction as well. It pulls you in and holds you close, and sometimes it just won't let go.

'The first time I saw it, I was about twenty. I had a run-in with a band of marauders on the Pavissia Steppes, and I went south to get away from them. I knew what was supposed to be there, but I was young and feisty, and I'd just killed my first man...'

He trailed off, pouring more cydrax and looking at Nomi and Ramus. *Trying to see if we're shocked*, Ramus thought. *Nomi is, I can see that. But I hope she won't give him the satisfaction.*

'Anyway,' Ten said, and drank some more. 'The feistiness didn't last. I got away from the marauders and kept going south. After a long time I found the Divide...or maybe it found me. It's a cliff that reaches into the sky.' He looked up into the clear blue above them, shaking his head. 'Here the sky has no scale. It's blue and beautiful, but there's no real sense of it. There, the Divide touches it, and seems to devour it. The cliff rises higher than the clouds, which seem to shroud its top permanently – if it even has one. It goes east and west as far as you can see, and disappears around the belly of the land. First time I saw it, I spent a whole moon camped a few miles from its base, thinking I would never get away. There was plenty of food; berry bushes, root crops, wild sheebok grazing along the foothills. I ate well. There were flying things that buzzed me, but they never came close again after I shot one down with my crossbow. In the evenings, I'd sit and listen to the tumblers rolling across the plains.' He took another drink.

Tumblers! Ramus thought. *I always thought they were*

legend! But still he reserved judgement. Ten was a good storyteller, yet perhaps that was *all* he was. Time, as Ramus's mother had said, would tell.

'That was when I first started thinking for myself. Until then, I'd never truly been a wanderer. I walked, yes. I travelled from here to there, but I spent most of my time simply surviving. There in the shadow of the Divide, I came alive. I spent the nights sitting by my fire and thinking on what the Divide could mean. What was at its top, if it had one? What was behind it?'

'There's nothing behind it,' Nomi scoffed.

'Then why is it called a Divide?' Ramus asked.

Ten smiled. 'So I sat there night after night, a good meal in my belly and the cool night air alive in my senses. I'd been drinking only water for a couple of moons, and I felt so much closer to the land. Almost as if I could plunge my hand into its loam and touch its magic.'

'Pah!' Nomi snorted. 'You're no magichalan.' She regarded such people with derision, Ramus knew, though he could never understand why. She was a Voyager and had seen many strange things in the marshes of Ventgoria. Why not believe in magic?

'No, I'm not. But the Divide makes you appreciate the potential in things. And this whole world is thrumming with potential.'

Nomi chuckled and took a sip of her cydrax.

'How long did you stay there?' Ramus asked.

'Three moons, camped in its shadow. At dawn I'd see a moment of sun, and then only dusk. After a while, I started thinking about finding where it ended.'

'I've always heard that there is no end,' Ramus said. 'That it goes on, out beyond Noreela's shores.'

'Maybe,' Ten said. 'But the closer I came to the eastern shore, the more treacherous the landscape became. Plain turned to marsh, and then bog. The bogs were venting poisonous gases, and there were creatures in there...huge. I never saw them, but I heard them, and I felt the ground shiver as they rose and rolled. So I worked northward, leaving the Divide's shadow at last. And by the time I reached the shore, I could no longer see the Divide. The bogs steamed, the clouds closed in, and wherever that cliff struck the coast was out of view.

'I would have stayed there, but the bog gas would have killed me eventually. And if not the gas, those things that lived there.' He opened the third bottle of cydrax. The alcohol seemed to be having little effect. 'I could hear them rising from the bog and dragging themselves towards me. Perhaps they were close. Or perhaps they were a long way off, and larger than I imagine. I didn't stay to find out.'

'Voyagers have tried sailing past the Divide,' Nomi said.

'Piss,' Ramus said. 'They've set out with that intention, but no one knows if they succeeded, because they've not been seen again.'

Ten nodded, a satisfied smile on his face.

'Maybe they're still sailing,' Ramus speculated.

'Or maybe,' the wanderer said, 'they're in the stomachs of the bog beasts, or at the bottom of the sea, or washed up rotting against the shore. Noreela is a hungry land.'

'You have a way of making it such an attractive place,' Ramus said, but his interest was piqued. 'Go on. What happened next?'

'I went west,' Ten said. 'I travelled again in the shadow of the Divide, heading for the western shores. I hoped that there

I would find what the east had hidden, but I was wrong.'

'What was there?' Nomi asked.

'A jungle. I started in, but the trees soon grew so close together that I could barely pass by. And there were creatures there, too. Spiders as big as my hand; snakes as thick as my thigh; ants; worms with teeth; flies that sucked my blood and left poison in its place. And other things, not animals. Not human. A *bad* place. I only touched its outer extremes, but I knew it went on for days.'

'So you went north?' Ramus asked. 'Tried to skirt the forest but keep the Divide in view? Only the forest grew north as well, and by the time you reached the western shores, the Divide was too far away to see?'

Ten stared at him for some time; so long that Ramus looked away, unnerved. 'You don't believe me,' Ten said.

'I've met a lot of wanderers in my time, and they're known to...elaborate.'

'Ramus,' Nomi said, her voice bearing a warning.

'I'm telling the truth,' Ten said. 'If any Voyager had made it back from that place, they'd tell you the same.'

'But you have more to tell,' Ramus said.

Ten glanced at Nomi, reached into his cloak and then decided against it. 'I'll tell you first,' he said. 'Then I'll show you.'

Ramus sat back and crossed his hands on his stomach.

'I walked back along the Divide. Camped here and there, ate well, listened to the tumblers in the north. It took me two moons to gather the courage to do what I knew I must.'

'You climbed,' Nomi said.

Ten nodded slowly. 'Up into the foothills first. And then, where the hills ended and the cliffs began, I started up.' He leant forward, elbows resting on the table, long hair hanging down to either side of his face. 'I never got very high, but I found signs that others had climbed before me.'

'What signs?' Ramus asked, but he could already guess.

'Bodies. Or what was left of them. Skeletons mostly, but some were…fresher. Looked as if they'd been chewed. And all badly broken, as if they had climbed higher, then fallen.'

'Fallen,' Ramus whispered. 'How many?'

Ten shrugged. 'Six? Eight? I climbed eight times at various points along the Divide. I made it three hundred steps high, maybe four hundred, and then…'

'No more routes,' Ramus said. 'Like the cliffs were never meant to be climbed.'

Ten shook his head. 'Not that, no. I could have gone further on at least two occasions. But every time I found a body, I lost my nerve.'

'So you never got as high as the clouds?'

'Nowhere near.'

'And no one else did, either?'

'I can't know that. If they did, and did not fall, then…'

'Maybe they're still climbing?'

'Or maybe they reached the top.'

'It's believed there is no top,' Nomi said.

'Of course,' Ramus said. 'If there *was* a top to the Great Divide, there would be something south of the cliff face. For most Noreelans, that's unthinkable. It's been a problem for thinkers for centuries. There are books full of it.'

'You've seen these books?' Ten asked.

'A couple. There's one in the Marrakash Library, not a mile from here. And I know people who keep books to themselves.'

'I could write one,' Ten said. 'And I could give it an ending.'

Ramus laughed again. 'You tell a good story, wanderer, but you need more than words and hearsay to…'

Ten reached into his cloak again, and this time his eyes were full of purpose. Nomi sat up straighter. She looked at Ramus, her eyes sparkling with something he had only ever rarely seen on her face: the thrill of discovery.

Ten brought out a rolled parchment, tied with a knot of leather.

'What's this?' Ramus asked.

The knot whispered as it came apart. 'I found these close to one of the bodies.'

'What are they?'

The wanderer flattened the parchment pages – three of them – across the table, his hands still obscuring the uppermost page. 'The body was broken,' he said. 'Every bone shattered, as though he or she had fallen from a great height.' He glanced around, sat back and revealed the pages. 'Perhaps all the way from the top.'

Ramus leant forward and turned his head, and for a heartbeat the images did not register.

And then he saw.

'Well?' Nomi whispered.

Ramus touched the top page and traced the first of the images. 'By every fucking god that ever touched Noreela!' he said.

'Not *every* god,' Ten said. 'Just this one.'

Ramus sent Ten away. Nomi objected, but Ramus gave her one of his harsh stares.

'Don't go elsewhere,' Nomi said. 'We're the Voyagers you need to deal with on this. I have the ear of Marquella, and he has the support of the Guild. If we feel that this is worth pursuing, I can ensure that you're paid everything you're due.'

Standing beside the table, the wanderer seemed taller than ever. The sun cast his shadow across Nomi's face, and she wondered what it would be like to live in shadow for ever. 'I'll be back at noon,' he said. But he seemed to find it difficult to leave the pages behind.

'You can trust us,' Ramus said.

'It's not about trust,' Ten said. 'I've had those with me for a long time.'

'We'll look after them,' Nomi said. She smiled her most charming smile, and the wanderer was looking at her as he walked away, not at what he had left behind.

Savi came to their table when he had left, and Nomi asked for some water and a bowl of river cherries. She felt like a treat.

'So what do you think?' she asked at last.

Ramus sat back in his chair, hands clasped in front of his face, eyes never moving from the parchment. His stubble was three days old, and Nomi could see the dirt beneath his fingernails. She knew the signs. He needed to go out again.

'How can we ignore this, Ramus?' she said passionately.

'It could be a hoax.' And there it was, his pissing cynicism, coming to the fore. He once told her something his mother had told him: *Everything is a lie until proven.* She hated that attitude, yet it gave him the endlessly inquisitive, questing mind that she so lacked.

'It's no hoax, Ramus. Look closer. You're a Voyager, and so am I. We have our differences, I know. But can't you see what this could be? The biggest find since Sordon Perlenni first went out! This could mean...' She swept her hand across the surface of the top parchment, wondering whose hand had hovered there to draw those images and symbols, and what it had looked like. 'This could mean a whole new race of Noreelans.'

'On top of the Divide?'

'Yes. And more, Ramus.' She pointed at the bottom corner of the second parchment, and at the curled thing, sleeping like an infant in its mother's womb. She'd already seen him eyeing the image and looking away again, terrified and excited. Her voice was a whisper. 'You know what that is.'

He looked at her, then back to the parchments. He stood quickly, his chair squealing back across the deck as he snatched them up. 'I have to examine these.'

'Ramus—'

'Why did you come to me?' he said, glaring at her.

Nomi could only be honest. 'You're the most brilliant person I know.'

Ramus dipped his head, acknowledging the fact rather than accepting the praise. 'Then let me take these to the library. I'll meet you back here a half before noon.'

Nomi watched him leave, the parchment rolled and hidden beneath his jacket. For a moment she went to call him back, offer to go with him. But books were Ramus's domain.

Nomi Hyden walked through the waterside market, trying to curb her excitement and think about all the arrangements she must make.

While Ramus examined the pages, she needed to put a voyage together.

Walking towards her home, unconsciously taking the quieter route so that she could think, the plan formed itself in her mind like a map. Naru May's was at the beginning, and at the end – two miles uphill to the south – was her home. Between those two points, other vital destinations began to take shape.

Nomi always thought this way – images, pictures, visions of what was to come. It came of being a dreamer, she supposed, but it was also a product of her map-making mind. A good map could light the way for even the most troubled soul. And a great map could change the lie of the land. Miss a troublesome street here, a run-down hovel there, and you altered the nature of the place you're mapping. Districts can be moved by a map-maker; not physically, but in the minds of all those who read their work. She could toy with people's perception of places, names and geographies, or she could make them see straight. Mostly she had no need for obfuscation, but sometimes having the talent could help.

She guessed she had gained this furtive approach to map-drawing on her first voyage to Ventgoria. There, nothing stayed the same. A path leading to this place one year would lead somewhere else the following year. A hill would become a marshy plain in the space of a long, wet winter, and ponds and pools drained and refilled with the frequency of leaves falling and fresh buds forming. It was a land that defied mapping, and those locals who would deign to talk to her blamed the steam dragons. They said the dragons came when the steam vents opened, snaked their way through the land just below the surface, straightening serpentine rivers and forcing hills of mud and stone from the sodden ground. And then they vented their steam and moulded the land into its new shape.

Nomi smiled at the stories, but she spent most of her first voyage there losing herself in the Ventgorian wilds. Even when she found a settlement, it might not be there the next day. The only things that seemed defined and fixed were the vast aerial grape plants, mile upon mile of vines networked between the Bole trees. The sun was hot and constant, the moisture from below billowing in occasional steam clouds, and she had found the best crop for the perfect wine.

The dependable plants had pinned her to the land, and their produce provided the wealth she now enjoyed.

If she walked fast and made her deals quickly, she would be back at Naru May's bathed, changed and ready to plan the voyage of her life.

With Ramus. That was exciting, but it troubled her as well. They had a complex history. So much time together, so many secrets. If she'd ever had siblings to compare him to, she might have thought of him as a brother.

Yet this was bigger than them. What Ten had brought would provide riches, glory, knowledge and danger enough for them both. And for the first time, the thought of what they were facing frightened rather than thrilled her.

Beko Havison lived in the basement rooms beneath a tavern. He was a Serian – a soldier from Mancoseria ready to sell his experience to the Guild of Voyagers – and he had accompanied Nomi on her second voyage to Ventgoria. It had been a relatively trouble-free journey, other than her sickness, but she had always seen the potential in him. They had talked a lot on that trip, and he had professed a love of free poetry, but the raw strength that had seen him through five voyages was obvious. He could talk endlessly about moonlight touching the stark branches of a lightning tree, but he could never hide his scars.

The tavern was still boarded up, and a drunk lay unconscious on its steps. Nomi thought of waking him and telling him that dawn had come and gone, but he did not look like the sort of man who'd take kindly to being surprised. There was a short curved knife in his belt, the blade keen, bone handle smooth and darkened from use.

She stepped over his splayed legs, cringing at the smell, and walked down the short flight of stone steps to the basement door.

It was open, and Beko Havison was smiling at her.

'Beko! You surprised me.'

'You come to visit, and *I* surprise *you*?'

'How by all the gods do you live here?' she asked. The drunk growled something indecipherable in his sleep.

'Nobody looks below a tavern,' Beko said. 'Makes me anonymous. Besides, it's not so bad here. A rough place, but the food is to die for.' He held out his hands and Nomi grasped them. 'Good travels.'

Nomi grinned. 'I hope so.'

'Ah!' Beko said. 'Work. Then welcome to my humble abode.'

The basement consisted of one huge room with a curtained bathroom in one corner and a large bed along one side. With the front door closed, the only outside light came from three slits just below ceiling level – one at the front and two at the rear. They were glazed with thick, misted glass, and dust on the outside further reduced the light. Candles flickered around the room, casting dancing shadows. The ceiling beams were low enough that the warrior had to duck in places.

All available wall space was taken up by weaponry.

'Very homely,' Nomi said.

'I have to store the tools of my trade somewhere.'

There were a dozen swords of varying shapes, lengths and designs. Several bows hung on the walls, the smallest the length of Nomi's arm, the longest as tall as the room. A collection of intricately designed quivers lay on the long table along the room's rear wall, and there were tall wooden pots from which the feathered ends of hundreds of arrows protruded like deadly flowers. Knives made from metal, bone and hardwood hung on strings, along with an assortment of other cutting, crushing or hacking weapons. She could also see the crossbow with which Beko had hunted fowl and wild pigs in Ventgoria.

Nomi shivered. She could not help wondering which blades, arrows and axes had killed people.

She knew that Beko had killed. They had talked about it. Hers was the most trouble-free voyage he had been on, he had told her. The one previous to that had been with a woman named Ghina Bleed, one of the most senior Voyagers of the Guild. They had gone south as far as the great lake south of the Pavissia Steppes, and whilst mapping the lake's shores, they had been besieged by a large, organised band of marauders, coveting the Voyagers' horses, equipment and weapons. The fight had lasted for eight days, and when the marauders finally fled, they left behind a hundred dead. How many of those Beko was responsible for he had not said, but Nomi did not believe that numbers really mattered. The voyage lost only four members, and it had become infamous in Guild history.

'Drink?' Beko asked.

Nomi's head was still spinning from her unaccustomed

intake of morning cydrax. She shook her head and watched Beko pour himself some root wine from a tall clay bottle.

'Please, sit,' the soldier said. He sat in one of the chairs around a low table and Nomi sat opposite, relaxing. 'Remember I promised I would show you this?' He indicated the table, shifting aside a plate dirtied with leftover food.

'Your trial carving!' Nomi leant forward and gasped when she saw the table's hardwood surface. 'Is that your seethe-gator?'

Beko nodded.

She touched the carving, and for an instant Nomi imagined the rough wooden edges to be seethe-gator teeth. She moved her fingertips across the deadly creature's image – its spines and serrated teeth, those long, hooked limbs which made it so deadly – and then she noticed the flicker of a figure beside it. It was so expertly carved that the candlelight revealed only its shadow: ridges and knots cut here and there to form the insubstantial image of a man. The seethe-gator was twice his size.

'I took it with nineteen throwing knives, fifteen arrows, six crossbow bolts, and a sword for its head.'

Nomi shook her head in awe. 'How can you and your people live in such a place?'

'My people have lived there for ever,' he said. 'Mancoseria is our home, and the seethe-gators have always been there, too. Yet for me…I don't live there anymore. I live here.'

'Of course,' Nomi said. 'I'm sorry. I—'

'It was a long time ago. And that was the creature that took her. I killed it. I've had my revenge. It's not every Serian who gets to kill such a seethe-gator for their trial.'

Nomi sat back, amazed once again at the soldier's history.

So much death, such harsh times. She tried to picture Beko fighting the terrifying animal carved in the tabletop.

'I'd like to offer you work,' she said at last.

'But not Guild work.' Beko rested his feet on the trial table, heels crossed atop the seethe-gator's head.

'No, not Guild. There are…reasons. And it would be myself and a friend.'

'Ramus Rheel?'

'Yes.' She'd forgotten how sharp Beko could be.

He nodded slowly, looking at her over the top of his mug.

What did I tell him about Ramus and me? She could not remember. They had spent many nights eating around campfires, and their discovery of Ventgorian airbacco had turned much of the voyage hazy and indistinct.

'He's a remarkable man,' she said. 'He reads, and not just the modern Noreelan languages. He's read *old* books, too. He knows so much, and for this voyage—'

'So it *is* a voyage. You were being a bit evasive, Nomi. It's not like you.'

'True. But with this one, there's nothing defined or known.'

Beko leant forward and placed his mug on the table. 'The very soul of voyaging.'

'Are you interested?'

'I'm intrigued,' he said. 'Which for me, amounts to the same thing. I've been here for almost half a year without a voyage. And the last one was with that fool Geary, a tiresome stomp down the Western Shores. We found nothing but sand and dead fish.'

'I'll want you as captain.'

He frowned. 'How many more Serians do you need?'

'Can you find five more who'll do private work?'

He nodded. 'Of course. But what do I tell them?'

'Nothing for now.' She looked down at Beko's trial table again, and the shifting candlelight made the seethe-gator move. 'Only promise them the voyage of a lifetime.'

'Well,' Beko said, picking his mug up and drinking more wine. 'I'm more intrigued than ever.'

Nomi caught him staring at her when she looked up.

'This needs to be kept quiet, Beko. I mean it.'

'I'm sure.' He smiled. 'But as captain, I think I deserve something to spur me on. Don't you?'

'Something...?' Not for the first time, Nomi felt uncomfortable in Beko's presence. He was a big man, intimidating when he wanted to be, yet gentle and caring when the mood took him. A man of contradictions; a lover of poetry who slept in an armoury.

'Tell me where we're going, Nomi.'

'That's your price?'

'I won't breathe a word.'

Nomi relaxed back into the chair. 'We're going to the Great Divide.'

The soldier's face did not change, but his eyes grew dark.

'The voyage of voyages, Beko! Perhaps the one to end them all.'

'What's down there?'

She looked away. 'We don't know yet.'

'You're lying.'

'I don't lie, Beko. We *don't* know what's down there. That's why we're going.'

He stood and walked behind her, a heavy shadow in the shady basement. In the tavern above them a piece of furniture scraped across the floor. Someone muttered, and somebody else laughed. 'Opening time soon,' Beko said. 'More drinking in the day, singing in the evening, and fighting in the night. More wine dripping between the floorboards. More puking drunks.'

'We could be drinking around a campfire two nights from now.'

'I'll come, of course,' Beko said. 'I made up my mind when I showed you my trial table.'

'You did?'

'I saw the excitement in your eyes. You don't hide much.'

She sighed with relief, but said, 'You haven't even asked about pay.'

Beko turned. He was holding a round stone, and he drew the blade of a short knife across its surface. 'I know that Ventgorian fruit has made you rich. Come back this evening and I'll give you a price.'

Nomi nodded, and jumped when something thudded onto the floor above them.

Beko rolled his eyes. 'Dragging out last night's drunks to make room for tonight's.'

'Yes. Very homely.' Nomi went to the door and opened it to the smell of vomit.

'Nomi,' Beko said.

She turned around, looking back into the cavern of a room.

'Thank you for asking me.'

'Who else would I go to?' Then she shut the door, climbed the steps into the street and went to find a runner.

CHAPTER TWO

Ramus sat just inside the library entrance, holding his head and hissing as the pain receded. His vision and hearing throbbed with each heartbeat, but the nausea was passing.

Not now, he thought. *Not while I need all my wits about me.* He grasped the rolled parchment pages in his left hand, and they too seemed to pulse with each beat of his heart.

It had started as a headache three years ago, one that lasted four days and seemed to reach out to every nerve in his body, drowning him in a pain he had never imagined before. He had thrashed and cried in his bed, unable to move or go for help. Even back then, Nomi was the only person who ever paid him a visit, and then not frequently, but she had been away on her second voyage to Ventgoria. He had suffered alone, and recovered without telling anyone what had happened. *One of those things,* he had thought at the time. *A sickness in the air, or bad food from one of the street vendors.* Looking back, he now considered it the period of impregnation, because every time an attack came he had visions: strange, obscure, sometimes disturbing, and other times quite mundane.

Ramus stood, resting his right hand against the wall for support. He gasped in a few deep breaths, trying to clear his head, and smelt the unmistakable must of age. This library was his home from home. He stood still for a few moments, feeling the last of the pain drift away, and then he reached for the library's inner door.

There were three other people at the tables immediately inside. One of them worked for the Guild, and she nodded at Ramus. He recognised the other two by sight, although he did not know their names. Scholars, probably, working for themselves or one of the local Chieftains. They scratched at rough paper on the tables before them, taking notes from a book here, a parchment there, and the frown of confusion on their faces was ever-present.

They don't know how to look, Ramus thought. *They may think they can understand language, but everything that matters is between the lines.*

The library was contained in a large, low hall behind a shop selling furniture, paintings, and exotic tapestries from Pengulfin Landing. It had been a storage building many years before, and the ranks of rough timber shelves were still there, free-standing down the middle of the hall and fixed to all four walls. When one of the old Chieftains of Long Marrakash had decided to gather as many books, scrolls and parchments together as they could, the shop's owner had sold the hall for a good price. The books and other recordings had been gathered and moved in, and since then this had been a virtual shrine to all those who strove to know the past. It was also a place of much frustration, as few books were written in exactly the same language. Most utilised some common

Noreelan lettering, but each writer had adapted the language to their own aims, using symbolism, unique dialects, graphical representations, imagery known and unknown, and preferences that often amounted to personal code.

Ramus walked towards the rear of the hall, passing the Burned Past. When the library was first gathered, a group of shamans came one night and tried to burn it down. They destroyed a thousand books before they were stopped, and the library keeper had left the damaged shelving as he had found it, a sort of shrine to all that lost history. It pained Ramus every time he saw it, because it represented knowledge that could never be regained.

There was no one else sitting at the tables and chairs at the back of the hall. He breathed a sigh of relief and sat down, closing his eyes as he let the smell and feel of the place envelop him. He loved it here. So much potential, so much history, and he was quite certain that many of these books, if translated correctly, would change the world as they knew it today.

And so could these, he thought, looking at the parchments. He smoothed them out on the table and spread them so he could see all three at once.

He did not recognise much of the lettering, although some of the root formations looked vaguely familiar. What he *had* seen – and he was certain that Nomi had not spotted this – was that the symbols and strange lettering were contained within defined borders. There was no way of telling whether or not the pages were supposed to follow one another, or even in which order, but each page displayed one fundamental similarity: a thick, vertical line dividing the page into a space taken up by writing and an area of blankness.

Ramus saw this as partial proof that these pages had come

from the Divide. And whoever had written them had acknowledged one of the elemental aspects to their existence: the cliff. One side there was life, the other side only open air.

He looked at the curled figure at the bottom edge of one page, like a serpent twisted into an egg. *You know what that is,* Nomi had said. He had seen and read much about the Sleeping Gods, and though descriptions of those mysterious deities varied hugely, this was a recurring image he'd seen in a handful of texts.

Usually, the gods were drawn as beautiful winged creatures. Not lizards or snakes.

He stood and went to one of the shelves, glancing around to make sure nobody could see the parchments. A sudden sickness rumbled in his stomach, and he recognised this for what it was: fear. Because as well as words and texts, he thought that much of what appeared on these parchment pages was more literal.

Part of it, including the curled image of a Sleeping God, seemed to be a map.

The first book he chose was a heavy tome, loosely bound with twisted gut ties and covered front and back with thin wooden covers. It had no title or name, and there was no indication anywhere inside about who had written it, nor when or where.

Ramus guessed it was maybe five hundred years old. Some of the glyphs used were similar to several other volumes from around that time. He had referred to this book several times over the years, and there was one page in particular that had jumped into his memory.

It took a while to find the page he wanted, inked on a rough sheet of layered silk-grass. The image there was, as he remembered, quite similar to that on the wanderer's parchment: a curled, serpent-like creature, only this one had a larger head, several limbs and hands. Each hand had six digits, and each digit was a person. Every person was screaming.

Ramus tried to read some of the glyphs around the image. He had never translated this page, though he had seen the glyphs used before, and it took him a while to edge his concentration in the right direction.

Fallen One put down, he read. *Down is the Fallen One. Deep is the god that Fell.* All saying the same thing in differing ways – and the more he read, the more he imagined a sense of panic overwhelming the writer. There was no information here; it was more like a statement of belief, a desire that would become more real the more it was written.

Every story he had read of the Sleeping Gods had sprouted from the solid foundation that the gods were benevolent, but extremely powerful. Some could move mountains, others were mountains themselves. Mention of a Fallen God was infrequent, a myth within a myth – one of those ancient gods gone insane and fallen from grace, its wings torn from their roots and the god itself buried deep in the land by the other Sleeping Gods. Those few times he *had* read about it, the language had been as frantic as this.

Superstition, he thought. Ramus liked to think of himself as a pragmatist with an open mind, but this was a tale designed to scare children at bedtime. That it managed to trouble him illustrated its power.

He reached for another page of the parchment. This one had a more regular spread of lettering and glyphs, and across its centre were images that looked like statues. Some were obviously people, with arms raised, heads thrown back, and mouths open. Others looked more like representations of people – vaguely humanoid shapes with extended necks, tall, thin heads, and arms that reached below their knees. These were drawn as frozen, or dancing, or perhaps paying worship to the other, more human statues. There was writing all around these images, and though Ramus recognised none of the lettering, he could already discern a pattern.

The third parchment was damaged and darkened, and some of the stains could have been blood. It was covered in fine writing, using the same unknown language as the other pages, and interspersed here and there were images of the sun, moons and stars. Each image had a face, and the faces all had teeth.

Ramus closed his eyes and leant back in his chair. Footsteps came close and he sat up quickly, turning the parchments over so they could not be seen. Nobody appeared, and he waited until the footsteps retreated again to the front of the library before turning the pages back over.

He looked at those thick lines once more, dividing the pages into thirds and two-thirds, the spaces to their left blank and sterile as if no ink would take there, no thoughts could hold weight.

These are real, he thought, his heart pummelling his chest and sweat beading on his forehead. He could pass the parchments over to the Guild, but then news would spread. Or they could go themselves – he and Nomi – to see if they could find what these pages alluded to. But the risks were great.

One thing of which he was certain: if they could prove that

the Great Divide did not rise endlessly, this would be the greatest voyage ever.

And if there was evidence of a Sleeping God up there, then they would change Noreela.

He closed his eyes and wondered what to do.

On her way home Nomi called in to the runners' rooms. She sent a runner to Pancet's Stables south of the city, with an order and promise token for ten good horses, riding and camping equipment, and all the climbing gear Pancet could procure in the next day and night. She deflected queries about why she was not going to the Guild with a handful of coins. The runners needed to make a living as well, and they were known for their honesty.

Then she returned home, readying herself to say goodbye. She lived in the hills above the river, her home one of twenty in a structure built around a central courtyard. In the courtyard were several young weeping trees growing from a small pond, and ducks and frogs made the high grasses and reeds their home. It was not a cheap place to live, but Nomi had the money. She'd been through a lot on her voyages, and she saw no shame in profiting from her travels. Let Ramus frown upon her all he wished. If it weren't for her, they wouldn't be able to undertake the journey they were planning right now.

Still, as she entered her home a moment of doubt assailed her. *Should I really have told Ramus about this? I could have gone on my own, perhaps with Ten as companion.* But the Great Divide was a huge distance to travel for a fool's treasure. She needed Ramus's wisdom, his knowledge of language and the printed histories of words, to tell whether the parchments were real.

Sometimes, she wished she were wise like him.

She walked around her main room, examining artefacts she had brought back from her two voyages. Carvings hung on the walls; woven materials swished from the ceiling in the shape of a hawk; a steam sculpture repeated itself in a tray of heated water. Bottles of her own Ventgorian wine lay ageing in one dark corner. A marsh harp hung above her fire, impossible to play unless you were a true Ventgorian. All precious items. No books, no crumbling scrolls like Ramus had in his own little hovel.

Nomi felt at home here, surrounded by the rewards of her life's chosen path.

If only Timal were still here, she thought. *He was the greatest reward.* But Timal had left her a year earlier, saying nothing, never returning. She heard from a mutual friend that he had left for Pengulfin Landing and the rich crystal farms that had started to thrive on its eastern shores. She still had some of his clothes in her sleeproom, and on nights when she was most lonely she smelt them and imagined him beside her.

She sighed. If he were still here he would not approve of this latest voyage, and maybe she would not even go. She'd let Ramus have the parchments and go on his own, make the find, reap the glory.

'Did I really love Timal that much?' she said to the empty room. The metal shields on one wall rang with a sonorous response.

Nomi lit the fire to warm water. She would bathe, change into fresh clothes, then go back down into the city to meet up with Ramus and Ten once more.

In her mind, the voyage had already begun.

❊   ❊   ❊

Ramus walked along the riverfront, past the traders he'd seen setting up that morning. They were still trading, but business had slackened somewhat as the sun rose higher, and the Cantrass Angels had vanished. He wondered what they had achieved with their morning's work.

As he approached the bridge out to Naru May's, he paused and looked across the water. It was almost half before midday and Ten was already there. He was sitting in the same seat he'd taken that morning at breakfast, head bowed, hands crossed on his lap. There was a mug on the table before him. Ramus guessed he had been there for some time.

Eager to see us again? he wondered. *Or eager to leave?*

He hurried across the bridge and stood before the table.

'Real?' The wanderer looked up, then stretched his arms above his head, clicking his fingers.

'Interesting,' Ramus said. 'They're written in an unusual language, and contain some intriguing imagery.'

'But don't you *agree* that they're from *above* the Divide?'

Ramus stared at the wanderer for a dozen heartbeats, trying to see past his eyes. 'Nomi will be here soon,' he said. 'Our discussion should begin when she arrives.'

Ten stretched again and looked around. 'Good. Can't wait to get away from here. My feet are itching already.'

'You didn't look around the city?'

'What's to see?' Ten asked, and Ramus surprised himself by finding nothing to say.

At Ten's signal, Savi came with cydrax and a mug for Ramus.

'Another mug?' Ramus offered, but Ten shook his head.

They sat in silence for a while, looking everywhere but at each other. The deck was filling rapidly with traders and buyers breaking off for their midday meal, and the chatter was upbeat and pleasant.

'So where did you really find them?' Ramus asked at last.

Ten frowned. He had been staring into the distance, lost somewhere beyond Long Marrakash. 'You don't believe what I said?'

'If there is a lie in your story, you'd best tell me now.'

'No lie.'

'Good. Because if there is one, Nomi will know it by now. Her mother's sister is a truthscryer.'

'That's superstition!' Ten scoffed.

Ramus raised his hands and shrugged. 'I'm not pretending to know how it works.'

Ten's eyes narrowed. 'You're just trying to play me.'

Ramus stared at the wanderer. 'Believe what you wish.'

Nomi arrived, a look of doubt and suspicion on her face as she glanced from Ramus to Ten.

'I thought we were meeting at midday?' she said to Ten.

The wanderer stared at her with that implacable expression. 'I was claustrophobic in the city. At least, sitting here, I can look out over the river.'

Nomi offered Ramus a brief smile. 'So do we have something to discuss?'

Ramus took out the parchment roll and placed it on the table between them. 'It's worth buying,' he said casually.

'And it is from where Ten claims?'

'I don't know. That's why I want to buy it, so we can pursue it further.'

Ten looked at Nomi. Even a wanderer could discern wealth. 'How much will you offer?'

'How much will you take?' Nomi asked.

Ten leant forward, glancing at the tables around them. He placed his hands flat on the table, fingertips just touching the parchment as though he had missed its company. 'There are other places I could go,' he said. 'Other Voyagers who I'm sure would be interested in these pages.'

Ramus looked at Nomi. She sat with her legs crossed, leaning back, presenting a casual air that he knew was anything but relaxed. He could see the small tic below her left eye which always began when she was most stressed.

I should have made sure we talked alone. I should have made her aware of what this really was. 'So what *will* you take?' he asked.

Ten leant back in his chair and rubbed his face. Then he looked down at the rolled pages, and smiled. 'If your first offer is enough, I'll take it. If not, I go straight to the Guild; I'm sure they can finance my needs. No negotiation.'

Ramus said nothing. Nomi shifted in her chair. Ten looked out across the river, and for the first time his scarred, weathered face seemed relaxed. *He'll take whatever we offer,* Ramus thought. *He's come a long way, but I think he likes us. I think he sees the adventurous spirit the three of us share.*

'Fifteen thousand pieces,' Nomi whispered. 'And a third of whatever we bring back.'

Ten smiled. 'As for the latter, the glory is all yours. I want no part in what you discover. But for the offer... I accept.'

Nomi let out a held breath and Ramus closed his eyes.

'I can give you a promise token now,' Nomi said. 'I'll tell you which banker to go to, or...?'

'Yes, that's fine. I trust you.' Ten poured a little more cydrax for each of them. 'Shall we toast our deal?'

Should we? Ramus thought. *Is this really something to celebrate?*

Nomi's nervousness vanished and she threw him her most dazzling smile. 'A toast to your own voyage, Ten,' she said. 'And good wishes for whatever will come for us all.'

Ten nodded and raised his mug.

They all drank, then Ten stood and stretched. 'Time for me to leave,' he said. 'I'll take your promise token with thanks, and if you could direct me to the banker, I'll be on my way.'

Ramus watched the wanderer and Nomi conclude business, watched him walk away after exchanging silent nods, watched him leave the bridge and disappear into the midday crowd along the riverfront. And every step of the way, he wondered what the wanderer was thinking. Was he laughing at them? Or did he feel only pity?

'So what did you find?' Nomi asked at last, obviously frustrated at Ramus's silence.

He picked up the rolled pages and put them back inside his jacket. 'When do we leave?'

'What makes you think I've already made arrangements?' Ramus raised his eyebrows.

Nomi laughed softly. 'Dawn, the day after tomorrow, from Pancet's Stables.'

'We should talk somewhere private. There's plenty to discuss.'

'Just tell me that one thing, Ramus,' Nomi said, her voice louder than she probably intended. The patrons sitting around them glanced their way, then went back to their business.

Ramus only nodded.

Nomi's eyes lit up. 'The voyage of a lifetime.'

❋   ❋   ❋

'A Sleeping God...' Nomi said.

They were back in Ramus's home, sitting in his main room with the remains of a sheebok and bread platter between them. Nomi had bought it from a street vendor a hundred steps from Ramus's home, and though still hot when they had arrived, neither of them had felt much like eating. The meat was tender and juicy, but the nervous tingles in her stomach had made her feel queasy.

'A myth,' Ramus said.

'Many people worship them. Await their return to lead Noreela into a Golden Age.'

'And many follow shamans, and others worship the life moon and the death moon.'

'Are you saying they're *all* wrong?'

'Not at all. I'm saying it's what may be atop the Divide that we must go for. Another land? Another race?' He shook his head again, looking down his greasy fingers.

'But if it *is* there? If we *do* find it?'

'Maybe this is a mistake,' he said.

'You said it looked real!'

'Not the parchment. I don't recognise any of the words it contains, so it must be from elsewhere. No...the mistake could be us.'

'Then I'll go on my own.' Hurt, Nomi turned away.

Ramus was silent for a long time. Nomi wanted to turn around to see what he was doing, but she felt it best to give him her back. She did not wish him to see the doubt in her eyes.

'I'm not saying I don't want to go,' he said at last.

Nomi spun around. 'Then what the fuck are you saying?'

'That we should not go blind. You called it the voyage of a

lifetime, and I agree. But it may contain the dangers of a lifetime, too.'

'Good. Duly noted.'

Ramus stared at her, unblinking. 'We can't tell anyone,' he said.

'Why should we?'

He smiled coldly. 'Not to retain the glory, Nomi. We need to keep this secret because of what just might be up there on the Divide. There must be very good reasons why no one has ever seen anything like this before.'

'One beat you're a sceptic, the next you're protecting Noreela from a Sleeping God!'

'Just being cautious.' He shook his head, sighing.

Nomi did not care. There were always dangers – her last trip to Ventgoria had proved that, though that was something she would always keep to herself.

'So we keep it a secret,' she said. 'You for your reasons, me for mine.'

He closed his eyes and nodded.

'So dawn, the day after tomorrow.'

'I have a few things to put in order,' Ramus said.

I have little, Nomi thought, but Ramus already knew that. She'd told him about Timal leaving, and there had been no one since. Sometimes Ramus seemed most at ease when she was not involved. He was like a brother watching over his little sister, and believing that no one was good enough for her.

'I need to see Beko and agree his fee, but that's all,' she said. 'I just wish you were more excited!'

'I can't change what I am,' Ramus said.

Nomi went then, giving him a tight smile before leaving his

rooms. Out in the street she leant against the wall and watched a few people passing by, trying to confine her mind to their own narrow concerns. She could not. Her ideas had been expanded, her horizons stretched. And the further she walked from Ramus's home, the lighter her step became.

CHAPTER THREE

The dream had assailed Ramus as he dozed off after seeing Nomi from his rooms: a Sleeping God rising from the ground, fearful, dreadful and unknowable. But the Sleeping God risen was a trifle compared to the sense that he was someone else.

What do we have if not our own identity? Even Nomi would agree. She had her home up in the hills, her ornaments and objects of worth brought back from voyages or purchased with her Ventgorian wine profits, but most of all she still had herself. Even Nomi – shallow perhaps, but still intelligent and broad-minded – would surely agree with that?

He groaned, holding his head as though to squeeze out the pain. The attacks were becoming worse, and more frequent. He should see the healer before he went, though the healer had already told him that there was little she could do for a disease of the mind.

Such a thing eats at itself, she had said. *And while I've never seen one like this before, I can see the swellings behind your eyes. There's a mass, and if it follows patterns I've seen before, it will get larger, the symptoms will worsen, and then you will die.*

The healer's words echoed back at him, as they often did when he was alone and suffering another strange dream.

Ramus sat up eventually, sipping water and trying to sigh away the dregs of pain. Strange how it never actually hurt during the dream, only after. Almost as if he really were being ripped away for a time, and the pain came from being forced back into his own body, his own mind.

'I should tell Nomi,' he whispered. But upon voicing the idea he instantly shoved it away. He had not told a soul, and he never would. This was his own final voyage, the greatest of them all, and he could share it with no one.

Next morning Ramus spent some time studying several maps of Noreela, trying to piece together clues about the uncharted terrain south of the Pavissia Steppes. Voyagers had gone that way before, but of those who returned, few were adept at mapping their routes. Ramus had painstakingly copied any voyage maps he could lay his hands on, either at the Guild or in the library, and he kept the copies in his rooms. He had never attempted to amalgamate them before, because a mistake repeated would only be doubled. But they were all he had.

Some indicated that much of the uncharted area was forest. Another map suggested that marshland took up a large proportion of the land down there. Both possibilities would offer differing problems, and Ramus hoped fervently that some of the terrain at least was plain or grassland. Some said that the land there was deceptive, shifting, as though it were a young land still trying to find its lie.

So he decided to create his own map, drawing together as much information as he could from the others, and he worked until well after midday. As he worked, he wondered yet again why it had taken so long for the Three Hearts – Long Marrakash, Cantrassa and Pengulfin Landing – to explore the rest of their world. Some said it was a leftover from the farming stock that they all descended from; simple folk who spent their lives working the land and rarely thought of moving on. Others suggested that it was a fear of the unknown set against the comfort in which much of Noreela lived. Ramus thought there was an element of truth in both, but that the real problem was a dearth of imagination.

Since the start of the Age of Expansion – with Sordon Perlenni's momentous voyage to, and naming of, Sordon Sound – things had been changing. The frontier was being pushed further south, but with each hundred miles advanced, it seemed that settlers regressed to a more savage state. There were vicious marauders down there, and talk of wars, sacrifice and cannibalism. That in itself was enough to put off prospective travellers.

And there was the barrier. No physical thing, but something more deeply rooted in the psychology of all Noreela. Their history was long and misty, but it was always underlined by the presence of the Great Divide. Many were aware of it, some even talked about it, but few acknowledged the effect that it had on them, whether they were three hundred or seven hundred miles away. Hardly anyone alive would ever see it, but everyone knew it was there. And with it came the enigma that would trouble anyone who thought for themselves: what was beyond the Divide? *Nothing* was the generally accepted answer. But the problems with that answer were many, and any alternate theories only encouraged more enigmas.

So the Divide pushed people away, like the opposing points of compass stones.

Ramus liked enigmas.

He worked on, and soon his room became a garden of parchment with him at its centre. He scratched away at the square of parchment he had chosen to write on, but even before he had finished, he knew that the map he had created was more than half guesswork. He noted the observations from Ten's story – the heavily wooded land at the Divide's western shoulder, the impassable marshes to the east – and the space before the great cliff he left blank. He wished he had quizzed the wanderer more on his journey, but something told him that would not have done much good. Wanderers were known for their secrecy. Ten had only shared his story to convince them of the parchment's worth.

By the time the sun had reached its zenith and started its own journey towards night, Ramus had done as much as he could. The map would offer them direction, if not accurate information. He gathered the various shreds and copies of older maps, rolled them together and shoved them beneath his bed.

He would sleep here for one more night. In the meantime, there was his mother to visit before he left, and his travelling gear to prepare. Backpack, weapon roll, compass stones, and the blank book he had been saving for such an occasion. Bound in strong leather covers, containing almost two hundred sheets of fine paper made in the mills of Pengulfin Landing, it had been a gift to him from his mother a dozen years before. *To keep track of your travels,* she had said, but even now the pages were still blank. He hated the idea that, once filled, the book would tell the tale of an average life.

It was time for the pages to bear ink. *The things we'll see,* he thought. *The images I can create, the routes I will map, the details I can write. And someday perhaps a future Voyager will pore over my book, and they will learn.*

Ramus opened his bottle of ink and chose his finest quill. On the first page of the book he wrote:

> The Final Voyage of Ramus Rheel
> Year 143, Age of Expansion
> In the company of Nomi Hyden

He sat back and stared at the page. When he turned it over, the stark white of the next sheet suddenly seemed emptier than ever.

Nomi went about shutting up her home. She gathered her travelling gear together, then started taking down the expensive wall hangings and other items of wealth. But she soon stopped. *We'll be back,* she thought. *Ramus is as doom-laden as ever, but we'll return triumphant. Let him worry about his foolish myths.* She left and went to the home of her sometime helper. The old woman and her three younger daughters had spent their lives in the service of rich clients, and now Nomi had a big task for them. She told the woman that she was leaving on a journey, and that her home should be maintained in its current state – aired frequently, plants tended, floors cleaned, shields and other metalwork polished. She gave the woman a series of promise tokens which she could exchange for pieces each month, and the old lady smiled and nodded her assent.

Her home and belongings taken care of, Nomi left to tell her friends. Some of them she visited at their homes, and over a glass of root wine she told them that she was leaving on a special voyage about which she could reveal nothing. None of them mentioned the Guild. Several other friends she met in the First Heart Wine Rooms. By mid-afternoon they were already merry from several bottles, yet Nomi found herself growing curiously distant. *Almost as if we're already halfway there.*

Afterwards, she walked down to the river and stood on its shores, staring across at the distant opposite bank and thinking of the Guild buildings huddled there. That made her feel good. Nobody was telling her what to do. This was her and Ramus, and though sometimes he enraged her, confused her, and intimidated her with his vast knowledge, she was glad they were doing this together.

She spent that last night in her rooms, and it no longer felt like home.

Ramus had slept well, and no nightmares welcomed in the dawn. He hoped that was a good sign. He'd spent the previous evening packing and preparing his voyaging paraphernalia, so when he woke an hour before sunrise, he only had to dress and leave. He locked the door and pocketed the key.

He had a very real sense that he would not be returning. No nightmares last night, true, but he could still feel the weight of the sickness in his head. Recently, whole days would pass when he forgot that he was ill, and then the brain disease would cut in with a shadow on the sun, a vision behind his eyelids or pure pain, and he would be dragged back to reality with a blink. *Chasing myself,* he thought. *Chasing my own mortality.*

He bought breakfast from an early street vendor and ate while he was walking. His bags were heavy, containing several books, his clothing and weapons, and a roll of maps, including the new one he had made yesterday. But he felt fit and ready, and he enjoyed breaking a sweat as he climbed the hill and headed south.

Though dawn painted the horizon to the east, shadows still ruled the streets, though most were shrinking back to wait out the day. Once or twice he heard a whisper as he passed, and he looked down at his feet, not wishing to attract attention. At one point, passing through a narrow path between high buildings, several shapes darted across the alley before him. He paused, then drew a knife and carried on. *Not people,* he thought. He heard no footsteps, no breathing. Wraiths.

By all the gods true and false, let me live to the end of this voyage, he thought.

He marched up the steep hill south of Long Marrakash, and when he stood on its summit he turned back and looked down at the city. It was coming to life now, the sun having broken the horizon and sent random shadows to ground. The streets became busier, noise rose to defeat the relative silence of night, and in the distance he could see the river glimmering through veils of mist.

He turned his back on the city with no regrets.

Pancet's Stables were nestled at the foot of the hill leading out of Long Marrakash. The lower hillside was taken with paddocks and grazing fields, while the stables themselves were a series of eight long, parallel timber buildings running north to south. The horses spent much of their days out in the fields, and most nights they were brought into the stables for safety.

There were things on the plains to the south that would eat them given a chance, and thieves worked the city's outskirts.

Beside the stables were several buildings made from logs, reeds and mud, and smoke rose cheerfully from a couple of chimneys. From the path leading down the hillside Ramus could see people moving around and, closer to the first of the stables, a group of horses was tethered. They were big animals with long manes and tails that almost swished the ground, ranging from dark brown to a light, sandy yellow. Cantrassan horses: tough, dependable and expensive. He hoped that this was a sign of Nomi's preparations.

He started down the hill, already feeling the sore spots on his shoulders where the backpack rubbed. *Getting old,* he thought. He blinked, his vision blurring for an instant before resolving itself again. Sometimes he forgot about his sickness and believed he really would grow old.

Going downhill felt good. Beyond the stables, past the small wood that sprung from the fertile ground at the hill's base, he could see the rolling land that led south and east toward the Pavissia Steppes. The border was less than a hundred miles in that direction, guarded by a series of outposts that were manned by the Chieftains' men. Beyond were the wilds, and Ramus suddenly craved that freedom with every heartbeat. Now that the voyage had begun, he wanted to be in the thick of it. He had always hated those first couple of days, moving across lands that were mapped, through settlements known and named. It was a false start.

He hummed to himself, an old Cantrassan song he often heard in the taverns down by the river, and the first he knew about the man shadowing him was when a knife pressed to his throat.

'Keep still and quiet and you'll see the sunset,' the voice said.

Ramus did as he was told. He did not know the voice, though he knew the sharp accent, the words quick and clipped. Mancoserian.

'Down on your knees.'

Ramus knelt and felt his weapon roll pulled away, untied and rolled out.

'Going for a long walk, eh?'

'A ride,' Ramus said. 'With Nomi Hyden.'

'And who'll you be?'

'Ramus Rheel.'

The man behind him grunted, not without humour. 'Good enough. Up, then, so I can introduce myself.'

Ramus turned as he stood, and smiled. 'I know you already,' he said. 'Nomi's talked about you.'

'Beko Havison,' the big Serian said. He held out his hands, and Ramus grabbed them.

'Good travels,' Ramus said.

'Let's hope so, eh? So we're to work together at last, on this voyage that isn't.'

'Oh, it's a voyage, believe me. Just because the Guild isn't involved...'

Beko waved his hand. 'They're a bunch of old pissers, though they do have money.'

'They have purpose, too,' Ramus said. 'Don't discard them entirely. So, has Nomi told you where we're going?'

'She has, though none of my Serians know yet. She suggested it should be kept quiet.'

Ramus looked at the soldier, and he had already decided that he liked him. Most Serians he found gruff and serious, and he still found their tradition of studding their leather tunics with a metal star for each kill troubling. Beko had many stars and carried an array of weaponry, but he seemed good-natured. And Ramus could read character well enough to know that it was not just eagerness to please.

'They can know soon enough. Once we're away from Marrakash, everyone can know.'

Nomi was there already. When Ramus held out his hands to wish her good journeys, she brushed them aside and hugged him hard. For a heartbeat he did not respond, but then he returned the gesture.

'These are great times,' she whispered in his ear.

All great times are painted in blood. But he smiled and nodded, and when she let go he had a chance to look around at their team.

Beko and five other Serians were helping Pancet's men load their gear on the horses. There was a mount for each of them and two spare, shorter, stockier packhorses with thick legs and wide bodies to carry their loads. The Serians had selected a horse each and were standing close by, some of them whispering to their mounts as they loaded their gear. He saw weapon rolls everywhere, and each Serian was already dressed in their usual garb of thin woollen trousers, heavy boots and leather tunics. All colours were neutral, intended to act as camouflage in whatever terrains they may be crossing. Each carried the usual array of knives and short swords on wide belts around their waists, and three of them had bows strapped across their saddles. There were also several crossbow cases still waiting to be loaded, and some other equipment which Ramus did not recognise.

'So what do you think?' Nomi asked. 'You've met Beko, yes?'

Ramus smiled. 'He seems pleasant enough.'

'He is,' Nomi nodded, glancing away when Ramus caught her eye. He felt a pang of jealousy, sharp as it was unexpected. 'He's a good captain, his Serians respect him and I've worked with him before. He comes recommended by others, too, and I've never heard bad words about him. You know how some of these Serians can get.'

Ramus nodded. Some Serians were occasionally prone to fits of temper, and sometimes rage. He'd never witnessed it himself, but he'd heard tales from Voyagers who had undertaken longer trips. He put it down to the normal pressures that any long journey would present; he'd heard of Voyagers losing their minds, as well. He tried not to judge a person by their faults, but by their qualities.

'Ramus!' Beko called, beckoning him over. 'Please, come and meet my people.'

Besides Beko, there were three other men and two women. None of them looked like someone Ramus would want to pick a fight with.

'Noon,' Beko said. Ramus grasped hands with the short, stocky man and wished good journeys.

'Unusual name,' Ramus said.

Noon nodded. 'The time of day I killed my seethe-gator.'

A tall woman appeared by Ramus's side, arriving like a shadow. 'I'm Rhiana. Sharpshooter with a bow, more kills than anyone here, and a great cook.'

'She does do an impressive spiced rabbit stew,' Beko said, smiling.

Ramus held hands with Rhiana, examining her tunic. There

were too many star studs to count, but he guessed thirty. 'Impressive,' he said.

Rhiana smiled. 'Thank you.' Her voice was cool and betrayed nothing.

'Over here are Konrad and Ramin,' Beko said. 'They're cousins, hence the similarity.'

Ramus nodded at Konrad, trying not to let his surprise show. The left side of the man's face was raised in a dozen ugly circular ridged scars, each of them the width of a thumbnail. He held out his hands and the men shook.

'Striking scars,' Ramus said. Not mentioning them would be false, and he did not want to set off the wrong way with any of these Serians. Over the course of the voyage, it was likely he'd rely on them to protect his life.

Konrad smiled, but the scar tissue pulled it into a grimace. 'You should have seen the 'gator.'

Ramin sighed and clapped Ramus on the shoulder. He was tall, dark-skinned and completely bald, and he looked nothing at all like Konrad. 'The 'gator was a baby,' he said. 'My cousin always likes to talk himself up. You have to forgive him, he can be...' He touched the side of his head and rolled his eyes.

'Rat piss, Ramin,' Konrad said.

Ramin laughed, startling the horses. 'Ramus, give me your bags and I'll load up your mount.'

Beko touched Ramus's arm and inclined his head. He frowned slightly before he spoke. 'And over here, meet Lulah.'

The short, slight Serian woman was strapping her gear to a huge sand-coloured horse. She had long beaded hair, skin the colour of Cantrassan chocolate and delicate hands. She glanced over her shoulder, and Ramus blinked back his surprise. She only had one eye. The other socket was covered by a brown leather patch, seemingly sewn into the skin and studded with one large metal star.

'Good journeys,' Ramus said, holding out his hands.

Lulah continued tightening the straps around a weapon roll, giving no sign that she had heard.

'Lulah?' Beko said, and the captain's voice was almost a plea.

Is he really in charge here? Ramus thought.

The woman turned fully and stared at Ramus. She looked him up and down with her one good eye – it was a startling gold colour, contrasting against her skin like the sun rising at night – and then stepped forward. Her expression did not change. 'Good journeys, Ramus,' she said, holding out her hands. They shook and she pulled away, turning back to her horse and continuing to load her gear.

Ramus swapped glances with Nomi. *Some stories to hear from that one,* he thought. He wondered who or what she had killed to get the stud in her eyepatch.

A huge man walked down the slope towards them. He carried a leg of some unidentifiable meat, chewing as he came, smiling through the grease and scraps of skin that clung to his beard. Several children hovered around him, eyeing the group of Serians with a mixture of awe and fear.

'Have you ever seen a group of finer horses?' the man said, spreading his arms as if to hug them all.

'Pancet, you've done me proud,' Nomi said. 'And all on a promise slip.'

'A promise from you is as good as its word, Nomi.'

Nomi was smiling, and Ramus was surprised at how this

man's charms affected her. He'd heard stories about Pancet, and not many of them were good.

Pancet chewed at his meat again, eyes straying over the rest of the group. They rested a little too long on Rhiana and Lulah, and Ramus could not help smiling. *I'd like to see him try.* 'An interesting group,' the horse-trader said. 'Long voyage, Mam Hyden?'

'Just a little trip into the wilds.'

'Which wilds would they be, then?'

Nomi's wide smile was still there. *She's so good,* Ramus thought. *So good that she sometimes fools me.*

'Just a jaunt,' she said. 'A trip, a walk, a ride through fields and pastures new, forests perhaps, some mountains and marshes and a few boat trips in between.'

'Can't help being curious,' Pancet said.

'I have your money, if you have my promise slip,' Nomi said. The smile had slipped at last.

'You like the horses?' he asked, ignoring her outstretched hand.

'They're perfect,' Nomi said. 'Well kept and healthy.'

'The runner you sent said not to give you any old nags.'

'Then she passed on my message well.'

'I don't keep nags, Mam Hyden. And if I did, I wouldn't sell them to you.' Pancet's voice had fallen in tone and volume, and the hand holding the meat was swinging by his side. The children hiding around his legs moved away, rushing back up the hill and giggling amongst themselves.

Nomi shrugged. 'The Guild uses other breeders as well, and sometimes they're not as scrupulous as you.'

'Scrupulous,' Pancet said. He smiled. 'Good word to describe me.' He looked at Ramus again, and the Serians standing beside their horses. 'Yes, quite a voyage I'm sure.'

'I have your money,' Nomi said, patting her chest pocket. 'And your silence is worth a little extra, if you'd like to discuss it with me in private.'

Don't pay the fat turd a piece more, Ramus thought. He knew that Nomi was not one to be bullied, but he hated the idea that this hoodlum would gain from their need.

Pancet smiled. 'I think not. That would be…unscrupulous of me.'

Nomi inclined her head but did not respond.

'And you're Ramus,' Pancet said, his attention shifting. 'I know of you. Wise man, a reader. And I know Beko Havison, too.' He turned and looked at the Serian women again, a small smile turning his lips. 'So, on your way Nomi. I never saw you.'

'I'm grateful,' Nomi said, taking a money folder from her pocket. Pancet dug in his own voluminous pockets and brought out a twist of cloth, the promise token Nomi must have sent with the runner.

Nomi and Pancet concluded their business and the fat man turned, sauntering back up the hill and opening his arms to welcome his herd of children once again. They jumped at him, laughed and darted between his legs, and he ruffled their hair.

'We need to move out quickly,' Ramus said to Nomi. 'First chance he gets he'll be spreading word about us.'

'Why should he?'

Beko joined them, signalling his Serians to mount up. 'Because he's a bully,' he said, 'and he couldn't bully our destination from you.'

'You've dealt with him before?' Ramus asked.

'Several times. He's not a nice man.'

'I've heard the tales.' Ramus nodded across the yard at a round stone structure. 'Rumour has it his first three wives are rotting down that well.'

'Nice,' Nomi said. 'And now that you've both convinced me, let's get the piss out of here.'

Beko grinned. 'Spoken like a true Voyager.'

The Serians were already mounted up and stroking their horses' necks, whispering and whistling to them, and at a word from Beko they moved out.

Ramus had not ridden for some time. Ramin had been good to his word, securing Ramus's travelling gear to the horse's saddle, but still Ramus felt like an amateur. He mounted easily enough, but he dropped the reins several times and his foot missed the stirrup. Nomi and Beko left the yard ahead of him, and as he finally rode out, he looked up the slope after Pancet. The big man was standing by an open door, one hand raised to his mouth holding a new chunk of meat, the other slowly raising to bid them farewell.

Ramus did not return the wave.

CHAPTER FOUR

Nomi rode beside Beko at the head of their small group. It felt good to be in the saddle again. Since the end of her second and last voyage to Ventgoria she had only ridden a handful of times. She sometimes went riding with friends up into the foothills of the Marrakash Mountains, but each such trip took several days, and it cost a lot in protection. Many people had gone into these mountains and never returned, and while Nomi believed most of them simply lost their way and fell victim to hunger, hidden crevasses, or cold, some talked of cloud-creatures in the high passes that viewed travellers as succulent treats. Many who spread such rumours were mercenary Serians who benefited from the protection payments.

She was glad that not all Serians were so deceptive. When she had ridden with Beko before she found him to be open, honest and simple. Not unintelligent – not at all – but his life was uncomplicated. He worked for the Guild, he went on journeys, and in between he lived a comfortable life in Long Marrakash, with no real worries or troubles. No harsh

Mancoserian wind-seasons to contend with. No seethe-gators slinking from the shallows when the moons were on the wane.

'Are you happy, Beko?'

He did not answer for a while and Nomi glanced sideways, thinking she may have surprised him. But he seemed calm, wearing his usual slight smile.

'Happier today than yesterday,' he said. 'I like to see the land. I like to work. Wandering has been in my blood since I left Mancoseria twelve years ago, and I sometimes think the further I am from that place, the better. So yes, happier today than yesterday.'

'And yesterday?'

He smiled. 'Yesterday wasn't so bad.'

'I'm glad.' *It's good to be riding with you again,* she almost said. But that could imply more than she meant...or more than she really wanted to say right now.

'These are good horses,' Beko said, saving her. 'You must know Pancet well.'

'I know what he is,' she replied. 'And I know how to play men like him.'

'He's a thug.'

'Yes. And a murderer, if all the stories are true.'

'You know how to play murderers?'

Nomi looked across at Beko's innocent smile. 'Captain, are you trying word games with me already?'

'Mam Hyden, I talk straight; you know that well.'

Nomi laughed.

Not long after setting out they entered Clyst Forest. It would take them until midday to ride through, and then the rest of their route out of Marrakash would be across the vast Clyst Plain: a hundred miles of grassland and moorland rolling through valleys and over gentle hills. It was an easy ride, and the dangers were few. There were a dozen small settlements between here and the border with Pavissia Steppes, and they would have tracks to follow and farmsteads at which to stop and buy food. Marrakash always offered a gentle start to a voyage, and Nomi was glad of the gradual change.

The shadows closed around them, the trees grew high, and there was a pleasant chill to the air. Ferns grew between the trees, taller than a person in places, and they swayed in time with tune birds singing in harmony. Every song was different, and some claimed that the birds felt the same emotion a person would whilst listening. The song this morning was upbeat and bright.

There was a path through the woods – a much-travelled route worn down to the rock in places. Before long, they passed a group of people going the other way, the men carrying heavy baskets on their heads while the women bore tools and water skins.

'Nolan berries?' Beko asked.

The lead man carefully lowered his basket to the ground, nodding. He was sweating and breathing hard, but he offered a smile.

'Can I buy some?' Beko patted his stomach. 'I've had breakfast, but nolans lose their freshness so quickly.'

'Help yourself,' the man said. 'Good crop this year, and I'll not take money for something you can pick a few hundred steps on.' He lifted the basket back onto his head and leant against Beko's horse.

Beko chose a dozen fat berries, handing a few to Nomi. 'Good journeys.'

'Same to you.' The man and his party headed off.

Nomi plucked the remains of a stalk from a berry then ate it. She closed her eyes, luxuriating in the taste. It was sweet, juicy and rich, and she could hardly think of anything more perfect.

Beko ate a couple of berries then turned his horse, passing the rest to Rhiana behind them. 'Pass them along,' he said.

'Should have taken a few more; they make a great filling for plain doves.' Rhiana grinned at Nomi as she chewed, a dribble of juice speckling her chin.

'Hey, Ramus!' Nomi called. Ramus was at the back of the group, looking around calmly as they ate and chatted amongst themselves. 'Come up and join us?'

He shook his head, smiled but said nothing.

'Please yourself. But I'll get there first!'

They moved deeper into the forest.

Nomi had not travelled this way in over a year, and when they came to the standing stones, she gasped in surprise.

The stones had always been there. There were nineteen of them; fifteen were arranged around the clearing in a rough circle, while four others stood beyond the circle at the four points of the compass. The glade was almost a hundred steps across, and at its centre lay a wide, flat rock with weathered carvings in its surface. Time had made most of the images impossible to discern, and the remaining indents were home to lichen. The stones were huge – the largest twice as high as a man and just as wide – and no one knew where they had come from, who had placed them, or how they had been manoeuvred through the forest. Their purpose was similarly vague. Temple, sacrificial altar, burial place of a Sleeping God

– all had been suggested. There had been digs over the years, but few people were really interested enough to spend much time here. Noreela, both known and unknown, was scattered with thousands of similarly intriguing sites.

This place had always appeared wild, primal and untouched; even the stone circle had seemed a part of the land, not the result of people upon it. But now all that had changed. The trees around the edge of the clearing were adorned with countless scraps of coloured cloth, some of them tied to lower branches or fixed to trunks, others hanging so high above the ground that whoever placed them there must have risked life and limb to do so. Blue, red and purple were the main colours, but amongst hundreds of these Nomi could also make out a few yellows, some greens and one or two black strips.

'What's this?' she asked, perplexed and a little awed.

'Remembrance trees,' Beko said.

The colours felt right here, not intrusive, and as a breeze rustled leaves and strips of cloth alike, they felt like a true part of the forest.

'I've seen remembrance trees before,' she said. 'But why here, so suddenly?'

Beko shrugged.

'The sightings,' Konrad said. 'There are rumours of wraiths being seen here, starting last winter.'

'I've not heard of that,' Nomi said.

'Then you don't drink in the right taverns. I've heard the tale from a few people – Serians, traders, a mercenary – and it's much the same whoever does the telling: the ghosts of children run here when the death moon's full. They say they were sacrificed to the moon a long time ago. Though the mercenary told me that the children are only recently dead. Still suffering their sacrifice, he said.' Konrad grinned. 'But then, he *was* very drunk.'

Nomi shivered. 'So why do people suddenly see this as a place of remembrance if it's so haunted?'

'Maybe because it's close to beyond,' Ramus said. He had ridden up quietly on his horse, and now sat an arm's stretch from Nomi. She wanted to touch him, but she was not sure how he would react.

'I don't like it,' she said. 'I did, but now I don't.' The strips decorating the stone circle clearing suddenly made her uneasy, and all she wanted to do was move on.

'Different colours from different faiths,' Ramus said. 'Death moon, life moon, the land. Sleeping Gods.'

'Which colour for them?' Nomi asked.

'I think probably the black ones.'

'Shall we move on?' Beko asked. 'It will be good to get through the forest in time for lunch.'

They skirted around the clearing. It did not feel right to break the circle.

Nomi found herself riding alone. Beko went on ahead with Lulah, the short woman dwarfed by her huge horse, and she heard them talking in subdued tones. Behind her rode the other Serians, mostly in silence but sometimes responding to comments or jokes from Ramin. She was already warming to most of them – though Lulah seemed cold and distant – and she hoped Ramus would become more friendly. They would be spending a long time together as a group, and she would far prefer if it was on good terms.

Ramus still brought up the rear. Nomi glanced back now

and then, and Ramus's movement on his horse was awkward. He still had to find his rhythm. He'd be sore after today's ride. Nomi's thighs and rump were already warm from the unaccustomed exercise, but her movement had quickly fallen in tune with her horse, and she sensed that it was at ease with her. *Over a thousand miles,* she thought. It was seven hundred miles there, assuming they did not have to divert for anything. And coming back the same, and who knew what they may be carrying on their return journey? She clicked her tongue and the horse's ears twitched.

'So, I hear women make better Voyagers than men,' Rhiana said. She had ridden up beside Nomi and now kept pace, moving with grace and poise. Even the cruel angles and curves of her weapons did not seem out of place.

'Of course,' Nomi said. 'We don't have anything to prove.' She smiled, but Rhiana's grin did not seem all humour.

'Piss!' the Serian said. 'Everyone's got something to prove. But is it true? This is my third voyage, and the first two were with men.'

'How did they go?'

'First one was with a turd called Blaken...'

'I know him,' Nomi said, nodding slowly. *A turd indeed.*

'We went south across the Pavissia Steppes, heading for the unnamed lake at its southern edge. He wanted to camp on the shore and catalogue its flora and fauna. But he hadn't researched the route, or even planned how long the voyage would take. We ran into a band of steppe marauders, disturbed them attacking a farming village, and we lost three people.'

'Serians?'

'Two of my friends, and a woman from Long Marrakash, one of Blaken's soft friends. When we returned, it came out that the marauders were known to be working in that area. Reports had filtered back from an earlier voyage, but Blaken had paid them no heed.'

'What happened?'

Rhiana touched her leather tunic, finger circling a patch of bare leather. 'Had a place just here for Blaken's stud. But Beko talked me out of it.'

'You're not the first Serian I've heard of who wanted Blaken's head. But good for Beko.'

The soldier offered a wry smile. 'I suppose so. Killing a Voyager wouldn't have put me in good favour with the Guild.'

'It would have got you executed, most likely.'

'Well. So, that was the first. The second was little better. I can't even remember his name, but he was nothing to speak of. Sailed us out to The Spine, dug up some plants, shot a few birds, sailed us back.'

'And now you're on a voyage with a man *and* a woman Voyager.'

'I am.' Rhiana glanced back over her shoulder, then leant across towards Nomi. Even then she rode with elegance, her long tied hair swinging down across her shoulder. 'He's a bit quiet,' she said.

'He does a lot of thinking.'

'And you?'

'What about me?'

'What's your drive?'

'To make women the best Voyagers, naturally.'

Rhiana stared at her for just too long. Then she grinned. 'I'll help,' she said. She rode on ahead and joined Beko and Lulah, and Nomi wondered exactly what she meant.

❈   ❈   ❈

When they passed the ruin, Nomi knew that they were almost out of the Clyst forest. The remains had stood here for as long as anyone could remember, and it was said that this had once been a temple to the Violet Dogs, a race of monstrous invaders that swarmed the Western Shores before history began. There was very little left now: a few scattered piles of carved building blocks, a heavy lintel half-buried in the soil, and one portion of a wall still standing. It was home to creeping vegetation and a colony of rock ants, weaving their sticky tube tunnels through grooves and cracks in the old stone.

Nomi had never paused to examine the ruin because it had never been her destination. She spared it a quick glance and noticed that it had been subsumed more by the forest since her last trip. The climbing plants' stems were slightly thicker, the lintel buried marginally deeper in the ground. A few more years and maybe this would become totally hidden, just another secret part of Clyst Forest that would fade from sight and memory until no one knew it was there.

She often wondered how many other such places had already disappeared.

She noticed Beko had paused ahead, Lulah and Rhiana just behind him. He turned around and caught her eye, and Nomi rode forward.

'Traders camped ahead,' he said.

The path through the forest was much wider here, the trees further apart. She could see movement between the trunks, and she caught the whiff of cooking meat and spices. 'Lunch,' she said.

'They're charm traders,' Beko said.

Rhiana spat. 'So long as they don't try charming me.'

Beko laughed, and Nomi felt momentarily excluded.

They moved on, rounding a slow bend and passing between the first of the traders.

A woman stood quickly from the woven mat she had been sitting on, holding out an array of fur tails. 'Ward away the dark,' she said, her voice tinged with the accent of the Pavissia Steppes. 'Wood cat tails to ward away the dark.'

'I just light a fire,' Noon said, laughing.

A young boy skipped along the track trailing a length of string behind him, dried leaves from a poison cactus waving in the breeze. 'Cure the ills in your head,' he said, laughing manically. 'Ill head! Ill head!' the boy shouted, darting in dangerously close to Konrad's horse.

'Away!' Konrad said. He kicked out, but the boy twisted aside easily.

More traders tried to parade their wares, dancing and singing, pleading and whispering, some of them saying nothing at all as they offered their products to view. There were petrified pieces of dead animals, plants, objects carved from wood or stone, fine clay pitchers of dark fluids, and one woman offered herself, pulling open her loose tunic to display heavy breasts and a stomach tattooed with swirling images.

They did not stop. Beko rode on and Nomi did not question his decision; there was a sense this could get ugly. When they had passed the traders Nomi turned around in her saddle to see how Ramus had reacted.

His horse stood abandoned, and Ramus was kneeling beside an old woman and her display of rope charms.

'What in the name of all the gods…?' Nomi paused and let the Serians ride by, only Ramin offering her a tight smile.

'Your friend in need of some help from beyond?' he asked.

'Not Ramus, no.' She shook her head. *At least,* she thought, *not the old Ramus.* But this was no longer the Ramus of old, was it? This was a new man, with a terrible new illness which he probably still believed nobody else knew about...

Ramus stood, dug into his jacket pocket and dropped some coins into the old woman's hand. She held his fingers and closed her eyes, then snatched up a rope charm from her extensive display. It was the length of her forearm, the knot in the middle thick and complex, and it had been dyed dark purple.

'I wonder what charm that one hides?' Nomi muttered. These were intricate knots, inside which the enchantments were supposedly trapped, expelled as a whisper from the charm breather. Untie the knot and the charm is released.

Ramus mounted his horse and kneed it on, approaching Nomi slowly. The old woman watched him go, then locked eyes with Nomi, her expression cold and hostile.

Nomi waited until Ramus drew close before speaking. 'You and a cheap charm trick, Ramus?'

He rode past her without a look. 'I'm interested, and there's no harm there,' he said.

'I know you. Interested you may be, but you'd never line the palm of a charlatan. You'd sooner steal it from her.'

'Who's to say who's a charlatan, and who is a true charm breather?'

She shook her head, incredulous and confused, then clicked her tongue and urged her horse onward. Now Nomi was at the end of the line.

They camped a mile beyond the forest. The Serians dismounted with ease, but as Nomi slipped from her saddle she realised just how much she'd lost the feel of riding. Her legs and rear ached, and her back, arms and shoulders were stiff from being constantly tensed.

'Got to ease up if you're going to make seven hundred miles,' Beko said. 'We've come about fifteen so far.'

'Well then, not far to go,' Nomi said. She gave him a sweet smile, which he laughed at before going back to his horse.

Ramus approached, his face a mask of discomfort. 'I forgot how much horses hate me,' he said. 'I think my balls are going to drop off.'

'Thank you so much for that information,' Nomi said.

Ramus smiled and nodded at the Serians. They were gathered a short distance away, drinking from their skins and talking quietly amongst themselves. 'They seem quite tight,' he said.

'I think they've voyaged together several times before. Beko called them his team, and I think they respect him as a captain.'

'Good.' He wanted to say something else, Nomi was sure. He stretched his arms and tried to massage feeling back into his legs, but he kept glancing up at her.

'What?' she asked.

Ramus shook his head and chuckled. 'Am I that transparent?'

'Yes.'

'Fine.' He brought the rope charm from inside his jacket. 'Don't tell me to piss off until I've finished what I'm about to say, because—'

'Piss off.'

He stared at Nomi without smiling, and she suddenly felt uncomfortable. *He's serious,* she thought. *And I just made fun.*

'I bought this for you,' he said.

Nomi's shock was such that she could not speak.

'We're voyaging into darkness,' he said, voice dropping to a whisper. 'I truly feel this. And though I know it's all about journeying into the unknown, I believe that we're heading for the unknowable. And I'm scared, Nomi. More frightened than I ever have been before. And I...' He put his hand to his eyes, rubbing above them as if suffering a headache. 'I wanted to give you a charm. You know I don't believe in shit like that, but it doesn't matter what I believe. If you believe, and it may help, then that's my aim fulfilled.'

'Ramus... I'm not sure what to say.'

'Well, take it first, at the very least.'

She took the rope charm from him. It was much heavier than it looked, as though the knot contained more rope than was possible. 'Thank you.'

'The idea is to—'

'I know. Untie the knot if I feel it's needed.'

Ramus smiled and turned away, heading off to talk to Beko.

Nomi turned her back on the rest of the team, blinking back tears that stung her eyes. *What am I?* she thought. *And what have I done? Whatever sickens him should have been mine.*

A tear ran down her cheek. She rubbed it away in case anyone saw its mark in the trail dust.

Ramus woke, the world crashing in around him in sound and smell, feel and taste. Grass and heather scratched at his hands and the exposed skin at the back of his neck, the smell of cooking meat assailed his nostrils, and he could hear the genial banter of the Serians. He smelt hot horses and humans perspiring in early afternoon sun.

He kept his eyes squeezed shut because the pain was so bad.

There are no children chasing us. He had dreamt of swarms of children pursuing them across the hillsides, picking off the Serians one by one and slaughtering them with hooked hands, and behind each child had fluttered a length of black cloth.

The nightmare was already fading, yet the pain still throbbed hard behind his eyes, as though the children really had caught him, pummelling down on his forehead with their tiny clenched fists while the black remembrance strips flittered around their arms.

He opened his eyes a crack and allowed in some light. It felt better than he had expected, and he slowly pushed himself into a sitting position, looking around at where they had stopped for lunch.

He couldn't have been asleep for long. Rhiana was kneeling beside a fire, stripping and gutting a couple of small rabbits. She worked with casual ease, no hint of distaste on her face at what she was doing. Guts and innards she dropped into a patch of ground where the sod had been lifted, and she used a small, sharp knife to cut off chunks of meat. She skewered these on two long metal spikes, placed them on brackets above the fire, then glanced over at Ramus.

'Nice sleep?' she said.

Ramus nodded, not trusting himself to answer.

'Smell of my cooking bring you awake?'

He nodded again.

'I do the best spiced rabbit stew you've ever tasted, but that'll wait for an evening. Quick stop for now, your friend tells us, so for now it's just roasted steaks. Good for you?'

Ramus smiled, surprised at the rumbles in his stomach. 'Sounds very good to me.'

Rhiana stood and walked over to him, squatting down and

leaning over to whisper some secret. 'Best spices for rabbit aren't violet skin and shred, like most will tell you. You know what they are?'

'Haven't got a clue,' Ramus said. 'Buy mine from street traders, and I don't know what they use at all.'

'Street traders,' Rhiana said, with disgust in her voice. 'For every good one, there are a dozen that don't know how to cook, let alone serve food at its best. I'll tell you, Ramus – best spice for roasting rabbit is porl root.'

'That's poisonous!' Ramus said.

'It is. Eat porl root and your guts will tie up, you'll puke blood and crap like the Violet Dogs themselves are after you! But if you use the porl root tendrils, they're not yet poisonous. Too deep, lots of water passing through them. Beat them, dry them and strip the brown flesh out of them, and they give you the best spice for rabbit you have ever tasted.'

'I'll take your word for it.'

'No you won't,' she said. 'You'll try it.'

Ramus looked at Rhiana's serious expression and burst out laughing. It felt good, driving down the memory of the dream and bringing him back to the present.

Rhiana walked away towards the fire and Ramus could not help admiring the shape of her as she went. *All this fresh air getting to me,* he thought. Beneath the aroma of roasting rabbit and hot horses there was the brisk, heady scent of the open plains. It all smelt good.

Rhiana took a leather pouch from one pocket, grinned at Ramus, and sprinkled generous pinches of dried white spice over the rabbit. The meat's juices were already running from the heat and the spices stuck, burning into the flesh and sending their rich, warm scent into the air.

Fresh air, he thought again. Half a day out from Long Marrakash and he felt different already. More alive.

Ironic, when the pain behind his eyes was giving him such horrendous nightmares.

They ate, and it was the best roast rabbit Ramus had ever tasted. Juicy, tender, rich, and the spice brought out the flavour and added a delicious heat that dwelt long after he'd finished the final mouthful.

'That,' Nomi said, 'was pissing good food. You cook like that for the rest of the voyage, Rhiana, and—'

'Wait,' the tall Serian said, holding up her hand. 'It's Konrad's turn to cook this evening.'

'But he makes everything taste like dust!' Ramin protested.

'Good food's bad for the soul,' Konrad said, but he could not keep a straight face.

'Rhiana's the best,' Noon protested. 'Why put up with anything else? Rhiana, I'm pleading with you, hang up your sword and take up the skewer. We'll split the pay with you just the same. Please!' He knelt and clasped his hands before his face, mimicking the moon worshippers who grasped moonlight between their palms to honour their gods.

'My favourite way of killing an enemy,' Rhiana said, 'is to fire a bolt into his spine, then slit his throat. That way he's paralysed, but he sees the knife coming.'

Silence fell for a moment, then Ramin said, 'And I bet you could even make an enemy taste good.'

'You said "his" throat?' Nomi said.

Rhiana shrugged. '*Most* of the people I've killed have been men.'

More silence. Ramus always found such talk uncomfortable.

He had seen fighting and he had fought, but for him it always marked an extreme moment, a time stamped into memory by its viciousness. For these people it was more a way of life, and he had to remind himself of that. The Serians were not just along for the ride. They were here to fight and kill if necessary, and if things went badly wrong some of them could die.

Oh, they will, he thought. *They'll go badly wrong, and some of those sitting around the fire will be dead.* He looked from face to face, feeling very distant. *Noon? Maybe. Konrad? He's scarred, already marked from violence, so yes. Rhiana?*

He did not like the idea of any of these soldiers dying on his voyage, but Rhiana felt different. He had spoken to the others, but *she* had chosen to speak to *him.* Perhaps as the voyage went on she could even become a friend.

Beko stood and stretched. 'Good food, Rhiana. Konrad, your turn to cook for us tonight. Dust will do fine. Let's move on. I want to make the Lowkie farmstead by nightfall.'

Everyone stood and started gathering their eating utensils. Rhiana emptied the remaining scraps of food – bones, skin and gristle – into the small hole she'd made, then stomped the sod back over it. She kicked out the fire and spread the ashes, then glanced up at Ramus watching her.

Ramus smiled.

Rhiana prodded a thumb between her breasts and drew a finger slowly across her throat. Then she laughed and turned away. Ramus shook his head, picked up his backpack and went to where Nomi was retying straps across her saddle.

'That food was something to remember,' he said.

'I can still taste it,' Nomi said. 'Rhiana though...she's a strange one.'

'Lots of Serians are.' Ramus helped Nomi tie a pack onto her saddle.

'It's going to be a long voyage,' Nomi said.

'Longest ever. For us, at least.'

'What do you mean?' she asked.

Ramus shrugged. 'Lots of Voyagers have gone missing over the years. At the Guild, I once heard a count of over three hundred. Who's to say some of them aren't still travelling, somewhere?'

She looked at him intently, eyelids fluttering as happened when she was angry or confused. 'That's not going to happen to us, Ramus.'

Ramus noticed the rope charm he'd given Nomi hanging from her saddle, tied within easy reach. *She hasn't packed it away,* he thought. He looked up at her but she did not meet his eye.

CHAPTER FIVE

Ramus did not speak to Nomi again that afternoon, though she fell back and rode beside him in silence several times. The quiet between them felt good, and he did not wish to risk such a feeling with misplaced words. Besides, if there had been anything important to say, one of them would have spoken.

They rode through a gentle rain shower, and as the water turned warm Ramus wondered what else would fall. Occasional squirm-storms on the Pavissia Steppes brought down insects and flies, and sometimes even scorpions, shell-spiders and small snakes. He knew a Voyager who had been paralysed for life by a scorpion sting, the creature having tangled in her hair when it fell from a dark, cloudy sky. Such storms were almost unheard of this far north, but something about this voyage already felt different. He would not be surprised if the land changed for them.

The trail passed beneath their horses' hooves, the sun dipped to the west, and this first day of their greatest voyage drew to a close. The Lowkie farmstead, the group's destination for tonight, kept a field free from planting so that travellers could make camp. Payment was a small fee and news from outside.

As the sun kissed the western horizon Ramus noticed a Lowkie marker beside the trail. 'Three miles,' he said. 'We've come a long way.'

Lulah had been riding behind him for a while, bringing up their rear. 'The Lowkies make good root wine,' she said. It was the first and last time she spoke to Ramus that day.

As the farm came into view, nature's sounds were changing, day giving over to night, and though the journey so far had been trouble-free Ramus felt as if they had been travelling for ever. He was saddle-sore and aching, and trail grime was already hardening in the creases of his skin.

'Is it only me who feels about a hundred years old?' he asked Nomi as they dismounted.

She groaned and rubbed at her thighs. 'We've become too used to the good life,' she said. Ramus almost commented, but thought better of it.

Beko had dismounted and approached the farmstead, and several people wandered out to meet him. After a brief exchange, Beko came back smiling. 'Plenty of room in their field, and they've bottled a new batch of root wine just this morning. Lowkie will be happy to give us six bottles, but he stresses we're the first tasters.'

'So if we wake with acid guts, it's not his fault,' Konrad said.

Beko shrugged. 'That's a chance I'm willing to take. You can drink water if you like.'

'Will he sell me some food?' Konrad asked.

Beko's eyes narrowed. 'What are you planning on cooking?'

The scarred Serian shrugged, then smiled. 'That's for me to know and you to taste.'

Beko threw a money pouch which Konrad caught from the air. 'If you give him good money for dust, I'll skin you myself.'

Konrad's undamaged eyebrow arched. 'You and which army?' He walked away from the group's quiet laughter.

Beko raised his arms. 'Home for the night, everyone. The field's past the farmstead, and Lowkie recommends camping in the shelter of the trees at its centre. He says there's no sign of any unpleasant wildlife around right now, so we'll get a good night's rest and set off at dawn tomorrow.'

'Does he have any young farm daughters who need irrigating?' Noon asked.

Beko shrugged. 'I'm sure if he has, they'll have already marked you out, Noon.'

Noon licked his fingers and rubbed them together.

'Sometimes I think I'd be better siding with seethe-gators,' Rhiana said.

Ramus laughed along with the rest of them, even though he had the distinct impression that Rhiana was not really talking to him.

They skirted around the farmstead, watched by two farm wolves lazing beneath a tree at one corner of the yard. Lowkie waved them on, then he and the others disappeared back into the buildings.

Ramus caught up with Beko. 'You know Lowkie?' he asked.

'I've camped here several times before. He's a good man, and an honest land worker.'

'Nice of him to give us free wine.'

'He said he'll bring it across to us later when the bottles are more settled. Honestly, I think he just wants time away from the farm, and sharing a bottle with us would only be polite.'

They walked together at the head of the line, leading their horses towards the spread of well-spaced trees on a small mound at the field's centre. The setting sun cast long shadows across the grass, which was wavering slowly in the slight breeze. It reminded Ramus of the sea.

He was looking forward to the first night camped out beneath the stars. Later, the nightly ritual of setting camp would become a chore, but right now it was something to enjoy. And after food and drink, he knew that the Serians would tell a story.

Like many tribes of Noreela, the Mancoserians passed on much of their past through storytelling. They were a proud, hard people, existing in harsh surroundings and facing severe risks every day. They fished and farmed, fought off frequent attacks from marauding seethe-gators, and then many of their children would leave the island and head for the mainland. Here they took employment as soldiers for the Guild of Voyagers or mercenaries. They were feared and revered in equal measures, and Ramus had never known a Mancoserian who could not fight.

And every Serian he had ever met had stories to tell. Many a time he had spent the hour before bed enrapt with tales of voyages gone wrong, fishing the violent ocean of the Bay of Cantrassa, or fighting seethe-gators that hauled their fearsome bodies onto the Mancoserian coastline to hunt, mate or kill.

When they reached the trees, Ramin and Noon relieved the packhorses of their loads, leading the animals to a nearby stream to drink. The other Serians started setting camp, and Ramus and Nomi erected their own tents. Ramus was pleased that he had not lost the touch. His tent was up before any other, and he sat and smugly watched them finish.

Nomi settled beside him and sighed. 'I'd forgotten how much I love the first day and night.'

'I hadn't,' he said.

'Sunset's going to be perfect tonight.'

'It's always perfect on a voyage. Clouds bleed it red, and clear skies turn orange.' Ramus closed his eyes and tried to will away the discomfort in his head. *I can feel it all the time now,* he thought. *It's only when I think back to how I was before that I really appreciate the difference.*

'I'm looking forward to my dust meal.'

Ramus smiled, realising that he was enjoying Nomi's company. Sometimes he thought she was a fool, but perhaps that was his problem more than hers. She was a Voyager, just like him. He breathed in her scent, and felt a momentary sadness at things that could not be.

'What I'm hoping,' he said, 'is that we have a group of Serians in the midst of a vicious culinary feud.'

Nomi laughed, and the sun went down.

Konrad spent some time back at the farm, and when he returned he was carrying a basket of mixed vegetables and a slab of meat wrapped in fine silk. After he had started a good fire, he took one of their cooking pots aside and started chopping and mixing. Nobody bothered him, and he acted as though he were camping on his own. With everything chopped and the pot starting to bubble above the fire, he ventured out into the field, heading for a marshy area in one corner, head down as he searched for a mix of herbs.

'I haven't seen him add the dust yet,' Nomi said.

'He does it so none of us can see,' Beko said. 'Probably rolled the meat across the farmyard with his boot.'

'Well, at least we'll know where it came from.'

Beko had come to sit beside Nomi when Ramus stood and went for a walk. Nomi had watched her companion pass beyond the influence of the campfire, and now he was visible only as a shadow out in the field.

'He's a quiet one,' Beko said.

'Ramus? I suppose he is.' She felt a brief flush of defensiveness, but it soon filtered away. Ramus was his own man and could defend himself.

'Is it him who wants to keep our destination secret?'

'It's caution, Beko, not secrecy. We don't want the wrong people hearing about this.'

'You mean the Guild of Voyagers? Why are they the wrong people?'

Nomi was silent for a while, considering the question. Finally she said, 'I think Ramus would best answer that. I'm here for the adventure, the discovery and the glory. I'll make no pretence about that. Ramus is here for something far deeper.'

'Deeper than discovery?'

'His own discovery. He set himself a challenge when he started voyaging, and that was to become the greatest Voyager of them all.'

'Quite a challenge. And quite a thing to tell someone.'

Nomi laughed softly. 'He's never actually told me that. But that's what his life is all about. I take pleasure in discovery, and if it can also earn my way through life, I'll take that too. Ramus has always looked down on me for that.'

'Ventgorian wine tastes just as good, even though you make a little money from it,' Beko said. He started sharpening a knife on a bladestone, a cool, smooth sound which Nomi found almost sensual.

'It does,' she said. 'But for Ramus, voyaging is his calling, his destiny. He thinks I cheapen it.'

'And you call him your friend.'

'Ramus is much more than just a friend.'

'Oh.'

Nomi glanced at the Serian captain, surprised by the suddenly lowered tone of his voice. A dozen responses came to mind, but the one she uttered surprised her even more. 'It's never been like that. It never will.'

Beko looked at her briefly, then went back to sharpening his knife.

'It's almost like we're the same person,' Nomi said, trying to move the conversation around where it had been heading, even though part of her truly wanted to stay there. 'We're friends like brother and sister are friends. Intense, but warring. Loving, but sometimes we get so angry at each other that...' She trailed off, not sure how to translate her thoughts into words.

'That?'

Nomi shrugged. *There he is,* she thought. *Just a shape in the shadows, and I wonder if he knows we're talking about him right now?* 'Haven't you ever loved someone so much, and for so long, and yet sometimes you want to kill them?'

'Never had the chance,' Beko said, sheathing his freshly sharpened knife.

Nomi closed her eyes. 'I'm sorry. Insensitive of me.'

'You're not insensitive,' he said. The sound of the

bladestone had not started again, and it took a few heartbeats for Nomi to look at Beko. He averted his gaze and started running the stone slowly, smoothly along his sword.

'Food!' Konrad called tersely. And much as the Serians had been denigrating his cooking, everyone dropped what they were doing to eat.

He had made a stew – chunky vegetables and cubed sheebok meat with snowspit petals adding a rich, warm aroma and a spicy taste. Everyone ate in appreciative silence. Lulah, the smallest of them all, went back to the pot twice for more helpings, and when Rhiana had finished she leant back against her saddle and let out a small burp. Then she started running her tongue along her teeth, frowning and reaching for her knife.

'Boulders stuck between my teeth,' she said.

Ramin nodded. 'That sheebok eat stones all its life?'

Konrad only smiled as the abuse came and went.

'I thought it was fine,' Nomi said. 'In fact it was better than fine. I've eaten some truly bad food on voyages, but I think this is the one when I'll be turning fat and lazy.'

'What do you mean, *turning*?' Ramus asked.

Konrad nodded to Nomi, acknowledging her praise.

'Thing is,' Nomi continued, 'the grit gives it texture.'

Konrad hefted his knife, but made do with throwing a discarded potato at her head.

As they cleared up, Lowkie – a thin, wiry man with a startlingly wild head of hair – appeared carrying a wooden box. He walked slowly and carefully, obviously not wanting to upset the newly bottled wine. Beko helped him open the first bottle. Rhiana collected each of their mugs and held them while Lowkie carefully poured.

'Who's first?' he asked.

'You, surely,' Ramus said. 'You brewed and bottled it.'

Lowkie grinned. He looked like someone who smiled a lot. 'And that's why I don't want to be the first to die from it.'

'Well piss, I've died from bad root wine a dozen times before,' Noon said. The stocky Serian seemed to have accepted that Lowkie had no daughters to entertain, so perhaps getting drunk was the next best thing. He took his mug from Rhiana and sipped. He held his expression for a while, but he could not hide the emerging smile. 'That,' he said eventually, 'is going to give us a good evening.'

They drank, answering Lowkie's many questions about events in Long Marrakash, and after a couple of bottles were emptied, Nomi stood close to the fire and looked around at the group.

'You can all guess one of the reasons why I like travelling with Serians,' she said. She nodded at Ramus. 'He may not be so keen to hear yet more stories, because he reads his fill, but I'm always ready for a new tale, tall or short. And as your employer, I believe it's my choice as to who gets to tell their tale on the first night of a voyage.'

She smiled at Ramus and was glad to receive a smile in return.

'So,' she continued, 'who's to be first?' She turned in a slow circle, hand held out and index finger dipped and ready to point. Beko...she had heard his tales, and knew that some of them were sad. No need of a sad tale this early in a voyage. And besides, she hoped she would be hearing more from him, and in private. Noon could be interesting, but she had yet to really connect with him. Rhiana and Ramin would both be amusing, especially the tall Ramin, who she was sure had some serious tales beneath his droll exterior. And Lulah…there was a story, for sure. That eyepatch, and where it had come from, and who she had killed to gain that stud.

But perhaps that was for another night.

'Konrad,' she said, pointing. The Serian affected a groan, but she saw his smile when he stood. *Picked the right one,* she thought.

Nomi went around the group with another wine bottle, refilling mugs where they were empty. Then she sat on her saddle, glancing to her left at Ramus.

She felt Beko's presence to her right, ten steps away yet still almost touching. *This could be awkward,* she thought. But when she looked at him she caught him looking away, and the campfire seemed to reach out and seed itself in her belly.

'I'll tell you about the first voyage I went on,' Konrad began, 'and a woman I met on that voyage, and how Mancoseria has never been a safe place to live.' He paced around the fire, finishing his wine and looking down at his feet as he mused upon his tale.

Nomi loved the way Serians told stories. She'd never heard anything quite like it; they combined personal tales with Mancoserian history, sometimes so seamlessly that she could not tell whether they were talking about themselves or their entire race. Their stories were always quite short, but they packed in enough to occupy her dreams and thoughts for days.

Nomi leant sideways. 'You should be writing this down,' she whispered to Ramus, but he acknowledged her with a blank smile and glittering eyes. He seemed to be enjoying the wine.

'I'm thirty-seven,' Konrad said, 'and I went on my first voyage when I was twenty-two. Two years before that, I had killed my seethe-gator and risen to adulthood, and I left Mancoseria with my 'gator carving, my weapons, and the clothes I walked in. My parents told me that Noreela was a safer place to be, and that I would find work in Marrakash at the Guild. My travels from my homeland to Long Marrakash…that's a telling for another night. A night when perhaps you'll want to hear about slave thieves and the wild-cat herds in Cantrassa's less accessible parts.

'Raiders are something Mancoseria is used to. They've been invading our western shores almost as long as the seethe-gators have been crawling onto the beaches in the east, but fighting them has never been a rite of passage. It's a necessity for our survival. No significant battles for over a hundred years, though even now there are occasional attacks from raiders hanging on to their past. But in the Founding Days of Mancoseria there was a constant trail of children travelling to the west, and adults coming back. Fighting knocks the childhood out of you – a youngster will be interested in combing beaches for strange creatures, shells and driftwood from which he can build elaborate stories. A Mancoserian adult back then would look at a beach and try to see where a raider may be hiding; behind that sandbank, beneath that convenient drift of seaweed, ready to leap from a beached boat? There's something devastating in the idea that a beach, home to waves and birds and patterns in the sand, is something other than beautiful. But back then, the raiders cut all the beauty away. And they sliced beauty from

Mancoserian women's faces with their knives.

'My first voyage was with a Voyager called Jeriglia, long dead now, a good man with a poor heart and a body not made for journeying. He took us to the northern tip of Long Marrakash. Many scoffed at his choice of voyage, but he insisted that so many wished to go far afield, that what lay close had still not been fully explored. And he was right. We went through the mountains north of Long Marrakash, where we found settlements of people who had fled the city decades before and never returned. We traded with them, though they were suspicious, and their food was good, though their wine was inferior. Their women, though...' Konrad closed his eyes, and by the light of the campfire his heavily scarred face looked suddenly serene. Nomi coveted such a look of delight. 'Their women were beautiful. Both men and women farmed the slopes, but it was the women who truly connected with the land. The men worried about mountain wolves coming down and stealing their livestock, but the women went into the mountains to feed the wolves and keep them away from the farms. The men concerned themselves that the goodness had gone from the ground, and the women planted each spring, moving fields across the slopes and giving the ground time to find life again.'

'More of their beauty, Konrad!' Ramin said, obviously having heard the story before.

'Beauty, cousin? I need a better word. Language can't reach them, but perhaps art could. If only I could paint, or charcoal with shred seed. If only I could recreate their image from this fire's smoke, this twilight's generous palette.'

'Get on with it!' Beko called, and Nomi felt an instant of annoyance at him for breaking the spell.

'Beautiful women,' Konrad said, looking down at his feet again. 'The raiders did not appreciate beauty because of the salt of the sea, the wind, the rains and snowstorms, the flying fish with their razor beaks...all raiders had their beauty stripped and scarred by the time they reached adulthood. So when they discovered beauty, they sought to tear it away. They would go at it with knives, or files made from urchins dried in the sun. Take out an eye, and a face is made imperfect. Take off a nose, and there's only ruin. But they went farther than that. Physically, they could wreak havoc on we Mancoserians, but with each raid they left more of our men without their balls, and more of our women damaged inside. We fought hard and well, but the raiders were not seethe-gators. At least the 'gators come at you one-on-one, their intentions merely to kill and eat. The raiders were more brutal. They killed on every raid. And sometimes they ate, too, tearing flesh away with their bare teeth. There are Mancoserians now, very old, who still remember the day a raider took a chunk of flesh from their breast, leg or face.

'But back to the voyage. So, north of the mountains, Jeriglia took us to the coast. We found a small village there on the shores of the Bay of Cantrassa, and in the small natural harbour were the remains of five boats. The masts still stood high, but the hulls were rotting, and sea creatures and birds had made them their home. Some of the village was built from wood harvested from the wrecks. Other buildings had been hacked into the soft cliffs, and still others were made from stone blocks, carved carefully over years. The people there feared us at first, especially the Serians among us. They looked at our swords, and my scars terrified them most of all. When they asked where I got them, and I told them about the seethe-gators, that seemed to relax them. A little. But it was only when we met their elders – saw their scarred faces and skin scored by decades at sea – that we knew for sure these were raiders.'

Konrad paused for a while and refilled his mug. This time there were no calls, no shouts to continue. He had cast his spell, and Nomi's attention was fully focused on the story. *Is this a tale of love or loss?* she thought. *Perhaps both...*

Konrad drank some wine, sighed appreciatively and continued. 'We wanted to kill them all. Though the frequency of raider attacks had dropped off drastically, still we knew them for what they were. Yet the younger ones among them did not have the look of raiders, and they mostly spent their days farming the fertile lands around the village, or fishing out in the bay from boats that looked barely seaworthy. The older ones, still bearing the scars, were friendly toward us, offering us food and shelter. Though they seemed confused as to why we were there, they opened their village to our presence.

'And then I met Neria. One of the few true raiders left among them. A lover.'

Konrad stopped pacing and stared down into his mug. 'I need more wine,' he said. Lowkie stood and poured, and worked his way around the group refilling mugs. There was no talk, no banter, because nobody wanted to interrupt Konrad's tale. It hung in the air unfinished, like a rock about to fall or a horse set to leap. Nomi sensed that the heart of the story was yet to be told, and everything up to now had been the preamble.

'Neria,' Konrad said. 'She looked a little like Lulah. Small, strong, rarely a smile on her face. She came to meet us down at the beach, and she arrived armed with all her raider weaponry. They used swords like us, and bows and arrows sometimes, but their favourite weapons were their throwing knives and stars. She had a belt of knives around her waist, straps of stars around each shoulder and down across her breasts, and more strapped to her thighs. As she came along the beach, the youngsters of the village ran to her, shouting in a language we had not yet heard them speaking. But I'd heard those words before. They sounded like waves hitting rocks, and it was the sea-banter of the raiders.

'We prepared to fight, though we knew this would not be much of a battle.

'The raiders were incredible warriors. We Mancoserians know how to fight, but our enemy is normally a seethe-gator. Strong enemies, cunning and vicious and powerful, yet they are animals, and they're all similar in how they fight. You could learn to fight seethe-gators by listening to elders and their experiences. Raiders were different, because each raiding party had its own methods, and sometimes even its own aims. Some came just to kill because they liked killing. Others came to steal Mancoserians for slaves, or to take women to rape, or men to work repairing their boats.

'One time, seventy years before I was born, a raider party landed and drove quickly inland, hitting a settlement that no longer exists today. But it was not the raiders who wiped it from the map; it was us. We fought back, so the telling goes, and when the raiders threatened to slaughter everyone in the settlement, we attacked, killing everything that moved – raiders and Mancoserians alike – chasing the last of the raiders back to the coast and pinning them to their boat with iron spars before sinking it. Some say that boat still sails, crewed by wraiths. It was one battle won, at terrible cost, but it led to three more lost, because the raiders grew more vicious with each attack that followed.

'How do you fight such an enemy? How can you hope to defeat people like that?' He drank, and Nomi could see that his eyes were glistening. It could have been the root wine, but she thought it more likely to be the story yet to tell.

Konrad walked around the fire, turned and went the other way, as if trying to warm both sides.

'Neria stopped a dozen steps from us and stared us down. She didn't go for any of her weapons – she knew that she'd be cut down before she could draw them – but she was defiant, and angry, and when she and I first locked gazes, something in the world changed.' He shook his head. 'I don't know how else to describe it. Even now, I don't think of what we had as love. It was more basic than that. I think it was more like respect. Two warriors, face to face, and if it had been fifty years earlier, our instincts would have driven us to fight until one or both of us were dead. But now there was something else happening, and I think we both felt a powerful sense of having moved on. I had left Mancoseria to find my way in the world, carrying these scars as a badge of my adulthood. And Neria, armed like the fiercest raider I had ever heard of, lived in a place where the raiders seemed to have found peace. Even their boats were sunk in the bay, like monuments to past crimes.

'Neria took out a knife, slowly, and cast it down into the sand. I drew my sword and lobbed it, and it landed a hand's breadth from the knife. And that ended the brief sense of doubt any of us had for being there.

'Our time in the village was short. My time with Neria was shorter. Though both of us had found peace, our visions were still vastly different. As the days passed, she became more determined to defend her village from anyone who came, and she was terrified that our arrival would herald more explorers in the future. I could not allay those fears, because Jeriglia was already talking of further voyages. And I had left Mancoseria to travel, because I had seen what staying in one place did to people. There were horizons to meet and cross, and I hated the idea of waking to the same view every morning. The life moon gave us legs for a reason.'

He knelt, his knees clicking, and Nomi wondered how far Konrad had already walked on those legs. *A long way,* she thought. *Farther than I have ever ventured.*

'What happened?' Ramus asked. Nomi could see how serious his gaze had become, and she was trying to remember where she had heard of Jeriglia.

'It all went bad,' Konrad said. 'And it was my fault. Mine and Neria's, at least. I schemed to take her back to Long Marrakash with us. And she had spent much of our time there conceiving an ambush in the hills to stop us from leaving. There were still a few raiders there with their ancestors' hot blood. And so our respect was...shattered. False. Even from that first moment when we locked eyes...false.'

'You can't be criticised for trying to help,' Nomi said.

Konrad looked at her as though he'd forgotten she was there. 'Help? What right had I? No right. She was proud and I was proud. We feigned friendship, but there was something rotten there from the start.

'The raiders had all but stopped striking at Mancoseria. No one knew why. Some thought they had moved farther along The Spine, that our increasing willingness to defend ourselves had driven them off. Others believed they had simply faded away as time went on. But now I knew what had happened to them. They settled; or at least some of them did. But there were always those still proud of their history, ready to honour the raider blood in their veins.

'Neria and I fought. This scar you see here...my seethe-gator scar...has another knife trail through it. And she scarred me here.' He lifted the right sleeve on his tunic to show the ugly pink welt across his forearm. 'And here.' A knife wound on his shoulder. 'And when I killed her, it hurt me here most of all.' His heart.

'Jeriglia never came back,' Ramus said.

'Dead, along with three Serians and the dozen raiders Neria had taken to her side. The survivors returned to Long Marrakash. Told the Guild we were attacked by cloud-creatures in the mountains. As far as I know, no voyage has gone to the northern shore of Marrakash since.'

'So Neria protected her village,' Ramus said. 'And you keep walking.'

Konrad stared at Ramus for a few heartbeats as though he would draw a sword and slay the Voyager. But then he smiled, shaking his head slightly. 'I tell myself so often,' he said. He sat beside Lowkie, picked up another bottle and refilled his mug.

Lowkie stayed with them for a while longer, finishing the root wine and rashly promising them a dozen more bottles to take with them in the morning. He finally left, swaying his way back across the field to the farm, wolves whining and yapping upon his return.

'One happy farmer,' Nomi said.

'For now, perhaps,' Ramus said. They had been sitting next

to each other all evening, listening to Konrad's tale and then chatting across the fire with the Serians. Nomi had spent some time trying to decide whether Konrad and Neria really had betrayed each other at all, but the wine had fuzzed her mind, and in the end she gave up.

'Tired,' Ramus said, yawning. 'Long day.'

'Lots more to come.'

He smiled, leant across and squeezed Nomi's arm. 'But it's a good feeling to be out here, isn't it?'

She nodded. 'A good feeling.'

'Good journeys, Nomi.'

They grasped hands, she returned the blessing, and Ramus went to bed.

Rhiana took first watch, stacking more wood on the fire and sitting close. None of them expected trouble, but that was when it would most likely come, and the Serian kept her weapons to hand.

Nomi slipped past the trees to piss, and when she returned to the influence of the firelight, Beko was standing outside the tent he would share with Noon, stripping off his tunic and undershirt and preparing for sleep. She caught his eyes, he stared back, and then she felt Rhiana watching them both.

'Dawn?' Nomi asked.

Beko nodded. 'Dawn, and a full day's travel tomorrow.'

'Good dreams, Beko.'

'Always,' he said. 'I have a clear conscience.'

Nomi nodded at Rhiana then knelt to crawl into her tent.

Good dreams, she thought. But it took her a long time to get to sleep.

❊   ❊   ❊

Nomi's night was unsettled, haunted by dreams of vicious raiders and seethe-gators trailing the black remembrance cloth strips of the Sleeping Gods. She and Ramus sat by a large pool and looked at the map he had made, and though they had been travelling for years, still their destination was no closer. It seemed that Noreela had stretched to ten thousand miles long, and the dotted line of their progress on the map was almost invisible. Ramus's skin was scarred with seethe-gator stings, his arms criss-crossed with battle wounds, one eye gouged out and all his teeth rotten and fallen from his head. In the socket of his lost eye, there was something moving, and as she urged him closer a small tentacle protruded from the bloody hole, searching this way and that as if looking for her. Nomi recognised the sickness inside him. She pointed at the map, wanting to shout and scream that it was time to go, but Ramus only laughed. He opened his jacket and showed her the scores of charms he had collected, all of them withered, dead, and ineffectual. She looked around the rough camp they had made by the pool, and although there were five tents, three of them had starting rotting. She could make out the vague forms of the Serians and she was sure that they were rotting too, the insides of the canvas slick and warm. Ramus laughed again, silent mirth that she could hear in her head even though he made no noise. She looked at the map. They had ten thousand miles to go. And she knew that Ramus, now mad, would voyage for ever.

Ramus slept well. When he woke before dawn he sat up in his tent, cricked his neck and sighed. It seemed that his nightmares were now confined to daylight.

CHAPTER SIX

Ramus spent the first part of the morning – whilst gathering wood for a fire, tending his horse, and washing and dressing down by the stream – trying to imagine what could be held within the rope charm he had given Nomi.

The old charm breather had asked him whom the knotted rope was for, and Ramus had found it difficult talking about Nomi. The details of why he wanted to buy it for her, what she meant to him, and perhaps what he meant to her, none of these were easy to scrutinise or describe. His words had ended up tripping over each other, and in the end he said nothing. But the woman had nodded sagely and reached for the charm, almost without looking. *She was fooling with me,* he thought, but that did not feel right. The rope had grown heavier the closer he rode to Nomi, and when he finally handed it to her, he had barely been able to hold it up. She had not noticed such weight.

He had met a hundred charlatans for every true charm breather, and he knew they all had their ways and means. A look from the old woman's eyes could have set a weight in his arms. A sprinkle of certain herbs from her hand could have made him momentarily weak without feeling tired. But he had found this woman to be more convincing than any he had ever met. Most of the alleged charmers in Long Marrakash were there for the money, but camped beside a forest path which was far from busy, she seemed to live for the charm of it.

'But what is it?' he whispered. His horse's ears twitched as it snorted, and he rubbed its nose. *Travel charm, friendship whisper…?*

Konrad and Ramin came across the field with their own horses, arriving at the stream and giving Ramus a cautious smile and nod.

'A good morning,' Ramin said. 'I usually like to start the day with a bath in whores' breast milk, a meal fit for the richest of rich, and a good humping. This morning? A wash in cold water, breakfast cooked by Lulah – which if we're lucky won't kill us until this afternoon – and my cock's too cold to rise.'

'Morning, Ramus,' Konrad said.

Ramus smiled. 'I enjoyed your tale yesterday.'

'Thank you. Never an easy one to tell, but the difficult ones are always the best.'

Ramus nodded.

'Just look at it!' Ramin said. He had stripped to wash and was staring down at himself, hands held out as if afraid to touch.

'Brisk mornings like this,' Ramus said, 'you can almost wonder how we continue as a species.'

Konrad laughed, Ramin grinned, and Ramus led his horse back across the field.

He knew that Serians led an extreme lifestyle. In their work, they were often involved in violence and death, and their play was hard as well. As such, their extremes of personality were to be expected. He was used to it. It made him feel as though they really were back out in the wilds, even though they would still be within Marrakash's borders for at least a couple more days.

As he approached the camp, Nomi emerged from her tent. She was the last to wake.

Ramus glanced quickly around the camp, spotting Beko strapping weapons to his horse's saddle. He sighed. *Nothing to do with me. She's her own woman, and...* He could think of no reason why he should care, but every reason why he would.

'Piss, I'm not used to sleeping on the ground!' Nomi said. She stretched in the open, her lithe body twisting beneath her undergarments.

'No heavy mattresses for months,' Ramus said. 'All these luxuries we forgo when we go on a voyage! Ramin was just bemoaning the lack of whores' breast milk in which to bathe. I'm just happy with hot food and ceyrat leaf tea.'

'You found ceyrat leaf?' Beko asked.

'Rhiana smelt a spread of it in the next field.' As he spoke the tall warrior approached, waving a handful of fresh yellow sprigs above her head.

'Then I'm with you!' Beko said. 'A Voyager's luxuries are hard-won and well loved.' He grabbed a leather skin and jogged towards the farm to fetch water.

Beko brought eggs and bread from the farm as well as the water, and while the ceyrat tea brewed, Lulah made breakfast. Ramus did not expect for a heartbeat that she would be a bad cook, and watching her work seemed to prove him right. She broke the eggs into a wide pan over the fire and whisked them with a frayed stick, adding a pinch of spice from a pouch she fetched from her saddle, stirring until the egg was lumpy, yellow and delicious-looking. She put the pan to one side and shredded the bread into finger-sized chunks, then she pricked each portion onto a metal skewer and toasted them quickly over the fire. It took five minutes to cook, and she clapped the skewer against the pan to tell everyone breakfast was ready. She truly seemed a woman of few words, and that intrigued Ramus more and more.

The food tasted even better than it looked. He could not identify the spice she had sprinkled into the egg, but it gave it a much more textured flavour, with pockets of heat that seemed to explode individually all across his mouth.

By the time they'd finished eating, the ceyrat tea was ready, and Lulah poured each of them a mug. Ramus watched her as she stood over him and poured, and when she glanced at his face he smiled. She looked away quickly and moved on to Noon.

The brewed ceyrat leaves – a favourite of predators before the hunt – buzzed into their muscles and limbs and chased away any shreds of sleep that remained. By the time they finished, the sun was pouring across the field. Long shadows from last night swayed in the opposite direction, and the light in between was brighter and fresher, and somehow more alive. Dawn breathed a heated promise of the day to come, and Ramus enjoyed the feel of it on his face.

They broke camp, packing tents and cooking equipment and leaving the bundles for Ramin and Noon to load onto the packhorses. The Serians worked efficiently and silently, and it was only when they were ready to move out that the banter began again.

Lowkie and his wife came to bid them farewell. The farmer's eyes were narrow and the skin around them dark, and Ramus smiled. Too much of his own wine.

'Stop by when you return!' he said. 'The wine will be better settled by then, I'm sure.'

Nobody answered with anything other than a wave. *When we return,* Ramus thought. *How many of us will there be?* He blinked at the weight behind his eyes, but his vision today was good, the pain absent, and if he did not think too deeply, he could even believe that he would see this place again.

They rode out, Lulah and Ramin moving on ahead to make sure the trail was clear. Ramus and Nomi rode side by side, excited that the first full day of their voyage had begun, comfortable in each other's company and relishing the feel of sunlight and open air on their skin.

Ramus noticed the rope charm still hanging exposed on Nomi's saddle.

'A good camp,' he said. 'I've not eaten so well in ages.'

'I always *think* I eat well,' Nomi said. 'You know me – the best food, the best wine rooms. But there's something about food cooked outside, the fresh ingredients, the meat just killed, eggs just laid, the smells…'

'It's called having a wandering soul,' Ramus said.

Nomi uttered a sharp laugh. 'That's us! Wandering souls.'

He had found his horse's rhythm much quicker this morning, and even before the Lowkie farmstead passed from view behind them Ramus was riding with a smooth, fluid pace.

'Did you sleep well?' Nomi asked.

'I did. Fresh air. The excitement too, I think, knocked me out.'

'And the wine,' Nomi said.

Ramus nodded, but when he looked across Nomi seemed distant and concerned. 'What is it?' he asked.

She stared into his eyes as though she had never seen them before. 'Are you really scared?'

'Yes.' There was no reason to lie.

She lowered her voice. 'But the Sleeping God...you don't *believe* in things like that.'

'Just because I choose not to worship them, doesn't mean I don't believe. There's too much written about them to discard them entirely.'

'We'll be fine,' Nomi said, but she seemed distracted.

'What is it?'

'Bad dreams last night. Change of diet, maybe.'

Ramus went to say something but Nomi clucked her horse on, cantering forward until she was riding side by side with Beko.

Change of diet, Ramus thought. *Or the map I made, the parchment Ten sold us, the place we're going, the thing we may be going to see. Yes, bad dreams are understandable.* He only hoped that this day would pass without him having another nightmare. He would do his best not to close his eyes for too long and allow one in.

Springtime in Marrakash was often quite warm, but today was more like summertime, the sun beating strongly against the subtle southern breeze, a combination which made the air light and sweet. Ramus stripped off his jacket and hung it from the saddle, and soon after Ramin was the first of the

Serians to take off his leather tunic. The others followed suit, and by mid-morning they were riding in their undershirts.

Ramus could already see an order developing amongst the riders. Ramin and Noon were obviously good friends. When they were not chatting, they rode in an easy silence, each of them guiding one of the packhorses with casual care. Ramus suspected that they had been chosen to lead the horses because they were closest to the animals, and some of their chat seemed to be directed to the horses as much as anyone else. Though Ramin's appearance was intimidating, there was a gentleness about him that Ramus liked. It made him easy to talk to, and the big man's good humour was always infectious.

Konrad was serious but affable, and he usually rode behind Ramin and Noon. Lulah would ride behind him, and she was the one Serian that Ramus had not even had a chance to fathom. She said so little, and when she did speak he always felt excluded, as though she were talking to her comrades and never to him and Nomi. He had attributed her solemnity to the studded eyepatch that must have such a story to tell, but he realised that conclusion was too hasty. Just because she displayed a terrible wound did not mean that she had been any different before receiving it. Maybe she was simply mistrustful. After all, she had been hired to protect Nomi and himself on the voyage, not make friends with them.

Rhiana usually rode up front, either alongside Beko or a few lengths in front or behind him. They seemed to change the lead regularly. Rhiana had boasted most kills out of all of them, and looking at her tall, imposing figure and honed physique, he could well believe that she could fight when called upon to do so.

It was he and Nomi who changed their positions most among the group. They could decide whether they wanted to be alone or in company, chatting to a Serian or each other. Ramus was already starting to find the Serians' ordered riding somewhat cloying. Others he had ridden with were much more casual, unless the situation called for more caution. Beko, their captain, had started the voyage as he meant to go on.

Ramus fell back and waited for the Serians to pass him by. Nomi had taken up position at the rear of the line mid-morning, and she had remained there ever since.

Lulah passed by without a glance. She had stripped to woollen trousers and a soft vest, and he could see now that the missing eye was not her only wound. Her entire left shoulder and upper arm was a mass of scar tissue, twisted and ugly in the blazing sunlight. Her beaded hair hung across it, and the textures of hair and skin matched.

'Hot today,' he said, wishing he could think of a better silence breaker.

Lulah glanced sidelong at him, up at the sun, and then forwards again.

Ramus shrugged, waited until Nomi drew close then fell in beside her. 'She's so quiet,' he said.

'Beko tells me there's some betrayal in her past,' Nomi said.

How free Beko is with his words to you, he thought. 'Maybe that's why she's so quiet during the day.'

'Of course,' Nomi said. 'But don't you hear her at night?'

Ramus frowned, shrugged.

'She doesn't sleep all night. She spends some of it praying to the death moon.'

'Praying for what?'

'What do moon worshippers usually pray for?'

'Same thing as most other people who choose one god over another,' Ramus said. 'Health, wealth, good harvests. Luck.'

They rode silently for a while, both watching Lulah moving easily on her horse.

'Somehow I think she prays for more than that,' Nomi said.

They rode through lunch, eating the bread left over from breakfast. It was still fresh, the crusts crispy. Rhiana leant almost sideways in her saddle to pluck at some tall yellow flowers, discarding the petals and crushing the rest inside her bread.

Ramus glanced down at the flowers as he passed, but he knew that he would end up falling from his saddle and making a fool of himself.

Around mid-afternoon, well on their way across the Marrakash plains, Beko rode back to speak to Ramus and Nomi. They had been riding in silence for a while, and Ramus welcomed the conversation. He did not know how Nomi felt, but sometimes the silence between them seemed to seethe.

'There's an old temple ruin a mile from here,' Beko said. 'I visited it once on a voyage several years ago. Deep, interesting, and it's relatively untouched.'

'What sort of temple?' Ramus asked.

'It's said that it's an ancient shrine to the Sleeping Gods.'

Ramus was aware of Nomi glancing sidelong at him but he kept his expression neutral. 'I'd like to see it.'

Beko rode back to the head of the line without another comment. He took them off the rough trail they were still following and into the grasslands proper, heading for a hill and the forest that started at its base. There was a stream there as well; Ramus could smell the water from here, and hear the chatter of wading birds. Cults of the Sleeping Gods had often built their temples close to running water, believing that the river or stream would carry their words across the land and beneath it, to where the gods still slept. More recent temples to the gods were less elaborate, and more likely to be built in residential areas, whether close to running water or not. It was as though civilisation engendered apathy, and people would only worship if it was convenient.

They passed from sunlight into the shadow of the hill, and the relief among them was palpable. Even the horses seemed to have more energy out of the heat. Beko led them into the trees and soon they could see some of the ruin – a collection of walls and tumbled stones much like a hundred others across Noreela. It was hidden away in a steep-sided ravine in the hillside that must have been caused by an ancient landfall.

They dismounted, and Noon and Ramin volunteered to remain with the horses. Ramus and Nomi followed close behind Beko, approaching the front lip of the ravine and the tangle of rock and undergrowth scattered there.

'Strange,' Nomi said. 'Worshippers usually wanted their place of worship on display.'

They made their way over the scatter of fallen rocks and the plant life that had made it home. There were new rockfalls here – jagged edges and dark pits not yet weathered by time – and Ramus glanced up at the sides of the open ravine. It must happen someday, he knew. Voyagers venturing somewhere unknown, and timing their visit exactly with the next fall of rocks. Why not here and now?

'Nervous?' Nomi asked.

'Cautious.'

Beko called a halt and stepped forward guardedly, stretching to look at something on the ground. 'Raynon cactus,' he said. 'Not blooming right now.'

Beko went on and they followed him, and Ramus noted yet again how curious everyone was about death, whatever their beliefs. Even Lulah peered at the squat, viciously spiked cactus, trying to see who or what lay dead beneath the flesh-eating plant. The fact that it was not blooming meant that the body was likely rotted away completely by now, and Ramus caught a brief glimpse of bone. It would only need the plant to catch a small bird or rodent, and then the flowers would blossom and the deadly pollen be released when someone or something walked by. He'd heard of a whole family being infected and killed when they ventured too close to a group of Raynon cacti in the Poison Forests. The wonder of this most fearsome plant was that it spread itself by making the infection slow and painful, so that victims wandered far and wide as the roots grew deep into their vital organs.

'Last visitor to the temple,' Ramus muttered.

'I think it was an animal,' Rhiana said, but no one commented because none of them could tell for sure.

They climbed into the mouth of the ravine, the Serians looking ahead at the ruins and up at the cliffs on either side. It was quiet and peaceful, but danger often hid in silence.

The temple was now in full view. It was much larger than many of the other ruins Ramus had seen on his travels, and it spoke of a fierce commitment to whatever it was built to honour.

'I always find these places chilling,' Nomi said.

'That's because you have no soul,' Ramus said, and he walked on with a smile.

'If you weren't such a friend...' Nomi muttered. He could hear from her voice that she wasn't sure whether he was joking.

He reached the first mound of rubble from a fallen wall and moved vegetation aside with his foot. There were no carvings or shapes in the stone here, so he went on.

'There's actually a doorway still standing around the back,' Beko said. 'At least, there was last time I was here.'

'How long ago was that?' Ramus asked.

'Three years. It feels just the same as it did then.'

Ramus looked at the captain, but he did not elaborate.

The Voyager climbed over a low wall that still stood a couple of blocks high, taking care where he was treading. The undergrowth was rampant here, tangled ground vines twisting in and around the stones, curled together and pointing roots to the soil, leafy fronds at the sky. They hid the ground from view, and every footstep risked a sprained ankle or worse.

The Serians had taken up position around the front of the ruin. Beko stood with Rhiana, while Konrad and Lulah had each gone to opposite sides of the ravine. They all looked alert and on guard, and Ramus felt comforted.

He moved some more vines away from a wall, and there were the first carvings. He traced them with his fingers, trying to make out the shapes and symbols, but weather and time had made them vague.

'What do you think?' Nomi asked.

'I can't tell yet,' he said. 'But your captain seemed certain.'

'*My* captain?'

Ramus glanced back and smiled at Nomi. She was half embarrassed, half angry.

Ramus headed around the back of the ruin to the doorway

Beko had mentioned. When he reached it, he moved back a few paces, trying to make out the whole facade of the temple before going inside. It was surprisingly well preserved, perhaps protected from the weather by the sheer walls of the ravine, which ended a dozen steps beyond the building. It was almost as though the ravine had been made for the temple, but he guessed it was the other way around. Whoever had built this place, however long ago, had meant it to fill this wound in the land.

'It's a weird place to build,' Nomi said.

Ramus shrugged. 'We can't pretend to know the minds of whoever built it. Could be a thousand years old, or even older.'

'Shall we go inside?'

Ramus swept his hand toward the ruin. 'After you.'

It was darker, but other than that there should have been no difference. There was no roof, and once through the door it was clear that few walls still stood higher than his head. But still Ramus felt as though he was moving into another place. In the ravine there was nature and shade, the Raynon cactus awaiting its next victim, and creepers using the tumbled walls as their home. Outside, time went on.

In here, time was frozen in place.

He could almost taste the final breaths of whoever had built this temple to the lost gods.

The remaining walls were lined with carvings. Most of them were badly weathered, but a few were still quite clear. Ramus read some sigils, translating as best he could, and he nodded in silent confirmation.

'Sleeping Gods?' Nomi said.

'Yes. Your captain was right.'

'I wish you wouldn't call him that.'

'And that's why I shall continue.' Ramus pointed at the base of one wall, where a sloped pile of debris was home to a vibrant purple heather. 'There were tiles on the wall once,' he said. 'If we could spend a year here piecing those together, we'd know more about the people who built this place than anyone else.'

Nomi whistled softly. 'That's a job for you on the way back, perhaps. Me, I choose travel over archaeology.'

'What is it you think we do on our voyages?' he asked. 'We dig up the past by discovering the present.'

'Very profound, Ramus. You should write a book.'

He smiled at her, opening the leather pouch on the side of his backpack and bringing out the empty journal. 'I'm going to start right here.'

'Recording your voyage?'

'*Our* voyage.' He showed her the title page he had written before leaving Long Marrakash.

'And what will you say about me in your book?'

'That's for me to know,' he said, 'and you to read.'

'You know very well I can't read.'

'Ah.' Ramus selected a hard charcoal stick from his writing roll and sharpened it with a small blade.

Nomi wandered away, idly kicking through the low undergrowth as if expecting to find something amazing beneath. She touched the walls, ran her fingers across some of the carvings, looked at Ramus and then headed for the opening through which they had entered.

'I'll see you outside,' she said.

'I won't be long.' Ramus did not look up from the open

book until he was sure he was alone once more.

And when he did look up and cast his gaze across the walls, and saw the carvings and images engraved by ancient hands, he was filled with a terror that punched straight through his chest and grabbed his heart.

For an instant he sensed this place as it had once been. People had worshipped here, but they had also feared.

A breeze rustled the undergrowth, like the satisfied sigh of a giant.

They are long gone and barely known, he thought. *So old that whether they really existed ceased to matter centuries ago. And now we're making it matter once again. We're going beyond the known Noreela in pursuit of what Noreelans have believed for millennia.*

He looked around the walls at the vague carvings. There were images he recognised from the texts he had read about the Sleeping Gods, and some shapes he had never seen before. He took out the parchment, unrolled it and tried to find a match for the image of the Sleeping God drawn thereon. He looked closer at the crumbling walls and—

Something moved before him. A shadow shifted, left the shade of a wall, crossed the ruined temple and faded slowly into sunlight.

A wraith.

Ramus gasped, reaching for breath, leaning his elbows on his knees and watching the book tumble to the ground. It landed with blank pages facing up, and his fingers spasmed and let the charcoal fall. It bounced from the paper, left its own random mark, bounced again. Ramus saw familiar nothing in the mark.

'Who can truly face their gods?' Ramus whispered.

The pain in his head slammed him once. Then he sat back and sighed, listening to the Serians chatting beyond the walls, birds calling from tree to tree, and he looked up and saw the same sky beneath which they all existed.

Nomi walked from the ruin towards the ravine walls. She did not like the feel of the place, and Ramus's strange behaviour made it worse. She knew that he could withdraw into himself when faced with something that fascinated or perplexed him, but she hated being subject to his sudden mood swings.

She glanced back at the old temple. She could just see him past one of the tumbled walls, sitting on a fallen stone with the book open on his legs before him. *He made me a part of his title,* she thought. *He's making me a part of his book.* The urge to learn to read was strong, and perhaps when this voyage was over she would do just that. The fame would ensure that she would never have to work again. But the thought of sitting in dusty, old libraries poring over the yellowed pages of books written centuries before she was born...she could find no allure in that. She'd much rather come out into the world, sit around a campfire and hear history related by the likes of Konrad. Tonight the Serians would tell another story, and tomorrow morning she and Ramus would know more than they had before. She had always thought word of mouth a more honest, immediate method of relaying history down through the ages.

Ramus seemed to drop the book and lean forward to pick it up. Then he leant back and looked around himself at the walls, the ruin, the sky.

Nomi turned her back on Ramus and stared up at the lip of the ravine. The wall before her was sheer, speckled here and there with tufts of moss and heather, and she could see a few birds' nests gripping the small ledges. The birds themselves were keeping well out of sight. She wondered whether their ancestors had nested here and watched this temple being built, and the richness of time washed over her. She wondered what language the builders had spoken, whether they had used slave labour, what they had looked like, what clothes they had worn. And for an instant she considered that a Sleeping God itself may have overseen construction.

Nobody knew just how long ago the Sleeping Gods had supposedly gone down.

She looked at Beko where he stood at the mouth of the ravine. *Ramus called him my captain,* she thought. *Perhaps I'd like that to be so.*

There was a sudden movement at the ruin and Ramus emerged, carrying his blank book by one open cover like an injured bird. He looked around, lost and frantic, until he set eyes on her.

'You were quick,' she said, but she could see that something had happened.

Ramus stared at her for a heartbeat too long before smiling and shaking his head. He looked down and closed the book slowly, deliberately, taking too long. *Composing himself,* Nomi thought.

'Not much new here,' he said.

'Except?' Nomi hurried to him, ignoring the flutter of activity from the Serians listening to their exchange.

'Except nothing,' he said.

'Ramus?'

He shook his head. 'Just a funny turn.'

'You feel unwell?'

'No. Maybe it's the heat, or...'

'This place.' She smiled and touched his arm. 'You always get so involved.'

'Yes,' he said. 'Involved.' He walked away, holding the book to his chest as though he had something to hide.

'Ramus!' Nomi called. *His illness?* she thought. *Or something else? I really need to know. Not for him or the voyage, but for me.*

He paused and looked over his shoulder.

'If you're unwell, we can turn around,' she said.

'I'm not unwell, Nomi.' He looked at the temple he seemed so keen to leave behind. 'Some places have echoes, that's all.'

Nomi listened, and watched, and when he walked away she saw Beko staring at her. She turned her back on all of them and looked at the ruins of the temple to the Sleeping Gods. A strange place, so old and well constructed for its time that much of it still stood. And she thought, *He's lying.*

'Let's get back to the horses,' Beko said. 'I have a camp site in mind for the night, but it's a good twenty miles on.'

'I'll ask him,' Nomi whispered. A bird took flight from one of the nests in the cliff wall, as though it had been listening for these words. She watched it fly, wondering how many other secret mutterings it had shared.

When he reached his horse, Ramus risked one more look at the book. Past the page he had titled back in Long Marrakash, the first blank page was now marked by the dropped charcoal.

When he had bent to pick up both book and charcoal, he had made another mark. An accident. A fumble, a slip of the hand.

But when he had grasped the book by its cover, and when it had swung down to hang at an angle from his hand, those random marks had manifested into images he could understand. It was Old Noreelan, with the pictorial quality so common in tomes about the Sleeping Gods.

He looked at it one more time, and even in the heat he could not withhold a shiver.

It said, *Never wake the fallen.*

CHAPTER SEVEN

They rode hard that afternoon, through the heat of the sun and dust thrown up from the dried ground, and by the time Beko called a halt they were all ready to stop. He rode on ahead with Rhiana and Konrad, the three of them spread out across the trail. Nomi knew that they were making sure the camp site he had in mind was safe. They were much closer to the border with the Pavissia Steppes now, and it was not unheard of for marauder parties to make sorties into Marrakash.

She dismounted and watched Ramus do the same.

He had said very little that afternoon. She'd ridden beside him much of the time, but the moment had never seemed right to ask what had bothered him at the temple. He had returned the book to his backpack and hung it on his saddle, and his expression had looked uncomfortable rather than disturbed. Whether that was because he knew she was watching, Nomi did not know.

'I'm sore and aching and I'd kill for a bath,' she said.

Ramin laughed. 'I wondered where the smell came from!

And there I was, blaming my sweet horse.' He leant forward and clucked and whispered into his beast's ear.

'Watch who you abuse, Ramin. I've decided that I'm cooking tonight.'

The Serian gave her an easy smile and touched his chest, lowering his head in a casual apology.

Nomi laughed. She felt fine. These Serians were good, and that gave her more comfort than she could have hoped for.

But Ramus...

She walked to him, tapped him on the shoulder and refused to drop her gaze when he turned around.

'Leave a weary old man alone,' he said at last.

'You're only ten years older than me.'

Ramus shrugged. 'I *feel* older. Probably all the hard living I've chosen, and the good living you've endured.'

'What's wrong?' she asked, lowering her voice. She did not want the Serians to think there was a problem. Beko she could talk to if necessary, but Ramin, Lulah and Noon were still unknown to her. They made her feel safe, but the farther they went from Long Marrakash, the harder trust was won.

Ramus glanced over her shoulder, obviously thinking the same thing. 'Just a bad feeling at the temple,' he said. He patted the backpack still hanging on his saddle.

'Ramus, in every story I've heard they're benevolent gods.'

'Of course they are. Benevolent *Sleeping* Gods. Who are we to wake them?'

'If they're even there. And who's to say we'll wake them?'

He came in close, his nose almost touching hers. Nomi was aware of Lulah looking their way, but she would not pull back. She could smell Ramus's breath, feel the heat radiating from his face.

'You really think that if we go there and find a Sleeping God, then things will stop there?'

'I don't know,' Nomi said. 'But we came on this voyage together. And nothing happens that we don't both agree on first.'

He pulled away, and uttered a noise that may have been a laugh. 'You've always believed you're so central to your life,' he said. 'But no one is. We're all small players in a much larger game.' He touched the backpack again. 'This is already way beyond us.'

'What did you write in your book, Ramus?'

'Nothing. There was nothing to write. I sat in the temple and read the walls. That's all.'

'Let me see.'

He smiled at her, but it was an ugly expression; not quite a sneer, but something with a dash of madness buried deep. 'You can't read,' he said.

'Beko's back,' Noon called.

Nomi turned around and Noon, Ramin and Lulah were watching her and Ramus curiously. She tried not to catch their eyes.

Beko and the others arrived, and the captain dismounted. 'The place I mentioned is just up ahead, on the other side of that low hill. It's even better than it was last time.'

'Better?' Nomi asked.

Beko smiled. 'You'll see. It's the last night we'll be camping in Marrakash, so I think it's only fair we take advantage of the safety.'

They mounted up and rode, and Nomi kept pace with Beko. She did not look back to see where Ramus was. She felt certain that she was being watched, but it could have been the

Serians' curiosity about their employers' exchange.

Let him play his games, she thought. *Let him see doom in every tumbled wall. This will be the voyage of my life, and I intend to enjoy it.*

She looked sideways at Beko and he grinned. And she wondered just what he had planned for that evening's campfire entertainment.

Nomi had been determined to cook their meal that evening. But when she mentioned it to Beko, he shook his head.

'Believe me, let Rhiana cook tonight. We've been here before, and she knows what she's doing.'

'What's so special about here and tonight?' Nomi asked.

'Rhiana,' Beko said.

The tall Serian dropped gracefully from her horse. 'It's a meal you'll remember for a long time,' she said. 'Or maybe not at all.'

Beko had certainly found them a beautiful place. Shielded from the cool evening breeze by a rocky outcrop, the level area was perfect for camping, with a soft bed of short grass and a scattering of stones with which to build a fire pit. A stream sprung from the ground to one side, gurgling merrily as though relieved to have found its way out of subterranean darkness. The marshy ground around the stream's birthplace was home to a profusion of small trees, bushes, orchids and a mix of berry shrubs. Some of them hung heavy with early fruit, while others rustled and shimmied with life. Nomi clapped her hands and watched small birds take flight. Lizards darted away into the cover of rocks and a larger, more cautious creature went deeper into the undergrowth.

'You sure you want us to camp this near to so much wildlife?' Nomi said dubiously.

'I've camped here before,' Beko said. 'I've never seen anything poisonous or harmful.'

Ramus sat across the clearing, leaning against a tree with hands on knees and eyes closed. He kept his backpack close. *Let him play his games,* she thought again.

She turned back to Beko. 'So, what are we eating?'

'That's up to you and me.'

Beko led Nomi across the stream, through a bank of heavy shrubs and down into the borders of a small forest at the bottom of the hill. It was cool beneath the trees, calming, the sound of the stream complemented by the gentle swish and sway of the canopy in the evening breeze. It felt as though they had entered nature rather than disturbed it; birds continued singing, and Nomi saw the shadows of three small deer nosing through the bracken deeper in the forest. She did not mention them to Beko.

That was another way Ramus mocked her. *If you had to kill your own food,* he would say, *you'd live on root vegetables and berries.* Well, now she was hunting with Beko. And if they were to eat as well as he promised this evening, something had to die.

But not the deer. She walked quickly ahead, stomping her feet and stepping on a fallen branch. The crack sounded like a whip. The deer shapes froze and then melted quickly away between the trees, almost as if they were shadows that could disperse rather than run.

'Don't worry,' said Beko. 'It's not deer we're after.' He walked past her and unslung the bow from his back. He looked up into the tree canopy, down at the ground, shifted the leaves and twigs around with one foot. 'We'll have to go deeper.'

'What are we hunting?'

'Green tree lizards.'

'They're poisonous!' Nomi said. When she was a young girl some of her friends had fed a green tree lizard to a farm wolf, and they had laughed and danced as it squirmed in agony and died. She could still hear its howls, and she could still hear her own hesitant laughter as she tried to join in.

'Don't worry so much, Nomi,' Beko said. He stepped close, grinned, and touched her on the shoulder.

A touch, she thought. *Not a squeeze or a clap. He touched me.* And as she realised that he was closer than he should have been, he turned and walked away.

Nomi put her hand to her neck as she followed the Serian, as though she would feel something different there. On their previous voyage they had grown close, but neither of them had let romance come between them. Nomi because she had still been involved with Timal at the time...and Beko? Why had he held back? For a while she had assumed that it was in deference to her own wishes, but as time passed and Timal left, she had believed that less and less.

Perhaps it was this new voyage, and where they were going, and the feeling that this was something different. She smiled at Beko's back and followed him into a bank of high bushes.

'Slow,' he whispered, crouching down and walking slower. He held the bow at his side so that it did not snag on undergrowth.

Nomi imitated his pose, trying to walk in his footsteps. She could not hear him; no breathing, no rustling clothes. She was certain that she would spoil this hunt. Her trousers whispered as she walked, and her open jacket caught on a sprig of bracken and whipped it back. She closed her eyes and breathed through her mouth, and when she looked again Beko was staring back at her.

He stared for a little too long.

'What?' she whispered, but she thought she knew. Her stomach was warm, her legs shaking under the stress of her pose and the influence of his stare.

Beko pointed up and to his left. Nomi looked and saw several green tree lizards roosting on a tree trunk, the largest of them easily the length and thickness of her arm. She gasped. She had never seen one so huge.

Beko was still looking at her, and he blinked slowly as he began to turn away.

She thought he would move slowly, getting into position, plucking the arrow from the quiver across his back, stringing it, turning, aiming and firing only when he knew the moment was right. But as she looked back up at the lizard, she saw a flutter of movement from the corner of her eye, and then an arrow struck home. The lizard hissed for a heartbeat and then hung still, impaled against the trunk. Its companions disappeared around the tree, and a heartbeat later Nomi heard them dropping to the forest floor and away.

'That was so fast,' she said. 'I didn't even see you move.'

'I'm hungry,' Beko said, grinning. He had already shouldered the bow and was heading for the tree.

'But they *are* poisonous,' Nomi said. 'I know for sure.'

'Only if you don't know how to cook them properly.' He reached the tree, drew his sword and stretched to hack through the arrow. The lizard fell and Beko caught it neatly in one hand. 'Waste of an arrow, but it'll be worth it.'

'We should go deeper,' Nomi said. Her heart suddenly beat faster, and her face flushed as she looked away from the captain and through the trees into the forest's deepening darkness. 'Might find some peace truffles. Good for relaxing.' *I'm not looking for truffles,* she thought, all too aware of Beko's gaze once again. She could almost feel where he was looking; her hair, her neck, her breasts. Or perhaps that was her own wishful thinking.

'No need for peace truffles,' he said. He was standing right beside her, though she had not heard him move. The dead lizard nudged against her leg. 'And no need to go deeper.'

Nomi closed her eyes. The coolness of the forest air soothed her hot skin as a breeze ventured between the trees. *What am I doing?* she thought. She knew well enough that a long voyage could be made awkward by an involvement such as this, but—

Beko's hand brushed across her stomach and stole down between her thighs, pressing there gently, weakening her legs and making her gasp.

'Beko…' she said, turning to him at last. She could hear his breathing now, fast and shallow. He was looking at her as though he could see her soul.

Timal never looked at me like that, she thought, and with her ex-lover's name in her mind, things fell apart. The pleasant coolness beneath the trees turned cold. Beko sensed it and moved away, looking down at the lizard swinging from his hand.

'It's me,' Nomi said. 'It feels wrong.'

'It doesn't feel wrong to me,' the soldier said, and there was something so vulnerable in his voice that Nomi almost went to him. She looked at his scarred face and remembered how awkward he had seemed when he first spoke free poetry to her, sitting alone in a Ventgorian stilt house. He had loved and lost, and only someone with such experience could recite like that.

'We've a long way to go,' Nomi said. And, as if that could explain everything, she turned and started walking back uphill.

'Nomi,' Beko said. She turned and smiled at him, because he was already grinning again. 'I can be very persistent. I should tell you, in case you see a problem in that.'

She raised an eyebrow. 'Then persist.' She turned away again, scolding herself as she walked, grinning, wondering what doors had been opened and which hidden places they would reveal.

By the time they returned to the camp, the others had lit a fire and started pitching tents. The horses were tethered loosely in the trees, saddles lay ready around the fire and Rhiana was foraging across the marshy ground by the stream. She eyed the green tree lizard appreciatively, then glanced quickly at Nomi.

'Good hunting?' she asked.

'I look forward to seeing how you feed us that and keep us all alive,' Nomi said, only half joking.

Rhiana opened her hand and showed Nomi a mixture of berries, leaves and dirt-encrusted root. 'Magic,' she said.

Nomi was glad to see that the Serians had also erected her tent. She slipped inside and pulled the flap closed. She sat down and sighed, wiping her hands across her face and feeling the grit and grime on her skin. The heat of her arousal was fading but the memory was still there, an imprint of Beko's brazen and confident touch. A stroke against her stomach, soft as a butterfly's wings, and then the firm pressure of his hand between her legs. He was a warrior and a poet, and she could not help but wonder which one had touched her. She was excited, but also slightly unnerved. She was not like some other Voyagers, setting themselves above their hired help. Yet she could conceive of nothing but trouble if she and Beko...

'There's nothing wrong with a hump,' she whispered.

But there *was* something wrong, and it took a moment of silence and privacy to acknowledge what that was: Ramus. The other Serians would likely offer jibes and make fun of them if they were together, but Ramus was something else entirely. Their complicated friendship made other aspects of their relationship equally intense; the jealousies, the resentfulness. *But I've never wanted him in that way. Not Ramus. He's too cold, too serious, too...*

Too much like I want to be? The voice and thought were her own, and yet seemed to come from elsewhere. Perhaps from the person she would have been had she returned from Ventgoria dying, not cured.

'Piss!' she hissed. 'Piss on it all!' She should go outside, watch Rhiana cook, and spend the evening with her travelling companions, doing her best not to let such concerns intrude.

After all, Rhiana had offered a meal that they would never forget.

'It's the liver that's poisonous,' she said. 'Make sure you remove that whole and the rest of the meat is wondrous. Watch.' Rhiana had the dead lizard on the ground before her, laid across a few wide sheets of bark.

The others were leaning against their saddles, relaxing in the warmth from the fire and sipping the remainder of the root wine from their mugs. Only Noon was absent, sitting somewhere away from the camp on watch. Ramus sat quietly against his saddle, his backpack still within easy reach. He was not actively ignoring Nomi, yet since their return from the hunt he had not gone out of his way to talk to her.

Beko was as relaxed and casual as ever. He smiled at her, and everything seemed unchanged. She was glad. She would hate there to be tension between them.

Rhiana heated her knife in the fire, turned the lizard onto its back and sliced. With a few deft swipes of the blade the animal lay open and bare, steaming slightly in the fading light. She leant back to view the corpse, then worked with the knife again, lifting out a glistening mass and dropping it into the fire. Then she took a root wine bottle and poured a good slug into the wound.

'There,' she said. 'All the nasty stuff burnt away, all the good stuff left. Now to really make the meal.'

Nomi felt a brief sense of disgust when Rhiana chopped off the animal's head and legs, stripped its scaly skin and started slicing chunks of meat and dropping them into a pot. But she thought again of what Ramus had said, and disgust turned to satisfaction that she had at least been involved in the hunt. She'd seen the animal killed, knew that it had died quickly and cleanly, and now it was being prepared with casual skill by someone who knew the value of good meat.

'This is when I turn good to great,' Rhiana said. She started crushing berries, slicing fine washed roots and tearing leaves into the pot with the meat. 'This is a good place for herbs and berries,' she said. 'It's the water that rises with the spring, fresh and clear and untouched by the sun or moons. Spends its life underground, picking up all sorts of hints of nature, and when it comes up here it seeps through the soil and gives these plants life. Don't know why it's so good. Just know it is.'

'*Very* good,' Ramin said. 'Sends your mind away!'

'What do you mean?' Nomi asked.

'He means we're going to get swayed,' Ramus said.

'Oh.' Nomi had never been one for such things. Wine, yes, in reasonable quantities, but she liked maintaining control of her mind. She glanced at Beko and their eyes locked briefly before they both looked away. *Thinking the same thing?* she wondered. Perhaps. She was thinking about loss of control. 'Is that really safe?' she asked.

'Give you less of a headache than that pissing root wine,' Konrad said.

'I mean with us camping so close to the border.'

'We can still fight if we're swayed,' Lulah said.

'And Noon is on watch.'

'Don't worry,' Beko said. 'It's not like the sky-root you get in the city. That's meant to lay you out cold. This is all natural, all fresh.'

Rhiana finished chopping, crushing and slicing and stirred the meat and plants together. Then she poured in half a bottle of root wine and hung the pot over the fire. 'It'll take a while. Time for a talk or a poem, a song or a story. Which will it be?'

'I'd like to hear a story from Nomi,' Beko said.

Nomi laughed and shook her head. 'I'm no storyteller. You Serians are the ones known for that. In fact, Ramus and I only hired you for your cooking and storytelling skills.'

'That's right,' Ramus said. 'We can look after ourselves.'

He spoke it so seriously that it was a few beats before everyone started to laugh.

❈   ❈   ❈

The smells from the cooking pot were wonderful. After some haranguing, Beko stood and recited a poem, part of something old augmented by some improvisation...or so he claimed. To Nomi, it sounded like something he had prepared long before. It spoke of the moons shedding their light on unknown lands, the curve of hips against rolling landscapes, the smell and dust of the trail washed away in pure waters, the caress of trees against a sky heavy with rain, and rivers flowing like Noreela's bloodlines. The camp remained silent and contemplative after he finished, and then Rhiana clanged the pot and announced that the meal was ready.

The meat was wonderful – rich, tender and moist, and the spices, herbs and root extracts complemented it perfectly. It cut a warm path down into Nomi's stomach, driving any chills from the inside out, and she found herself chewing and swallowing with eyes half closed. Every one of her senses was focused on the meal. She looked at her plate and perceived patterns in the food there; a face with one eye, a bird impaled on a thick thorn of a lightning tree, clouds striving to resemble something else. The smell was continuous, warm and smoky. Tastes grew and faded with each mouthful, the meat providing a perfect canvas on which the other ingredients painted their own particular images. Her mouth and tongue became her prime organ, swilling the food around to make the most of its touch, listening to the sound her teeth made grinding through meat, cracking seed pods and crushing leaf stalks. It was a sensory experience, and the satisfaction the food brought to her empty stomach was almost an afterthought.

When she had finished, she ran her finger around the plate, gathering juice and errant herb shreds and licking them off.

Her eyes were still almost closed, and she was revelling in the results of the meal. Because, though the eating was over, she was beginning to understand what Rhiana and Beko had said about camping here. It was indeed a special place. She was more aware than ever of her body, where her limbs lay, the sensation of the ground pressing at her rear and legs, the touch of the evening breeze through her hair and across her stomach where Beko had touched her, and in her fingertips she felt the memory of that touch as though she had made it herself. She frowned, inhaled quickly and remembered the other way he had touched her soon after, and then she felt the heat of that touch in her own hand. She opened her eyes dreamily and checked that her hands were not drifting anywhere they should not, but no, it was an imagined sensation.

'That was a meal,' Ramus said. He nodded slowly, thoughtfully, and said the same thing again, as though keen to make sure everyone knew.

'This is good,' Beko said.

'Not too bad, Rhiana,' Ramin said. 'Meat could have been...a bit more tender.'

'Piss on you,' Rhiana said.

'What, out here where the moons can see us?'

Rhiana giggled softly. 'You wish.'

Ramin stood slowly – Nomi watched, and it seemed to take almost for ever for him to stand – and stretched, fingers reaching for the mysterious stars as though there was a very real chance he could grab them.

'What a statue he would make,' Lulah said. 'Dark as the night, bald as a baby, ugly as a seethe-gator's cock.'

Ramin laughed out loud, holding his stomach and bending

over when it became too much. He laughed until he gagged and then fell to his knees. 'You're only jealous of my finely sculpted body,' he said. He crawled to her on all fours, tongue lolling like a tamed wolf.

Lulah laughed. It was a low, rumbling chuckle, like a basket of stones being rolled, and Nomi found it endlessly fascinating. She sat up straighter and stared at the one-eyed Serian in frank amazement, wondering what she would say next, what she would do.

Lulah's legs fell open, Ramin crawled forward, and then she clamped her legs closed around his neck. He still giggled, even as she started gently slapping him around the face. 'Ramin should learn manners,' she said, punctuating each word with a slap. None of them were hard, and the affection these two had for each other was palpable.

Nomi stood and swayed with the rapid influx of information. It was as though she had suddenly grown a hundred steps tall and could see much farther, hear more, taste and feel more of the land than she ever had before. She was standing on a living map of the area, rising up and reading it. Beyond the trees there was more hillside, and then an old fence marking the boundary of an abandoned farmstead. The buildings were low and dark, but even though it was a mile distant and hidden by the folds in the land, she knew it was a ruin. She wondered where the farmers had gone, and suddenly their fate was clear to her; the disease and death, all of them rotting into the ground or being taken by carrion creatures. It was sad, but part of the risk of working the land. She turned slowly and saw past the stream, the horses and the marshy ground, down into the woods where they had killed the lizard. She could picture the paths and hillocks, the streams and fallen trees, the nesting birds and the marching ants as though she were there. And, if she breathed in deeply enough, she could smell that place.

She looked across the campfire at where Beko lay against his saddle, eyes closed and hands crossed on his stomach. And she knew that he was there as well.

'What is this?' she said.

'Swayed, that's all,' Rhiana said. 'Something under the ground, maybe. Something that flows with the water. It touched the plants, we eat the plants, and we're swayed.'

'Poor Noon,' Konrad said. 'He's up there in the shadows. Can't see him, but...'

'Picking his nose,' Beko said, and he snorted laughter. Others joined in, and Nomi turned and looked uphill to where Noon had hidden himself away. She could sense him up there, and when she closed her eyes she could almost see him as well.

And then suddenly she was back in the forest once more, below that tree where Beko had killed the lizard. She went slowly down to her knees and stared at him across the fire, and he was looking at her with hooded eyes, his face shimmering with the heat rising from the flames. Nomi blinked and smelt the forest, and she wondered whether she would feel him touch her again.

She lay down with her head on her saddle and closed her eyes, eager for more.

Ramus had never felt anything like this. He had been swayed on dried sky-root several times back in Long Marrakash, and each time its effect upon him had lessened. It was a relaxant that slowed the heart and made bad things seem good, and good things seem better. He drank root wine regularly, and sometimes Nomi would give him a bottle of her Ventgorian wine as well. He had even tried flail – a liquid drug derived from the spawn of wolf frogs in the wetlands west of Long Marrakash. It had pumped through his system and lit the darkness, but the illumination hurt like fire. Flail had been unpleasant, hurtful and probably addictive, and he had never returned to it.

But this…this was different. His perceptions were opened, not relaxed, sight and touch enhanced as though he could rise and expand from the weak flesh and blood thing he was.

He could feel the landscape around them. The sun was down now and darkness had fallen, but the lie of the land was more illuminated than if it had been daylight and he stood atop the hill, looking out and seeing rather than feeling. He was afraid to test how far his senses went, but he knew this hillside and stream, the forest and barely used paths beyond, the deserted farmstead to the east and the hill rising above, back the way they had come.

It was extraordinary. He could even feel the black heart of his illness, a shadow on his senses like a blank spot in the vision of someone going blind…which he supposed he was. The growths behind his eyes could crowd in at any moment and steal his sight, and if he was five hundred miles from home when that happened he was finished. Swayed, perceptions so much wider and clearer than ever before, he even tried to interrogate his sickness. But though it was a shadow within him, it offered up nothing. It would take more than some unknown drug from the ground to help him see that deep.

He opened his eyes and glanced around the camp. Konrad was sitting on his saddle with his head bent back, looking up at the stars and moon and the darkness in between. Lulah still sat with Ramin clasped between her legs, and he could hear the gentle mutter of their voices. There was nothing at all sexual about their pose, and affection radiated from them in waves. Rhiana had returned to the cooking pot and seemed to be picking scraps of something from what was left of the food, making delighted noises as though it was the first time she had tasted anything. Beko and Nomi…

Ramus was sure that they were still there, but when he looked directly at where they had been, they were there no more. Nomi's saddle was bare, gleaming in the moonlight, and Beko's weapon roll and saddle lay some way off across the other side of the fire.

No one else seemed to notice that they had gone.

Ramus closed his eyes and sensed the camp. It was like looking at a map of the place, and he was one of the best map-makers he knew. There was the fire, the Serians and himself lying within its influence, the horses standing still and quiet in the trees, the ring of tents, and beyond the fire's light and within the undergrowth to the east, Beko and Nomi.

Ramus sat up and opened his eyes. It was not his business. Timal had not been his business either, not really, but…

They were only sitting together, barely touching. Perhaps they were not even talking.

Ramus felt tired. His eyelids drooped and behind them he felt exhaustion closing in, blanking out the effects of the food, swaying him back down from high to the lowness of true sleep. He looked around the camp and saw the others drifting off as well, and the empty spaces where Beko and Nomi should have been, and as sleep took him he looked to the east once more.

They were still there, within those bushes, but now he could only make out one form. Entwined, moving beneath the moonlight, and as he was dragged down towards unconsciousness he did not know whether the cry he heard was Nomi in ecstasy, or himself in pain.

It had never been like this. She could feel Beko within her, and she could feel herself around him, and as she looked up into his eyes she knew that he was feeling the same, sensations from both of them mixing and merging as though drawn from the same warm spring. She was gasping with the wonder of it all and Beko breathed into her mouth, and she locked her legs around him to make sure they stayed together.

They had come here to talk, and even then she had not been sure whether she was dreaming. Beko had been mumbling something about the lie of the land and how beautiful shadows were in the darkness, and then the world had turned onto its side and her cool skin had grown warm where he touched her.

He lowered his head so that they were cheek to cheek, and Nomi looked up through the trees at the sky. Light danced as leaves shifted in the breeze, reflecting campfire and stars. Beko began to move faster, she clasped him harder, and then she heard a cry that should have been both of them together, but was not.

'The voyage starts so well!' Ramus shouted, his laughter high and uncontrolled. 'It starts so well, and then our Serians get us swayed, and then the fucking begins!'

Beko withdrew and knelt, and Nomi cried out at the overwhelming sense of abandonment. She sat up and reached for him, seeing the same feeling reflected in his eyes. But there was something else there, too. Anger.

She pulled her shirt closed and brought her knees up to her chest.

'Don't cover up for me!' Ramus was carrying a burning brand from the fire, and Nomi noticed the taint of scorched hair and skin on the air.

'Ramus, what have you done?' she said.

'What have *I* done? *Me*?' He took a step forward and Beko stood, tucking himself back into his trousers and moving between Ramus and Nomi.

Ramus laughed. Shook his head. And Nomi saw the tears on his face, though whether they were from the pain of the burn on his arm or something else, she did not want to know.

She was still swayed, but the shock had driven much of the effect away.

'This is nothing to do with you, Ramus,' she said, hating the appeal in her voice. *Isn't it?* she thought. She could not hide a flush of guilt, but at the same time she wished that he would piss off and let her and Beko finish what they had begun.

Ramus staggered slightly, and when Beko moved aside again, Nomi could just make out the ugly burn on his arm.

'Your arm!' she said aghast.

'I woke myself up. They put us to sleep but I woke myself up, because the truth needed seeing.'

'The truth of what?'

'You,' Ramus said, but already the anger was leaching from his voice. 'You two.'

'As Nomi said,' Beko said, 'it's nothing to do with you.'

'No?' he said, and his voice sounded weaker than ever. 'Really?'

Nomi stood. 'Oh, Ramus, I didn't realise... I didn't know...'

Ramus fell and Beko caught him, knocking the still-smouldering brand from his hand and lowering him gently to the ground.

'Rhiana!' the Serian called. He glanced across at Nomi. 'You should dress,' he said quietly.

Nomi pulled on her trousers, the cool breeze no longer pleasant against her damp skin. She wanted to go to Ramus, hold him, but now there was a shadow between them deeper than simple night. It was shaped from his surprising anger, and her own resentment at what he had done.

'Is he all right?' she asked.

'He's fainted,' Beko said. He was still holding Ramus, one hand behind his head to keep him comfortable. The Serian could have let him fall to the ground. And though there was anger in his eyes when he glanced at Nomi, she saw compassion there as well.

'You're a good man,' she blurted, looking away in embarrassment. Brought down from their sway by the sudden events, the sex hung heavy between them, and now Nomi was complicating it even more.

'I feel like slitting his pissing throat,' he said, then chuckled. 'Couldn't he have left it another few beats, eh?'

Nomi laughed gently.

Rhiana burst through the undergrowth. She carried an oil lantern in one hand, a short sword in the other. She glanced around the small clearing beneath the shrub's overhang and seemed to make sense of things in a heartbeat. She threw a brief smile at Nomi, sheathed her weapon and knelt beside Beko and Ramus.

'He's burnt his arm,' Beko said. 'We'll need to treat that so it doesn't become infected.'

'What's he likely to be like when he wakes?' the tall Serian said.

Beko shrugged. 'He wasn't violent. Just angry. I never heard of anyone having a bad sway from this place, have you?'

Rhiana shook her head. 'Everything still feels good and fine to me.' She took a small roll from her jacket pocket. It contained herbs and pastes; she had come prepared.

While Rhiana went to work on Ramus's wound, Beko stood and came to Nomi. He touched her shoulder, hesitated then pulled her close, pressing his cheek against hers. 'Perhaps it was a mistake,' he said.

'No!' Nomi said.

'You young lovers piss off and take it somewhere else,' Rhiana said. 'Whatever happened here, I don't want him waking back into it. It's a light faint. He'll come around soon.'

Nomi half-expected Beko to berate Rhiana for talking to him like that, but he grabbed Nomi by the arm and guided her away.

They emerged back into the camp to find the other Serians sitting around the fire, brewing red root tea and obviously doing their best to come around.

'No problem,' Beko said. 'But that tea's a good idea.' None of them asked any questions, and for that Nomi was glad.

'Beko…' she said. *Can we talk?* she wanted to ask. And she wanted to tell him about her and Ramus, how their friendship was fraught with complications, and how there had never been anything more serious between them. Not physically, and not in her mind. What went on in Ramus's head had always been a mystery to her, and now, rather than being enlightened, she was more confused than ever.

But the big Serian looked at her and shook his head slightly, then went back to his saddle. He sat and stared into the fire, accepting a mug of red root tea from Noon, and by the time Rhiana helped Ramus back into the camp they had been sitting in silence for some time.

Ramus, cowed and in pain, still uncertain on his feet, still trying to shake the sway from his system, allowed Rhiana to help him settle beside his saddle. He leant against the smooth leather and rested his wounded arm across his lap. The burn scorched a path of pain all through his arm and seemingly down to the bone, but the Serian had told him it would heal well. The paste she had chewed and then smeared against the wound was dark in the moonlight, but better than the sight of his own blackened skin. He was grateful to her, and he told her so.

'Just rest,' she said. 'I'll redress it in the morning.'

Ramus nodded and looked down at his arm. If he looked up he'd be with everyone else, but at least if he could not see them he could pretend he was on his own. *Hiding,* he thought, and the shame warmed his skin as well as the fire. Someone had piled more wood and firestones into the blaze, and now it threw sparks skyward and lit the entire camp. Sway rapidly fading, it seemed that events had brought an end to sleep.

What was I thinking? The memory came back to him, Beko and Nomi entangled in the moonlight, skin pale with a silvery sheen, gasps like wraiths in the night. *What a fool,* he thought. *That's what they'll think of me. A fool who gets swayed and loses control.*

He glanced across at Nomi. She was sitting on her saddle, elbows on knees, leaning forward and staring into the flames. Over the years, the more he considered they could be together as more than friends, the less likely that scenario seemed. And they were *good* friends, the *best*. If only he could have been content with that.

Ramus rose, standing still for a moment to make sure he had his balance. Then he walked a dozen steps to where Nomi sat, knelt down and waited for her to look at him.

She knew he was there, but her gaze never left the flames.

'Nomi,' Ramus began, but he got no further.

'You've always been jealous of me,' Nomi said. Her voice was low but filled with bitterness. Still she stared into the flames. 'My money, my lovers, my friends. They always make you feel low and sad, and pathetic.'

'No,' Ramus said, shaking his head.

'Yes. And my voyages.'

'Your *voyages*?' He laughed, and it sounded more mocking than he'd intended. 'Why would I be jealous of them? You've been out twice, and you came back with nothing but meaningless maps and fruit.'

'And what's wrong with that?' She had turned from the flames to stare at him now, and fire still seemed to dance in her eyes.

'It's hardly pushing the boundaries of discovery,' Ramus said. He was aware of heads turning as he and Nomi raised their voices.

'And that's another reason you resent me,' she said. 'You go out and strive to be famous – discover things, write books, bring back news of places and people and things never seen or known before. But what do you have? Piss all. You walk around a mountain range for a year and return with news of rock and snow.'

'I don't resent you for being a wine trader,' he said.

'And why *shouldn't* I benefit from my voyages? You have this belief, Ramus, that true explorers need to suffer for their calling.'

'Not suffer. It's about purity of purpose.'

'My purposes *are* pure. I go out and discover, and if something I find can make me some money, I see nothing wrong in that.'

Ramus stood and turned away. 'I only came to apologise.'

'Then say it. Say you're sorry.'

The Serians were watching them, and to Ramus their faces all suddenly seemed the same.

'Tell me you're sorry for interrupting me and Beko while we humped, Ramus!'

He shook his head. 'Not when you're like this.'

'Like what? Angry because you act like some spurned lover? If you think like that sometimes, then I'm sorry, but it's only you. We're friends, that's all. And sometimes barely that.'

'Maybe you're right,' he said.

'Of course I am.' But he heard hesitation in Nomi's voice, and that allowed him to defeat his self-doubt.

Ramus turned back to face Nomi. 'But maybe not. Because I think the truth is, it's you who are jealous of me.'

Me, jealous of him? Does he really mean that? Does he really believe…? Nomi laughed and shook her head, but the uncertainty lingered. There was his illness, after all.

'Don't be a fool,' she said.

'It's you!' Ramus said, voice louder now. 'I came here to apologise, because I was wrong. Who you fuck is up to you, not me, and you're right, it really is none of my business. But don't accuse me of being jealous of you…your safe little voyages…your fancy wine and nice home and mindless friends. What could I possibly want with any of that, Nomi? Your life is a blank, and you're barely a shade across it.'

'I like my life,' she said, and she told the truth. She *did* like her life. What was there to not like?

'But I'm a real Voyager,' Ramus said. 'And you're jealous of that. You covet my knowledge, my intelligence, my ability to read, the places I've been and the things I've seen.'

'And your humility?' But this was ice that could not be broken.

Ramus shook his head sadly. 'I'm just saying what I see, and what I know you feel. You want to be a Voyager who'll be remembered, but I've given more back to the Guild than you'll ever attain.'

'And now we're out here without the Guild,' she said. 'Explain that.'

'We both know this is beyond even them. We talked about it, and agreed. And you wouldn't have a clue about where we're going if it weren't for me.'

'Ha! Don't give yourself all the credit, *Voyager*. Ten brought the pages to *me*, not you, so—'

'And you *still* don't have a clue. Not an inkling. This is just another little adventure for you, and you'll be looking with money eyes. The importance of what we may find is *nothing* to you, so long as you can still have your wine, and your humps, and as long as your safe, rich friends are ready to congratulate you if we ever get home.'

'Of course we'll get home,' she said, nervous at where this was going. Two days out from Long Marrakash and already Ramus was announcing their possible doom. Surely he could not mean that. He was angry and confused, and probably embarrassed.

'Maybe,' he said, and looked into the fire. She did not like his expression when he did that. He looked like a man with secrets.

Nomi stood and approached Ramus, and though she felt Serian eyes upon her this was all about the two of them. 'Ramus? Don't you dare go quiet on me now, not with what you've said.' She reached out – to shove or to touch, she was not sure – but he looked at her hand with contempt.

'Admit it,' he said.

'Admit what?' Through the flames she saw Beko watching them, his face quivering and melting in the heat. She wished she could see his eyes properly, take strength from them.

'Admit you want to be a little like me.'

Nomi smiled. Grinned. Laughed out loud, and with every heartbeat she saw the bitterness in Ramus's expression increasing. *If I keep laughing,* she thought, *it won't be long until he hates me.* The idea was ridiculous and absurd, and it made her laugh some more.

'I know about Marquella of the Guild,' Ramus said.

His voice, so quiet that the crackle of flames almost swallowed it, cut into her laughter and killed it at the source.

'Marquella?' she said. But there was no way she could deny her treachery. Not with Ramus, because he was too sharp for her to win such an argument. And not in front of these Serians – and Beko – because to do so would make it all seem worse.

'Marquella!' Ramus said, turning to the Serians and acknowledging their attention for the first time. 'Very high up in the Guild echelons. He was a Voyager himself, many years ago, and a great one, too.'

'Ramus, don't do this,' Nomi said, trying to remain as dignified as she could. 'Please?'

'Please?' he repeated, glancing back at her only once. 'Piss on you, Nomi. Piss on you and your pathetic jealousy. You can't undo your wrongs with "please".'

'Can we at least talk about this together?'

Ramus nodded. 'We are! We're talking about Marquella, and how you persuaded him to refuse a voyage plan I had submitted. It would have been my *greatest*! Once I heard whispers of what had happened, I tried to find out exactly *how* you persuaded him, but it wasn't as if I could ask Marquella himself. By then he would barely acknowledge me in the Guild buildings. Looked at me as though I was something he'd stepped in at the markets.'

'It wasn't like that,' Nomi said.

'Then what was it like? Tell me the reason you had to destroy my plans?'

Nomi shook her head, and she realised that she could not tell. Because there was no reason.

'Envy?' Ramus said. 'I *told* you I was planning a voyage to the Poison Forests, and over the weeks you got wind of the fact that the Guild was about to sanction it, with a full complement of Serian guards and porters. And that was more than they ever gave you, so...?'

'I was worried for you,' Nomi said, and every time she had thought of her betrayal since it happened, that is what she tried to tell herself. The Poison Forests were a dangerous place, barely travelled and mysterious. Of the people who had gone in there, more had gone missing than returned.

But it was also one of the great prizes of voyaging. And Ramus's take on such a journey – a mapping of the outskirts, classification of plants and animals into differing poison strengths, and the collection of samples that could allow potential cures to be created – had won the Guild over.

Her reaction to that, thought but never spoken, had been, *It should have been me.*

'I thank you for your concern, *friend*,' Ramus said, and never had that word been spoken with such venom. 'So how did you persuade Marquella to embargo the plan? A word in his ear, a promise of a lifetime's supply of Ventgorian wine? Or did you just suck his cock?'

Nomi lashed out. She missed, her hand skimming from Ramus's shoulder, and it was only then that she realised she was crying. The tears caught light from the fire and fractured her vision, and she turned away from Ramus and faced out into the night.

'How pissing *dare* you even suggest that,' she said. 'I never laid a finger on Marquella, and he never touched me.' She wiped the tears from her face and spun around to face Ramus again. Her voice was low, and it came from somewhere deeper and darker than normal. 'You piece of shit, Ramus. How fucking *dare* you?'

'How dare *I*?' His face changed a little when he saw her tears, and she was certain there was a hint of regret. But regret can only go so far. And once some things were said, there was no unsaying them.

'You're right,' Nomi said. 'I didn't want you to go on that voyage. What we're doing here, now, is what I've wanted for a long time. To share in discovery. Why do you think I came to you with Ten's parchment, and not the Guild? I know I can learn from you, and I was hoping... Hoping that you could learn from me.'

'What could I *ever* learn from you?'

'I know I don't read books or understand the old languages, but at least I live a little.'

'*Live* a little?'

'Yes! And there's nothing wrong with that, either. I don't just bury myself away in Long Marrakash between voyages, sulking in my rooms, wishing I were greater than I really am. I *enjoy* myself, Ramus. You should try it one day. You're *pathetic*!'

Ramus smiled. 'Well, so you live a little. But that's not the end of it. Marquella was only the beginning.'

Nomi went cold. A chill passed through her, resistant to the fire and the flames burning in her chest, anger and shame and...fear. Ramus had her scared. And a large part of that fear was because of things she had yet to tell.

I never can, she thought. *Some things die as secrets, and that's only right.*

But then Ramus's smiled stretched into a grin, and she thought that perhaps this was a time for all dead secrets to be given life one more time.

'I knew about Marquella soon after my voyage plan was rejected,' Ramus said. 'I knew you were somehow involved. And I never thought I was one for revenge. Such a clumsy, wasteful endeavour. But sometimes opportunities present themselves to you, and a few glasses of root wine...a few bad days...'

'I don't know what you're talking about,' Nomi said.

'That's because I was always content keeping it a private vengeance. Keeping things even. But now, after this...' Though smiling, inside Ramus was nervous, like a boy dipping his cock for the first time. Perhaps his perceptions were still tinged with whatever had been in their meal, but this night seemed one of potential, and change, and he already knew that things between him and Nomi could never be the same again. *Remember the voyage,* he kept thinking, *and don't destroy it.* But perhaps events had already gone too far. Nomi's brushing aside of her ruining his voyage...her and Beko...

Inside, far from where the heat of the campfire could ever hope to reach, Ramus was on fire.

'Timal was no fool,' he said.

'Timal?' Nomi's face fell, going from defiant to vulnerable in a beat.

'He was good for you, Nomi.'

'Yes.'

'Appreciated the fine things, but he was also a wise young man. He can read, you know that?'

'Of course I know.'

'He's a future-seer. You know that, too?'

'He told me he wrote stories.'

Ramus shook his head. 'Not stories at all. Stories are tales from the past, twisted through the telling. Timal wrote projections.'

'Why are you talking about Timal?' she asked.

Ramus grinned at her, and he could see in her eyes that she already knew. How could she not? Because in reality, Nomi was also no fool. 'He came to me,' Ramus said. 'The night he left you, he came to me to talk.'

Nomi closed her eyes and lowered her head. Ramus looked around at the Serians, and they were all blank-faced. Not judgemental. Not yet. But everything was going to change.

That frightened Ramus, but he also knew that it was now inevitable. It shamed him – the Great Divide and what may be sleeping up there meant so much more than him and Nomi – but he could not help being human.

'I was in the Bay Lee Tavern, and he found me sitting in the corner. I'd had a bottle of root wine by then, and the tavern owner had just started brewing his own golden ale. It tasted like sheebok piss but it was cheaper than wine, and it helped me travel in my mind. You know where I was dreaming of travelling right then, exactly when Timal came to see me?'

'My guess would be the Poison Forests,' Nomi said.

'Good guess. Care to guess more?'

'I'd rather hear it from your mouth, Ramus.' Nomi's voice was level and neutral, but there was something about her stare and expression that he found threatening. He had never seen Nomi violent, but suddenly the potential was there. He could see it, feel it. Drinking in the sorts of places he favoured, it was something he had come to recognise.

'Then from my mouth, Nomi. Timal disturbed me from my drunken dreams of the Poison Forests, and he asked me what there was between you and me.'

Nomi blinked slowly, extinguishing and relighting the fire reflected in her eyes.

One of the Serians shifted, betraying their curiosity.

The fire burst a sap bubble and spat.

'He was suspicious. You and I spend a lot of time together, and perhaps your confidence and brashness made him...insecure. So I put his mind at rest. I told him we were humping. Every morning, I said, when he left your home to go to his studies, you came to my rooms and we humped until lunchtime. I told him how we did it, and what I liked. I even told him what you liked, Nomi, because I know you so well. And that's what convinced him I wasn't lying.'

'You bastard.'

'Really?'

'You bastard, Ramus!'

'You really think so? No. I think that just about makes us even.'

Nomi's calm exterior was melting. She had started to shake, her hands were fisting, she blinked quickly and unevenly. *She'll either come at me now,* Ramus thought, *or run.* Either possibility filled him with dread.

'I messed up a voyage,' she said. 'And a lot of the reason is because I wanted us to travel together, learn from each other, and—'

'Learn!' Ramus said, almost spitting the word.

Nomi raised her hand. 'And in return, you intrude into my life, destroy a relationship...' She shook her head and angrily wiped away a tear.

A shadow fell across them, Beko walking around the fire and going to stand between them. He glanced at Ramus, then looked at Nomi until she returned his stare. 'It's time to bed down for the night,' he said.

Nomi was still shivering. She started shaking her head, lips pressed tightly together, and then she gave Ramus the most humourless grin he had ever seen.

'Nomi,' Beko said. 'Your tent. And Ramus, you should bed down too. Daylight will ease this and make things easier for—'

'Stay out of this, Beko,' Nomi said. The Serian tensed as if about to speak, but she looked at him and shook her head. 'I hired you.'

Beko raised an eyebrow. 'So I obey your orders?'

Nomi said no more, but Beko turned and walked away. 'Just keep your voices down while we try to sleep.'

'How's your head, Ramus?' Nomi asked.

His breath hitched, his heart stuttered. *How's your head, Ramus?* He blinked and the weight was there, it was always there, the extra weight behind his eyes that he should never have been carrying.

How's your head, Ramus?

Nomi glared at him. She looked as if she had just stepped from a cliff, and the fall would be a long, long way.

Nothing can be unsaid, Nomi thought. *No backing out of this one. Perhaps if Timal had come back to me after he saw Ramus, we could have undone what he said together. The lies. The cruel lies.*

But not this.

'Does it ache?' she asked.

Every beat altered things, but this was when the world changed for ever. For both of them.

'Have nightmares that don't feel like yours?'

His shock cut her, but the pain in her soul was not bad. It didn't feel like vengeance, not exactly. But the guilt she had suffered was breaking free, being shredded and whittled down by what Ramus had revealed to her.

'Something heavy, Ramus? Behind the eyes?'

But this all happened before Timal, she thought. She drove that down. It didn't matter. The vagaries of time had no place juggling with such sins.

'What do you know about what's wrong with me?' he said slowly, quietly.

Nomi sensed the Serians listening again, and she glanced

right through the heat haze above the waning campfire. Beko was there, and the way he looked at her now was nothing like earlier.

'Nomi!' Ramus shouted. He stepped towards her and she stumbled back, expecting a blow that did not come. 'What do you know?'

'I think you know already,' she said. 'You're the one with the brains.'

He frowned, putting his left hand to his temple as if to question the thing growing in there. The cancer. 'You gave me this?' His frown smoothed out, his hands fell to his side and he grew terribly still. 'How?' he asked. Not why, or when, but how. Ramus, ever the seeker of knowledge.

'I caught it from a steam vent in Ventgoria,' Nomi said. 'I was tracing the track of an old vine-hanging field when the vent erupted. No sign of it one second, and the next...an explosion. Mud, rock, steam and gas, and something else from the ground. I didn't see or sense it at the time, but later I heard about these things from the Ventgorians. They're the eggs of giant mind-worms, things that twist up and down from and to the heart of Ventgoria. I...didn't understand. Still don't.' She was aware that she had an audience, but her words were only for Ramus. And herself. Expressing what she knew, putting it into order, made real what she had been living with for two years. It was like dragging a ravenous beast from the depths of a black pool and up into the sun. Revelation, realisation and perhaps understanding. But at the same time, its full horror would be appreciated.

'You told me you were ill,' Ramus said.

'There was a woman – a shaman – and she used magichala to tend wounds and treat illnesses. They kept me in one of their highest stilt houses, fed and watered me, and they wouldn't let anyone come to visit. Not Beko, not anyone.' She looked at the Serian captain to make sure he heard every word, because this was a confession for him, as well.

'Go on,' Ramus said.

He lost me Timal, Nomi thought. But her anger had suddenly drained, and she felt hollow and devoid of emotion.

'The shaman woman came to me morning, noon and night for three days. She made me talk about my dreams and nightmares, and gave me potions. I had no idea what was in them, but she wanted to help me. Even though I wasn't Ventgorian... It was as if she was ashamed that I'd caught such an illness there.'

'What was it like?' Ramus asked.

'Something inside me that shouldn't be there. Growing. A cancer, but fast. And as my eyesight began to fade, the shaman told me there was only one way to save my life.'

Ramus nodded, a terrible acceptance. 'Pass it on to me.'

'She came with a doll made of mud and reeds. No features, just a torso with arms, legs and a head. She pressed it to my chest and said it had to feel my heartbeat for a night. In the morning I would imagine a person and name them, and the shaman would pass the sickness on.'

'You're lying,' Ramus said. 'You know there's something wrong with me – I don't know how. And you're sick that I ruined it with Timal, so you're trying to go one better. Make me believe you're responsible for this.'

'You have nightmares that aren't your own,' Nomi said. 'That's because they're mine.' It was a stark statement, making her feel so exposed.

But Ramus's face dropped and he believed. His anger

simmered behind his eyes, but still he wanted to know. Perhaps he wanted to kill her...but not yet. He was Ramus the Voyager, Ramus the explorer, and here was something beyond his experience and knowledge.

'How...?' he muttered.

'Someone I knew well, the shaman told me. Someone whose soul I had felt. And all our differences aside, you were the only one.'

She could see Ramus trying to work things out, casting through the dates in his mind, and she knew that it would make sense because it was true.

'You cursed me to die,' he said.

Nomi's tears came. This was revenge of a sort, but she was cursing herself as well. 'It hurt so much, I didn't know what else—'

'It's your fault that I'm going to *die*.'

'You took Timal from me,' she sobbed.

'*After* you did this to me!' he screamed, slapping at his head as if to loosen the illness. 'That's nothing! I didn't *kill* you! I didn't *doom* you!'

'The shaman said—'

'She said you'd die?'

'Yes,' Nomi whispered. 'In great pain. Soon. And I'd only just met Timal, and I didn't *want* to die.'

Ramus's anger had withered and now he looked lost, alone. He looked shrunken. He glanced around the camp at the tents, the rapt Serians and the quietly nodding horses.

Then he looked back at Nomi and she realised his anger had not vanished at all. It had simply grown so cold and concentrated that it had taken on the colour of night.

'Neither do I,' he whispered. And he went for Nomi.

The change was startling. The camp went from motionless to chaotic, and even the fire seemed to leap and spark. Nomi stumbled back as Ramus came at her, his hands reaching for her throat. She tripped and fell, and as she went down she kicked out, her right foot connecting with Ramus's wrist. He grunted and let his momentum carry him forward and down, sprawling onto Nomi and crushing her into the heather.

Nomi let out an involuntary laugh. This was so ridiculous, so unbelievable, that it could not really be happening.

Ramus's right fist crashed into the side of her head and knocked aside all such thoughts. The fire illuminated his face, his wide eyes, his mouth drawn into a savage grimace as he struck again, fist glancing from Nomi's shoulder and head.

'No!' she shouted, but he was raised above her now, entwining his fingers and bringing both hands up ready to crash them down into her face. 'Ramus!'

The horses neighed and snorted, startled from their sleep.

The fire spat and threw sparks at the sky.

Nomi surged up and lashed out, feeling her fist drag across Ramus's teeth. He shouted and fell sideways away from the fire, and Nomi kicked his legs from her and reached for a burning stick.

Anger and shame, fury and sadness, her tears bled all of them across her skin.

'You killed me!' Ramus shouted, spitting blood.

Nomi turned and knelt in one motion, bringing the burning stick around with her.

'You think I'm afraid of fire, Nomi?' he cried, slapping the dressed burn on his arm. 'My brain's dying, and you think you can scare me with that?'

The Serians were around them then, Beko standing before

Ramus with his arms outstretched, Noon behind him, and Lulah kicked the stick from Nomi's hand as Ramin pressed down on her shoulders.

'Both of you calm down and keep quiet,' Beko said. He spoke softly but his words carried a great weight. 'I won't watch you fight, and if either of you try, you'll get hurt.'

'I pay you to protect us, Beko!' Nomi said.

'And I'm doing just that.'

Nomi shrugged Ramin's hands from her shoulders. His face appeared beside hers. 'Very well,' he said, 'but don't move.'

'Ramus?' Beko said. 'Are you calm?'

Ramus seemed unable to answer. He stared at Nomi with hatred. Shame as well? She wasn't sure. She hoped so but...they should both be ashamed.

'Ramus,' she said, 'we need to end this.'

'End?' he said, incredulous. 'It's ended already! I'll be dead soon, and that's the only end you wanted, isn't it?'

'I *never* wanted that!'

'You gave me your disease!' he roared, and Noon grabbed his arms when he tried to stand. 'How could you? You fucking sheebok bitch, how could you?'

Nomi started crying but the tears only seemed to spur Ramus on even more. He shouted and raged, and Noon and Beko guided him away to the other side of the camp.

'I didn't mean it,' Nomi said, fighting back the tears. She thought of Timal and what could have been, and the voyage she had ruined for Ramus, and she had never been so confused. Her own intentions seemed to have altered with time, and as she considered them, they changed some more.

'Tell that to your dying friend,' Lulah said.

Nomi looked at Beko where he stood talking to Ramus in

calm, even tones. Beneath his shirt the Serian bore scratches on his back from her nails, but that seemed like a dream now, something seen away by the changes and violence of the last few moments.

And what's going to happen now? she thought. The voyage was over. But it could never be over, not this journey, because it was still the voyage of a lifetime.

'We can make up,' she whispered.

'Can you cure him?' Lulah asked. Nomi had not meant for anyone to hear, but she looked up at the Serian and shook her head.

'No. But I can be sorry.'

'Only now?'

'I was sorry when it happened.'

Lulah laughed and shook her head. 'The madman's right. You *are* a sheebok bitch. By every god that cares, I hope I never have a friend like you.'

You can't talk to me like that, Nomi thought, but she knew that Lulah could. Back in Long Marrakash perhaps there was a pretence at respect, but out here, on the borders of the wilds, they lived by baser rules.

Lulah walked across to calm the horses with Noon and Rhiana, and Ramin knelt down beside Nomi.

'Don't worry about her,' he said. 'She's always angry.'

'Don't give me sympathy,' Nomi said.

The big Serian held up his hands. 'None from here.'

She closed her eyes and sighed. Her head ached, two of her knuckles were split from where she had punched Ramus in the mouth, and she thought back to that illness that should have killed her. She'd had nightmares she could not explain, and the shaman had told her they were the unknowable dreams of the thing that had passed the illness to her. *And now Ramus is living* my *nightmares,* she thought. *He's under my skin, in my head. And what nightmares will this night bring?*

When she opened her eyes Ramus had already started taking down his tent.

'Who will come with me?' Ramus said. 'I can't pay as well as Nomi Hyden, but I'll promise rewards at the end, when we're back in Long Marrakash.'

He had rolled his tent and folded the poles, and Noon agreed to bring him his horse. He was leaving. There was no way he could stay, and much as he thought of this voyage as his, he knew that Nomi had paid for everything.

And he would make her pay for more.

'I'll go,' Lulah said.

'Lulah—' Beko began.

'Captain, I terminate my employ here and now. My apologies, and I hope we can serve together again. But it's the start of a voyage, not the end. I don't feel that my absence will trouble you in any way.'

'I do,' Beko said.

Lulah did not reply. She had not even glanced at Ramus yet, but she stared at her captain until he sighed and relented.

Beko stepped forward and clasped Lulah's hands. 'Good journeys, Lulah.'

'And to you, Beko.'

She walked to Ramus then, her one eye giving nothing away.

'Thank you,' Ramus said. 'We can discuss—'

'Plenty of time for that,' Lulah said. Noon arrived with Ramus's horse then, smiling sadly at Lulah. 'Pack your horse,'

Lulah said. 'I need to gather my things and say my goodbyes, and then we'll be on the trail.'

'It's still dark,' Ramin said.

'There's no danger here.' Lulah went back to her tent and started packing. Ramin, Rhiana and Konrad went to her while Noon went for her horse. They helped her pack and saddle her mount, and all the time they whispered things Ramus could not hear.

'Ramus…' Nomi began, her voice small and lost.

Ramus shook his head and turned away.

'The pages,' she said. Her voice was still weak, but she was not about to ask for mercy. Not now. Things were said and decisions made.

'The parchment pages?' Ramus said. He touched the backpack already slung over his shoulder. 'In here. Come and take them.'

'They're mine. I paid Ten for them.'

'You don't have the first idea what they say. You can't even read!'

'They belong to me, and I want them back.'

Ramus posed mock-thoughtful for a while, tapping his foot and looking up at the death moon. 'Well, perhaps we can perform an exchange,' he said. 'My life for the parchment pages.'

Nomi shook her head sadly and turned away.

Ramus saw her talking to Beko, both of them looking past the horses into the darkness that still surrounded them.

'I'll fight whoever comes for them!' Ramus said. He drew his knife and shifted it slightly so that it reflected firelight.

Beko turned and watched Ramus, completely unconcerned. *If he wants the pages, he'll take them*, Ramus thought. *I'm being a fool.*

'You'll have to kill me,' he said. 'I'm dying already. If Hyden tells you to take the pages by force, you'll have my blood on your sword before they're in her hands. You want that?'

Beko moved away from Nomi, shaking his head at her insistence. He stood six paces from Ramus, looking at the backpack.

'Nomi says they're hers,' he said. 'I don't know what's on the pages, nor do I care right now. But she'd like them back.'

Ramus's lip bled from where Nomi had punched him. He sucked in a dribble of blood and spat it out. 'You heard me,' he said, turning the knife to throw a reflection at Beko's face.

The Serian could probably kill him in the space of five heartbeats.

Beko sighed and turned away. 'I'll not fight him,' he said. 'And I'll not risk him fighting me, because then he'll be dead.'

'Beko, please, those pages are—'

'This is your fight, Nomi. If you must, try and take them from him yourself.'

For a moment Ramus was sure she would do just that. She was younger than him, fitter, faster. But she was even less of a fighter than him.

'Please, Ramus,' she said.

'Piss on you, Nomi.' He turned his back on the camp, grabbed his horse's reins and set off. Ramus would have been happy knowing he would never see Nomi again. But that was not likely.

This voyage of a lifetime had become a race.

CHAPTER EIGHT

It took a while for Lulah to catch up. He even began to fear that the other Serians had persuaded her to stay behind, and he went slowly, trying not to consider the prospect of travelling on his own for so long.

When he heard her coming, he breathed a long sigh of relief.

'We'll ride until dawn,' she said, 'and then we need to pause and take stock. Noon gave me a parcel of food and a skin of water, but we have little else.'

'We have to gain a lead on the others,' Ramus said. 'We won't be stopping.'

Lulah fell in alongside him, their horses moving slowly across the darkened landscape. Ramus knew how dangerous it was to travel by night. They were not only risking their horses stepping into a hole or tripping on a loose stone, but there could be different perils easily avoidable by day.

'I'm with you for my own reasons,' Lulah said. 'Maybe you'll hear them, maybe not. That's my choice. But I'm here as an equal, and I'll not take orders from you.'

Ramus actually laughed. 'Lulah, I never for a moment thought you would.'

He wondered if she smiled, but it was too dark to tell.

Dawn came and burnt the sky. They stopped, took a drink, ate some dried biscuits from the parcel Noon had sent with Lulah, and Ramus took out his map.

'I drew this from everything I have at home,' he said. 'It's well mapped where we are now, but even so there are differences. We're closing on the border. We need to take care.'

'Last night you were all for riding on regardless,' Lulah said.

Ramus nodded, looking up at dawn's spectacular blaze on the eastern horizon. 'I'm more tired now. More angry.'

'You and she were good friends?'

He shook his head. 'Not really. More like lovers who never loved.'

'A simpler life is better,' Lulah said.

Ramus glanced up but she had already said enough. He did not want to push her. They had a long way to go, and plenty of time for talk.

'You're sure about this?' Ramus asked.

'About a simple life?' Her eye glittered with defiance, as though he had issued a challenge.

'No, no. About this. Coming with me instead of staying with your friends.'

Lulah shook her head. 'I don't have friends. I like my own company. Voyaging with you may be the next best thing.'

'I *will* pay you,' Ramus said, the lie burning still.

'I believe you.'

'After what you heard back there? I'm surprised you can trust Nomi *or* me.'

'I said I believe you. I don't trust anyone.' Lulah knelt beside Ramus and started looking at the map. She pointed to a spot south-east of Long Marrakash, where two valleys met and the hills faded away towards the Pavissia Steppes. 'So we're here?'

'Near enough,' Ramus said. He picked up a small twig and leant over the map. 'We've just come down this valley. Maybe five miles to go until we reach the beginning of the plains, and then thirty more until the border.'

'It's guarded,' Lulah said. 'We'll get news from the guards about any recent marauder activity, and that should help us plan a route.'

Ramus nodded, his eyes drawn back the way they had just travelled to the approximate location of last night's camp. He wondered whether the others were still there, eating breakfast or perhaps packing and preparing to set out. He thought not. Nomi was no fool, and she'd appreciate that the race was on.

He had already decided what to do. 'We need to hang back.'

'What? Make your mind up.'

'We need an advantage. And I can't just have her think she drove me away.'

'Surely we're past all that?' Lulah asked.

'I need her to know I'm not beaten.'

Lulah shook her head and sighed.

'And it's not just about Nomi and me, I promise you,' Ramus said. 'You don't know what we're going to find when we get to the Great Divide.'

'And you do?'

'I have a suspicion.'

'So why is it more important for us to get there before the others? *Is* it simply competition and revenge?'

'No,' he said. 'It's a lot more than that.'

'Then tell me.'

He looked at the Serian, unnerved as ever by her single eye, her unwavering gaze. It was as if losing an eye had given the one remaining twice the intensity, melting through his skin and seeing the dark heart of him.

'I can't,' he said. He expected protestations, but Lulah simply shrugged.

'Maybe later,' she said. 'But you won't be able to do anything to Nomi, not with Beko and the others guarding her.'

'I don't want to do anything to Nomi.'

'Really?'

He thought about that for a while and could not answer.

'You're not dead yet,' the Serian said, and the hint of compassion in her voice surprised him.

He laughed, short and harsh. 'Maybe not, but time belongs to my sickness now, not me.' There was so much more to say – what the illness did to him, why he was undertaking this final voyage, the dangers he saw in its aims – or nothing at all. For now he chose nothing. Just as there would be time later for Lulah's secrets, so perhaps he would tell his own campfire tale.

Lulah looked around, and indicated a place high on the hillside to the east. 'Cover there,' she said. 'I don't like this.'

'I told you, nothing too bad. I just want to slow Nomi down for a while.' Ramus folded the map and returned it to his backpack.

'So what's on the parchment?' Lulah asked.

She was surprising Ramus more and more. He had assumed her to be cool and uninterested, here for the voyage and little more. But away from the others, she seemed to be developing an intense curiosity. Maybe she realised that this was riskier than she first thought.

'They're from an old book. Do you read?'

Lulah shook her head. 'What do they say?'

Perhaps if she'd asked six hours ago he would have told her about the Divide and the Sleeping God. Encased in the night and the dark memories of what it had brought, his sadness and pain may have brought the truth out of him. But now dawn was here, and the sun had seemed to burn some of the badness away. Given him hope.

'That's what I need to find out,' he said. Only a small untruth, because though he recognised some of the images on the parchment pages, the language was still a mystery.

He would have many evenings to examine the pages by campfire light.

Lulah led them up the hill, and as they approached the cover she had spotted they had to dismount and guide the horses by their reins. They reached a rocky overhang, its flattened top home to small trees and a tangle of undergrowth. The horses were easily tethered out of sight, and Ramus and Lulah lay on the thin mountain grass and kept watch along the valley.

'We could have all stayed together,' Lulah said after a long silence.

Ramus stared at her eyepatch and the stud that decorated it. 'You came with me for a reason. When will you tell me what it is?'

Lulah smiled. 'We both have secrets. That's good. It's not healthy to know your travelling companions too well.'

'Why not?'

'Boredom can be deadly on the trail.'

'Here's a deal,' Ramus said, intrigued by this warrior woman. 'When I can translate the pages and tell you what they say, you tell me how you lost your eye.'

Lulah nodded. 'Fair enough. Though the real tale is in how I gained this stud.'

They waited for a long time. The sun rose and passed its zenith, drawing steam from the valley's hidden places that drifted and eddied on unseen draughts. Ravens floated down from the north, out of the hills and into the valley that petered out into plains just visible to the south. They circled Ramus and Lulah for a while, until Lulah loosed an arrow in their direction. Then they soared down into the valley, crying their upset at the sun, and some of them settled on a large dead thing by one of the streams. Ramus concentrated, but he could not make out what the dead thing was.

'Too far away,' he said.

'I see it well enough,' Lulah said. 'Mountain goat.'

Maybe my eyesight is fading already, he thought. He looked elsewhere in the valley, seeing blurs where perhaps he should have defined trees, but he commented on it no more.

Mid-afternoon came and went, and Ramus began to fear that the others had somehow passed them by. He consulted his map again to check. If they had taken a different route it would have added at least a day to their journey, and there was no reason for them to do that. They would have nothing to fear from Ramus and Lulah, after all.

'I'm stiff as a corpse,' he said to Lulah. 'I need to walk. I'll be gathering some stuff, back there past where the horses are tethered. If they appear, please come to get me.'

'What are you planning?'

I trust no one, Lulah had said. And yet she came with him, hid with him waiting for her old comrades, asked after the pages he had and what they meant. And it was not even that he could promise her more pay than Nomi. She felt some link to him, and whether she trusted him or not, he would have to respect that if they were to carry on together.

'I'm going to poison their horses,' he said. 'Slow them down for a day or two, and that will give us the head start we need. After that we ride hard for the Great Divide. Camp only at night; during the day we eat as we ride.'

Lulah nodded slowly, weighing up what he had said. 'They'll buy more horses at the border.'

'Maybe. But we'll be well ahead by then.'

'You know I can't help you harm Nomi?'

'I know that,' Ramus said. 'I don't want to harm her.'

'Why?'

The question, blunt and brutal, surprised him. And he could not answer. Because considering a response confused him even more, and melted away the comfortable afternoon sun that had been soothing his nerves. Ramus wondered whether, come dusk, his anger would rise again.

He checked on their horses and then passed them by, clambering up the slope and looking for signs of rock ants.

On his voyages into the unnamed mountains he had met the Widow, though he was unsure whether she had ever been wed beneath the moons, or in the eyes of any other god. Widow was what she called herself, and though he had probed, she had never offered any other name. He had come to believe that she had none. She practised magichala and displayed a knowledge of herbs, spices, roots, plants, animals, poisons and balms of the land more extensive than any he had ever known. When he uttered his astonishment, she had scoffed, saying that she knew nothing. Real magic is beyond plants and charms, she had said. *It's in the land, and perhaps one day it will be in me.* She hunted and haunted those mountains – the peaks she said would belong to her, given time – and she had imparted huge knowledge to Ramus. Not everything she knew, he was sure. In fact, the last time he left her for home she had smiled at him for the first time ever, and in that smile he had seen the superiority of a hawk over a dust sparrow.

She knew so much more.

From the Widow, he had learnt how shred and snowspit could be combined to make a tincture that would clean wounds and stop bleeding. Flail, used in its basest form in Long Marrakash, could be dried and refined into a chewable paste, suitable for calming tensed muscles and nerves, without all the side effects of the pure, untreated form. Certain rocks, found only in the Widow's peaks, could be bled of a useful tonic by long immersion in salty water and then distillation to remove the salt. The resultant fluid would ease coughs and clear thick chests.

And for every good drug, tonic or balm, the Widow told him about poisons, toxins and pollutants of the soul.

He moved through the rocks, looking for the telltale shimmering that would show where rock ants were active.

The land is far richer than anyone knows, the Widow had told him. *We live upon it, plant our crops in its skin, but deeper down there are more worlds, places where secrets lay*

hidden awaiting discovery. And even up here, there are
wrinkles in that skin, layers upon layers, fake sheens overlying
the true reality which most people will not understand, or
cannot bear to believe.

Have you been down? Ramus had asked.

The Widow had given him her customary glare, as though
considering whether he was suitable to hear truths. *There are*
depths and there are depths, she had said. *I've barely been*
farther than the sunlight can still kiss.

Ramus had asked why. She was the Widow after all, dweller
of these peaks and an explorer of Noreela as much as he,
though she chose to explore without covering great distances.

This time, she chose not to answer. But he had seen the fear
in her eyes.

Things down there, he had thought, and sometimes he
dreamt of what those things could be.

On his way home from that last voyage, he had already
been planning his next: a journey back to the Widow's peaks
and then below, following the caves, finding routes deeper and
deeper still. He would burrow beneath the false skin of the
world that the Widow so mocked.

But then his illness had struck, and his planned voyage had
never come about.

He paused, balancing with his feet against one rock and his
back against another. The sun did not find its way down here,
and in the narrow crack below him he could hear the subtle
rustlings and hissing that could reveal what he sought. He
moved sideways, trying not to let his feet slip down and
damage the rock ants' structures. When he reached a larger
rock, he slid onto it and lay down, lowering the upper half of
his torso into the crack. And there it was, the silvery trace

work of a rock ants' nest, their extruded silk marking the paths of minute cracks and fissures in the rock. The Widow had told him she could read a language in the structure of their nests, but she never told him what that language was, nor what it said. He supposed it was the language of the land, the vague idea of order behind chaos that she alluded to on occasion. But though he changed his angle of viewing, narrowed his eyes and turned aside so that the nest was almost out of sight, he could read nothing.

Across the larger cracks were more elaborate structures providing bridges and tunnels for the ants, solid as the rock itself. The creatures were as long as his little fingernail, abdomens swollen with the poison he sought.

'So now to find some berry bugs,' he said. He stood from the nest and climbed the rocks, glancing down at the grassed ledge where Lulah still lay. He whistled briefly and she looked back.

'Any sign?'

Lulah shook her head and turned away from him again.

Behind the rocky overhang and further up the hillside, he found a swathe of yellowberry bushes, their fruits still small and hard. He examined the berries until he found what he wanted – fruits fattened by the larvae laid inside. Splitting the skin, pulling the small larvae out and letting them squirm on his hand, Ramus felt the thrill of forbidden knowledge coursing through him. It was as though the Widow was looking over his shoulder, and he was certain she would be pleased.

He found no more than thirty berry bugs, but he hoped that would be enough. He might not be able to infect every horse in Nomi's group, but if only two or three of them were sick, they would still be delayed.

Back at the ants' nest, he lay on the rock again, reached down and scattered the bugs across several of the thicker bridges.

It took a while for the creatures to react. The berry bugs squirmed in their unaccustomed exposure, twisting and flexing in a vain attempt to crawl back into darker places. A few ants stopped and examined the new arrivals, exploring their bodies with front legs, smelling and tasting them, and when these ants hurried away and disappeared into cracks in the rocks, Ramus knew that it was going to work.

The soldier ants emerged. Larger than those he had seen before – some were as long as the top segment of his little finger – their abdomens were swollen and red with poison. They swarmed from the rock nests and across silver bridges, hanging from fine threads that Ramus could not see and dropping onto the berry bugs.

As the ants' poison commenced melting the bugs' insides, they began to squirm more violently. Ramus reached down to pick them up, dropping several deeper between the rocks as he desperately tried to avoid being stung. *Slow learner,* he heard the Widow saying over his shoulder, and he grinned as he dropped the bugs into a small pouch on the side of his backpack.

When he returned to Lulah, she waved him down. He dropped to his stomach and crawled to the edge of the overhang, leaving his backpack behind.

'Movement,' Lulah said. 'Opposite side of the valley.'

'Level with us?' he asked, fearful they would be seen.

'No, lower.'

'Is it them?'

'I think so. Look, there. See that spread of trees in the shape of a raven's wing? They'll appear south of there any time now.'

They lay and watched together, squinting against the sun as it began its slow descent into the west. The travellers emerged from the cover of trees, the group snaking its way down the hillside and towards the valley floor.

Ramus could make out no details at all. He closed his eyes, and asked.

'Yes, it's them,' Lulah said.

Ramus nodded and sighed. 'So now we follow. We'll leave it until they're camped, cooking and telling tales. Then I'll do what I have to, and you and I can leave.'

'It won't be that easy,' Lulah said. 'They'll post a guard. And now we're closer to the border, I suspect they'll have two on watch at any time.'

'I'll go quietly.'

'You can barely see in the daytime. At night you'll be caught. I'll go.'

Ramus looked at Lulah, trying to see any hint of deception in her expression. *We need trust,* he thought, but she had already stated that she trusted no one. That made him uncomfortable.

'I can create a diversion,' he said.

Lulah nodded. 'That will help.'

'Thank you for coming with me.'

She nodded again. Opened her mouth as if to say more, but said nothing instead.

Lulah ran on ahead and left Ramus to guide her horse. She would be more silent on foot, she said, and more in control. She knew how Beko and the others worked, and she was confident of being able to track them without being seen.

Ramus remained a mile behind, always keeping a fold in the land between him and them, until dusk began to draw shadows from hiding and Nomi's group stopped moving for the night.

Lulah returned, panting hard and her face slick with sweat. 'They're camping by a stream,' she said. 'The stream's between us and them. It's wide, but shallow enough to cross on foot. The land's lightly wooded, so there's plenty of cover, and they've already lit a fire. They don't feel threatened.'

'Nomi probably thinks we've ridden on ahead.'

Lulah nodded, catching her breath. 'How far are we from the border?' she asked.

Ramus had already consulted the map while she was away, using the last of the sunlight to try and place their position. 'About twenty miles,' he said. 'South-east are the Pavissia Mountains, and directly south the Steppes begin.'

Lulah nodded, catching her breath. 'You know you'll only get one chance to do this?'

'We'll only need one chance.'

Lulah mounted her horse and led them off.

They gave the camp a wide berth, and by the time they stopped again the moons were high and the sun long gone. They tethered the horses and each took a drink. It was going to be a long night.

Ramus handed Lulah the pouch. 'Don't scatter them too far or they'll get lost. We only need to get three or four horses, not all of them.'

'What will your distraction be?'

'A noise. It'll draw them long enough.'

'You're sure you can do this in the dark?'

'I'm not completely blind.'

'Not yet.' She stripped her weapon belt and slung it on her saddle.

Ramus raised an eyebrow.

'I'm not fighting anyone,' Lulah said. 'I'm sorry for your illness, but they're my friends. They catch me, that's it.'

Ramus remained silent, but he could not help thinking to the future. There was a long ride ahead, and at the end of it, if they climbed the Divide and found that a Sleeping God really was there, such petty conceits as friendship would cease to matter.

'Go well,' he said, holding out his hands. Lulah glanced down, nodded once and vanished like a shadow. He did not even hear her leave.

Ramus went south, then west. He moved slowly and cautiously, not wishing to give himself away. His head was throbbing and the pain behind his eyes gave a false light to the scene. What he saw as solid ground was marsh, and where he saw marsh was a spread of shale, slipping and sliding beneath him, loosened by the rain that had begun as soon as he started to move. His clothes were wet and heavy, his hair lank and plastered across his face. He held out one hand ahead of him, knowing that, if he caused too much noise, he would likely encounter a Serian in the darkness.

When he judged he had gone far enough past the camp, he turned north once more, going carefully until he saw the glow of a campfire in the distance. He should have asked Lulah how far from the camp the Serian guard or guards could be, where they would choose to keep watch, and how they would be armed. He could see the fire from here, but if he set the distraction he had planned, it was possible they would not hear it. Lulah would be waiting way past that fire even now, hunkered down in shadows, ready with the pouch of berry bugs.

Ramus moved closer. He entered a lightly wooded area, slipping from tree to tree and doing his best to avoid the undergrowth that grew around their trunks. There were noises from all around; scurrying things, leaves rustling and caressing in the breeze, raindrops dripping from above.

This is not for me, he thought. *Give me a warm library, a musty book and a bottle of root wine any day.*

As if to mock him, the raindrops grew warmer, and he felt the occasional impact of something harder against his scalp. He held out his hands and caught a slick serpent, the length of his index finger. It flexed and snapped at the fleshy pad of his thumb. He dropped it, and more landed around him, slithering away into the damp grass. Something larger struck the ground to his left, and he heard the meaty sound of something bursting.

Ramus moved on, cringing when something other than rain hit him. He stamped on the small serpents when he saw them, kicked at running, many-legged shapes, and stepped over the wet mess of other things that had split upon impact. They steamed into the night; some had legs, a few had the stubs of rudimentary wings.

He slipped on a slick of leaves and went down, sliding into a gulley he had not even seen. His head struck the ground and the pain flared, sending spears of light into his eyes. The heat of agony did its best to draw a groan or a scream from his mouth, and he ground his teeth together to hold it back.

Lulah needs her distraction, he thought. This strange

downfall would not suffice – this far north, squirm-storms only ever lasted a few beats. If he left it much longer, she would assume that he had been caught, and he suddenly had the image of her walking back into Nomi's camp. Once that happened, he doubted she would be able to leave again.

As he sat up and slipped off his backpack, the storm turned to simple rain once more.

It would have to be here.

Ramus had brought several souvenirs from the Widow with him, and one of them was a handful of screeching lizard eggs. These creatures were limited exclusively to one valley in the Widow's mountains, but their reproductive technique was so unusual that Ramus had felt compelled to bring some home. Not with any intention of hatching them, or selling them, or even presenting them to the Guild for its museum. It had been pure curiosity. These were the only animals Ramus knew of that were hatched by fire.

The rain had eased, for which he was glad, and he found it easy to dig down through the leaves to a level of drier soil. He worked by touch, making a nest from an old paper map and dried kindling from his bag, and placing the eggs on top.

He wished the Widow had told him more about these screeching lizards. She had said that they lived mainly in caves and crevasses, their eggs exuded a sticky fuel when heated, they were hatched by fire, and they made a terrible sound once born into the world. Being woken from peace into pain did that, she said. But Ramus had no idea how long their hatching took, nor whether the tiny lizards would even still be alive. These eggs were old.

I could just shout, he thought. *Scream and crash around in the woods.* But that would give him no time to escape. And he had to accept that Lulah had been right about his eyesight.

Shielding the nest from the rain with his body, he used his flints to throw sparks, and it did not take long for the old paper to catch on fire. The kindling caught next, then came a shower of crackling sparks as the eggs began venting their own fuel.

Ramus ran. Hands held out before him, he darted between the trees, tripping several times before he burst back out into the open. South a little way, then east again, always aware of the vague glow of the campfire through the trees to his left. *Is this right?* he thought, and cursed his weakness. Why have doubts when the deed was done? He may well be a man of words and not action, but that had to change.

The sounds came sooner than he had expected. Several loud cracks first of all, like branches being snapped in the night, and then soon after the screeches of the newborn lizards rose up. The eggs were small, but the noise they made was tremendous.

Ramus ran faster still, distancing himself from the crying lizards and the small fire that had birthed them. The rain continued falling, and now his wet clothes were musty and warm from the sweat rising from his body.

He soon slowed, heart thumping, vision clouding, and he had to sit beside a fallen tree to regain his breath.

Shouts came from the direction of the camp. It was too far away to make out who was calling, but if he concentrated he could hear the voices moving into the woods, seeking out whatever made the noise.

He wondered where Lulah was and what she was doing.

And then he began to wonder about Nomi; would she be scared, worried, concerned? Would she suspect that this was

Ramus's doing? She would be in the camp, guarded by Ramin and Beko perhaps while the others searched the trees for the source of the sounds.

Ramus rested his head back against the tree and closed his eyes. The lizards' cries still pierced the night, and the pain behind his eyes sang as though in harmony. He had run further than he had for a long time. Exhaustion took him, and before he knew it he was drifting away from this rainy night and into the more complete darkness of a nightmare.

He is at the centre of things. To his right is a fire burnt down to glows and ashen sculptures, to his left are unoccupied tents, and ahead of him is the wood from which a howl of rage continues to rise, going higher and higher and yet somehow never passing beyond the realms of hearing. Moonlight bathes the trees and silvers a thousand sword blades across their leaves. Raindrops and limp serpents gather and drop from the tree canopy, and each impact is the footfall of a killer. Steam rises and flows where there should be no steam, and the ground gapes open as it vents its own nightmares to the night.

He is at the centre of things, and events radiate outward. He sees the running shapes darting away in their search for whatever threatens them. Moonlight streaks across the grass, as though illuminating routes for those who have gone, or those who have yet to go. And then events radiate inward as well, and the trees begin to part as things emerge and come for him. He has never seen or imagined these things before, but he recognises them as something personal and secret to someone other than him.

❀   ❀   ❀

Ramus screamed himself awake, huddled against the fallen tree. For a beat everything startled him, but then the nightmare – *Nomi's* nightmare – faded rapidly, and it was as if he had never dreamt at all.

Nomi's nightmare... He had seen her fears, and they were terrible. He should have felt happy.

He stood, shivering and wet, listening for movement or voices. But he heard nothing, and when he looked around he could no longer see the glow of Nomi's campfire. Looking up he could see no stars, and the rain was heavy again, blinding him. He had no idea how much time had passed.

Lulah could be back at the horses by now. He had to hurry.

But she came to him. As he struggled across the sodden ground, lightning cracked and thunder split the darkness, and shadows manifested before him. He drew his knife but quickly made out the shapes of two horses, one of them ridden by the slight but impressive figure of the Serian.

'Are you well?' she asked.

Ramus nodded, and it felt as though a ball of fire seethed behind his eyes.

'Mount up,' Lulah said. 'Lean forward and rest if you must. I'll lead your horse.'

'Is it done?' he asked. His voice came from very far away.

Someone was helping him then, and every heartbeat was disjointed. He was suddenly astride his horse as Lulah rode ahead, his mount's reins tied to her saddle. *Is it done?* he tried to ask again, but even his voice had failed him.

Nomi must think I wish her dead, he thought. And as pain and exhaustion dragged him back down to a deeper, darker sleep where even nightmares would never reach, he could not feel pleased.

Part Two

THE STONE MAN
CURSE – WIDOW'S WARNING – ASCENT

'Voyaging great distances – through forests, from island to island, across plains and into the mountains – is all about finding ourselves.'

Sordon Perlenni, the First Voyager

CHAPTER NINE

Nomi saw shadows moving into the camp, and she knew that they were Ramin and Rhiana, yet still the fear had settled in her and refused to let go.

'Well?' Beko asked. He had remained close to Nomi from the moment the first strange cry rose up in the night.

'We found a small fire, nothing else,' Ramin said. 'Whatever was making those sounds spread out and disappeared into the landscape. First it came from one place, and then many.'

'I've never heard anything like that before,' Rhiana said.

Beko stood quietly for a beat, listening to the darkness with a frown on his face.

'Animals,' Nomi said. 'That's all.'

'Some steppe marauders use animal calls to communicate,' Rhiana said. 'Birds, frogs, lizards.'

'Didn't sound like animals to me,' Ramin said. 'Sounded like someone having their nuts squeezed.'

'Charming.' Rhiana came closer to the fire, squatting to warm her hands.

'If it was marauders we'd have seen some sign,' Ramin said. 'I've dealt with them before. I know what to look for.'

'Different clans have different methods,' Beko said.

Ramin shrugged. 'I'm telling you, there was no one out there. Maybe it was something that fell with the rain.'

Beko turned to Nomi and included her in the conversation for the first time. 'Nomi?'

She looked around at the three Serians. Konrad and Noon were still out there somewhere, hidden away to watch and listen for anyone or anything approaching. They had all acted with confidence and professionalism, but although she felt safe, still there was a sliver of fear. She saw Ramus's face and remembered the sickness that had once afflicted her. 'You're the experts,' she said. 'I'll do what you say is best.'

'I just don't like this so soon after what happened last night,' Beko said. 'The voyage is young, but already it's feeling ruined.'

'It's not ruined!' Nomi said.

'But he took those pages—'

'I know where we're going, Beko, as do you. The pages were something else, and I can remember them.'

'All of them?'

'Enough.' *Even though I cannot read,* Nomi thought. *I can remember the pictures...some of them...but that's like remembering the colour of a map, but not the contours or scales. I know where we're heading, but now it feels as though we're travelling blind.*

Beko nodded. 'Right. We stay here for the night, because we all need rest. We won't be flustered by phantoms or wraiths. Konrad's out there to the south, and Noon will remain with the horses. Rhiana is close to the camp but in the shadows. The rest of us will sleep, watch rotation every two hours.'

'You don't sound flustered,' Nomi said lightly.

Beko glared at her, then smiled. 'Just being cautious.'

She lay in her tent, listening to the night noises and wondering where Ramus was now. He was probably miles ahead already, using his rage to drive him and Lulah on, and when daylight came he would be examining those pages from Ten, searching for any advantage he could gain over them.

She tried to recall what they contained. Closed her eyes, absorbed the safety of Beko and the others outside, settled her mind and cast it back to Long Marrakash. She could picture the parchment in her mind, but when she tried to organise the various images, they became clouded and hazed. She concentrated some more, remembering her first meeting with Ten. The image of the Sleeping God was clear, and given a quill and paper she could reproduce it herself. But she had nothing like that with her. On this voyage, she had agreed to leave the mapping to Ramus. He had that journal of his, and he would be filling its pages with each new discovery. And each page filled would lead him one more step ahead.

Nomi slipped from the tent and stood close to the fire. Much of the wood had burnt down now, and Rhiana was feeding it just enough to keep it alive. There were whole worlds in there; ash caverns, burning wooden ravines, forms in smoke and fire, and Nomi blew on the flames to see whether they gave her any shapes she could remember.

She wrapped a blanket around her shoulders and pulled her saddle close to the fire. The Serians came and went about her, changing watch and moving off into the darkness. Nothing else disturbed them that night.

Dawn came gradually, lighting the bushes and trees around them, then showing individual blades of grass. She was exhausted.

'We need paper or parchment,' she said when Beko came to her. 'I need to remember what was on those pages.'

'Very well. But you do know we're close to the border with the Pavissia Steppes?'

'Yes,' she said. 'And so, out into the wilds.'

'I'd say we're in the wilds already.'

As Rhiana peeled some ground-fruits, Noon rushed into the camp. 'There's something wrong with the horses!'

Nomi followed the others past the tents and into the trees, and with every step the sense of dread weighed heavier. Ramus was in her mind – in truth, he had not left her since the night before – and she could picture his cool smile.

'I thought you were here watching them?' Beko said.

'And so I have been!' Noon said, anger and confusion in his voice. 'By that tree over there, watching, listening. But now the sun's up I can see that I was fooled. I think we've all been fooled.'

Nomi could see nothing wrong. Eight horses stood there, loosely tethered to the trees, neighing softly in the cool morning mist. Some chewed grass and soft heathers; others still seemed to be asleep. It was these that Noon went to first.

'Touch them,' he said

Beko and Rhiana went forward and touched the motionless horses. Stroked their hair, put their hands beneath the creatures' mouths, and then passed them before the open eyes. The open, glazed, lifeless eyes.

Rhiana slapped her horse hard on the side. It swayed, and then its two far legs crumpled and it tilted heavily to the ground.

Nomi cried out and stepped back, stamping on Ramin's foot as she did so. The big Serian held her arms and kept her steady, but she could hear his own panicked gasp.

The other horses pulled back tight against their reins, one of them rising on its hind legs and breaking free of its tether. It turned and galloped between the trees, slipping on wet leaves and stumbling to a stop a hundred steps away.

'The other two as well?' Beko asked.

Noon nodded. 'Dead. Cold. Stiff. They must have been dead for some time.'

'Poisoned,' Nomi said.

Beko turned. 'How can you tell?'

'It's a guess. Ramus knows a lot about poisons from his travels. The Widow in the peaks taught him.'

Noon knelt before the dead horses still standing and scanned the ground, shifting grass with his hand. 'I can't see anything,' he said.

Nomi closed her eyes and fear pressed in. *This is all my doing,* she thought. *I should have said nothing to Ramus. I should have taken his anger and turned it back on him, not made it worse.*

'We ride on,' Beko said. 'Perhaps we can buy new horses at the border.'

'Perhaps,' Nomi said.

'Six people, all our equipment, five horses,' Ramin said. 'Numbers not being my good point, I'd say we're pissed on already.'

'Nomi will ride with me,' Beko said. 'Konrad and Ramin, you share a mount. The spare will be our packhorse.'

'One horse can't carry everything we have,' Noon said. 'We'll kill it just as well as poison.'

'Then we lose what we don't need. Share tents. Compromise.'

Nomi nodded and looked around the group. Fear was suddenly replaced with determination. *Only until the sun goes down again,* she thought, but she grabbed on to the positive and tried to drive the negative away. 'We should ride through the day,' she said. 'Try to buy horses at the border. I have money and Ramus has nothing, so he's only inconvenienced us for now.'

'He could have ridden on ahead,' Rhiana said. 'Could have gained thirty miles on us last night. But he chose to stay back and do this.'

'And Lulah with him,' Beko said.

The Serians fell silent, and Nomi wondered whether they saw this as betrayal by their friend. Or perhaps it was all just work, and they were admiring a job well done.

They broke camp and mounted up, leaving the spare saddles behind and loading the empty horse with a pack-saddle. The creature did not seem happy with this imposition – it was obviously bred to be ridden, not loaded – but Noon whispered soothingly into its ear, and soon they were ready to leave.

Nomi sat behind Beko, and even before they left the camp site she felt the saddle cutting into her lower back. This would be an uncomfortable day.

'We've left it a mess,' she said. The Serians were usually very particular about how they left a camp site, burying waste, scattering the fire's ashes and giving the impression that no one had ever stayed there. This time things were different.

'We can stay and spend another hour clearing up if you like,' Beko said over his shoulder.

They wended their way between trees and emerged eventually onto the plains. Leaving the hills and woods behind felt good to Nomi, but the landscape before them had just as many places to hide. Clumps of trees grew here and there, the land rolled and dipped subtly toward the near horizon, and there were signs of half-hearted attempts to work the land: hedge lines, tumbled walls. They urged the horses into a trot.

She and Beko said very little. After their intimacy, the air between them felt loaded and tense, a potential that kept Nomi warm, nervous, and expectant. But since finding the dead horses, breaking camp and heading for the border, the tension had evaporated. He had hardly looked at her, and the warmth in her belly had faded to a cool distance. So she sat behind him and smelt his familiar smell, and any thoughts she had of reaching out and holding herself against his back were soon dispelled.

'Are you worried?' she asked at last. The morning was drawing on and the sun was high. They would be at the border with the Pavissia Steppes soon, and the next stage of their troubled voyage would begin.

'Concerned that things will fall apart.' He sighed and stretched his arms above his head, the horse trotting on of its own accord. Nomi heard his joints click and saw muscles tensing beneath his shirt. *Are my scratches still on his back? I fear they'll fade, never to be replaced.*

'Ramus...' But she was not entirely sure what she wanted to say.

'We had a strong group, Nomi,' Beko said. 'Two Voyagers with high hopes, myself, and five Serians I trust with my life.

Enough horses and equipment. But now we're fractured. And we've hardly even begun.'

'What do you think of what Ramus said?' The question had been burning, because none of the Serians had commented on the argument and what had been revealed.

Beko shook his head but did not turn around. 'That's none of my business, and I've no right to judge.'

'Thank you,' she said, though she was not certain he had spoken through kindness.

They rode in silence once again. She looked back at Noon, Ramin and Konrad bringing up the rear, and ahead at Rhiana where she scouted their route half a mile away. She could just see the tall Serian as her horse climbed a slight incline, looking around confidently. She wished she could feel as much...but she also wondered at the simplicity that Ramus claimed she dwelt within. *Nothing in my life is simple,* she thought bitterly. Ramus was so wrong there.

'And us?' she whispered, surprising the silence.

Beko turned around and looked at her, and she could read nothing in his eyes. That frightened her. She remembered his face above hers, eyes half closed, hair damp with sweat and hanging beside his face. There had been desire there, and a fulfilment of an aged lust.

'That caused problems,' he said. 'Right now, and for the duration of the voyage, I'm your Serian captain.' He turned away and took up the reins, urging the horse to catch up with Rhiana.

As the day wore on, so Nomi's anger grew. It was like a flower blooming in the sun: stunted with shock that morning, stretching high at midday and spreading into an encompassing bloom come late afternoon. The heat of the day, the wear of the saddle, Beko's cool silence, the dust and flies and sunburn, all conspired to make her irritable and annoyed – bad companions for anger. When they finally stopped within sight of a border post, Beko slid from the horse and held out his hand to help her down.

'I can get down on my own,' she said. 'Keep your hands to yourself, warrior.' She had not meant to sound petulant, but Beko's surprised reaction meant little to her right then.

Ramus stole from me. This was the thought that had implanted itself in her mind, seared there by the sun. *He stole from me. First Timal, and now those parchment pages that Ten brought to me, and which I paid for. He rode away with them, self-righteous and superior, and it was not only* me *who wronged* him.

The anger simmered, ideas surfaced and sank again – dangerous ideas, and some of them brutal. If such thoughts did not concern Ramus, he might even be impressed at her maliciousness.

They had been approaching the border along a rough trail, lined on both sides with young trees which had evidently been planted in some attempt to mark the route. They could have gone cross-country and avoided any contact with the border guards, but Nomi had insisted that they converse with the Chieftains' militia. And now the border was at last in sight.

'Small border post,' Rhiana said, riding back to join the main group. She and Beko had ridden together several times that afternoon, chatting about the terrain, the weather and what they might meet when they arrived at Marrakash's southern extreme. The border guards were a hard breed, but they often had valuable information about the state of things on the Pavissia Steppes. Both had agreed with Nomi; it would be worth suffering their surliness to gain knowledge.

'Have they seen him?' Nomi asked.

Rhiana looked at her like a mother regarding a naive child. 'I haven't been close enough to ask. They're not the sort of people you talk to on your own, Voyager.'

Nomi stared at the Serian, refusing to look away. *Piss on you*, she thought, and she hoped it gave her expression feeling.

'How many?' Beko asked.

'I saw eight. Four at the post, four more spread along the ridge. Which means there are sixteen, maybe more.' She smiled. 'But they'll not give us trouble.'

'No?' Beko asked, surprised at her certainty.

'Ever hear the saying "small world"? I saw their leader. Bastard called Volkain.'

'And you know him?' Nomi asked.

'I fucked him.' Rhiana stared again and this time Nomi looked aside. There was an uncomfortable silence.

'Can you give us details, please?' Ramin called, and his jocular tone went a little way to melting the atmosphere. But only a little.

'Later, when you're eating dinner,' Rhiana said. 'My turn to cook. And Pavissian giant stoats have the tenderest testicles I know.'

'You're supposed to cook and eat them, not fondle them!' Ramin laughed at his own joke and the others joined in. Even Nomi managed a smile.

'We all go together,' Beko said. 'Show of force. The fact that Volkain and his militia know you only aids us.'

Rhiana nodded, and offered Nomi a tight smile which she took as an apology.

Nomi smiled back, but inside her thoughts were all of

Ramus. *Has he been through, what did he tell them, what did he say, what can they tell us about him...?*

And beyond the border, in the wilder lands of the Pavissia Steppes, perhaps she would feel ready to permit less civilised thoughts.

The border post was set back from the trail. It was a randomly constructed building of timber, rushes and mud, extended here and there over the years into a disorganised sprawl. The long curved wall facing the trail was built of stone. It contained several arrow slits, and one end was stained black by an old fire. A movable fence of woven rushes spanned the trail level with the building. It looked almost comical, because the grasslands on either side were just as passable. But the three guards standing beside the gate did not encourage laughter.

Nomi had rarely seen such mean-looking militia. The woman was short and fat, hair completely shorn to show a network of spider-web scars across one side of her scalp. She carried a spear and wore a variety of swords and throwing knives around her waist. Her expression did not change at all at their approach. The other two were men, both huge, looking as though their rolls of flesh could swallow arrows and bolts.

'Suppose there's not much to do here but sit and eat,' Nomi muttered, and was pleased when she heard Beko's short laugh in response.

'I saw Volkain from a distance!' Rhiana called. 'Best way to see him, too. Can you not come out and greet us, Volkain?'

'No Volkain here,' the web-scarred woman said.

'Rhiana!' a huge voice boomed. A shadow moved in the shade of the building, emerging stooped because the reed canopy was too low to accommodate him. And if the men at the gate were huge, this man was a giant. A head taller than Ramin or Rhiana and perhaps twice Beko's weight, he walked with a self-assured gait and wore a comfortable grin. 'By all the pissing gods, Serian, I never thought to see you again for a while.'

'I've been looking for you ever since that night,' she said. 'You hit all the right spots, Volkain. I haven't slept a wink since without feeling your weight in the bed beside me.'

He bellowed laughter and slapped his hip. Two other militia emerged behind him, these carrying bows with arrows already strung.

'Sorry to disappoint,' Volkain said. 'But last week I met a pretty mountain wolf. She howls!' He strung out the last word, performing a passable impression of a wolf's call.

It was only as he leant back into the howl that Nomi noticed his third arm. It curled out from his left shoulder, erring forwards instead of sideways. There was a small crossbow strapped around its wrist, and in place of hand and fingers, three metallic spikes protruded from the wrist.

She'd heard of the Cantrassan chop-shops, but this was the first time she'd seen one of their subjects. It was rumoured that nine out of ten who went there died on the table, before the places had been shut down.

Rhiana joined in the howling, and Volkain coughed, spat and laughed.

Nomi was unnerved by the display. She wondered how many travellers these militia met, and what payment they extracted for anyone wishing to pass through. And beneath Rhiana and Volkain's bluster, she sensed something more sinister.

'What is this?' she whispered.

Beko half-turned and whispered over his shoulder. 'Testing the water.'

'Who are your friends?' Volkain asked.

'I'm glad you asked.' Rhiana dismounted and stretched, and Nomi was sure there were more curves to the Serian than she had noticed previously. 'Curses, that saddle makes me sore in places I never knew I had.'

Volkain eyed the Serian greedily, the look in his eyes unmistakable.

'So, my friends and I are on a bit of a journey,' Rhiana said. 'Indeed, a voyage.'

'You have a Voyager among you?' Volkain said, and his voice changed immediately, from vaguely threatening to fascinated. He lowered his third arm, as though to hide it away, and scanned the small group. When his eyes alighted on Nomi, she offered him a half-smile.

'Voyager Nomi Hyden,' Rhiana said.

Volkain came forward, out of the shadows and into the sunlight. 'We're honoured!' he said, and Nomi saw that he meant it. *And here I am,* she thought, *judging by appearances.*

'It's my honour,' she said, and Volkain laughed at that, but politely.

'Can I ask where your voyage takes you?' he said. 'We've had a few of your colleagues come this way since I've been in charge here. A year? Two? Maybe even three years.'

'Any recently?' Nomi asked.

He ignored her question. 'They always pay their way.'

'What's the fee?' Rhiana asked.

Volkain shook his head, as though deeply offended. 'For you, Rhiana? You have to ask that?'

A brief silence, a nervous pause.

'There's no fee for a friend.'

Rhiana smiled and gave Volkain a brief bow.

'Although… I lie,' the big man said. 'The fee is to drink and eat with us. We have some fine root wine, and the best air-snake steaks for a hundred miles around. And I'm sure you'll want news of steppe marauders and the like, yes?'

'If we could trouble you,' Beko said.

Volkain turned back to the building, flapping one of his natural hands as if at a bothersome fly. 'No trouble! Maybe you'd like to buy some horses too, eh? I'm sure there's a tale behind that.' He chuckled to himself.

'No horses here,' the woman at the gate said. Her expression had not changed at all.

The inside of the guard building was surprisingly well appointed, considering the haphazard exterior. Each militiaman seemed to have his or her own sleeping niche, and many of them were personalised with wall hangings, clothing and charms. The central living area was scattered with chairs and several low tables, and from the ceiling hung yet more charms: rope knots, luck crystals woven into dried reeds, and an array of animals' parts to which were ascribed various fortunes. The whole display swayed in unison when Volkain slammed the heavy door, and he was tall enough to have to wave them out of his way as he crossed the room.

'Sit,' he said. 'My people will care for your horses.'

'You live in luxury,' Rhiana said.

Volkain laughed again, but the unabashed good humour had slipped slightly, as though he was upset at her veiled criticism. 'We do well,' he said. 'We trade with people crossing the border.'

'Charge them passage, you mean?'

Volkain shrugged. 'They pay us for safe passage and information.'

Rhiana looked around and Nomi thought, *Don't say anything else against him, we need him on our side right now.* Of course, she had no idea of the history between these two. And yet, other than Rhiana, playing her games with Volkain, the Serians seemed relaxed and at ease. Beko had sat down and was leaning back in his chair, perusing the display of charms. Noon and Konrad had gone to find the toilet room, and Ramin was walking slowly around the large room, casually but obviously exploring the building.

'We'll take whatever hospitality you can offer,' Beko said. 'And we'll happily pay our way.'

Volkain sat opposite Beko, his chair creaking ominously. He leant back and mimicked the Serian's relaxed pose, his third arm resting across his stomach. 'As I said, Serian, there's no charge for a friend. And as you're a friend of a friend, no charge for you either. Well...'

Here it comes, thought Nomi. *Here's the reveal.*

Volkain looked at Nomi and smiled. 'The only charge – and you'll forgive my childlike enthusiasm – is that your Voyager tells me a tale from one of her journeys.'

'And that's it?' Beko asked cautiously.

'What can I say? I'm fascinated. And though I sit here in my luxurious border post, a wanderer's heart beats in my chest.'

Nomi smiled, and found that she was warming to this man. 'I'd be happy to,' she said.

Volkain sat forward, expression eager. 'So where have you been?'

'My area of interest before now has been Ventgoria.'

Volkain stood quickly, chair grinding across the wooden floor behind him. Nomi saw Ramin tense, and Noon's hands fell to his belt.

'I have wine!' the border chief said. 'Good wine! I'll get it.' He drifted into one of the side rooms and returned beats later with a large, dusty bottle of Ventgorian wine. He grinned. Then he used a spike on his third arm to pull the cork.

They drank and ate, and Nomi told Volkain tales of Ventgoria. He absorbed them like a child learning new words, reserving his questions until she had finished her tale. And there were *many* questions. The Serians seemed to enjoy the rest, and occasionally another militiaman would appear at the door to ask questions about the horses. Noon eventually went out to oversee the care of their mounts and, when he returned, several of the militia came in with him. He was laughing and joking with them, and Nomi felt herself relaxing even more. The wine, the atmosphere, even the company went some way to distracting her from what had happened over the past two nights.

Stories told, hunger and thirst satiated, Nomi asked the question that had been pressing her ever since they had arrived.

'Two of our group came on ahead,' she said. 'My friend and a Serian companion. A woman. Did they come this way?'

Volkain's smile changed. No muscle twitched, but though the smile was still there it left his eyes. 'Ah, so now here's the thing,' he said. 'You've lost horses, your friend has moved on ahead of you, and you're on a voyage you choose not to share with me.'

'It's difficult to explain,' Nomi said. 'It's shared with no one.'

'The Guild?' Volkain asked.

Nomi shook her head slightly, and the militiaman raised his eyebrows.

'Well then, perhaps when you *return* this way, you'll share your tale with me.' He stood from his chair, the movement effectively ending the conversation. As he went to leave, Beko stood as well, and the men faced each other across the room.

'Did they pass through?' Beko asked.

Volkain looked from him, to Rhiana, to Nomi. Then he glanced up at the charms hanging about his head, and Nomi thought, *I could pay him with the charm Ramus bought for me. I've no need of it, and whatever the charm breather placed inside will likely do me no good.* But then the big militiaman smiled again.

'No need for secrets,' he said. 'He was a troubled man. And pained. I asked him for tales of his voyages, and he refused. But he left me with a promise that was payment enough. He told me that his was the greatest voyage ever, and that I would be the first in Marrakash to hear of it upon his return.'

'He spoke the truth,' Nomi said. 'And we're on that voyage together.'

Volkain shook his head. 'I may be a mere border guard, Voyager, but be kind to my intelligence.'

Nomi smiled and nodded.

'He bought a charm from me, and we talked about the current state of the Pavissia Steppes. He told me you were coming – mercenaries and murderers, he said. And then he went on his way. His Serian said nothing, just stood at the gate with their horses and stared through my guards. They didn't eat or drink with us, and I was happy to see him leave.'

'Happy why?' Rhiana asked.

'Firstly, because he tried to poison my horses. We found dead grass-rats in the stable half a day after he left, and the remains of a few tainted berry bugs.' Volkain looked up, tapped a charm above his head and set the bone swinging. 'Main reason, though: if ever I've seen a cursed man, it was him.'

Cursed, Nomi thought. *True. And if Volkain knew it was me that cursed him, I wonder what his reaction would be?*

They went around to the stables. There were a dozen horses there, all in good condition, and Nomi paid Volkain well for two, along with saddles and gear. Noon chose which mounts to take and led them away, talking softly, his voice making their ears twitch and flick.

'What of the Steppes?' Beko asked.

'It's been quiet for some time,' Volkain said. 'We fought a small marauder party half a year ago, but they only come against us for what they think they can steal. If they want to get into Marrakash, they go through the hills. But from the travellers we've spoken to these last few moons, I've heard of no marauder attacks. There are rumours of a big party coming across from the mountains. But that's just whispers on the breeze.'

'It's warning enough,' Beko said. 'Thank you.'

Volkain again offered that false smile that evaded his eyes. 'You should watch out for marsh wisps.'

'In the Pavissia Steppes?' Nomi asked. She had heard of the wisps in Ventgoria but never seen them herself. She had started to think of them as myth, though the Ventgorians she knew held them as fact.

'In the lowlands,' Volkain said to Nomi. 'It's only what I've heard, but you ask for news and I'm telling it.'

'I've never heard them mentioned outside Ventgoria,' Nomi said. *Is he pissing with us now?* she thought. *Maybe Ramus planted a seed of doubt, and now Volkain is feeling it bloom.*

'What are marsh wisps?' Beko asked.

'Just tales,' Nomi said. 'Sprites from the depths. About as real as steam dragons.'

They exchanged farewells with Volkain and went to where Noon and Konrad stood with their horses. The two Serians took the new mounts, patting their necks and talking in soft tones.

Nomi mounted her own horse and gave her thanks once again to Volkain, but his final comments about the wisps had soured their brief stay. As the militia eased the gate aside and Nomi's party rode through, she looked once again at the web-scarred woman. Her face had not changed, her expression neutral, as though her flesh had burnt and melted into a mask of indifference.

As they left the border post and rode onto the plains that marked the edge of the Pavissia Steppes, and the sun cast purple and yellow streaks in the heathers, Nomi's thoughts were complex. Fear and excitement vied as she took her first steps into Pavissia. Her voyaging spirit revelled in the miles of unknown ground laid out before her, and yet she mourned what she was leaving behind – the familiarity of Long Marrakash.

And before her, dangers more numerous than she had imagined even a few days previously. Back in Long Marrakash, sitting in Naru May's and contemplating the seeds of this voyage as the river flowed by below and around them, she already had a partner. Ramus was wise and responsible, and they would travel together as friends. There would be threats, yes, but they would have Serian guards. They both understood that Noreela still had many hidden dangers yet to be discovered. Risk was a big part of the thrill of discovery.

Now the perils were known as well as unknown, and more terrifying because of that.

Ramus had killed their horses to slow them down. The idea that he could have poisoned them as well had crossed her mind more than once. She did not see him as a murderer, yet she could not imagine him as a horse killer, either. Perhaps he could have slipped into their camp and infected their food; perhaps not. She was not certain either way, and the uncertainty played with her imagination, painting images there which she did not welcome. And he was out there somewhere now, riding ahead of them with Lulah, and perhaps plotting fresh assaults to slow their progress even more. The thought of the Serians fighting each other seemed almost alien to her, but she also knew how persuasive Ramus could be if he wanted. In the unknown wilds of the Pavissia Steppes, perhaps Serian steel would be tainted with Serian blood.

Ramus was like a ghost, gone from her life but haunting her all the more. He could be watching her right now. She looked right, across the rolling plains towards the sea that lay well beyond the horizon. To her left the land was more undulating, with a thousand hiding places and endless possibilities. And ahead...

Marsh wisps? Marauders? Ramus, furious and perhaps

mad, buying charms when he claimed never to believe in their worth?

She had a horse to herself again and, though more comfortable, she missed the nearness and warmth of Beko's body.

In her backpack she carried a sheaf of rough parchment which Volkain had given her. He had no quills and ink, but he had rooted around in a large wooden box and found a handful of charcoal fragments. It was enough. When they camped that evening, she would set about recalling Ten's parchment pages. For what use she could not be sure…but the idea that Ramus had stolen something vital to the voyage stalked her, more worrying than unseen watchers, and more certain than marsh wisps.

'Ahh, the wilds at last,' Ramin said, riding alongside her. 'According to the map-makers, at least.'

'It's what lies at their end that interests me.'

Ramin laughed, but it was more out of habit. He had a merry soul. 'That's fine if you know,' he said. 'Great Divide is all I've been told.'

'Isn't that enough?' She was hardly surprised that he knew their destination.

Ramin nodded his head from side to side, considering. 'For now,' he said. 'But when things get harder, be warned we may need more to drive us on.'

'*When* things get harder?'

'I like horse meat as much as the next Mancoserian, but dead horses on a voyage aren't good news.'

'You think he hasn't finished?'

'It's not my place to say,' Ramin muttered.

'You started this conversation, so finish it.'

The Serian sighed. 'I don't dislike you, Mam Hyden. And if I didn't know better, I'd say you have no harm in you. But what I heard…well, if I were your absent friend, I'd be a long way from finished.'

'He wants to get there before me,' Nomi said. 'He won't waste his time with more games like last night.'

'I play games,' Ramin said. 'Back in Mancoseria, I was very good at them, before I took my seethe-gator. Head ball, whip slash. They take dedication and determination, but a lightness of approach. Go in simply to win and you're guaranteed to lose. Believe me, last night was no game. And if he wants to reach the Divide before you, speed is not the only way.'

They rode together in silence for a while longer, but neither of them spoke again until Beko called camp.

That night's camp had a much more restrained feel than before. Even the previous night, with what had happened between Ramus and Nomi fresh in their minds, there had been no real sense of danger. But now that they were on the Pavissia Steppes, Beko and the Serians took their purpose more seriously. Rhiana had scouted ahead a couple of miles until she spied a suitable camp site, and upon her return the others had waited while she and Beko went to check it out. After pronouncing it safe they rode the last couple of miles. There were always at least two Serians on guard while the camp was set up, and the fire they built was smaller than usual, shielded by screens built of stone and mud.

Nomi felt a little safer. But only a little.

The dark skies were the same here as back in Marrakash. The stars shone the same light in the same patterns, the moons had barely moved, and the scattered clouds knew no borders.

And yet everything felt different. It took Nomi until after their meal to realise that much of the difference was within her.

Ramin told a tale, standing close to the fire and talking in low tones. He eschewed Mancoserian history and instead relayed a story about when he had first come to the Noreelan mainland. It involved a tavern, a huge whore and the intervention of the whore's lover, but though Ramin coloured it with effortless humour and a natural storyteller's grace, Nomi could not find it in herself to laugh. Perhaps it was because of the exchange she'd had with Ramin that afternoon. He could tell them about fat whores and livid lovers, but nothing could erase his belief that they were heading towards bad times.

After the tale, Ramin went out to relieve Noon for his watch, and Nomi made her excuses and went to her tent. Beko did not even acknowledge her leaving the campfire, and that was another factor contributing to her sudden loneliness. Away from familiar territory, in the wilds, Ramus was perhaps out there seeking to do her harm...and the man who had become her lover was shunning her just as quickly.

She sat before her open tent and took the parchment pages from her backpack. They were dry and brittle, but the charcoal was soft and fine. She placed the first sheet on the ground before her, and if she leant aside she could see its surface quite clearly in the moonlight.

Nomi drew the largest rectangle she could on the uneven parchment, and then she tried to remember.

By the time Beko and Rhiana went to their tents and suggested she did the same, Nomi had moved on to the second sheet. The first was a tangle of scribbles and crossings-out, and she had crumpled it up and thrown it behind her into the darkness. Now she stared at a sheet with a drawn border and one vertical line. She could remember nothing else. If she closed her eyes, she knew that there had been pictures, letters and glyphs, and though she could recall seeing a page with many images she could not place or define any of them.

Resisting the urge to curse and shout, Nomi cast a long stare at the darkness around the camp before entering her tent.

That night, she slept with her knife still strapped to her thigh.

CHAPTER TEN

It took Ramus most of that day to recover. Lulah had ridden them through the rest of the night cold, wet and tired, and Ramus had been slipping in and out of a troubled sleep for several hours. He remained aware enough to hold himself upright on the saddle, but little more. There were no nightmares. When he awoke to feel dawn's virgin light warming his skin, he could recall no dreams at all.

They passed through the border without incident, Ramus gaining information about the Pavissia Steppes and a bone charm from the big militiaman in charge of the border guards. When Ramus asked him what the point of a border post was when anyone could cross at a thousand places either side, the three-armed man had smiled. *People cross here for the same reason you do, Voyager,* he had said. *Information.*

He did not trust the border militia, even when they pledged not to sell horses to those following on. *Murderers, mercenaries,* Ramus had said, but as he spoke he knew the militia would respect such qualities.

So before they left, he threw the remaining berry bugs into the militia's stables.

Then they rode hard, pausing only so that Lulah could hunt rabbit for their evening meal. The landscape changed slightly, shrubs and bracken giving way to heathers, and the hills were lower, the valleys shallower. The Pavissia Steppes was a new place for both of them, and by the time they halted that evening Ramus was pleased with the progress they had made.

He thought of Nomi, and wondered how far she and her Serians had travelled with dead horses.

The dusky light took on a purplish tinge. Lulah was stripping, gutting and preparing a rabbit for dinner, and Ramus went to a nearby stream to fill their water skins.

The sound of the stream was so familiar that he sat beside it for a while, taking comfort in its soporific tones. He did not need to see Lulah's edginess to acknowledge that they were somewhere different now, a place both more dangerous and less known than the Marrakash border territories they had ridden through the night before. Here could be marauders and aggressive wildlife, and the militiaman had also mentioned marsh wisps. He had refused to elaborate, probably because they would not pay him enough, and it had taken Ramus until midday to remember where he had heard of them before: Nomi, from her travels in Ventgoria. She had maintained that they were creatures of myth, but it would be dangerous to completely disregard such stories.

As he leant over to fill their water skins his new charm swung out from his neck. He had never put much value in such fancies, but something niggled at him constantly now, a worry that kept itself dark and hidden away. Much had changed – he and Nomi, for a start, and the fact that he was sometimes living her dreams and nightmares – but this felt like something more. It felt like…intrusion.

Many people he knew wore charms to ward away certain worries. So he bought one, and named it as he put it on. He knew it would not work, but neither would it do any harm.

He looked down at the twist of bone suspended from the cord around his neck, spinning, swaying…and past it, below the surface of the water, he saw a light-coloured stone. He picked it out. The water was cold and took his breath away.

The stone was flat, about the size of his palm, and it had a perfectly round hole straight through its centre. The Widow had shown him a similar stone many moons ago, and as she held it up to the sky she said, *Look at the moons through the hole, breathe through it three times and wear it, and it's said your heart and mind will be well for a long time.* Ramus had scoffed at her beliefs back then, asking how a worn stone could influence someone's health. But the Widow had scolded him, as she often did, berating him with superior knowledge and breadth of vision.

How can you know this is only a worn stone? she said. *You know precious little of the Noreela we live in now, but what of the past? It's said by some that a great shaman once cast such stones. He moulded them from his own seed, and clay from the shores of the southern sea that you now call Sordon Sound. He was the first charm breather, and he breathed goodness and health into the clay before it hardened. When all thirteen pieces were firm he strung them on a rope of twisted hawk gut and hung it around his neck. The weight of the charms bore him down but he never took off that necklace until the day he died. And when he died, he was almost three hundred years old. He had friends in life, but in death they coveted what he had possessed, the talents and charms, the shreds of early magichala which none of them could begin to understand. And they tore his body apart, seeking to make their own charms from his bones and organs, knotting his guts to string his toes around their necks, and his fingers, and his incorruptible eyes. The necklace was destroyed, each individual stone carried from there by the people who had proven themselves no friends at all. And in their betrayal lay their doom. Some of them lived almost a year after the great shaman died, but certainly little more than a year later all thirteen were dead. Rotting into the land, eaten by carrion creatures, taken apart just as they had taken him apart. And the stones that gave him such long health sank into Noreela. Sometimes, they're found.*

The Widow had held the stone out to Ramus, but he smiled and shook his head.

Don't believe me, Ramus? she had asked.

Those same words echoed in his mind now. He held the stone up and viewed the darkening sky through the hole at its heart. The life moon was out already, low to the horizon and half full, and he turned until he could see it through the charm.

It was superstition, a story of a story, and he was a Voyager. Committed to truth and fact, science and discovery.

He breathed through the hole three times. Nothing felt different.

'I'm not sure, Widow,' he whispered. 'Not anymore.' He placed the stone gently on his knee and took the bone charm from around his neck. The militiaman had denied any knowledge of what the charm was for, but it had called to

Ramus as it swung from the ceiling, set spinning when the man nudged it in passing. Now he unknotted the leather thong and fed it through the hole in the stone.

It was no bother wearing something like this. If it did not work, he had lost nothing. If it did, then perhaps he could maintain his health until they reached the Great Divide.

He carried the water skins back to camp, and if Lulah noticed his new adornment, she did not mention it.

The food was good but not great, almost as if Lulah had lost heart after leaving her companions. Afterwards, she said that she was going to patrol the area for a while, and left Ramus sitting alone by the fire.

He took the parchment pages from his backpack. Placing them carefully on his knees he touched them first, feeling the texture of the pages and wondering whose fingers had touched them before him, and how many, and how often. He smelt them, brushed them against his face, listened to the rustle as he waved them past his ear.

The Pavissia Steppes smelt different. He was used to the aroma of heather, but the heather here gave off a warm, earthy stink. The air was richer and wilder. The parchment smelt almost familiar, and Ramus felt a sudden, surprising pang for Long Marrakash, now far behind.

Lulah appeared from the shadows to ask if he was all right.

'I'm fine,' he said. He felt uncomfortable with the pages exposed on his lap, as if anyone else viewing them would detract from their power. Lulah stood by his shoulder and looked down. When she reached out to touch the pages, Ramus covered them with the map he had drawn.

'Sorry,' she said.

He shook his head. 'It's just...' An awkward silence was broken by something calling in the dark, a low cry from far away.

'I should do another circle of the camp,' the Serian said.

Ramus nodded and watched her walk away. *She's on my side*, he thought. But that idea was naive. There were no sides here, only those with knowledge and those without.

He took out his journal and charcoals, skipping the first page, resisting the temptation to scrub Nomi's name from sight. He could not change the past. He turned past the page where he had made the mark in the temple, and when there were blank sheets before him again, he placed it on the ground between his feet.

Ramus concentrated on Ten's parchments again, turned them, viewing them all at once, staring at one at a time, laying them side by side across his lap, letting the information enter his mind without dwelling upon it too much. He accepted that some of the symbols may be strange lettering, and some of the letters he thought he recognised could be obscure symbols. The illustrations were obvious in places, not so in others, and even these could be glyphs or symbolic representations of words or phrases, rather than simple drawings. He was already certain that whoever had written these pages was at least as advanced as the most literate scholars in Marrakash. If it truly was a language from long ago, it was utterly unique.

And yet...

Ramus closed his eyes and let the imagery wash around in his head. His mind's eye opened onto a blank grey slate, and the images from the parchments floated there. He let it arrange itself at first, then he began shuffling and changing, altering shapes here and there or turning them upside down, left to right. He touched the stone charm resting around his neck, wondering who else had worn it and when.

By the time Lulah returned again, Ramus was feeling a closer affinity to the language. It was as though the truth lay a hundred miles away, but he was slowly drawing closer. If he watched, and listened, perhaps he would see it soon.

'All quiet,' Lulah said. She squatted by the fire, hands held out to warm.

'But something still bothers you,' Ramus said.

Lulah laughed, a short bark. 'Plenty bothers me about this voyage.'

'But here and now?'

The Serian glanced up at him, her eye glittering in the firelight. 'Just a niggle,' she said, touching her cheek below her missing eye.

'Seeing something that isn't there?'

'I've learnt to trust my intuition. And something around here feels out of step.'

'It's a different land,' Ramus said. 'The smells aren't the same, the air is heavier. Perhaps the unknown carries weight.'

'I like strange lands. I thought you would, too, Voyager.' She shook her head and reached for a water skin. 'Just something odd. But I'm not too worried. Perhaps daylight will tell us more.'

'You can't stay awake all night,' Ramus said.

'Just for tonight. Then tomorrow it can be your turn to lead my horse.'

'I can keep watch, maybe—'

'Have you ever killed anyone, Ramus? Fired an arrow into a man's face? Fought off something come to eat your flesh?'

He shook his head.

'I can look after you, but let me do it my way.'

Ramus watched her leave. *She's so strong,* he thought. *But she doesn't trust me at all.*

He revealed the pages again and narrowed his eyes, letting firelight illuminate the unfamiliar language. He picked up the journal and began making marks. Words flowed, old languages combined, his knowledge of writing and past times acted as the filter through which the parchment images were sorted. And soon he began to discern sense in chaos.

When Lulah returned again, the fire had burnt down, and Ramus had never felt so awake.

'Some of this is speaking to me!' he said.

'That's good, Ramus. But you need sleep.'

'No! No! This is vital, Lulah. I need to read these pages for us to get where we're going.'

'I know how to get there,' she said. 'South, 'til we hit the Divide.'

'And then?' he asked, wide-eyed.

'And then you do your Voyager things, and we come home.'

'No. We reach the Divide, and then up.'

'Up?' He saw realisation dawn. 'Are you truly mad?'

Ramus shook his head. 'There's sense here,' he said. 'Sit down, look.'

'I really don't know anything about—'

'Please, Lulah. Let me talk it through with you, and that will illuminate it for me as well.'

Lulah sighed and dragged her saddle closer to the fire. She took one more look around before sitting down, and Ramus noticed that she kept her sword hand free, her bow and quiver within easy reach.

'See here,' he said, leaning towards her and revealing one of the first parchment pages. 'The imagery is so literal that it took a while for me to see. Here's the cliff – the Great Divide. This much I know already. There are images of sun and moons, and people dancing or paying homage to one or the other or all three.'

'What's that?' Lulah asked. She pointed to the curled image of the Sleeping God, surrounded by a clear space on the page.

Perhaps she knows more than she admits to, Ramus thought, panicked. 'Sleeping God,' he said, trying to sound casual. 'See, the space around it on the page? They shun the cult of the Sleeping Gods and worship the heavens.'

Lulah nodded, and glancing sidelong at her Ramus could see that she was scanning elsewhere on the page.

'I thought these were the words of a story,' he said, pointing at some of the lettering surrounding the more literal imagery. 'I was searching for a link between the images and the words, but now I think they're more than a story. I think some of them form a spell.'

'A spell?'

'A curse,' Ramus said. 'Maybe a warning against... something.'

'Why do you think that?'

'I recognise some of the words.' It was almost as if he were talking to himself now, and Lulah's questions were what he had been asking himself as he sat by the fire. His concentration focused inwards, and speaking through his thoughts gave them more weight. 'I was looking backwards to older languages, to see whether any of the lettering or glyphs matched any that I've read before. But I should have been searching differently. If this is from the top of the Divide, whoever wrote it is cut off from the rest of Noreela, and their languages have developed in isolation. So I took some of the older, dead languages and tried to present them forwards, imagining how they could have developed had they survived. And I started to see things.' He pointed to a splay of words halfway down one page, surrounding the image of a tall, thin humanoid figure with hands raised into a cloud above its head. 'Old Narumian,' he said. 'Except the structure is all turned around, and some of the words don't make sense. And there's a definite Old Cantrassan lilt to some of the spellings. Strange, but that's how it seems. It's like the roots of these languages were the same, and...' He shook his head and blinked rapidly a few times, trying to clear his eyes. Then he spoke a few Narumian words similar to those he saw, attempting to incorporate how the alteration would affect their articulation. It felt wrong in his throat and the words hung heavy on the air.

'What was that?' Lulah said.

'I'm not sure.'

'Well, I'm going to walk around a bit more,' the Serian said, but Ramus barely felt her leave. He was there on his own, those just-uttered words hovering around his head as though waiting to be unspoken.

He traced his finger across other pages, different lines, until he saw another line of writing that bore resemblance to an old Ventgorian tongue. Nomi may have heard these words, but she would not recognise them written down. The lettering was different – there seemed to be more letters in this alphabet, at least thirty as opposed to the twenty-four in modern Ventgorian – but Ramus whispered his way along the line.

Something touched his cheek. He started, dropping the pages, standing and stumbling back. He scanned the camp quickly and saw that there was no one there. Putting his hand to his face he found a few specks of dust clinging to his stubble, wind-blown grit that had struck him like a soft fingertip.

'And now I'm spooking myself before sleep,' he said, but in truth he was enthused by his breakthrough with the parchments. He would sleep for a while now, let his unconscious work on the problems. And in the morning, while Lulah prepared breakfast, he would peruse the pages once more.

The time would come when he should tell her what they might find at their journey's end. But until he could make more sense of the parchments, he would keep such possibilities to himself.

He slept with the holed stone still around his neck, and that night he dreamt of the Widow. She was younger than she had been when he met her, and there was something almost beautiful about her appearance. But she was still aloof and alone, exuding a haughty indifference when he tried to tell her of things beyond the mountains. He had Ten's pages in his mind, though he did not speak of them, and the Widow came close, fixing him with bright green eyes that would fade to grey with age. *Do not fool with curses you do not know,* she said. And he smiled, because he did not believe in curses.

But you do believe in charms? the Widow asked. That gave Ramus pause, because even in the dream he felt that weight around his neck.

He awoke to darkness, the dream melted away, and he understood that the Widow's warning and question were really his own.

The smell of cooking roused Ramus from a light doze, and when he exited his tent he found Lulah stirring a stew of the leftover rabbit. She looked edgy and nervous, and she barely acknowledged him when he sat on his saddle beside the fire.

'Have you slept at all?' he asked.

Lulah shook her head. 'You could?'

'A little.'

'Daylight makes me more nervous,' the Serian said. She dished a portion of stew into Ramus's bowl then stood, strolling slowly around the camp while he ate. 'There's no real threat, but my guts ache, and I know there's something wrong.'

'You've seen or heard nothing?'

She shrugged.

'Then we break camp and go on. I'll lead your horse and—'

'I won't be sleeping until I feel better about this.'

'That may be a long time,' Ramus said. 'You've not been here before. The Pavissia Steppes is a strange place. Have you heard it called the Land of the Lost?'

Lulah shook her head.

'It's a Voyager name. Foolish, perhaps, but it shows how uncertain many people are travelling this way. Many people have vanished here, and not every disappearance is down to marauders. Some have witnessed their travelling companions fade away in a blink, as though passing through a doorway from Noreela to somewhere else. Others have fallen victim to rokarian traps.'

'Rokarians?' Lulah shook her head. 'Myth. There are no plants big enough to eat a person whole.'

'True, I've not seen one myself,' Ramus said. 'But the Pavissia Steppes hides its secrets well.'

Lulah fixed him with her eye, then shook her head and looked away. 'I'd still rather stay awake,' she said. 'If the time comes when I *have* to sleep, then I will.'

Ramus thought of the parchment pages he had hoped to work on again that morning. But as they packed up camp and he hoisted his backpack, he did not feel sorry. There would be plenty more nights, many more mornings.

His dream of the Widow's warning sang to him as they rode out.

He could smell the blood from a long way off. Lulah glanced back, but he nodded at her before she had to say anything. *Maybe this is the wrongness she was sensing.*

The Serian stopped her horse beside an ancient cairn. 'I'll go on ahead, on foot. I don't think it's fresh.'

'You can tell that?'

'You stay here,' she said, ignoring him. 'Behind the cairn. Keep the horses quiet. And take this.' She unwound her weapon roll and handed him a small crossbow. 'You have your own knife, yes?'

Ramus nodded. He felt uneasy holding the crossbow, yet he could see that Lulah would not allow him to return it.

'Going for a look.' She tied the horses' reins to a stone protruding from the cairn and then stood there for a beat, tapping her hand against her thigh.

'Lulah?'

She looked at him, tight-lipped. 'There should be at least

two of us,' she said. 'I can't watch my own back.'

'I'll come and—'

'You'll give us away.' She looked past the cairn, then up at its summit maybe twenty steps high.

'You said you don't think it's fresh?'

'Doesn't *smell* fresh.' She climbed carefully, testing each foothold before transferring her weight from stone to stone, higher, pausing twelve steps up and lying flat against the stones.

Ramus wondered briefly which Chieftain or clan leader was buried beneath the stones, but he had already seen the opening where a barrier of sticks and mud had once shut the tomb. Someone had looted the cairn long ago, and he doubted there was anything inside but dank air.

Lulah slid back down to the ground.

'What did you see?' Ramus asked.

'There's a building half a mile away,' she said. 'It looks like a small temple of some kind, though I can't tell to what.'

'And?' he prompted, sensing that there was more.

'Bodies,' she said.

It's a temple to the Sleeping Gods, Ramus thought. *I know that already. It's inevitable, and I've fooled with curses I cannot know. It's sensing me, it knows I'm coming and its marking my route and giving me warnings I cannot read on these old pages.*

Such thoughts shocked him, but they did not feel as foolish as they should.

'We *should* go around,' he said. 'Head east for a while and…'

'I suppose that would be safest,' Lulah said uncertainly.

They stood in silence for a while, the rising sun reflecting heat from the light stones.

Can I ignore such a message? he thought. Lulah was

staring at him, aware of his discomfort.

His head throbbed suddenly, as if something was moving inside his skull, and as he swayed he felt the Serian's strong hands grasping his biceps and changing his collapse into a controlled fall. Sweat ran cool, daylight shimmered, and then he could see clearly again. A brief burst of pain, but a reminder nonetheless. *Time,* Ramus thought. *I have so little.* He held on to the stone charm around his neck and craved for the moons, but he felt foolish doing so.

'No,' he said. 'No, we must go on. If this was marauders, hopefully they're long gone.'

'I'm not so sure,' Lulah said.

'There's no time to go around! We have Nomi at a disadvantage, but they'll catch up. She won't give in.'

Lulah sighed, then nodded. 'You hide in there, I'll check.' She pointed at the tomb.

'You'll not leave me waiting for you in an old tomb, empty or not! I'll come with you. Besides, you can better protect me at your side.'

'But your head, your—'

'I'm fine.'

'I saw lots of bodies, Ramus.'

'I've seen dead people before.' He stood without her help, untethered their horses and was the first to mount. He thought he hid his queasiness well.

He *had* seen dead people before, but never ruined like this. Ramus stopped counting after fifteen. Piled against a wild hedge some distance from the bodies were several dead horses, fleshy gashes gaping pale in the sunlight where rain and dew had washed away dried blood.

Beyond the bodies was the temple. And as he suspected, it bore all the characteristics of an ancient building raised to the Sleeping Gods, even older than the temple they'd visited in the ravine. There were carvings in the stone plinth, words and symbols both known and obscure, and evidence of a gully dug around the outer wall to channel worshippers' prayers downward.

The blood of the dead was splashed up its sides.

It has painted itself red so that I can see it better, Ramus thought. His heart was racing, and his head seemed clearer and more certain than ever.

The temple was set in a stand of trees. The bases of its walls were stone, several steps high, and above this the walls and roof rose in roughly hewn timber, bleached by weather. The carvings in the stone were splotched black with dried blood.

The bodies crawled with ants, beetles and flies, and many of them had been chewed by larger things.

It knew I would come this way, Ramus thought, but even then his panic was being countered by something that seemed to bear more sense.

'Definitely marauders,' Lulah said. 'The dead wear no jewellery, and there are no children.'

'No children?'

'The marauders trade them as slaves,' Lulah said. 'Some marauder clans flay and eat them alive. Old flesh is tough.'

Their horses had stopped of their own accord, skittish from the sight and smell of the dead.

Marauders, Ramus thought, *not the Sleeping God reaching for me...* His doubts swayed, rising and sinking. 'But the militia said there was no marauder activity close by.'

'And what do they know, sitting fat and drunk in their border building?' Lulah said. 'Try telling that to him.' She pointed at the closest corpse, a man whose throat had been sliced to the bone. His eyes had been taken, and his death grin was stretched by days of blazing sun, and nights of withering cold.

Ramus looked again at the old temple, and the blood smeared across the carvings. He could see no bodies close by – they had all been dragged away from the building to be killed – so whoever had spread the blood must have done so on purpose. No accidental splashes. No dead falling against the stone and leaving their final mark there.

A message from It to me, a warning, a guide, a sign, an acknowledgement—

'Ramus?'

'The temple,' he said. 'None of them were killed close to it.'

Lulah shrugged. 'So marauders have their superstitions as well.' But she looked warily at the temple, as if it had more to tell.

'We should leave,' he said. 'The stench of death and blood is heavy here. It's upsetting the horses.' He kneed his mount and turned away from the slaughter, but as he trotted towards a shallow dip in the land where a small stream found home, pain erupted behind his eyes so powerfully that he thought they had ruptured, his vision scorched away in a blinding light. He cried out and reached for his head, pressing the heels of his hands against his eyes. His horse darted to the right. Ramus fell.

He is standing on a low ridge from where he can see all around, and he knows that he is alone in all of the Pavissia Steppes. There is no other human here but him, and no signs that there ever have been; no walls, no old hedges, no scars of campfires, buildings, chopped trees, ruins, cairns or trails. He is long before or long after the time of humans in Noreela, and to the south the sky burns a palette of reds, purples and maroons. He feels at once insignificant and the centre of attention, but the attention of what he cannot tell.

It, he thinks. *The Sleeping God.*

But it is not him thinking this, it is Nomi. And the guilt of an old illness burns behind his face.

The nightmare vision changes quickly. The land darkens all across the horizon as something flows over the land towards him. The skies remain the same colour, ignorant of what is happening to the landscape they cover, and the flood closes in, resolving itself into people. Thousands, hundreds of thousands, and perhaps a thousand times that, more people than have ever lived or will ever live on Noreela, and they are closing on him like an inexorable tide, unstoppable and determined, all carrying a fearsome burden of blame.

He wants to cry out but he has no voice. He looks down at his hands and they are not his own; soft, long-fingered, he has seen them painting shapes in the air many times before.

As his high-pitched scream begins, he sees the faces of the incoming hordes about to engulf him, and every face is his own.

Lulah was with him when he awoke. Her face blocked out the light. He thought she would be angry or concerned, but her expression was one of confusion.

Ramus closed his eyes again and mentally felt around for injuries. He'd been thrown from the horse, not just fallen. He must have broken bones at least, and maybe there were injuries inside. *To add to what I already have,* he thought.

'Don't go back to sleep,' Lulah said.

I'm not, Ramus tried to say, but his mouth was dry and his tongue felt heavy and covered with grit. He shook his head instead and opened his eyes again.

Lulah held a water skin to his mouth and he drank, swilling it around his mouth.

'The horse?' he asked.

'Safe. It stopped as soon as you fell.'

'My head... The pain was too much.'

Lulah nodded, distracted. She was looking around Ramus, not just at his face.

'Are we safe?' he asked.

She nodded again, not meeting his gaze.

'How long have I been gone?'

'Not long,' she said. 'It's mid-afternoon. You were talking in your sleep.'

'What was I saying?'

Lulah looked at him then, fixing him with her one piercing eye. 'I don't know,' she said. 'I didn't understand.' She reached out and brushed at his jacket, his throat and face. 'You're covered with dust.'

Ramus sat up, Lulah pulling gently on one arm. They were in a gentle dip in the land, a stream running past nearby. It made a pleasing sound in the quiet afternoon. A few small birds frolicked in bushes across the stream from them, chirruping and jumping from branch to branch, scraping their beaks on the wood and pecking insects from the air. There was no sign that death and murder lay so close.

'Marauders?' Ramus asked.

'I went back to have another look while you were sleeping,' the Serian said. 'Your voice... I didn't like it. It sounded like the words you spoke last night, from those pages you have. So I was pleased to leave you to your nightmares. I turned a couple of the bodies and found arrows crushed beneath them, and there was a spear hidden in undergrowth. Lots of hoofprints too. Marauders usually work on horseback.'

He looked down at himself and brushed more dust away. Some of it felt sharp, and he brought his hand close to examine it. 'What's this?' he asked.

Lulah shrugged. 'Must have blown in from somewhere.'

Ramus looked around, seeing only heather, grass and undergrowth spotted here and there.

'We should go,' she said. 'If you're feeling up to it?'

Ramus nodded, though the pain in his forehead still made him nauseous. He fisted his hand, not sure that he had seen what he thought he'd seen.

They mounted up and Lulah rode thirty steps ahead, and when he was sure she was not looking Ramus opened his hand again. There, amongst the grit shaped like nothing, was a small grey fly. Grey, because it seemed to be made of stone. He crushed it between his fingertips and let it drift away on the breeze.

He wondered what Lulah had seen in the dust while he slept.

CHAPTER ELEVEN

Nomi was doing her best, but the memory of those parchment pages was vaguer than ever. Her parchment was scored, scratched and scribbled with crossings-out. The more she tried to cast her mind back to her meetings with Ten, the more nebulous the images became.

Worse, she knew that Ramus would be laughing if he knew what she was going through. He was a constant critic of her stubborn refusal to read. *If it's written down,* he would say, *it's written down for ever.* Her argument had been that a lie written is a lie that endures. She was much more trusting of verbal storytelling, histories passed down from father to son, mother to daughter. It was far more difficult to wipe out a tale in the telling than one in the writing.

Beko had noticed her distraction and commented upon it, but she had been riding alone for most of that day. She let her horse follow the others, stared into the distance, waiting for inspiration to strike but fearing that it was actually bleeding away.

And even if I did remember, she thought – the voice small, vicious and painfully honest – *what would I do with that knowledge?*

That barely mattered. Her desire to recollect those pages was partly for the voyage, but mainly down to the bare fact that Ramus had stolen them from her.

They would be useful. They *must* be. He had said that they were a mixture of writings, imagery and even maps, and she needed them. It was still a moon away, but the closer they came to the Great Divide, the more serious Ramus's theft would become.

She saw Beko fall back from the lead, waiting for her to draw level with him. She offered a smile and he nodded in return.

'Noon just came in from scouting ahead,' he said. 'He's found evidence of marauder activity.'

'Volkain said there was none this close.'

'Volkain sits in his border post and listens to stories told him by travellers and traders,' Beko said, his distaste evident. 'We're our own eyes and ears now. And Noon saw the results of an attack.'

'What results?'

'Bodies. Not fresh. West of here, close to an old building.'

Nomi nodded and scanned the horizon, expecting to see dark shadows rolling in to overwhelm them at any second. The idea chilled her, as if touching on a forgotten nightmare.

'We'll move in closer formation,' Beko said. 'Noon and Konrad will ride ahead and report back with anything troubling.' He looked up at the sun. 'We'll make camp earlier tonight.'

'No!' Nomi said.

'Nomi, we can't rush on regardless.'

'We have to catch up with Ramus.'

Beko shook his head. 'He's taken his own path in this.'

'You think he's right to do what he's done?' The suspicion had been burning at Nomi, a burrowing paranoia sinking from the blush of her embarrassment to the guilty core of her.

'Steal your parchments?' Beko said. 'Or leave because of what you did to each other?'

'You have no idea about me and Ramus,' she said.

He nodded. 'And I'm just a simple soldier. I don't need complications.'

But I need to talk to someone, Nomi thought of saying, trying to ignore Beko's sarcasm. But that would sound too much like begging. And she would not beg anything of Beko.

'We need those pages,' she said instead. 'I've been trying to remember them since last night, but I can't. The more I try, the more unclear they become.'

'You said you can't read.'

'They contain more than words.'

Beko sighed. He looked away and Nomi examined his strong profile, appreciated the ease and grace of his movements on the horse. 'Let's talk about it when we camp,' he said.

'You'll send someone?' she asked, surprised. She had been considering going after Ramus herself, but if Beko agreed to send the Serians after him...

'I said when we camp.'

'You could track him? You could follow?'

Beko only glared at Nomi this time, before urging his horse ahead to catch up with Rhiana. Noon and Konrad joined him at a signal, and beats later they galloped ahead together, disappearing into the landscape to scout ahead.

Nomi rode alone. Behind her she heard Ramin and the packhorses keeping pace, and she felt his gaze on her back. And the guilt was there again, a burning conviction that the Serians thought her the wrongdoer rather than the wronged.

'We're in your employ,' Beko said. His words broke the uncomfortable silence that had hung around them since finishing their meal. Rhiana was on guard somewhere beyond the fire's influence, but Nomi and the others sat close. Beko had insisted upon it. No slipping off between the trees, no wandering alone to gather thoughts. If there were marauders in the vicinity, he wanted everyone close. 'If you request something of us, we'll carry it out if it's safe to do so.'

'Safe for you, or safe for the voyage?'

'Both.'

Nomi stared into the flames. She thought of the parchment page with the thick vertical line, and all she could recall was the side with no writing. She had convinced herself that this was not simply anger on her part, and that having those pages back was essential to the voyage.

'Could you track them?'

Beko sighed and turned to Noon.

'Some of the bodies I found had been recently disturbed,' Noon said. 'Examined, not mutilated.'

'And you think it might have been them?' Nomi asked.

'I found two horse trails,' Noon said, and he shrugged.

Nomi nodded and looked back at the fire. She closed her eyes. 'Beko, I'd like you to send two of your Serians after Ramus and Lulah. I need the parchment pages he stole from me. They're mine, and Ramus is involved simply because I decided this journey was too important for one Voyager alone. But this is my voyage.'

'And Ramus?' Beko asked.

'This is about the parchment, not him and me.'

'He may fight,' Beko said. 'But we won't fight Lulah. Serians never fight their own.'

'I'm not *asking* you to,' Nomi said.

Beko glanced at his people, then back to Nomi. 'None of this feels good,' he said.

'None of it *is* good.' Nomi picked up a stick that had fallen from the fire and used it to stir the flames. Sparks rose and knots spat.

'I've never been on a voyage spoilt by the Voyagers,' Ramin said.

Anger surged through Nomi but receded just as quickly. She could not deny her guilt.

'Ramin, Konrad?' Beko said.

Konrad nodded. 'I'm the best tracker here.'

'And the humblest,' Ramin said, laughing.

'Just telling the truth. I can track well. And you're probably the most persuasive. You can joke Ramus into submission.'

'I want your guarantee that he won't be hurt,' Nomi said.

'If you send us to get those pages, you accept the consequences,' Ramin said. The joking had gone from him now.

'I just don't—'

'What happens when he refuses to hand them over?' Konrad was on his feet, pacing back and forth before the fire.

'He's right,' Beko said. 'You send us, Nomi, and we'll get what you want.'

It was a strange way of stating it, but Nomi heard the

honesty behind Beko's remark. They would not fight their own, they had made that clear. She respected that completely. But no one was willing to say they would not fight Ramus.

If only he won't be a fool, Nomi thought. She bowed her head. 'I need those pages.' The fire drew her attention again, and she was happy to see shapes in the glow. Around her, she heard the bustle of Konrad and Ramin checking their equipment before the light faded altogether.

They left the following morning. They all breakfasted together, and then Konrad and Ramin said their goodbyes to Noon, Rhiana and Beko. It was a ritual that excluded Nomi, and she walked some way off across the plain while they clasped hands and touched each others' shoulders. They looked her way as they mounted up, and she raised her hand. They gave no sign that they had seen.

She watched the two Serians ride south. They carried everything they needed on their own horses – a pack animal would slow them down – and they urged them into a trot as soon as they left the camp. They had opened their weapon rolls and now looked like true soldiers, with swords, knives, bows, arrows, crossbows and bolts adorning straps across their chests and around their waists.

The moment they disappeared into the landscape Nomi felt an instant sense of dread. Days ago, at the start of their voyage, she was excited to be out again. She had put the team together herself, paid for everything from her own pocket, and along with Ramus she was in complete control. Then everything had gone wrong, falling apart in such a short space of time that the voyage felt moons old already, not merely days. Control had become an illusion.

I'm trying to regain control, she thought. *Take back what's mine.* But however much she clung on to that idea, it did not hold.

One group was now split into three. They were on the Pavissia Steppes, marauders had killed people only miles from here, Ramus was probably running as fast as he could for the south...and worst of all, she felt like the cause of everything.

If only she and Beko had not made love. The shock of that had snapped Ramus – and she still berated herself for not perceiving his true feelings for her – and the rest had tumbled from there. She squatted down in the heather and closed her eyes, feeling Beko's hands on her thighs and delving in between. When she looked back at the camp Beko was scattering ashes from the fire and muttering something to Rhiana and Noon. This was a different man.

Beko fell in beside her as soon as they set off. Rhiana was in the lead with Noon close behind. Nomi sensed that the Serians were nervous.

'If they don't pick up the trail today or tomorrow, I've told them to return to us,' Beko said.

'What? Why?'

'Noreela's a big place. Ramus may have gone due south instead of south-east. Maybe he's trying to take a different route. I'll not have Ramin and Konrad chasing phantoms when there are enough dangers out there already.'

'How big do you think the marauder party was?'

'Noon thinks a dozen horses, maybe more.'

Nomi considered that, and though she was no warrior, it was easy to recognise superior odds.

'Remember, I've fought them before. They're vicious, but

not trained. Brawlers, not warriors. Weapons are usually old ones stolen from people they've attacked. And there's as much fighting between marauder clans as there are attacks on travellers.'

'Are you trying to tell me we'll be safe even if we do meet them?' Nomi asked.

'I'm saying we'll have a chance. Hopefully we'll ride right past them, but if we do meet up I'm hoping they'll avoid a fight.'

'They fought at the temple,' Nomi said.

'No, that was a massacre.'

The day was long and hot, and the air seemed to abrade her skin. Nomi could not settle. Every heartbeat could bring something new, and anything new would most likely be bad.

What if they come back and they've killed him? What if he fights? What if Lulah fights for him, and they have no choice but to kill her? She went with him for her own reasons. Maybe she's much more for him than for her Serian friends?

What have I started?

What have I done?

She remembered the days of her illness and how terrified she had been, told that she was going to die and helpless to stop the sickness growing in her brain, sending its tendrils through her skull and forcing her to face mortality far sooner than she had ever expected. There had been nightmares that she could not recognise, alien visions of drowning and fading away, and then the option for survival placed before her by the Ventgorian shaman. The guilt had preyed upon her ever since, but it was a price she had paid for life.

Poor Ramus, she thought. Damn *Ramus*! She hoped she would never see him again, but she could not imagine events working that way. There was much about this voyage that breathed destiny.

Just before midday, the land they rode across started to turn to marsh. And after midday, when the sun had more life behind it than in front, Nomi saw her first marsh wisp.

The heat brought steam from the ground, and the landscape was reminding her more and more of Ventgoria. The horses' hooves squelched down into the soft loam, and spreads of stagnant water reflected dark rot at the sky. If she closed her eyes, she could almost smell the scent of Ventgorian grapes on their suspended vines.

A shape darted across the ground, leaving no footprints or splashes in its wake.

When Nomi blinked and looked again, a huge shadow bore down. It blocked the sun and enveloped her, a darkness rising, crushing light from her senses and flooding her with gloom. It pressed against her and Nomi vomited, great heaves that she could not see in such blankness. She was torn away from the world and taken elsewhere – somewhere deeper, where less existed, a place farther away in perception and looser in her mind, like an idea of Noreela instead of Noreela itself. There was nothing to hold on to there, and she tumbled, feeling a warm splash across her face and throat as she vomited again. The shape was in her now as well as around her, filling her spaces and flooding her organs, bones, flesh.

She struck the ground and saw the shadow shrink to a tiny speck before her.

Nomi tried to cry out but spat chunks of half-digested food instead. It was thick and hard in her mouth, and the sensation made her retch again.

'Nomi!' It was a shout that came as a whisper.

She looked at the hovering thing, close to her and no larger than a fingernail. It was blank as a hole in the world. It shifted left and right, passing over a long-stemmed flower, skirting around a twist of sun-dried wood. Was it teasing her? Playing with her? Or was there no sense to it at all?

'Nomi!' It was Beko, kneeling beside her and supporting her shoulders with his hands.

'Stay away from it!' she heard Rhiana say, and Noon appeared in her field of vision, wielding his sword as though it could help.

'Don't...' Nomi said, '...don't let it...please...' She spat again, trying to void her mouth of gritty vomit. Beko helped her sit up and she clasped his hands, relishing their reality.

'Stay back, Noon,' Beko said.

The shape fluttered here and there, like a butterfly looking for somewhere to land. Nomi suddenly perceived a repulsive sentience about it, and a sick humour in every skip and swerve.

'It knows me,' she whispered.

The wisp floated away, expanding between blinks into something the size of a horse, featureless, dark and blank. As it retreated, it crushed flowers and rolled across heathers. The path it left behind was marked by plants fading from purple and green, to brown and pale.

'It's just a thing,' Beko said, and Nomi almost laughed.

'A thing?'

The wisp flicked back to a minuscule taint on the air once

more, seemingly without passing any size in between.

'It's laughing at me,' she said. Beko tried to let go of her shoulders but she clasped his hands, holding him there. He was keeping her in the world.

'What the piss was *that*?' Noon said. The Serian sounded scared, and that did nothing to settle Nomi's fears.

'Marsh wisp,' Rhiana said. 'The things that don't exist.'

Nomi felt the tall Serian looking down at her as she spoke, but she did not return her stare. *More than I know*, Nomi thought. *There's so much more than I know. I didn't believe in them, but they don't need my belief to exist.* Some of what Ramus had said to her came back with a sting. Perhaps she *had* restricted herself by only choosing Ventgoria for her voyages. 'I *am* a searcher of new things,' she said quietly, and Beko slipped his hands out from beneath hers.

'We should get away,' he said. 'No saying when it'll come back.'

'What did you see when it was over me?' Nomi asked.

'It was like you had a bit of night around you,' Noon said. 'What about you?'

'Nothing,' she said. 'I saw nothing.'

'So, do you want to hear about my eye?' Lulah asked.

They had stopped for a brief rest just after midday, and since then they had ridden hard. Lulah had gathered some bread mushrooms, moist and wholesome, and they had been eating as they rode. Ramus chewed thoughtfully, dwelling on what had happened and what may come.

He fumbled his last mushroom and watched it disappear in the grass.

'You're sure?' It was a foolish response, but Lulah had truly surprised him. Strong and silent at first, it seemed that being away from the crowd had allowed her to lower some of her defences.

She turned in her saddle and smiled. 'I don't offer something like that unless I'm sure.' She untied Ramus's reins from the back of her saddle and he kneed his horse, riding alongside her so that he could hear better.

'It's relevant, isn't it?' he asked. 'How you lost your eye.'

'Made me the way I am, and that's why I came with you.'

'You said you'd tell me when I finally translate these pages.'

Lulah's expression grew dark and Ramus, looking at her from the side, found it strange being unable to see her good eye. It made her inhuman. 'I think you're close already.'

'There may be a Sleeping God on top of the Great Divide,' he said. Rather than feeling annoyed at blurting the secret, sharing it suddenly seemed to lift the weight from his mind and ease the pain behind his eyes.

'You didn't have to tell me that,' Lulah said.

'You're going to tell me about your eye. Just sharing trust. We've got a long way to go together.'

'A Sleeping God...' she said, trailing off and looking away from him across the Steppes. She was quiet for a while, and Ramus tried to imagine the thoughts turning over in her mind. Superstitions, fears, and doubtless a hundred questions. 'I knew that already.'

'You *knew*?'

'I'm no fool,' she said. 'I saw its image on that parchment. There are people in a village in Cantrassa who worship such an image.'

'They worship a Fallen God?'

'Fallen?' Lulah said, frowning.

Ramus shook his head. *She doesn't know the name. But that doesn't mean anything.*

'I'm travelled, Ramus. I probably know more than you think. And I promised you my tale, so I'll save my questions until that's done. Most of them. But here's one: does Beko know?'

'I'm not sure,' Ramus said. And truly he did not. But he suspected that Nomi would tell him if she had not already. She was wilful and confident, but not very strong, and she would want him on her side.

Lulah suddenly laughed out loud. 'This is more than just a voyage, isn't it?' she asked.

'If there *is* a Sleeping God there, it could be the final voyage. Some say they were the First People, others that they moulded the land, and only went to sleep when it was ready for humanity to follow them on. But it's also said that Noreela is theirs, and we are merely tenants. If such knowledge awoke, the Age of Expansion would end, and Noreela will be known to us.'

She nodded, still smiling, and then began her own story.

'I'm no Konrad. I can't spin a fine tale like him. Rhiana too, and Ramin, you'd have heard their stories if we'd stayed together. But not all Serians are natural storytellers, though we have that reputation. And when it comes to my eye, I don't dwell on it too much, and speak of it even less. But you should hear why I chose to come with you and not stay with Nomi. I understand betrayal, and pain, and the stuff of friendships.'

'You told me you have no friends.'

'I don't now. But I did once. You and Nomi...that all seems so complex.'

'I barely understand it myself.'

'My own friendship – and the rules that governed it – was very simple. He was a year younger than me, and just to begin with there was romance and attraction. But that soon became far too complicated, because he was really only just getting to know himself. He had doubts. Sometimes he was attracted to me, and at other times he had trouble deciding why he was attracted, because his heart and mind were telling him otherwise. I valued our friendship enough to talk to him about it and suggest we ease away. It wasn't too difficult for me, and I thought he'd found it equally easy. We saw a lot more of each other, got on very well. We went on hunting trips to The Foot, the island north of Mancoseria, and there we fought golden pythons the size of five men. We took their heads and ate their meat, and we became a good hunting team – one of the best. We spent much of our time with each other, until I took my seethe-gator. After that, things went sour.'

'That's your mark of adulthood, the seethe-gator,' Ramus said.

'Yes, socially at least. There are Serians as old as I am now who have never taken a 'gator, for one reason or another. They're not the easiest of animals to kill, and though there are thousands of them, it does sometimes happen that they become cautious and elusive. It comes in waves. We've never pretended to understand them; we just kill them, before they kill us.'

'So some Serians never reach adulthood?'

Lulah frowned. 'It's not that simple. It's acceptance and standing that are affected. A Serian who takes their 'gator when they're in their teens will likely have a comfortable life, respected and involved within the community. Either that, or they do as I did and travel to Noreela.'

'Come to make your fortune,' Ramus said, a smile in his voice. He was pleased that Lulah laughed softly before responding.

'There are some who say that, yes. But most of us know there's no fortune to be made. It's more a case of broadening horizons, seeing more of the world. Mancoseria becomes a very small place when you have to kill seethe-gators simply to protect your people and cattle, rather than to prove yourself.'

Lulah took a drink from her water skin and passed it across to Ramus. He accepted, swilling the water around his mouth to clean the dust from his tongue and teeth. He said nothing, eager to hear the rest of Lulah's story.

'His name was Pargan. A strong boy, but he faced a lot of prejudice when he told his family he and I were only friends. They wanted their son to take a wife and have children, and when they realised that was unlikely, they shut him out. When I took my seethe-gator, he saw that as a betrayal of our friendship.'

'Why would he believe that?'

'He thought I wanted to leave him behind. He transferred his family's prejudice onto me and painted me in their colours. However hard I tried to convince him that he and I were still friends, he took my ascent into adulthood very hard. And seven days after I killed my seethe-gator, he killed himself.'

Ramus was stunned. Ever since meeting Lulah he had been convinced that there was some tragedy in her past, something to explain the physical evidence of her missing eye and also her coolness and detachment. But believing in some vague tragedy and hearing the facts of it were very different.

'You can't believe that was all because of you,' Ramus said, and Lulah's head snapped around, and she fixed him with her eye. 'I mean, you were his friend. He can't have *really* thought you betrayed him.'

She shook her head. 'No, I don't believe that at all. This stud here...' She tapped her eyepatch and the star embedded within it. 'This is for Pargan's father.'

'You killed him?'

'I challenged him. It was at the Cliff of Souls, just as Pargan's body was dropped from Mancoseria into the sea below. I...lost control. The tears of loss had come and gone, and now I cried with rage. I saw my friend wrapped in black-grass and tipped into the sea, and he was younger than me, and both socially and physically he had yet to become a man. And now he was dead, and I blamed his family for it first and foremost. So I did something that I believed would define our friendship and honour him. I challenged his father, struck him down with my fist. And when he rose again, he had a knife in his hand.

'We fought, but it was quick. On his first strike, he hit my eye and I felt it pop. He laughed. The rest of Pargan's family, the others gathered there, were shocked at the violence – this was Pargan's funeral, after all. But what better place for a fight to the death than above the Cliff of Souls? He came for a second strike. I deflected it, broke his arm, took his knife and slit his throat. Before anyone could stop me I sent his body over the cliff after his son's, and that was that.'

Lulah fell silent again, almost as if the story had ended. But for Ramus it had just begun. Surely there was so much more to tell?

'And you escaped justice, after killing him in front of so many?'

'Justice?' Lulah asked, and she was so close to tears that Ramus looked ahead, not wishing to see her cry.

Lulah's story *was* told. Whatever had happened between her killing of Pargan's father and her arrival on Noreela seemed moot, because she was here now and she wore her patch with pride.

'So I understand betrayal,' she said a long time later. 'And I understand being wronged. And that's why I came with you.'

'You see the betrayal I've suffered?' Ramus asked.

'Nomi's killed you.'

And in that bald statement Ramus tried to discern the truth of things. *Nomi and I should have been lovers,* he thought. He wondered how lovemaking with one's executioner would feel.

That night they made no campfire, and Ramus had to study the parchments by the light of the moons. Perhaps it was a strange property of the material, or a trick of his eye, but the blank third of the page seemed to glow with life-moonlight, and the other two thirds – where words were written and images printed – shone yellow. The death moon touched the Sleeping God and gave its image shape.

Lulah had prepared them a meal consisting of dried meat from the day before, stuffed with soft herbs and a variety of crushed root. It tasted cool and foul, but she insisted that it would give them strength. Ramus had eaten it whilst holding the round stone charm in his other hand, and he felt effects from neither.

Now Lulah patrolled the camp once again. He could not hear or see her, and that gave him great comfort.

And the pages Ten had found at the base of the Great Divide breathed at him.

Ramus knew that translating old languages relied on a small stroke of insight to give large benefit. Some languages

262   Tim Lebbon

from Old Noreela had never been broken, and probably never would. There were stone tablets from the great burial mounds of Cantrassa that must contain the histories of an entire race, long since gone. But though the tablets were filled with symbols, there was nothing with which to compare them. Some believed they came from a race that landed on Noreela many centuries or millennia before, and that their people were long gone to dust. Others alleged that they were from a civilisation wiped out when the current Noreelans first started to appear, a genesis lost to the mists of time, myth and superstition. If the new race wiped out the old, it would follow that the history of the old race would be wiped out as well. Victors write history, not the vanquished.

Still more said the tablets were lined with the terrible history of the Violet Dogs.

But he knew now that the language used on these pages had a basis in some of the Old Noreelan tongues, and may even be derived from one or all of them. This was a mystery that he would uncover, and the thought of what he would find numbed the pain behind his eyes.

Yet he could not clear that small stone fly from his mind.

Ramus worked long into the night. Lulah returned to the camp after midnight, mumbled something about having travelled for miles and seen no threat, and fell asleep close to Ramus. He could hear her breathing and took comfort from their proximity.

He muttered words he had discerned from the pages the previous night, and once again felt a fine fall of dust around his head. He frowned, because he did not know what was happening, though suspicions were taking form.

On one page, the words were surrounded by a series of

images – a humanoid figure repeated thirty times around the page in various poses, one seeming to follow the other. At first he had believed it to be an illustrated dance, one form of expression displayed by another. Now he had other ideas. In the morning, perhaps he would find out for sure.

He traced other words with his finger, trying to shape his mouth around them, and they felt alien and old. They gave him only a whisper, because their vocalisation took much strength from his body and mind.

There is magic deeper than magichala, the Widow had said. She often spoke of the potential in the land, and sometimes he believed she viewed Noreela as a living thing. She would pick up a stone and hand it to him. *Touch this. Feel it. Sense its shape, its smoothness on one side and the jagged edge on the other. Imagine who or what has touched it before you, what it has seen, what it has borne witness to. How did it break? A footfall, a strike, caving in the skull of a person or thing? There's magic, Ramus Rheel. The land's memory and future. The land's soul. It's deep, but when I'm asleep and I look far enough inside, I can sense it there, waiting to be born. And one day I will possess it, and these peaks will become mine.*

His eyelids drooped and his head nodded forward, and Ramus carried the pages from waking into sleep, aware that he was dreaming yet still trying to translate. And though he could not hear or speak the words fully, they began to make some sense.

Ramus awoke to daylight, slumped on his saddle with the parchment pages clasped in his hands, and something was moving across his face. He lifted a hand before he could open his eyes fully, and the beetle was cool and hard in his fist. Its pincers sliced for his thumb but missed. Its feet spiked his skin, feelers tickling the hairs on the back of his hand as it tried to crawl away. And from the depths of sleep words echoed at him, and he muttered them aloud.

They stuck in his mind, as though pinned there by barbs of sunlight.

The large insect's feelers turned from black to grey, snapped and crumbled. Its carapace lightened, and it stopped moving when three of its legs snapped off. Their stumps scratched at Ramus's hand, sensation paying witness to the impossible thing he saw. He wanted to throw the thing away, yet it was of his own making. His sleep-staled breath, his words, his muttered dreamtime exhalations were turning this beetle to dust.

Its body was grey now, and all movement had ceased. He heard a subtle cracking sound and the animal twitched in his hand, breaking in two as impossible stresses were forced upon its structure. When its outer shell was ruptured, its innards flowed out onto his hand. Dust and grit.

Lulah appeared from behind a high bank of shrubs and Ramus closed his hand, crushing the dead beetle beyond recognition.

'What's wrong?' she asked, pausing when she saw his face.

'Nightmare,' he said. He stood, pressing both hands to the ground to do so. As he stepped forward he passed his foot through the smear of dust.

'We should move on,' she said. 'It's bright now, but there's rain coming.'

Ramus looked up at the clear blue skies, enjoying the sunlight on his face. *My words did that,* he thought, but immediately the lie was apparent. They had not been his own words, but those of some unknown civilisation. He could only wonder whether they still existed atop the Great Divide, and what other wonders they may possess. They wrote a charm that turned a living thing to stone. *Maybe you were right, Widow,* he thought.

'I see only clear skies,' he said.

Lulah looked grim and more withdrawn than before. Perhaps this morning she was regretting telling her tale. Ramus knew more than most how a person could change from day to day.

'Believe me,' she said, 'heavy rains by midday. I smell it, shred flowers droop and the birds are gathering food. And the farther south we go, the more the rains might bring with them.'

They rode out after a light breakfast, and by early afternoon the sun was blotted out by clouds, daylight had turned almost to dusk and the rains were thrashing down.

The storm hid them from threats, but seemed to bring dangers closer. Rain fell vertically, splashing from the ground to create a mist of water around their horses' hooves, dirt and muck rising and muddying their legs. Lightning flashed; thunder cracked. They both wore the heavy leather groundsheets from their tents that doubled as cloaks, and much of the water ran off, but not all. It found its way down Ramus's neck and through his trousers until he was cold, wet, and shivering. Such discomfort did not concern him, however. For now the storm brought only water, but Ramus felt for the impacts of something heavier.

He watched Lulah's back as they rode and he was somewhere else, a blank place of thought where possibilities collided and coalesced into things beyond belief.

He knew of people who disbelieved magichala. They were fools and he told them so, because it was simply the arcane knowledge of plants and roots, dust and rain, and such things seemed impossible to those who lacked such insight.

But now...

That was no trick, he thought. *I saw what I saw. And when I fell yesterday, the dust of dead flies was upon me, turned to stone by my nightmare mutterings. And Lulah, stern Lulah, she did not hear exactly what I was saying, she was too far away. But if she had come to see, brought close by my rantings? She would not know the words, but neither did the flies or the beetle. I could not fashion a sword, yet one could kill me despite my ignorance.*

Magic, Ramus thought. *Widow, I have touched the magic you so covet.* And yet he was still not sure. Was this magic, elusive and unknown, a myth with no histories to back it up? Or simply another form of magichala? Perhaps those that dwelt on the Divide performed their own magichala, permitted by nature and the land but known by few.

The more Ramus mused upon it, the less the differences seemed to matter.

He felt those words engraved in his mind, like the prayers carved on the stone temples to the Sleeping Gods.

The whole day was dark, and dusk seemed a long time coming. They passed across the Steppes and encountered no problems, though Ramus felt watched every step of the way. He saw no one, and Lulah claimed to be unconcerned, but the rain felt like a weak barrier against who or whatever observed them. At one point there were slugs and snapes falling with the rain, and they brushed the sticky creatures from each other's capes. But for now, nothing dangerous fell.

And in his sickening mind, Ramus sensed the monstrous attention of something non-human. The cancer was a weight behind his eyes, and this was a void inside his mind, an area of nothingness that he could never possibly know. *How can it truly be sleeping if it sees me from afar?* he wondered. He shook his head, tasted the raindrops, and wondered whether the parchment pages were affecting him more than he knew.

Late that afternoon, Lulah stopped and waited for him to draw level. She rode beside him, neither of them looking at each other, and he felt the weight of expectation bear down heavier than the torrential rain.

'We're being followed,' she said at last. 'Don't turn around and don't speak.'

How do you know? he wanted to ask, but it was a foolish question. The Serians spent much of their time hunting things that wanted only to eat them. He knew that Lulah's senses could see and hear through such simple stuff as rain.

'When I fall back, ride hard,' she said, and without giving him a chance to ask questions, she turned her horse and galloped back the way they had come.

Ramus kneed his mount and lifted himself from the saddle. He squinted against the rain as his horse first trotted, then galloped ahead, veering left around a large outcrop that loomed from the gloom, heading down into a gulley that carried a shallow flood, crossing the stream and riding up the other side. Even in this weather he knew that a good tracker could follow, but if he lost hoofprints in streams, floods and marsh then perhaps he could shake whoever pursued them.

Pain thudded in behind his eyes, perhaps aggravated by the

sudden increase in his heartbeat. *Not now,* he thought. *Not now!* He listened for the sounds of fighting; metal on metal, the thudding of hooves. But he heard only the rain and the sounds of his own flight.

Be safe, Lulah, he thought, and he imagined the father of her dead friend taking her eye.

He climbed from the shallow gulley and the plains stretched before him, with little cover other than a few scattered trees. He paused for a moment, looked back the way he had come in the hope of seeing Lulah following him. But she was not there. *I should go back,* he thought. *If the marauders have been stalking us…*

But if this *was* marauders, then at least Lulah could be giving him a chance to escape.

He waited there a moment longer, then started across the Steppes. The rain was heavier than ever, and at times it felt as though he was traversing the bed of a deep sea. He passed a huge rock, veering aside in case someone or something was hiding in its shadow. Half a mile further on, he paused beside a burial mound, letting his horse snort and foam into the rain, feeling the thumping of its heart through his legs. The pain behind his head was constant now, but he willed it down. *Stay away,* he thought. *Just for a while, stay away.* At least it blanked out the other thing he had felt in there.

Ramus was confused. Should he remain here, waiting for Lulah to come and find him? Should he go on? If so, how far ahead? He didn't want to lose her, and if she'd been mistaken and there was no one following them, she would be looking for him.

His doubt seemed to seep down to his mount. The horse started snorting and stomping its feet, raising splashes of mud.

'Steady,' Ramus said, patting the animal's back, but he had never been close to horses. Not like the Serians. Not like Nomi, who seemed to have a special empathy with the creatures. 'Steady.'

He heard something beyond and behind the rain, and immediately he knew that Lulah was dead.

Horses, coming his way fast and unflinching. Whoever rode them were not being cautious.

Ramus hauled on the reins and kicked at his horse's ribs but it remained motionless, snorting and foaming at the mouth, eyes wide. 'Come on!' he shouted, his voice drowned in the rain.

He could see three horses coming his way. They were following the exact route he had taken, and he wondered how they could see his trail in such terrible weather.

If they're marauders I could buy them off, he thought. But he had no money, and if they *were* marauders Lulah would have already taken them on. Who knew how many there had been before she met them? They'd be in no mood for bargaining.

It was too late to fight.

Where are you now? he thought, and it was the first time in his life he'd issued anything like a prayer, to anything like the Sleeping Gods.

He dismounted, drew his pitiful knife and darted behind the cairn. At least if he hid he may be able to surprise one of them.

Where are you now, if you really want me to find you?

'Ramus?' a voice shouted.

Lulah!

'Ramus, nothing to fear.'

Still holding the knife he stepped from behind the rock. The three horses were thirty steps away, and he could already make out Lulah on the lead beast. The other two bore Konrad and Ramin, the big man's face split into a grin, rainwater dripping from his teeth like the blood of the sky.

'Ramus,' Konrad said, his voice quiet yet carrying through the storm. 'Put the knife away or you'll prick yourself.'

They found an overhang on one side of the cairn, and it sheltered them from the weather. Until the four of them were seated and a fire was lit, the subject of why Ramin and Konrad were here was successfully avoided.

'Ceyrat tea,' Ramin said. 'That's what we all need right now.' While he brewed, Ramus tried to catch Lulah's attention. But she was not looking at him. She stared at her feet, a worried frown creasing her features.

'Nomi sent you,' Ramus said.

'Of course,' Konrad said.

'Or maybe we decided to come and join you?' Ramin said, but Ramus saw that he was joking. A cruel joke, perhaps.

'No,' Ramus said. 'She sent you. And as she's killed me already, I assume it was not for that.'

'We're not mercenaries,' Konrad said. He stared at Ramus as if challenging him to disagree.

'Then you came for the pages,' Lulah said. 'Nomi sent you to track us and take those parchment pages from Ramus.'

Konrad smiled tightly and nodded.

Nobody spoke. Ramin continued brewing the tea, and soon the sweet smell filled the air. The rain fell in a torrent from the overhang, loud and unremitting. When the tea was ready they presented their cups and Ramin poured, careful not to spill a drop. They each sipped, and Ramus felt its immediate effect chase tiredness from his muscles and sharpen his eyes.

'You can't have them,' he said, and the atmosphere changed instantly.

'After brewing you such a nice drink, I think you'd at least consider our place in this,' Ramin said.

'You have no place. You're Nomi's soldiers, and she's sent you after me for something she cannot have.'

'Are you a soldier, Ramus?' Konrad asked.

'You know I'm not. But you also know I was ready to fight you three when I thought you were marauders.'

'We're not here to fight you,' Ramin said. 'Either of you.' He glanced at Lulah but she was still looking at her boots.

Ramus dropped his cup, stood, pulled his knife and backed against the rock. He felt the backpack pressed between him and the stone. To get the parchment pages, they would have to come through him.

'Serians don't fight each other,' Lulah said. She stood slowly, no real threat in her movements.

Ramin and Konrad remained seated, but Ramus recognised the look in their eyes. They were ready.

'They don't,' Konrad said, 'and they won't. Stay aside, Lulah.'

'You threaten me, Konrad?'

The scarred warrior sighed and put down his cup.

'Because you have to threaten me, both of you. If Ramus does not wish to give up the parchment pages, I have to support him in that.'

'You'd stand between us?' Ramin asked.

Lulah took three steps and turned her back on Ramus, so close that he could smell her wet hair. *Answer enough*, he thought.

Konrad stood now, the two sides facing each other across the fire. No one but Ramus had drawn a weapon, but the false casualness with which they had been drinking their tea was now gone. Their faces were the masks of fighters, and they gave away nothing.

'They can't have them,' Ramus whispered, just loud enough for Lulah to hear.

'You think we have any choice?' she said out loud. Ramin and Konrad glanced from her to Ramus and back again.

'We can stand like this all night,' Ramin said. He took a step closer to the fire.

Ramus tensed, clasping the knife tighter in his hand.

'Just getting out of the rain,' Ramin said. Water glistened on his dark skin and ran from his long hair. 'It's running down my back. Uncomfortable. But I don't mind, Ramus. I'm strong. Really, we can stand here all night.'

Ramus's breath came faster and lighter, and he felt the beginnings of panic. Lulah was right: what choice did they have? But he had so much work left to do on the parchments – he had read some of it, and seen what it could do, and what more would there be? What other wonders from beyond the Noreela that was known?

The stone was cool at his back now, its cold pressing through the backpack and soaking into his flesh. Beyond the stone, inside...? He had never been into one of these cairns, because they were unique to the Pavissia Steppes, and this was as far south as he had ever come. Perhaps now was the time to expand his horizons.

He rested his forehead on Lulah's right shoulder and whispered, knowing that the rain and fire would hide his words from the two men. 'A dozen beats,' he said. 'Give me that if you can.' And then he ran.

He did not look back. If he did he could stumble, or he would see what he so did not wish to see. So he ran blind, scraping his shoulder around the roughly circular base of the cairn. He gasped at the sudden shock of rain as he emerged from the overhang, but kept on running.

He heard shouting behind him, and the harsh hiss of swords being drawn. Lulah roared, loud as a female mountain wolf protecting her young from a rogue male. Ramin and Konrad growled something back, someone hit the ground, more loud voices in argument and then conflict...but Ramus did not hear metal on metal. *Don't fight,* he thought. He did not want Lulah's death on his conscience.

He circled around another quarter of the cairn, then searched for hand and footholds. Water was pouring down the structure's outer skin, and where moonlight lit silvery splashes against protuberances he found the purchase points he wanted. He climbed quickly, scaling the sloping wall of the mound, scrabbling with hands and feet and trying not to make too much noise. A dozen steps higher and the wall sloped in towards the top of the cairn. He began to crawl.

Let it be here, he thought. Moss and grass sprouted from cracks and joints in the stone below him, and when he reached the highest point of the curved roof he found the entrance hole he was searching for. It was covered by a thin mat of heather, but he tore through into the darkness below and knew that no one had been inside for a long, long time.

He lay there for a while, looking all around and fearing that he'd see Ramin or Konrad appear over the edge of the cairn at any moment. He still heard shouted threats and curses down below, but now he could only hear one male voice.

She's keeping one of them occupied, he thought. *But she can't take on two.*

With another glance around he lowered himself into the cairn.

He was trying to remember everything he had read about these places. There were hundreds scattered all across the Pavissia Steppes, the tombs of important tribal leaders from long ago. Most of them had steps leading down from the uppermost entrance, and Ramus supported himself on his elbows as he felt around with his feet. *There!* His memory was good.

They would come down after him, of course. But he had not come here to hide.

It was completely dark inside the cairn. Ramus could not see his hand before his eyes. There were thirteen steps and then the flat floor, a gravelly surface that allowed the rainwater to soak down into the ground. It smelt of age and forgotten things, and it was almost silent, as though the burial structure had no concern with today's world. Even the wraiths here were too ancient to make themselves known.

He walked forwards with his hands held out before him, still trawling his memory for more facts. Voyagers had been into some of these places, and though the constructions, shapes and sizes were often similar, the contents were vastly different. Built by different tribes and clans, a huge variety of beliefs were displayed in the way their Chieftains and holy people were buried.

Ramus felt his way along a wall which soon ended in an open area. He squatted and moved on, shuffling his feet and reaching out to sense whatever was before him.

This place is for the dead, he thought. His head thumped in a sudden wave of pain and he slipped to the side, reaching out to prevent himself sprawling to the floor. In this darkness, light burnt behind his eyes, but it was a false light of agony. He groaned, then felt something curved and smooth beneath his hand. A skull. There was no mistaking it. And something moved in its eye socket, something wet and round, an incorruptible eyeball seeing him in the dark and marking him...

Ramus cried out and pulled back his hand. *A grub,* he thought. *An insect, a blind rodent. Something alive, not long dead. Don't be a pissing fool.*

A noise came from behind him, deadened by the thick stone wall. He recognised it as feet slipping on the wet steps that led down. *So here it comes,* he thought, and he closed his eyes and began to concentrate. His breathing became slow, he shoved the irrational fear of the dead from his mind, the sound of rainwater flowing down the entrance steps seemed even farther away, his shivering ceased as he found warmth in the darkness, and then the words were in his head, waiting to be spoken.

I cannot, he thought, but the knowledge was brash and insistent.

I should not, he thought, but events had created enemies for him. And even then, contemplating what may be murder, Ramus believed in the greater good.

'Ramus?' a voice said. It was a whisper, respectful rather than afraid. He could not tell whether it was Konrad or Ramin, but that mattered little.

'Leave me alone,' Ramus said. 'I don't want to hurt you.'

The Serian slid across the floor, the noise of his movement

echoing briefly from the walls and confusing Ramus. He turned left and right, unsure now where the man stood. He could be directly before him, and if he reached out his hand...

'I don't want to hurt you,' Ramus said again, softer this time, more heartfelt.

'Nomi wants what is hers,' the voice said. The cramped, flat tones inside the cairn hid the identity of whoever had come down after him.

'They're no use to her,' Ramus said.

'I don't care,' the Serian responded. 'I'm here until I find you. I'm here until I have those pages. If that means my sword is stained, then so be it.'

Ramus closed his eyes and it was no darker. He sighed. His mind felt full, ready to spew what he knew.

'Nomi said—'

Ramus spoke *those* words. They sounded just as unfamiliar as the last time he had uttered them, and equally unwelcome in his mouth. As the final word trailed off the darkness seemed to sigh.

'What's that?' the Serian shouted. 'What speaks? What shouts?' Ramus heard movement to his left and there was a brief shower of sparks as metal slashed against stone. 'Away!' the man shouted. 'Come no closer! Ramus, *run*!'

It was those last two words that made Ramus close his eyes and hold his face, as if to clasp the pain pulsing behind his eyes.

The Serian shouted again, a word that turned into a pained, disbelieving growl, and then fell to the floor. More sparks came as he swept his sword left and right, and all they illuminated was the stark, wide-open eyes that held a dark fear that nothing could illuminate.

Ramus could not move. He should flee now, he knew, but his body would not obey.

The Serian stood again, growling instead of speaking, and started scuffing along the wall back towards the entrance. Ramus heard his laboured breathing, the sound of leather against stone, metal clinking here and there...and then a single loud crack. Stone against stone.

The Serian cried out. It sounded as though his voice came through gravel.

Ramus listened to the agonised retreat, and when he could hear no more movement, he followed. The sound of flowing water led him around a corner, and then he could see the weak ochre illumination of the death moon fingering through the entrance hole.

What have I done? he thought as he climbed. But there was something other than guilt plaguing him. Something very much like excitement.

'Oh, Ramus,' Lulah called. 'What have you done?'

'Ramus!' It was Ramin, roaring into the night yet not moving a step from where Konrad lay sprawled at his feet. The Serian must have rolled from the cairn and landed below, close to where Ramin and Lulah argued by the campfire, and the rain now fell into his wide-open eyes.

Ramus walked from the darkness and into the fire's light. 'I gave him the words Nomi seeks,' he said. 'Now he can carry them back to her.' He was aware of Lulah and Ramin staring at him but they were only shapes, shadows beyond what he really had to look at – Konrad, squirming on the ground. A continuous low groan came from his mouth, changing tone every few beats, and Ramus realised it was the sound of the Serian's breathing.

'He's dying,' Ramin said. There was disbelief in his voice, and then anger as he stepped around his fallen cousin. 'He's *dying*!'

Lulah pressed her sword across the side of Ramin's neck. He was a head taller than her and the weapon rested at an angle, but it was still obvious that she could inflict a terrible injury with just a flick of her wrist.

'We shan't fight,' Ramin said.

'No,' said Lulah, 'and so you shan't fight him.'

Ramin glared at Ramus, then turned and knelt beside the writhing Serian. 'Konrad,' he said gently. But he could only look on hopelessly as the man suffered.

'This is what Nomi wants so much,' Ramus said. He tried to inject venom into his voice but he felt suddenly wretched, looking down at the man he had doomed. Konrad's eyes were wide open, the eyeballs turning pale. *I did that,* Ramus thought. A bout of queasiness hit him and he closed his eyes, pain thumping down his spine.

'Help me with him,' Ramin said, but he was no longer talking to Ramus.

Lulah helped Ramin lift Konrad to his feet, the stricken man screaming as his joints ground and popped. They dragged him across to his horse, moving carefully but still unable to prevent the pain. Together they helped him up onto his mount. Ramus was excluded now, the cause of this pain and yet not allowed to help.

And can I? he thought. *Perhaps if I translate more of the parchments I'll find a cure?* But unlikely as that seemed right now, some deeper part of him – the new part that hearkened to the Sleeping God, perhaps – knew that this was an example that needed to be made. When Nomi discovered what he could do she would pursue him no longer. She would *fear* him.

I did that, Ramus thought again.

Lulah stepped back with a startled cry when two of Konrad's fingers snapped off in her hand.

She helped secure the dying man to his saddle.

'Is there a cure?' Ramin asked, looking to Ramus. His voice was quiet, and in that hopelessness he already knew the answer.

Ramus shook his head.

For a few beats, he thought that Lulah would mount up and ride away with the Serians. If that happened, he would not call her back, because Lulah could make up her own mind. He hoped that she would stay.

She stood beside Konrad's horse for a while, touching the slumped man on the cheek and snatching her hand back. She said something to Ramin, but Ramus could not hear her words through the rain.

Konrad's right arm looked grey and dead. His face was pale. His right hand was cracked and crazed, and it bore stumps instead of fingers.

Ramin mounted up and grabbed Konrad's reins, riding away without another word. He threw Ramus one final glance. There was hate there, and something else besides. Fear, Ramus thought. It was a new experience for him.

Lulah returned to the fire, keeping it between her and Ramus. 'You did that?' she asked. 'You did that with words?'

'More than words,' Ramus said. 'I'm not sure what they are. I...was afraid.'

Lulah threw something through the dying flames, and they landed at his feet. 'Konrad's fingers,' Lulah said. 'You turned them to stone, and the rest of him is following. You've breathed another charm.'

Ramus took a step back, looking at the dark, wet things before him. Firelight touched them and cast harsh shadows from their broken edges.

CHAPTER TWELVE

They saw no more marsh wisps. Nomi had ridden the rest of the previous day deeply troubled by the encounter, feeling as though the wisp had left her with something, changed her in some way. But she could not make out exactly what that was.

'Maybe you changed yourself,' Beko had said the previous night. They had sat close together at the fire for a while, and she relished their proximity.

'How do you mean?' she had asked.

'You didn't believe the wisps existed. They do. Perhaps your world is opening up.'

'My world has never been closed,' she had said, but even while uttering those words, the lie shone through.

Now, riding through the midday sun and starting to dwell upon whatever lay beyond the Pavissia Steppes, Nomi was startled by Rhiana's shout from ahead. The Serians blustered around her, Beko and Rhiana riding off to the east while Noon rode close to Nomi. She looked after Beko, trying to make out what had caused the upset, and then she saw the two shapes moving across a low ridge in the distance.

'Marauders?' she asked.

'Serians,' Noon said, but his voice was troubled.

Nomi squinted against the sun but could not see clearly. 'And?'

'Two horses, only one rider,' Noon said.

Nomi brought her horse to a standstill and dismounted, walking slowly through the long grass to meet them.

It was Ramin. Konrad had gone. The tall Serian rode in between Beko and Rhiana, guiding Konrad's riderless horse.

When they arrived Ramin dismounted, sparing a brief glance for Nomi that held more than a little anger.

'Where's Konrad?' Noon said.

'Ramus killed him.'

'Ramus?' Nomi blurted. 'He…' *He wouldn't?* Was that what she was going to say? Because she no longer believed that. Too much had changed for her to pretend to know him anymore.

Ramin began fumbling at Konrad's saddlebags.

'Have you brought the pages?' Nomi asked.

He looked at her properly this time, untying a heavy bag from the saddle as he did so. 'Piss on your pages,' he said. He knelt beside the horse and opened the bag, rolling down the edges as though whatever was inside could be damaged by the gentlest of contacts. 'And piss on you.'

Nomi let out a cry when she saw what the Serian had uncovered.

Beko slid from his saddle and backed away.

Rhiana closed her eyes.

In death, Konrad's stony visage still carried the terrible scars he had borne through life.

❊   ❊   ❊

'Is this a sick joke?' Noon asked. He stared at the stone head, unable to look away.

'Why would he make a cast of Konrad?' Rhiana asked.

'It's no cast,' Ramin said. 'When I left Lulah and that bastard, Konrad was sitting on his horse behind me. I had to tie him on. Whatever Ramus had done had frozen him, and all he could do was scream. And even his screams...' He trailed off, and Nomi thought, *The head will finish his sentence. The head will speak!* But its face remained unmoved.

'His screams?' Beko asked.

'Not his own,' Ramin said. 'They were changed by whatever was changing him.'

Beko shook his head, as though to make sure he still could. 'What happened?'

'Before we left Lulah, Konrad lost fingers. They broke off. Snapped. And as we rode I tried talking to him, listened for his reply, but he could not speak. I'm not sure he even heard. He kept his head down and barely moved, as if he'd forgotten how to ride. His horse became agitated. I was trying to watch out ahead and around us, as well as keeping one eye on Konrad. The rain was heavy, and for a while I felt things hitting my shoulders and head. Spiders, I think, though I couldn't see in the shadows. So I was looking out for them as well, and I wasn't looking when he fell from his horse. I only heard. A heavy impact. His horse kicked and stomped, happy to be free of the weight, perhaps. When I went back to Konrad he was...broken.'

Nomi looked at the stone head and wondered whether it was changed all the way through.

'Shattered,' Ramin said. 'He shattered when he hit the ground, and I couldn't just leave him there. But the rest of him was too heavy for the horse. So...'

Beko stepped forward and knelt before the head, just out of touching distance. He looked at it for a while, then stood and backed away. 'He still has his silver earring.'

'And Ramus did this?' Nomi asked. 'You saw him?'

Ramin shook his head. 'He ran from us, hid inside a burial cairn. Konrad went after him while Lulah and I faced each other down. He wasn't gone for long, and when he returned he was already...infected.'

'How did he do it?'

Ramin shrugged. 'I don't know. But he said he'd given Konrad the words you seek, and that he could carry them back to you.'

'This is bad magichala,' Rhiana said. 'Very bad. This is cursed work, and we should have nothing to do with it.'

'Just where are we going?' Ramin asked. He darted at Nomi, his usually cheerful demeanour now hard as stone.

Nomi took a step back but the big Serian stopped before her. 'The Great Divide,' she said.

'I've known that for a while. But what's there? Where do those pages come from that you and Ramus are so keen to own?'

'*I* own them,' she said. 'I bought—'

'Nobody owns such cursed magichala,' Rhiana said. 'It's of the shadows and wilds. Beko, I'm telling you, we should turn around and go back.'

'What's there, Nomi?' Beko asked. 'You said you'd tell me when the time is right. I believe now is that time.'

'I can't—' Nomi began, shaking her head.

'You *will*,' Rhiana said, 'or I'll be the first to leave. And once one goes, others follow, and soon it'll be you, Ramus and that fool Lulah with no one to protect you from whatever it is you seek.'

'Can't be protected,' Nomi said quietly. 'Not from a Sleeping God.'

Silence fell like a mist of rain, cooling them all and concentrating their attention back on Konrad's head. His eyes were half closed, mouth open in an endless scream of pain.

'They're a myth,' Rhiana said, but Nomi saw the fear in her eyes.

'A wanderer found the parchment pages at the foot of the Great Divide,' Nomi said, 'on the body of someone who had fallen. I bought them. They showed what Ramus believed to be an unknown language that could have come from the top of the Divide, and images that hinted at a Sleeping God buried up there.'

'You should have told us,' Beko said.

'Would you have come?'

'No,' Rhiana said.

'Yes.' Beko nodded. The others were silent, but Nomi sensed their uncertainty.

'I can't tell you any more than this,' Nomi said, 'because it's all I know. But Ramus has been edgy ever since we left. Almost afraid. He must have started translating some of the parchments. What happened to Konrad is a tragedy, and I'm sad for the loss of your friend. But it shows that whatever is up there has or had knowledge no one else on Noreela possesses, or has ever possessed. Except in story.'

'I've never heard a tale like this,' Rhiana said, 'and I've heard many.' Nomi sensed the Serian's interest now, buried beneath grief but still there in the lilt of her voice, the tilt of her head.

'So we bury Konrad,' Beko said. 'And then we eat. And then we decide, and we all honour the decision we make.'

It's already made, Nomi thought. *I can see it in their eyes; the fascination, the excitement, the thrill of adventure. They're more adventurers than I've ever been, and far more deserving to be called Voyagers.*

Rhiana drew her sword.

Nomi stepped forward, took it from her gently, and started digging a hole.

I'm digging to bury, she thought. *But one day soon I may be digging to unearth.*

Nomi had been right; the decision was already made. After she buried Konrad's head the Serians performed a small ceremony over his grave, and she backed away to give them privacy. Watching from afar, she realised yet again how different from them she was. They had lost a close friend, yet she was fascinated at the murder Ramus had performed. *He'll want that for me,* she thought. *If and when we meet again, he'll have some words to say to me.*

The Serians conversed briefly after the burial and then rode, and for the rest of that day they journeyed in silence. She brought up the rear, never falling back too far but wanting to give them all space. Around mid-afternoon, they passed a series of streams and small pools, and Nomi untied the rope charm Ramus had bought from her saddle. She paused by a pool and weighed it in her hands, wondering what the charm breather had tied into the knot, what Ramus had told her. It felt heavier than it should, as if the knot contained much more than rope and air.

Nomi threw the charm. She gasped as it left her hand,

knowing that some believed it bad luck to dispose of a gifted charm unused. But this rope had the taint of Ramus's sweat upon it, the memory of his breath, and her feelings for him had changed. Now, she feared him as well.

The knotted rope struck the surface of the pond and sank. Nomi was not sad to see it go.

The mood that evening in camp was sour, and Nomi took to her tent to try and recall more of the parchment pages, but her memory was failing her. And even if she did remember, she knew that it would do her no good. She had to be content with reaching the Divide and climbing, knowing that they had the equipment to do so. Ramus and Lulah did not.

Next morning, the atmosphere was somewhat lighter, bathed in bright sunlight instead of rain. Serians were used to losing friends, she knew, because theirs was a dangerous life, whether they remained on Mancoseria or journeyed to Noreela to work for Voyagers. But she did not expect for an instant that this made their loss easier to bear. And she believed it was her silence more than anything that brought them back to her. Beko first, then Rhiana, and by the end of that first full day after Konrad's death she felt almost comfortable amongst them once more.

She thought of Ramus often. It was as if in riding away from her he had left many recognisable parts of himself behind, and now she was imagining a stranger on a parallel course. *Is he stronger as each day goes by?* she wondered. *If he continues translating those pages, what else will he find?* The thought was chilling, and as dusk fell she tried to shut it out and replace it with the blank, comfortable presence of campfire stories.

❉ ❉ ❉

Their voyage across the Pavissia Steppes continued. They camped at night and rode during the day, passing an old settlement destroyed by fire long ago. There were no bodies, but a mile farther on they found a sculpture of bones a dozen steps high, and on the skulls making up its head sat several ravens.

Skull ravens. Nomi had heard of them, but never seen them. They fed on dreams and revelled in nightmares, excavating them from sleeping victims' heads by pecking holes through their skulls and eating their brains.

The birds showed no fear as Nomi and the Serians rode by.

Three days after Konrad's death, they reached the wide, unnamed river that marked the southern border of this wild place, and the uncharted regions beyond. Most of the land between here and the Great Divide did not even have a name. They camped that night beside the river, and as Rhiana told a tale and Noon cooked a meal, Nomi felt her thoughts carried away on the water. Beko and the others surmised that Ramus and Lulah were to the east of them, and perhaps even now they were camped next to this same river. Nomi sat for a long time that evening watching the waters roll by, looking out for twigs, leaves or branches that Ramus may have laid eyes on hours or days before. Between one blink and the next she spied something that caused her heart to stutter – a shape that can only have been a body. It bobbed by, carried by the strong current, arms held wide as though halfway through a swimming stroke.

At her alert, Noon ran along the bank, dived in and swam out to retrieve the corpse. They watched him pull it towards the shore, his expression unreadable, and Nomi felt a sense of dread envelop the group.

Don't let it be Ramus, she thought. And she knew that the others were thinking something else entirely.

But it was neither Ramus, nor Lulah. The body was a young man, dressed in ratty leathers, torso and face pierced in a dozen places by spears or swords. His chest was spiked with the stumps of three snapped arrows. His face and neck were heavily tattooed, and his left ear was sliced off.

He had wings. They hung limp and wet from his back, protruding through slits cut into his jacket for that purpose. They were sparsely feathered around their edges, leathery and thick elsewhere, and one of them had been slashed through to its thick, bony edge.

'I know this marauder clan,' Beko said. 'Graft these onto their young when they're designated as warriors. How they grow through time, I don't know.'

'Do they really work?' Nomi asked, amazed and fascinated.

Noon stared at her and blinked slowly. 'Of course not.' He gave the body back to the river and they watched it spin away into the strong central current.

They travelled upstream for several miles until they found a place where they could cross. It was a tense operation, but Pancet had been good to his word, and the horses were strong and capable. They went on immediately after crossing, even though they were all exhausted. Nomi sensed the excitement the others felt at being away from known territories, and she was starting to feel the draw of the Divide.

All the time she thought of Ramus, and she knew that he was thinking of her. It was not an idea that gave her peace.

❋   ❋   ❋

Lulah had been joking, but Ramus made a charm from Konrad's fingers.

He picked off the loose flakes of stone first, then tested to see whether they would break into small pieces. They did not. They seemed strong, which was befitting their origin. Then he cut a thin thread of leather from the bottom hem of his jacket, rolled and twisted it into a thong and tied the two fingers together. He knotted it around his neck without Lulah seeing, dropping the stone fingers inside his shirt. He was not certain what Lulah would do if she knew. It was very possible that she would kill him.

Later that night, as Lulah scouted ahead, Ramus paused and cupped the stone fingers in his hands. He breathed across them, whispering the same words that had made them. Nothing changed. In a way that comforted him. The magichala which the Widow performed followed the laws of time well, and so it seemed did these words from atop the Great Divide.

Lulah remained distant. She often rode ahead to explore their route, make sure it was safe, save time if they were heading for a ravine, deep river or some other obstacle. She never found one – none that they could not pass, at least – but she used the excuse nonetheless.

Ramus would have preferred her to ride with him. He had seen in her a kindred spirit, and he sensed it there still, though swallowed by grief and a dash of pride. But he would give her time, and perhaps time would wash away some of the hurt.

Riding alone gave Ramus the opportunity to speak to the Widow.

She had been on his mind for a long time. In truth, she had been a part of him ever since he met her on his first voyage, a voice in darker times and a companion when he was lonely. He was certain that she did not cast herself this way, and yet he had given her that role. She was a wise woman who acted wiser, and it seemed to Ramus that every time he saw her she was younger, though possessed of more knowledge and exploring deeper into arcane matters that few would even consider. There was no limit to her ability to believe. Most people treated magichala as a slight against whichever god or gods they worshipped, a betrayal of natural laws as opposed to a deeper understanding of them. The Widow was a purer explorer of the mind and the powers in the land than Ramus, even though she had never travelled beyond her own mountainous home. She knew Noreela deeper, appreciated its nature more fully than he ever could.

Now he could go back to her, his imagination stretching north to her mountains. He could sit in the cave that she called home, eyes burning from the scented smoke from her fire, nose stinging as the acidic fumes were drawn in, and the Widow smiled. *Tell me what you have, Ramus,* she said.

I'm not sure. Something beyond magichala. Something belonging to the potential you see in the land.

Instead of being amazed, she shook her head and sighed a tunnel through the smoke. *There's always a cause,* she said. *Always a source, a home, a well from which such things rise and spread. Because this land is far from ready, and we are young and innocent of our purposes here.*

My purpose is to explore and be a discoverer.

Exploration? the Widow said. *Perhaps.*

Ramus whispered those words from the parchment in his mind, and the Widow's eyes went wide, the smoke from her fire slowed. But then she smiled again and the fire roared higher than ever. *Tricks in the smoke,* she said. *Twists in your mind. Magichala is more than roots, leaves and steam dragon teeth, and you know that, Ramus. Riding where you are, seeking what you seek, you know that there are whole new vistas waiting to be opened in the land, and the minds of those who live upon it. But those words...do you really think they're anything other than a hex?*

'Are they?' Ramus said, blinking away sunlight or staring into the night, and Lulah remained away from him.

Perhaps it was hatred. He had seen it in her eyes that first day following Konrad's death, but it had mellowed since. So perhaps that, yes, though in a waning state.

But maybe more than anything, she was afraid.

'I won't turn you to stone,' he said to her whenever they came close enough to speak.

Lulah shook her head and rode away. 'You talk in your sleep.'

Two days following Konrad's death, they came across a band of marauders. Lulah rode back quickly to warn Ramus. She said there were maybe a hundred of them, some hauling wagons heavy with equipment, others riding fully armed. A few riders guided a small group of chained fodder, a race of fat, pale humans bred for food in the southern parts of the Pavissia Steppes. There was a way to skirt around them, but it involved a long, careful march, watching out all the time for marauder guards and preparing for attack at any moment.

It turned into a wearisome afternoon, mostly spent walking so that they could guide their horses along gulleys and through a heavily wooded area. Twice they saw marauder sentries miles out from their camp, and Lulah took this to be a sign that this was a war party, as likely to be attacked as to attack someone else. 'So there are more out there,' she whispered in Ramus's ear.

By the time dusk fell, they had covered only fifteen miles, and they were more exhausted than they had yet been on the voyage. Ramus's head was thumping and his eyes swam with colours he did not know, and for a while he ranted and raged as Lulah gathered herbs and roots to make him medicine. Later, huddled together for warmth because they dared not light a fire, Lulah admitted that she feared he would curse her without knowing. 'You were raving,' she said. 'Just for a moment, but it was long enough. Words I didn't know came from your mouth, your hands drew strange shapes in the air, and I stuffed my ears with moss. Do I have to hear these words for them to change me? If they touch my skin, will that be enough to turn my blood to dust?'

Ramus told her he was not sure, though he knew the true power of those words. He hoped that the more he examined the parchments, the more he would understand.

They were almost across the Pavissia Steppes and there was a longer ride ahead of them, through places unmapped and landscapes unknown. They would navigate now via hearsay and tales passed by word of mouth from wanderer to wanderer, instead of using maps drawn and refined by Voyagers dedicated to the task. Everything that had happened up to now had been in a place of relative safety.

'These are the dark lands,' Lulah said as they stood on the shores of the great river. 'These are places untravelled.'

'Not untravelled,' Ramus said. 'Simply unknown. Doesn't that excite you?'

Lulah smiled at him, and it was the first time she had shown him anything other than resentment and fear since Konrad's death.

They crossed the river and moved on, Ramus driving them with his silent sense of urgency. Lulah never questioned his swift food stops, his early mornings, his insistence that they cover another few miles before making camp. She rode with him, and as time went on Ramus began to believe that she really was the kindred spirit he had sensed before his words had turned Konrad to stone.

Every evening, after food and before sleep, he studied the parchment pages, fingering the charms about his neck – the bone, the stone, the fingers. He filled his journal with notes and observations, and Lulah watched from a cautious distance. He never revealed to her what he discovered, because in truth there was little to reveal. More words which he dared not speak. More sentences that held no meaning for him, but which perhaps would turn air to glass, rock to salt or flesh and blood to something more terrible.

Yet these words held no fear for him. He remembered them, and sometimes when he was alone he whispered them to the wind.

What did frighten him were the frequent references he found to a Sleeping God gone mad. And one line in particular that said, *Never wake the fallen.*

A day after fording the river, Nomi and her Serian riders entered the first of the great forests. Some rumours held that much of the uncharted area to the south of the Pavissia Steppes was wooded, and that was part of the reason it remained uncharted.

Such landscape was notoriously difficult to negotiate. At first they found rough trails worn between the trees, but these soon vanished as though who or whatever made them had simply faded away. They took to wrapping their lead horse's chest and front legs with their leather groundsheets so that it could force its way through thickets of brambles and ferns, forging a path for them all to follow. Sometimes the going was easier, trees more spread out and the spaces in between taken with grass or purple and green moss. Other times the route became completely impassable, and they either had to turn back and retrace their steps or push left and right.

Some of the trees here were huge. Their trunks took thirty steps to walk around, and their heads were hidden so high in the canopy that they could not be seen. Thick creepers hung from tree to tree high up, swaying slightly even when there was no breeze, and Nomi saw fleeting shadows passing along these fine connecting lines. The Serians saw them too, and they looked up nervously every few beats, weapons ready. Sometimes Nomi was sure they were being followed through the forests at high level, though the shadows never resolved themselves, and the followers never came.

They found several fruits dropped from one of the highest trees: round, spiked things as large as a human head, that seemed to pulse with inner life. One of them had extruded several spiny limbs and was slowly hauling itself away from its parent's shadowy influence, searching for somewhere new and sunlit to sit, take root and grow. Some of their fruits' spines were home to dead creatures: rodents, large insects, even a few birds. The skin below these pierced animals was a bright crimson, and the spikes throbbed as they ingested blood and insides.

Many of the trees seemed to have much of their root systems exposed above ground. Long, thick roots snaked up to a hundred steps from the trees' huge boles, and behind several trees the voyagers found wide drag trails. The evidence was compelling, but though they camped close to a tree for one long afternoon, they saw no signs of movement.

Ramus would love this, Nomi thought. However much she tried, her old friend would not leave her alone.

The trunks of lightning-struck trees were often home to giant fungi that grew in wide, thick plates. Ramin carved a slab from one of these growths, but threw it away, cringing at the smell and wiping his hand for the rest of that day. The fungi displayed holes here and there the size of a fist, and Nomi saw an occasional spiny leg draw slowly back into the darkness as they passed.

The landscape was not at all even. The forests covered hills and valleys, and sometimes deep and deadly ravines were spanned and camouflaged by thick creepers and vines. More than once the lead rider stumbled and almost fell, and it was more the horses' instincts than anything else that saved them.

They found occasional signs of wanderers: old campfires, shelters built between trees, and a platform constructed up in the branches that seemed more permanent. But they saw no one. Every sign they found was old, and if there were wanderers still travelling these parts, they were keeping to themselves.

And there were dangers other than the lie of the land. One morning Noon was stung by a huge wasp, a creature the size of a small bird, and when Rhiana brought it down with an expertly fired arrow, it spat and spun on the ground, wings kicking up a storm of leaves as its stinger slapped into the soil again and again. It took Beko's boot to silence it fully, and then Rhiana sliced off its sting and squeezed the remaining poison onto a wide green leaf. Noon had already fainted by then, and the lump on the side of his neck was swelling rapidly.

Nomi felt useless as she watched the Serians work, so she sat behind Noon and cradled his head in her lap, making sure he could feel her touch on his face. She talked softly to him, hearing only moans and hisses in return. His skin grew hot.

Rhiana did something with the poison. She gathered fallen leaves, selected the few she wanted, chewed them into a paste, and dripped wasp poison into the mix. Then she added a few pinches of stuff from her belt pouches. Nomi could not see what it was, and she did not ask, because the concentration on Rhiana's face was absolute.

A hundred beats after Noon had been stung, Rhiana knelt before him, short knife in one hand and the leaf holding the dark green paste in the other. She looked up at Beko and Ramin, her face stern with concern, and then pricked the swelling on Noon's neck. Blood gushed out, followed by a clearer liquid that seemed to have small shapes swimming within it. Nomi blinked quickly and bent to look closer, but the fluid had already soaked into Noon's shirt.

Rhiana nudged her aside and pressed the leaf to his wound.

He screamed for a long time.

They stayed there for several hours while Noon recovered. His screaming dwindled to a cry, and the cry to a deep, troubled sleep. When he finally came around, the wound on his neck was little more than a vivid spot, and his skin had returned to its normal temperature. Rhiana showed him the wasp that had stung him and he examined it for some time, either fascinated or disgusted.

After eating they moved on. Noon was weak but eager to continue, and he rode the rest of that day beside Rhiana, their bond obviously close.

Camping in the forest was a nerve-racking affair. By day it was filled with the sound of birdsong, the hum of insects and the surreptitious rustle of small creatures in the undergrowth. There were dangers – they saw more of those huge wasps, and for one long afternoon they passed through a ravine crawling with snakes – but during the day at least they were mostly visible, and avoidable.

By night the place changed into somewhere else. Insect noises grew from a hum into a loud, persistent buzz, tone and volume changing as clouds of flies parted to make way for larger, less easily identifiable creatures. They saw things with wingspans the length of a person's arm, and the canopy above them was briefly lit by a vivid display of orange and yellow flames. Roasted nuts pattered down around the camp, and the shapes swooped down and plucked them from the ground almost too fast to be seen. A few were left, smoking aromatically upon fallen leaves, and when the buzzing shapes had departed, Beko collected some and handed them to Nomi. They tasted gorgeous, still warm and sweet from the cooked sap oozing from within.

Noon was still recovering from the sting so he was allowed to rest, but the other three Serians took turns standing guard. One would stay nearby, close enough to be seen by the light of the campfire, and the other would creep into the forest and perform slow, cautious circuits of the camp.

Things called, screamed, cried, yelled, howled, bayed and buzzed, each species doing their best to outdo the next in volume and persistence. Bushes shook leaves, branches whipped back, and several times in the depths of the night, the sound of trees splintering and falling was clear in the distance. One creature – Beko identified it as a bellows ape – cried like a newborn child being slowly murdered. It was a shocking and wrenching sound, even though they knew it came from an animal and not a dying child. It bore down on the whole camp and made sleep next to impossible, and when dawn came the next morning, Nomi was still exhausted. Her sleep had been intermittent at best, and she felt ill-prepared to go on. The sun seemed to rise on a different world – a forest more inimical to humans than the day before, and more determined to eject them from beneath its sheltering canopy.

They moved off that morning feeling the comfort of known places slipping farther and farther behind.

He is in the forest and it has sprung a trap on them, luring them in with the promise of mysteries too enthralling to resist, serenading them with the songs of nature, gathering them beneath its protective canopy so that the sun cannot witness its crimes. And now that dawn has come, there is no let-up in the monstrous sounds of the dark. Animals screech to each other way above the forest floor, sharing secrets that no humans should know or could understand. Things move just beyond his vision, dashing through the undergrowth with the padding of many feet. He hears them, but by the time he looks all he can see is a waving branch or the flutter of a few leaves drifting slowly groundward. Further away trees are uprooted and thrown across the forest like leaves on the wind.

Something is coming...

He senses this through Nomi's fleeting nightmares, and he looks around desperately to see whether there is anything here he needs to know. Beko is sitting across the camp, his visage shimmering in the heat from the campfire. The other Serians are out of sight somewhere, and that realisation brings a scream from the forest, and then something splashing down onto the waning fire. It's the torso of a Serian, arms, legs and head ripped off to leave streaming wounds that paint the forest red.

Before the screams can begin something huge rumbles into the camp, shattering trees, crushing everything before it, and it is a monstrous thing made of stone, crunching down on six legs, head higher than the tallest trees, and it only has eyes for...

'Nomi!' Ramus shouted. He snapped awake and sat up, pressing one hand to his mouth to prevent another cry. The camp was quiet and the fire small but strong, and somewhere out there Lulah was circling the camp. He had decided not to sleep in his tent tonight because not seeing his surroundings made him feel even more vulnerable. *Nomi,* he thought, *what nightmares you share with me!* He supposed he should have felt elated that he scared her so – the stone thing coming at her through the trees was testament to that. But did she really think of him as such a monster?

It could have been worse. He breathed long and deep to quieten his thumping heart, and gave thanks that Nomi did not fantasise about Beko. That was one dream he had no desire to visit.

Being here seemed to be focusing Ramus's mind. Though

the sickness was ever-present, ranging from a dull throb to a bright white agony, he seemed able to think around it, applying himself to problems without his creeping death putting a barrier in their way. Eight days in the forests now, and he spent much of his time whilst not travelling examining the parchment pages. He was building a vocabulary of words that he still did not quite understand, and sometimes he whispered them to the breeze, a leaf or the insects that landed on his arms. Little seemed to change, but he knew that somewhere in there lay something vital to the voyage.

How the Widow would so love to talk to him now! He was sad that he would likely never see her again, but he was also content in the knowledge that she would champion this voyage and be pleased to see him upon it. And perhaps one day, the repercussions of what might happen south of here would reach her in her mountains.

My killer is in these forests, Ramus thought. *She rides through, expecting to beat me to the Divide, expecting to gain the top first, find the god.* But the Sleeping God was guiding *him* in. It left his dreams to him, whether they were his own or Nomi's skewed visions. But it gave signs to his waking self. Some words he read from the parchment were held within the twisted boughs of trees, spelt out by the fall of certain leaves, cast into the sky in cloud formations that whispered to him when he saw them through the forest's ceiling. Shapes in chaotic undergrowth spoke in languages he could not understand, but their underlying meaning was so clear to him, and so he followed, closing in, nearing the goal of this his final voyage, and all the time he learnt the parchment words that one day could mean so much.

He did not mention the shapes, words and signs to Lulah.

She was too busy protecting them from more worldly threats: poisonous insects, beasts that kept their distance, and the enduring idea that they were being followed. He thought perhaps she was paranoid, but at least it kept her away from the trail he was following.

The tenth night they spent in the great forest, Beko came to her. Rhiana was sleeping in her tent on the other side of the fire, and Noon and Ramin were out in the forest on watch. The night noises were different here, the fauna quieter and more restrained, and Rhiana had suggested it was due to the proximity of the huge river they could hear in the distance. None of them had seen it yet, but that afternoon they had crested a rise and been able to look through the trees at a wide valley ahead of them. Much of it was obscured by mist, and they had headed down the gentle gradient with a keen sense of anticipation. Nomi swore she could feel the ground shaking from its power.

It was the sound of unknown Noreela, waiting to swallow them up.

'Tomorrow could be a real test,' Beko said, settling down beside her. 'Have you heard tales of this river?'

Nomi shook her head. 'I know of few Voyagers who have come this far.'

'Hmm.' Beko was sitting beside her, staring into the fire with his shoulder touching hers. The contact had shocked her initially, and she was sure it was the first time he had touched her in days. They'd ridden close, yes, and talked often, but this was what she craved. Superficially, it was Beko's acceptance of her again, after the startling revelations that had driven Ramus away. She'd hate to be thought of as a jinx on the voyage. But beneath that was something more complex, deeper than Nomi could really bear to look. With Timal, she had used the word 'love' many times, bandying it around like an accessory while he rode her, lived in her house, and spent her money. Now she could barely think of the word when she considered Beko, and it felt as though she would curse the very idea by doing so. But his closeness warmed her, in her mind and elsewhere.

'What does "hmm" mean?' she asked.

'It just seems strange,' Beko said. 'Maybe when Voyagers *do* make it this far, they don't come back because they've found somewhere better.'

'Voyagers are driven by discovery, and most of them want to share. To flaunt what they've found. But that's a nice belief.'

He laughed quietly, his voice merging with the river's distant roar. 'A hope more than a belief. If they didn't return because they were hurt or killed, then we have a rough ride ahead of us.'

'We've had a rough ride already,' Nomi said, and she leant into Beko as she felt tears burning. The first dribbled down her cheek and she wiped it away.

'I've certainly had easier,' he said.

'You've lost friends before?' she asked.

'I don't think I'd ever consider Ramus to be your friend.'

'I was talking about you and Konrad.'

Beko sighed. 'Oh. Yes, I've lost friends. Saw a woman called Tresay killed in the forests to the north of Pengulfin Landing, cut in half by a razorbill lizard. Two friends taken by sea raiders on the western shores of Marrakash. And back in Mancoseria, of course. Seethe-gators. Not every Serian survives their encounter.'

'But never like that,' Nomi said.

'No. Never killed by the Voyager who hired us.'

'*I* hired you, Beko.'

'And I'm still grateful you sought my service.' And perhaps it was the heat from the fire, or her unsettled state of mind, or even the elemental roar and groan of the river filling the air and vibrating through the ground, but Nomi heard more in his statement than the literal. She placed her hand gently on his thigh and he did not turn away, did not object, and she knew then what she had heard.

'My tent?' she said quietly.

He turned and looked at her, smiling. 'If you're sure.'

'And all these days I've been thinking you were the uncertain one.'

Her tent was cool and filled with the sighs of the river.

The river burrowed beneath the ground. It entered the valley from the east, cascading down a set of violent rapids and waterfalls, and then across the valley it ploughed into the western hillside, disappearing in a constant cloud of heavy mist that drifted towards them on the breeze and soaked them to the skin. Nomi guessed that the valley had once been a lake with a small drain to some subterranean river, but an ancient cataclysm had opened the ground and swallowed the water, sucking it down into unknowable depths and giving the fertile valley sides and much of its floor back to the trees.

The sound was tremendous, and the clouds of mist thrown up by the tunnelling river soaked the air with a permanent fog. The plant and animal life had adjusted to the environment. Soon after descending the slopes and entering the cloud the group found themselves surrounded by huge butterflies that seemed to swim through the moisture-laden air, wings flapping intermittently. The creatures were friendly and curious, and Nomi found it amusing to watch the Serians carrying a dozen gorgeous butterflies on their shoulders, arms and head. There were many more lizards than they were used to as well, most of them harmless creatures that basked on trees, their glistening skin adapted to moisture rather than sunlight. But there were also creatures less than harmless, and Rhiana was the first – but not the last – to kill a poisonous salamander with an arrow.

They also saw serpents that seemed to float on the curtains of mist. Their bodies were transparent, their wings wide and gossamer thin, and occasionally they converged on a giant butterfly and burrowed into its body, driving it to the ground and consuming it from within. Thankfully, these serpents seemed to have a taste only for butterfly meat.

They skirted wide around the sinkhole into which the river disappeared. They had to keep at least a mile away, because to go any closer meant visibility was down to a few steps. Besides, their mounts were petrified. Noon and Ramin went from horse to horse, comforting them, whispering in their ears and stroking their necks and backs, but still the animals were jumpy and nervous.

Far from disturbing her thoughts, the shattering roar of the river allowed Nomi to think more clearly. And most of her thoughts related to Beko. Their earlier lovemaking had been clouded by being swayed, and her memory of it was further sullied by the events that had interrupted it. But last night was clear in her mind, and as they rode through the day, she could not help replaying it again and again.

Beko smiled at her and rode by her side, but he did not

TIM LEBBON

neglect his duty as captain of the Serians.

It was late afternoon by the time they rode out of the valley, and as the western horizon caught fire and the damp air gave them a glorious sunset, they rode into the forest to escape the river's clammy influence. They were exhausted, wet and hungry, and their ears were ringing from the thunderous river. They could still hear it in the distance, but now it was merely a murmur.

Rhiana vanished so quickly that it took them a few beats to register what had happened.

Her horse galloped away between the trees.

'Rhiana!' Noon shouted. The other Serians had drawn their bows and spread through the trees, taking up defensive positions as Beko rode close to Nomi and urged her across onto his horse.

'Hold on to me,' he said quietly, as she sat behind him.

'Hey!' Rhiana's voice cut through the loaded atmosphere, but still they could not see her.

'Where are you?' Noon slipped from his horse and moved forward cautiously, looking down at the ground and up at the trees, probing undergrowth and stepping carefully over trailing tree roots.

'Watch your step,' Rhiana said. Her voice was muffled. She started singing a bawdy song to guide Noon, and by the time she reached the second verse he was kneeling on the ground thirty steps from Beko and Nomi.

They gathered around and looked down into where Rhiana had fallen. It was a trench in the forest floor, maybe twenty steps long and taken up with five wide, deep, violet plants. The plants' leaves were cylindrical and ten steps deep, and Rhiana had become wedged at the bottom of one.

'Hurry,' she shouted. 'I don't like the company I'm keeping down here.'

Noon lowered a rope, Rhiana grabbed on, and he began to pull.

Nomi winced at the stink that wafted up from the trench. It was sickly sweet, a bewildering odour that made her hungry and nauseous at the same time. When Rhiana crawled over the edge of the rent in the forest floor, her trousers were glistening and sticky with some noxious liquid.

'Oh, nice,' Noon said, leaning over the Serian and looking down into the giant plant leaf.

Nomi looked as well. There was a corpse down there, mostly submerged in liquid, flesh black and rotten, bones showing through in places. It was human, but beyond that she could tell nothing. As if seeing it brought the truth home, she caught another waft of rot. The smell was so thick and meaty that she was sure it coated her skin.

'Clever,' Beko said.

'Clever?' Nomi turned away, clasping her stomach and trying to hold on to her last meal.

'What, this doesn't fascinate you? It's perfect!' Beko knelt by the trench's edge, trying to restore the carpet of roots, moss and dead leaves that Rhiana's horse had stumbled into.

Nomi shook her head and glanced at Rhiana. The Serian was wiping down her trousers with handfuls of dirt and dried leaves.

Nomi smiled. 'Any of you seen or heard about anything like this before?'

'I've heard of them,' Beko said. 'Rokarian traps. Don't know anyone who's ever seen them.' He peered into the other huge leaves to see what meals they had caught.

'Then it's now renamed as Rhiana's Trap!' Nomi said. 'A fitting plant to give your name, Rhiana?'

Rhiana grinned. 'At last, I have my place in history!'

Nomi and the Serians laughed, mounted up and moved on, riding more cautiously now that they knew of another peril to avoid.

When they made camp that evening, Rhiana and Noon went hunting for meat and collecting roots and herbs. Ramin patrolled their perimeter. Beko and Nomi built the fire together, their glances lighting fires elsewhere.

And that night, after food and tale-telling and before love, Nomi began to feel that her voyage was on course again.

After fourteen days travelling through the forests, Ramus and Lulah at last reached their southern extreme, beyond which lay a bizarre landscape of interconnecting waterways and standing stones.

And then the grey people came.

They waited until the travellers had passed the last of the trees before emerging from their hiding places and launching their attack. They scurried from the forest like massive ants, hands and feet slapping the ground, their movements so fluid that they seemed to flow. Ramus saw them first, a flash of movement from the corner of his eye. He shouted to Lulah. The Serian was standing a few steps ahead of him, horse reins in one hand and the other held up to shield her eyes as she looked at the view. For some reason the grey people bypassed Ramus, and it was Lulah they went for first.

He smelt them as they drifted by, like old, musty, forgotten things. Their long hair flowed behind them, and seen through its trailing strands the forest lost all of its colour.

Lulah cried out, batting the first grey person aside and stepping back as she drew her sword. But there were too many and they were on her, sticking like mud, wrapping their arms and legs around her torso, knocking the sword from her hand and driving her to the ground. Her arm flashed out and one of the attackers screeched, a high keening cry that sent a shiver down Ramus's spine. Blood splashed the air – surprisingly red – and the thing fell away from Lulah, clasping a hand to a vibrant wound across its shoulder.

Lulah's screams changed from fear to pain, and Ramus wondered what they had done to her.

He looked back into the forest and saw more of the grey people coming at him. They emerged from the gloom between the trees, and then he realised that some were materialising from out of the trees themselves, parting from trunks like smoke taking shape and form.

Lulah's screams changed again. From fear to pain, and now from pain to wretchedness.

What are they doing *to her?* Ramus drew his knife and stepped forward, but then the grey people fell on him as well. He had imagined them as mere wraiths, but their weight surprised him, crushing him down and squeezing him inside. His head pulsed with pain, but what they sought existed far deeper.

Ramus felt the swell of old knowledge, much of it hidden away in the darkest corners of his mind, and at last he knew where Lulah's desolate scream had originated. He screamed as his own terrible memories rose.

His mother cries as he laughs at her, and it's a childhood wickedness he would never forget. She has had a hard life bringing him up on her own, every painful day etched in her face, and she nurses her bruised arm, loving him far too much to ever curse him for striking her. He is nine years old. He continues laughing, because to stop would be to allow access for the shame and shock pressing in from all around. She looks at him and loves him, and Ramus laughs some more.

More wrongs, more faults, more sources of guilt. A shopkeeper who Ramus stole from in his teens, his mother's look of hurt when he turned down a gift she had bought for him, and Nomi, sitting in her home after Timal has left for the last time, her tears icy spears in his heart.

And the grey people grinned and grew fat on what he was experiencing. Their weight increased, their eyes sparkled, the rotten teeth in their mouths gained weight and colour, their sunken cheeks filled out, and more and more of them were coming from the forest.

He grasped the round stone charm and struck out, feeling the warm patter of blood across his face.

The Widow spoke to him and he clung to her voice, feeling surprise simmering through the beings splayed across his prone body. *Magichala is instinct,* she said. *You're born with it, and it can never be forced. You* breathe *it. There's no technique other than that.*

Ramus uttered the words he had read from the parchments and they flowed from him like stale breath. He kept his voice low so that Lulah could not hear.

He grabbed Konrad's stone fingers hanging around his neck and they felt warm, a strange heat as though it was from somewhere other than his own flesh and blood. He looked up into the eyes of a woman as the final sound left his mouth. At first her grin changed into a look of surprise, and then her eyes stopped glittering as they turned to pale, dead stone.

Ramus did not know how long Konrad had taken to die. Perhaps back then, whatever power the words held was still developing in him, growing from the seed planted by his readings of the parchment. But this time, within a dozen beats of him muttering the words, everything had grown still.

When Ramus moved, the crackle of breaking stone limbs startled him. The grey people around him were still grey, but now they were motionless and dead. Here and there he could still see the soft texture of flesh and skin instead of the dulled tones of stone, but as he watched even these hardened. His attackers were statues, frozen for ever into one moment in time. He heaved away the people who had been crawling and clasping across him, pulling himself from beneath their dead weight and feeling the rough edges of their fingers, teeth and hair scratching the exposed skin of his face.

An arm stood in his way, fingers turned into the soft ground where its owner had been grasping for balance. One thump with the heel of his hand snapped it from the shoulder and it tipped over, fingers still splayed like a dead spider.

Gasping, still barely believing what he had done, Ramus stood and looked across at Lulah.

Her grey attackers still smothered her, but now they were looking at him with suspicious eyes. They did not seem perturbed by what had happened – indeed, none of them seemed to be looking at their dead, petrified companions – but the threat had bled from them. One stood on Lulah's chest, stepped off and loped back between and into the trees. Soon, the others followed.

Lulah remained motionless on the ground. Ramus wanted to go to her, but then his legs began to shake, and he went down to his knees.

All instinct, the Widow said in his memory, and he relished his vision of her. He closed his eyes, and drove away all the sour memories the grey people had dredged up. He answered her, and it felt good to have his own voice back.

'Much for you to see here, Widow. Plenty for you to know. You'd be proud of me.'

'Ramus,' Lulah whispered again, and she was looking at him in fear. 'You have the power of the gods.'

Ramus shook his head, unable to meet her eyes. 'Maybe just one of them.'

Lulah stumbled around the dead people, staring down as if they would move again at any moment.

'I spoke without thinking,' he said. He frowned, not understanding. The Widow's words of advice echoed in his mind, but she was not really here, did not really know what he had.

Lulah kicked at a stone man's leg and it came off, thumping to the ground. She looked at the broken part, running her fingers across the insides and rubbing dust between fingertips. She avoided catching Ramus's eye. She had yet to thank him, and he felt a brief rush of annoyance, but smiled at such foolish petulance.

'They were preying on bad memories,' Ramus said. 'Sucking them out of us.'

'Not me,' she said.

Her denial surprised Ramus. 'You were screaming.'

Lulah rubbed her chest and neck. 'They were hurting me.' She looked away again, retrieving and sheathing her dropped sword.

I heard you, he thought. *I know what you were going*

through, because I went through it myself. But if Lulah
wanted her distance and privacy, so be it.

For the rest of that day, as they left the great forest behind
and set out across the strange landscape of water and standing
stones, Lulah said little. And Ramus wondered what dark
deeds were swilling in her mind, trying to lose themselves in
the past once again.

CHAPTER THIRTEEN

Twelve days after entering the forest, it ended by the side of a lake, and beyond the lake, Nomi saw a plain of standing stones. When they skirted the lake and realised how huge the stones were – the largest were ten times the height of a person – they paused for a while to admire them, and Nomi wondered how they had ever been placed. Nobody suggested that they might be natural.

They saw no sign of Ramus or Lulah.

Days passed, spent mostly on horseback except for short breaks for food or to explore some of the more extraordinary standing stones. Nights were often spent camped beside a monolith for shelter. Some nights, Beko spent in Nomi's tent, and others he chose to remain outside. They did not speak much about what was happening between them. The time would come for talk, Nomi knew, but now there were things that felt greater – the places they were seeing, the voyage, and what they may find at its end. So she was content to let lust take its course and hope that love would find its own way.

Sometimes when night came Nomi became wary of falling

asleep. She knew that Ramus sometimes dreamt her dreams, and the thought of that made her naked before him, exposed and open to his scrutiny. She tried to steer her thoughts certain ways, but she could never dictate her dreams. Or her nightmares. She dreamt of making love with Beko, dying in the forests, killing Ramus with a blunt knife, Timal appearing before her and fading away again, and the Divide falling to crush all of Noreela once they had climbed and discovered its secrets. She invited none of these dreams, and always awoke wondering which ones Ramus had shared. Whichever he saw, she hoped that some sense of her remorse would show through.

Their route was not direct because of the many waterways that sliced the landscape in all directions. Sometimes, the surfaces of these streams or channels appeared to be frozen, but as they drew closer the effect would shimmer and disappear, leaving little more than ripples in its wake. Other times the streams would be steaming, the ground close to them almost too hot to walk on. Geysers erupted, not large but unpredictable, and several times a horse was startled enough to bolt.

As Nomi took in their strange surroundings, she hoped that Ramus would be fascinated enough to stop and take notes, write at length about the frozen and steaming streams and whatever things may live in them to cause such effects. She wondered where he was. Close? Watching her watch for him?

And if he ever spoke to her again, what language would he use?

Despite the stones – which became more infrequent the further south they went – and the streams, small lakes, and areas of marshy ground, they made surprisingly good progress. Food was plentiful, both meat and vegetable, and they ate three good meals every day.

A couple of times they saw tumblers in the distance. Nomi was delighted. She'd heard mention of them before, but when Ten had spoken of them back in Long Marrakash, they had still struck her as the stuff of legend. Now, even from such a distance, she could make out their great rolling shapes, part animal, part plant, that would supposedly crush and consume anything in their path. They rolled south to north, against the slope of the landscape and the direction of the wind. The Serians kept a wary eye on them until they vanished, while Nomi watched with wonder.

The waterways became less common, and when they arrived at the final standing stones, they looked south and saw a shadow along the horizon.

'Clouds,' Beko said.

'Hills,' Rhiana said. 'And shadowed valleys.'

Nomi shook her head and urged her horse forward. They passed through the shadow of the final standing stone, and the landscape before her was stark and bare. 'Neither,' she said. 'That's the Divide. A couple of days' ride, perhaps, but it's already there. Too far to see properly.' She looked up above the shadow and saw only the slate grey of distance.

The Serians were silent, letting Nomi look upon the target of her journey and think her own thoughts. But, in truth, all her thoughts were about Ramus. She wondered whether he was looking at this same sight right now, somewhere far to the east or perhaps closer. She looked that way, across the gently undulating land, and she closed her eyes and tried to imagine him looking back at her. But her visual landscape was a blank. It always had been; her imagination was limited, a trickle compared to Ramus's roar.

'We should camp here,' Beko said. 'Beside the final stone.'

'I want to ride on and—' Nomi began, but the Serian captain gave her a stern stare. 'We have equipment to check,' he said. 'We've all climbed sea cliffs before, but none of us have ever faced anything like this. We should eat well tonight, prepare ourselves to ride into the Great Divide's shadow.'

'I've heard things,' Noon said. 'I've heard it said that the shadow is a curse, and once it touches your skin you're the Divide's meat for ever.'

'I've met someone who defies that curse,' Nomi said. But still, it gave her a chill. *There'll be something final about entering the Divide's shadow,* she thought. *Cutting off the sun. It'll be like leaving Noreela.*

'This is the far extreme of the land,' Beko said. And Nomi thought, *Please don't fall apart on me now.* He looked at her and smiled. 'What a voyage!' he said. 'To the edge.'

Nomi smiled back. 'It's only just begun.'

'How high can it be?' Ramin asked.

'Do we have enough climbing gear? Enough rope?' Noon said.

'Let's camp and eat.' Beko's voice was calm and assured. 'Around the fire, we can talk about these things. And I'm sure Mam Hyden, if she knows more than she has let on thus far, will have plenty to say.' He smiled again, but this time his eyes held a glint of something cool.

He doesn't trust me, Nomi thought. *But after what I've done to Ramus, it's hardly surprising.* And she realised, looking south at the shadow of the edge of the world, that whatever there was between her and the captain could never be more than it was now.

❋   ❋   ❋

Noon and Ramin unloaded the packhorses and started going through their climbing equipment. Beko watched with half an eye, but most of his attention was directed southward, at the darkening stain that marked the edge of the world they knew. Nomi felt the draw. It called her, inviting her from the camp to bathe in its gloom, and she wondered what could possibly grow there at the base of that great cliff, a place where the sun rarely touched. Mystery lured her, and the unknown, but something pushed her as well. Ramus. And the thought that he could get there before her.

I should send two Serians ahead, she thought. *Get them to patrol the base of the Divide, try to stop Ramus from starting his climb.* But Konrad's fate hung around her neck like a rock, and she had no desire to be the cause of more deaths. Ramus had something powerful and remarkable, and had shown that he was not averse to using it.

'He took no climbing gear,' Beko said. He stood beside her where she leant against the standing stone, both of them looking south even though the gloom of dusk meant that they saw little.

'I've thought of that,' Nomi replied. 'But he's determined. He and Lulah will climb nonetheless.'

'With no ropes? No crampons? No slings? One slip and they're both dead.'

'Maybe,' Nomi said. 'But that won't hold him back.'

'Why should it?' Beko said quietly.

Nomi glanced sideways at him but he did not meet her gaze. 'Why indeed?' she said. 'He's dying anyway. But Lulah isn't.'

'She may be dead already,' Beko said. 'Ramus is obviously...not of his own mind. Whatever he has – whatever knowledge can do that to a man – can't have come without a cost.'

'He's no killer,' Nomi said, realising as she spoke how ridiculous that sounded.

But Beko understood. 'Konrad threatened him, I know. But maybe Lulah has as well.'

'Serians are loyal.'

'Yes, but not to madness.'

'You think Ramus is mad?'

Beko touched Nomi's back casually, then slipped his arm around her waist and leant into her. 'There was something mad about him the day we met.'

'My fault,' she said, and Beko's arm brought her no warmth. 'I gave him that sickness, so Konrad is my fault, and…'

'Blame will crush you,' Beko said, 'and guilt will chew your bones.'

'An old Mancoserian saying?'

'An old Beko Havison saying.' He rested his forehead against hers for a few beats, and it was the smell of his breath more than the contact that gave her some comfort. She was here among friends, and whatever she had done, they still chose to ride with her. She was paying well, true, but their actions spoke volumes.

'It's going to be a hard climb,' she said.

'I know. And we may not reach the top.'

'If there is a top.'

Beko sighed. 'We should set a limit. A point at which we stop and come back down.'

'Ramus won't.'

'No, but Ramus is crazy.'

Nomi nodded slowly and listened to the noises made by Noon and Ramin checking their gear. Tomorrow they would ride toward the edge of Noreela. This was the greatest time of her life. Why, then, was she filled with such dread? She had the sense that the climb would be like plunging into a bottomless lake, doomed never to surface again. She would sink out of Noreela, leaving behind not even her shadow.

'Let's eat,' Beko said. 'Rhiana has made us something special.'

To begin with, Ramus wanted to stop at every standing stone.

He dismounted and circled the first one, using his foot to shift aside the tall grass around its base, running his hand across the smooth weather-worn surface, trying to discern shape, purpose or intention in its placement. He carried his journal with him, reversed so that any notes he made here were in the back. He did not want to interrupt his translations and observations of the parchments.

Lulah, still shaken from their encounter at the edge of the forest, remained mounted. She rode a circle around Ramus and the rock, looking outward instead of in. She had hardly exchanged glances with Ramus since the grey people. *Every day I'm driving her further away,* he thought, but that hardly mattered. They had passed well into the uncharted territories now, and his rough map was taking on shapes and contours as he added information. It was knowledge for knowledge's sake, because he knew he would never return.

Soon they would be at the Divide. And perhaps these stones would guide him in.

Is this you? he thought, but no voice answered.

No markings, no carvings, no signs of who or whatever had placed them, and yet placed the stones must have been. Ramus pressed his back to the stone and looked in a slow half-circle from east, to south and then west, and from here he could see six other stones. Most were quite small humps – either through distance or quirks in the landscape – but the largest stood proud from a small hilltop to the south-east.

He closed his eyes and heard only the sound of Lulah's horse's feet plodding across the soft ground to his right. He whispered some new words to the air – the language he was coming to know better and better, but which he had yet to understand – and nothing changed. But he felt the power there, and he suddenly wanted to see the parchment pages again.

There was something about one of the pages, the one without writing but swamped in images...

He sat against the rock, opened his backpack and unrolled the parchments, flattening them out on his outstretched legs. The one he sought he had examined least, because much of it was filled with imagery that spoke no words. But Ramus knew that you did not need language to tell a story. This page had the customary line dividing the sheet into a third and two thirds, and among the abundance of images and shapes were twelve pointed images that could have been standing stones. They started smallest away from the Divide, and the closest one was largest. The line of the Divide adjacent to this largest stone was stepped inward briefly, as though indicating a special place.

The easiest way to climb, Ramus thought. *Either that, or a route into a trap.*

By the time Lulah had passed behind the standing stone and emerged again on his left, Ramus knew where they had to go. 'That way,' he said, pointing at the largest rock in the distance. 'And from there to the next largest, and the next.'

Lulah nodded and stopped her horse, waiting for him to mount up again.

But Ramus turned once again to the monolith, opening his arms and pressing his hands and face against a surface slightly warmed by the sun. The rock seemed to throb at him, a brief sensation that was not repeated, and for a moment the pain in his head receded. Like the slow, ponderous heartbeat of something asleep for a very long time.

The shadows grow from the south and advance towards him, and they have teeth. They are made of darkness and ambiguity but are sharp and deadly, and one bite from their unseen edges will kill him for sure. He looks around for his travelling companions, but he is on his own. They have abandoned him or been killed, and even his horse glances to the side now and then, foaming at the mouth, blood in its spittle, its mad, rolling eyes accusing him of some wrongdoing and issuing the promise that it will be gone at the first opportunity. But it is a chance it will never have, because the shadows roll fast across the landscape. Every time they touch one of the standing stones, the rock transforms into a nebulous, writhing shape that runs and frolics within their embrace.

And there it is: the unknown, that sea of darkness containing all the knowledge he can never have...even though the source of this dream is Nomi, not him, and the insecurity showing through is both chilling and heartening. *I'm lost,* he thinks in the dream, but in the part of his nightmaring mind that is aware of where this comes from, those words are spoken in Nomi's voice.

The shadows bear down on him and their leading edges are raw, seeping wounds in the land.

He laughs.

Ramus sat up quickly, still laughing, and wondered whether he could reverse the process of his worsening sickness. It burrowed in his head and gave him her nightmares, and though the pain flooded in again and drove him back to the ground, there was one ray of light that kept his smile. The hope that, somewhere in her sleep and across the miles, she would hear him laughing at her dread.

They navigated their way south from rock to rock. Sometimes it was obvious which distant monolith was the largest, but other times it was difficult to tell. Whenever they had been placed, it would have been impossible to account for future shrugs in the landscape, fallen stones, growing trees or drifting mist. If he could not tell which was largest, Ramus consulted Lulah, and together they followed their best guess. It did not concern him unduly. The pages were right, and he had felt that beat through the land. He was confident that if they did stray from the trail, they would soon find it again.

He hugged every rock they came to, and each time he felt another encouraging beat. And there was the sickness, and the deeper, darker portion of his mind that no longer belonged to him. It was watching him, and he revelled in its attention.

A day out from the forest, Lulah started to settle again. Whatever dark memories those grey people had encouraged to resurface must have been dark indeed. Either that, or Ramus was far more able to deal with such guilt.

Because I'm going mad. But he would shake his head at that idea, even though it hurt to do so. *I'm not going mad. I'm going* sane. *I'm looking for the future, and when I find it I'll make sure it's safe.*

But he wondered...

When he sat down during the evenings and examined those pages, he wondered where he was leading himself, and just how much he was being led.

Ramus knew what it was straight away, and Lulah seemed terrified.

'That's the edge of the world,' she said.

'It's the Great Divide. Not the edge, just a boundary. Every boundary is there to be crossed.'

'No,' Lulah said, shaking her head and somehow transferring her unease to her horse. It stomped its feet, skittish and snorting. 'No, it's the edge. Can't you see that? Can't you feel it?'

Ramus looked at the stretch of shadow across the southern horizon and tried to decide exactly how he felt. Excited, perhaps. Nervous. Behind them stood the final huge standing rock, and between here and the horizon was an unremarkable plain of rolling grassland swept bare of trees. Across that landscape, where it met the horizon, the first part of their voyage would end.

'I've been examining the pages every evening,' he said. 'There's nothing that tells me this is the end. Everything indicates that the Divide is the beginning of somewhere else.'

'A place where words can turn people to stone?'

Ramus looked at Lulah – her face nervous, belying the image of the strong woman bristling with weaponry – and shook his head. 'Those words are special.'

'The words of a Sleeping God?'

'Perhaps.' But when he looked south again he thought, *Perhaps sleeping, or more likely fallen, because some of what I see on those parchments...* But that was a myth within a myth, and the more he thought of it, the more those doubts were swallowed by the presence in his mind, leaving only the good behind.

'If there is a Sleeping God—' Lulah began, but Ramus cut her off.

'They were good. And only good will come of finding it.'

Ramus went first, keen to head as far south as possible before darkness fell. He felt a terrible moment of sickness later that afternoon and the sun seemed to explode, casting a bright light into his eyes that he knew originated from within. The pains scorched his skull and he lowered his head, letting the horse carry him on. When he could look up again, he lifted the charms around his neck – the bone from the border guard, the circular stone that Lulah had seen, and Konrad's snapped-off fingers which she had not – and pressed them to his lips. He exhaled past each and inhaled again, hoping to breathe in charmed air.

The pain subsided, barely, and he imagined Nomi standing before him naked, her body pierced by bolts fired from a crossbow held in his hands. The bolts went in slowly. They hurt. She screamed, and he aimed at the parts of her he had never seen. *Let Beko kiss them better,* he thought. The daydream went on for a long time, and when his horse stumbled and jarred him back to reality, it took a while to lose the image. It did not shake him as much as it would have a score of days before. He had never realised that he had changed so much.

CHAPTER FOURTEEN

The sky had become overcast a few miles back, an even greyness that filtered weak sunlight, and the cliff itself seemed swallowed by its blandness. But distance was very difficult to determine. When they first saw the cliff face – the ridges and textures of rock instead of the haze of mist – Lulah guessed that they would be there within the hour. Ramus was not so sure. He concentrated on the landscape rather than where it ended, and he could see hills and plains disappearing into the distance. He thought another day's ride. This was something neither of them had ever seen or been able to imagine before, and scale seemed to obey no laws. The sky looked huge, but it was dwarfed against the cliff.

Ramus could feel the weight of the Divide pulling him onward. It was unbelievable, this bulk, this mass, and the pain in his head seemed to be coming from somewhere just in front of him rather than inside. He stopped paying attention to things close by and instead looked ahead, focusing on the wall of rock that sprouted from Noreela and disappeared into the level grey cloud cover above. How high up those clouds were he could not tell; they felt low, but sometimes he saw the specks of birds or other things circling and drifting high up, and on occasion these specks disappeared to nothing as they rose even higher. A mile, perhaps two, maybe three...he could not know. And they would not find out until they started climbing.

Around mid-afternoon, several shapes drifted toward them from the south, wings flapping now and then but mostly riding the air currents. It was difficult to tell how large they were, but they kept formation; two in the lead, three more behind. Ramus listened for their calls, but there were none, and they did not deviate from their path.

As the shapes began to lose height, Lulah rode before him and drew a crossbow from her saddlebags.

'Hold this,' she said, lobbing the weapon back at him. Ramus caught it in one hand, rested it across his saddle and then caught the rack of bolts Lulah sent after it.

The shapes had four wings each, bulbous eyes and silvery legs that trailed behind them as they drifted lower. Each was the size of a man.

'What are they?' he asked. 'Livid eagles?' But livid eagles were so rarely seen that some thought them myth, grabbing their victims with metallic claws and exuding a cloud of acidic vapour from their feather tips to strip skin, melt flesh.

'Hardly matters right now,' Lulah said. She took the bow from her back and strung an arrow without taking her eyes off the creatures coming at them.

The animals did not circle or stalk, but dived in to attack without any preamble.

Lulah loosed three arrows quickly, and one of them found its mark. As Ramus saw more detail of the lead creatures –

two sets of webbed wings folded as they dived, vicious curled claws trailing behind, fur rather than feathers lining their chests and backs, narrow heads and long hooked beaks slung low and ready to attack – the arrow pierced one of the creature's shoulders and broke its wings on that side. It shrieked, a terrifying sound reminiscent of a sheebok being slaughtered, and then veered to the left as its good wing folded under the pressure.

The others came on, seemingly unfazed by their companion's fate.

Lulah tipped sideways on her horse and hauled it to the left, and Ramus did the same to the right. The birds – if that name could be applied – screeched as they flapped by, and Ramus felt something score across his upraised arm. Blood splashed the air and he smelt it, combined with the rank stink of wet fur.

Trying to sit up on the horse again he overbalanced, falling to the ground and kicking his feet from the stirrups. He rolled onto his side, raised the crossbow and fired at the birds as they swung around for another pass. The bolt missed, but Lulah was already firing arrows again. She took down two more of the creatures, and when the last two came in again, it was higher than before, more cautious.

Ramus primed the crossbow and fired directly up as a thing passed overhead. He heard rather than saw the bolt rip through a wing, and it swayed in the air for a beat before finding its balance again, wings flapping harder than before to keep it airborne.

Ramus ran to his horse and remounted, guiding it close to Lulah.

The birds were flying back the way they had come, silent

and seemingly unconcerned at their missing companions.

'What the piss were they?' Lulah said. She was breathing hard but her eyes were wide, her face flushed with excitement. *She's a warrior,* Ramus thought, *though she's had little chance to fight so far.*

'Weird and angry, that's what they were.' Ramus looked down at his left arm and felt immediately queasy when he saw the gash there.

'Let's dress that,' Lulah said. 'I'll clean it first. No saying what illnesses those things carry.'

Ramus almost laughed, but thought better of it. She was right. He may be dying, but there was no need to let complacency kill him quicker.

What if there are hundreds of those things down here? he thought. *What if they roost on the Divide and we can't even get close? And what of the tumblers that Ten mentioned; we haven't even seen one of those yet.*

They rode on beneath the clouds, only able to make out the position of the sun from the paler, lighter spread of sky to the west. And the closer they drew to the Divide, the closer the sun came to touching the cliff, until the time came when shadows grew even deeper, the air cooler, and the Great Divide cast its shadowy influence over them.

'I've heard things—' Lulah began, but Ramus cut her off.

'It's not true.'

'How do you know? How many people do you know who have returned from where we are right now?'

'One,' he said. 'But that's proof enough for me.'

'I don't know,' Lulah said shivering. She pulled a rolled blanket from her saddle and placed it loose around her shoulders, ready to throw it off should the birds approach again. 'I don't know, I feel different. Don't you? Can't you feel the shadow?'

'It's cooler,' Ramus said. He looked down at the ground and saw that grasses had given way to moss and a type of stumpy herb, with wide leaves and a thick, low stem. 'The sun doesn't shine here for very long. But that doesn't mean anything.'

Lulah shook her head but looked unconvinced.

The flora changed rapidly the closer they rode to the Great Divide. Ramus knew that there would come a place soon where the sun never shone, through all the seasons of the year. A place where the shadow of the Divide always fell, and where its influence dictated what could live there, and what could not. That would be where Lulah made her choice.

And can I assume I'll pass by that place without a moment's doubt?

He knew that the answer was yes. He was going to be the greatest Voyager of them all. And though nobody would remember his name, that had never really been his desire. For Ramus, the thrill of discovery was a very personal thing.

It was almost dusk when they reached the place where much of the flora changed. If Lulah noticed she said nothing, and Ramus did not bring it to her attention. By then the Divide dominated their view, rising high before them until it disappeared into the cloud cover, and stretching left and right as far as they could see. It was magnificent and terrible, awe-inspiring and shocking. And the thought of climbing that great cliff almost made Ramus weep.

He kept thinking that they were close enough to see surface imperfections that could mark a route up the Divide, but then they would ride for another hour and still seem to be no closer. Perspective was shattered by the wall of rock.

The end of Noreela, Ramus thought. He tried to imagine what he would see if this cloud cover ever shifted or faded away.

They found an old camp. There were two tents crushed into the ground, the material torn, tattered and mouldy. Other signs of habitation were scattered around; a rotting saddle, some cooking utensils rusted into the soil, and a bow without its string. They dismounted and explored the camp for a while, kicking things over and trying to make out what had happened to its owners.

'They didn't just leave,' Lulah said. 'There's too much here that anyone would have taken. They must have been killed or taken by force.'

'Perhaps they went to climb?'

Lulah shrugged.

They moved on another few hundred steps before making camp. Lulah quickly lit the fire and produced food she had brought along from the previous night. The meat was not as fresh and the herbs not as fragrant, but neither of them felt like being left alone. The light from the fire darkened their view of the Divide until it was a huge looming blankness that swallowed sound and sight.

'How do we climb?' Lulah asked.

'We'll find something to help us.'

'How do you know?'

Ramus shrugged. He knew she sensed the movement because they sat close to each other, sharing warmth and comfort. 'There's no alternative,' he said. 'We haven't come all this way to turn back now.'

'We should have brought some of the climbing equipment.'

'As if Beko would have let us.'

Ramus stared into the flames and wondered what nightmare he would share with Nomi tonight.

But there were no nightmares, because Ramus did not sleep.

When morning came, and the sun rising in the east smeared itself along the Great Divide, Lulah jarred awake from a troubled dream. Ramus had been keeping the fire alight all night, and they shared the last of the stored food.

'We'll find stuff to eat as we climb,' he said.

'Or something will eat us.' Lulah stretched and strolled away to find somewhere to piss.

An hour after heading off, they came across another old camp. This one had been larger than the first, though without tents or cooking equipment. There were skeletons, though. At least six of them, though some were so tangled and twisted together that it was difficult to tell exactly how many people had died here. There were no signs of arrows, bolts or other weapons, and when Lulah examined one of the skulls she found what she thought were claw marks across the cracked dome.

Ramus was searching for something else. And he found it just outside the remains of the camp, buried beneath a leather groundsheet that was smothered with a growth of pale pink fungi. There were ropes, crampons, waist straps and other climbing gear, even down to a bag containing gloves and spiked boots. Some of the ropes had become brittle and decayed, and the first big coil that Ramus picked up virtually crumbled in his hands. But as he dug down into the store, he found several coils that were dry and tough, and he and Lulah unwound one and pulled to test its strength.

They left the camp, keen to distance themselves from that scene of death. Ramus had felt a sense of something there, a wretched thing aware of their presence but unable to change. A wraith, perhaps, seeking comfort from the place where it had been made. He saw nothing, but he felt observed, skin itching under that unknown attention.

Lulah was more nervous than ever, and she kept her bow drawn and an arrow strung as she rode.

When they stopped for lunch, Ramus knew that things were about to change. The ground was becoming steeper, the slopes varied from shale to damp soil to compact moss, slippery and sickly to the touch. The horses were becoming agitated, and the huge cliff loomed over them as if ready to fall at any moment.

'We need to leave the horses now,' Ramus said.

Lulah nodded. 'I know. But what about when we come back down?'

When you *come back down,* Ramus thought, but he could not say that. 'We worry about that when it happens. Nomi and I had planned on leaving one of you down here with the horses as the rest climbed, but I don't want us to split up. We'll take off their saddles and let them go. Who knows, they might even wait.'

'They'll be dead or long gone by the time we come back down from there,' she said, staring up at the rock face. She shook her head. 'I've climbed sea cliffs before, but never anything like this. Ramus, I've never *imagined* anything like this.'

'That's why I'm here,' Ramus said. 'Because it's beyond imagination.'

They unsaddled their horses, both of them working slowly because neither really wanted to lose this link to the north. Even though Ramus was sure that once he started climbing, that would be the end of his time in Noreela, the option of turning back would no longer be his once the horses left.

The animals stood close to them, stripped of their gear yet still ready to ride on. They cooked and ate a bird that Lulah shot from the sky, a small creature whose meat tasted tough and bitter. Then they shared out the climbing gear and stood to leave.

'You're sure?' Lulah said. 'If we're tied together up there and you pass out from your illness...'

'Then we won't be tied together. We climb close, but uncoupled. I'll not take you with me if I fall, and if you fall...'

'I won't fall,' she said, and that simple statement seemed to cut through her uncertainties. She was unsettled, yes, but she was a Serian.

And me? Ramus thought. *Am I really that sure?* He closed his eyes and his head swam, the weight of the growing badness behind his eyes leaning him forward towards the Great Divide. *No, not sure at all. But I don't have any choice.*

The slope of the ground increased, the surface soon became more rock than soil, and the shadow of the cliff lured them on.

Nomi and Beko debated leaving one of the Serians with the horses, but Nomi did not like the idea. Whoever they left – and either Noon or Ramin were the obvious choices – would be on their own, relied upon to defend the horses from whatever threats may exist down here. Several times they had spotted creatures circling high above, as if watching their group approach. No one could identify them, but they acted like birds of prey. There were also the tumblers they had seen on the plains, rogue marauders that might come far enough south to wander the foot of the Divide, and whatever other dangers existed here that had not yet made themselves apparent. Planning the voyage, it had been easy to suggest leaving a Serian to guard the horses. But now that they were here, the immensity of the Divide made the climb seem something even more treacherous than Nomi had imagined.

Besides, Konrad was dead and Lulah had left with Ramus. She did not want to lose anyone else.

They decided to let the horses go. When they came back down they would be faced with a long, hard march northwards, through those seemingly endless forests and back to the Pavissia Steppes. But once there, they could trade or steal horses once again. And there was no telling just how long their ascent and whatever may follow would take.

While Noon and Ramin unloaded the horses and went about making a store for the equipment they would leave behind, Nomi, Beko and Rhiana stood staring up at the solid grey wall before them. None of them spoke for a while; no one was used to the sight yet, and Nomi guessed they never would be.

'Edge of the world,' Rhiana said at last. It was almost a whisper.

'Maybe not,' Nomi replied. 'Maybe it's just the beginning of another.'

The cliff before them was streaked with smears of pale plant growth. Rhiana had suggested that this was a good sign because it indicated there were crevasses, cracks and ledges upon which soil had accumulated. But there were many places where the sun never touched the cliff surface, and Nomi was worried that the plants would be brittle or slick with damp.

'There's our starting place,' Beko said, pointing slightly to the west. 'A mile that way. Cliff looks textured and cracked; could be easy going to begin with.'

Nomi's stomach fluttered and doubt pressed against her chest. Was she arrogant to believe that she could voyage all this way and then lead a climb to the top? She had rarely climbed before, and when she had it had been on safe, known peaks in the hills north of Long Marrakash. She'd been with experienced climbers then, people who knew the routes they were taking and the risks they would face, and even then there had been accidents.

If anyone fell here...

'Which of you has climbed the most?' she asked.

Beko turned and nodded to Rhiana. 'Rhiana, you used to do the Painback Cliffs back on Mancoseria, didn't you?'

The Serian did not seem happy at being singled out. 'I did three rescues from there, yes. Foolish children who thought themselves old enough to take a seethe-gator, mostly. But...' She looked up at the cliff and Nomi saw its bulk reflected in her eyes.

'Same techniques,' Beko said. 'Just a bit higher.'

'A bit?'

'The light's pissing awful,' Noon said. 'What happens when it goes altogether? Do we just hang there till morning?'

Nomi turned her back on the Divide, hoping the gesture would paint her with confidence she was not feeling. 'When mid-afternoon comes, we start looking for somewhere to spend the night,' she said. 'A crevasse, a ledge, maybe even a cave if we're lucky. We wrap up warm, tie ourselves in and wait until dawn.'

'And if we don't find anywhere?' Rhiana said.

'If that happens, we tie ourselves to the cliff face.'

'And sleep?'

'If you want strength for the next day, yes.'

'What about wildlife?' Ramin asked. 'Get stung up there by something like the wasp that got Noon, and piss on all of us.'

'Nobody knows the sort of things that live this far south,' Nomi said.

'Exactly,' Ramin said. 'It's always gloomy here, even when we can see sunlight on the ground to the north. Always dusk. Creatures that come out at dusk…sometimes, they're not too nice.'

Nomi felt a twinge of annoyance. 'You think there are things up there worse than your seethe-gators?'

'I doubt that,' Ramin said, standing straighter.

'Then that's why you're here,' she said. 'Because you're all warriors and I'm not.'

'I'm glad this is all so well planned,' Rhiana said, and Nomi almost cursed. But then she recognised her own annoyance for what it really was – embarrassment. If Ramus were here he would probably have better answers for these questions. Nomi had essentially followed him, because he was one of the best.

What did that make her?

'We go now,' Beko said. 'We leave the horses here and walk until we can't walk anymore. Then we climb. The only way is up.'

Nomi smiled and thought, *I hope so.*

CHAPTER FIFTEEN

Nomi was exhausted. She had never felt so tired or drained. Her arms and legs shook, sweat soaked her back, and she could not bring herself to look back, down or up. The rock before her was her whole world, and to look farther afield than the next handhold would be to doom herself to terror.

Because Nomi was scared of heights. That had come as a shock, but the realisation also struck her with a force too powerful to deny. In Ventgoria, she had sometimes felt nervous climbing the vertical ladders to their stilted dwellings, but now she was higher above Noreela than she had ever been.

I won't look down.

Rhiana had gone first, rope slung over her left shoulder and belt jangling with hooks and crampons. She took her time to begin with, selecting handholds with care, hammering the crampons in and marking the route with rope. But within an hour of beginning she was far up the cliff, and Noon and Ramin had followed. Beko insisted that Nomi go next.

I won't look down.

Another hour into their climb, Ramin had slipped. He cried out as he slid down the vertical stone face, hands slapping and scraping for purchase, knees bent and feet held back in case they struck a protuberance and flipped him out into space. Noon shouted up to Rhiana and the two braced themselves, taking the weight as Ramin jerked to a halt.

'It's OK!' he had shouted, finding a grip and scrabbling at the rock with his feet. 'It's OK!' But his voice had sounded far from OK.

I will not *look down.*

She tried to follow Ramin as best she could. He called down to her now and then, guiding her hands or feet left or right to where he had found handholds. She did not look up to acknowledge him. If she did that, she would see Noon past him, and then Rhiana higher still, and the clouds way above her, and something about the scale of what they were doing would suddenly hit home. Then she would have to look back down at Beko…

I will not pissing look down!

…and that could well be when her real problems began.

She did not want to freeze. Panic ran its fingers through her chest and down into her groin, a curiously intimate sensation, like a malevolent ex-lover. If she froze, Beko would come up for her and try to ease her fears, and if she knew there was no one below her she would…

'I'm going to look down.'

Panting, sweat cooling on her skin and chilling her whenever the breeze blew, Nomi looked down between her feet.

Dizziness struck and tried to prise her from the cliff. 'Oh

no,' she said, 'oh no, oh no...' *Have we really come so far?* Below her she could see Beko's head as he worked at a crampon, easing it loose with a pick so that they could relay them up to Rhiana when the time came. Past him, an outcrop in the cliff that they had passed barely an hour before. And past that, further down, deeper into the dusky light that seemed to be the Divide's daytime, the horses and camp they had left behind. Two of the animals had vanished, but the others still lingered around the camp, chewing half-heartedly at the scant vegetation. They looked unbelievably small. *If I fell, it would take me a dozen beats to reach them,* she thought, and she wondered what would go through her mind as she tumbled past Beko, and death welcomed her down.

'Nomi!' Ramin called. The rope before her was taut.

She pressed her forehead against cool stone and took in a few deep, slow breaths.

'Nomi?'

She looked up. Ramin stared down at her, sweat glistening on his bald head. 'Taking a breath,' she said.

'Are you all right?'

She nodded.

'Are you sure? Need me to come down?'

And this from the man who just fell, Nomi thought amazed. 'No,' she called. 'Wait. I'm coming.' She started climbing again.

Space pulled behind her, seeming to grapple at her clothing, tug her hair, claw into her insides and wrap itself around her organs as it hauled her out and away from the cliff. And the rock before her held a weight as well, keeping her pressed against it and only letting go to allow her to move higher. For now the weight of the rock was winning. If she turned around again, or looked down, she might well upset that balance.

I'm scared of heights, she thought, curling her fingers into a crack and pulling hard. *Isn't that just fucking great.*

She felt the day melting away, and the thought of trying to sleep hanging like this was terrible. Nomi could not face that. She called down to Beko and asked him how long they had to go, then she turned and called up to Ramin, asking him the same thing. Their shouted responses sounded flat and distant, as though the rock refused to echo them.

'One more hour!' Ramin shouted down to her. 'Rhiana thinks she sees a ledge.'

So they climbed on, and as her heart beat out a rapid time, Nomi became more and more certain that they would be hanging here all night.

She turned and looked down at Beko again. *I won't let it beat me,* she thought. *I can't. That's pathetic.*

Beko smiled up at her. 'Fantastic view of your arse from down here,' he called.

Nomi laughed out loud. 'Oh, I bet it's marvellous.'

She looked past him to the ground and the horses were no longer visible. Maybe they had all gone, or maybe they were just too small to see. It was difficult to tell. She took a deep breath and looked behind her, out across Noreela, and wondered how far north they would be able to see. She thought she could make out the last of the standing stones they had passed, but it could have been an optical illusion. The expanse of landscape was stunning, and quite beautiful. Some birds flew past below her.

Somebody shouted, a distant call at first too far away to hear, but it was repeated by Ramin. 'Ledge!'

Thank all the gods, Nomi thought. She pressed herself against the rock again, then forced herself to start moving. The more she thought about what she was doing, the worse it would become. And if she fell...?

Beko would catch her.

She saw Ramin reach the ledge and swing his leg up onto it, sliding out of view for the first time since their climb began. His head soon appeared again over the edge, accompanied by Rhiana and Noon.

None of them looked very happy.

When she reached the ledge, Beko not more than a dozen steps below her, the Serians reached out to haul her up. She collapsed beside them and tried to relax, but her muscles spasmed and continued to knot as though she had to hold herself even here.

'Nomi,' Ramin said.

She kept her eyes closed and nodded her head.

'We have a place for the night, but someone was here before us.'

Ramus! she thought. She opened her eyes and tried to sit up, but her body rebelled. Instead she raised her head just as Beko was pulled over the lip, and she saw that her first reaction was wrong.

There was a skeleton splayed across the ledge, selfishly taking up its widest part. A few shreds of clothing remained around the clean white bones, but there was little else.

'Well, now we know why some people don't come back,' Ramin said.

'Been here a long time,' Rhiana said. 'Nothing to show who it was.'

'No climbing stuff?' Nomi looked into the skull's eye sockets and then around at the scattered bones, and it was the first thing she'd noticed.

'Nothing,' Rhiana said.

'Bones are spread out,' Noon said. 'Shattered. They fell.'

Nomi sat up and shuffled towards the back of the ledge, terribly aware of the wide open space behind her. They were all panting with exhaustion, and Beko lay out along the far end of the ledge, perhaps eight steps from her. She was glad she was not the only one who appeared exhausted.

'But having no climbing equipment…' Nomi said.

'I could have got this far without ropes,' Rhiana said. 'Difficult, but I'm sure I could if I was determined enough. And maybe whatever they brought with them has been blown from the ledge. Or washed away by rain.'

'The bones would be gone too.' Nomi looked back at the skull and saw the cracks around the eye sockets, flakes of bone missing here and there. The back of the dome was also smashed, as though something had broken it open for the brain inside.

'I don't like it,' Noon said. 'Shove it over. I won't sleep here if that thing's with us.'

'I'm not touching the dead,' Ramin said.

Nomi shook her head and picked up one of the leg bones. It was completely separated from the knee and foot. *Smashed to pieces,* she thought. He or she must have fallen a long way. She threw the bone out into space and they all watched it arc away from them, tumbling end over end until it disappeared into the gloom. Then she shoved the rest of the bones with her feet, kicking them away. She heard Rhiana gasp as she did so.

'Just a dead climber,' she said when she'd finished. 'I'm sure he or she won't mind us taking their ledge.'

But the skeleton troubled her more than she showed. As the Serians pinned ropes in around them to prepare for the night, Nomi looked out across the darkening landscape of Noreela and wondered who the climber had been. Or maybe they had not been a climber at all.

The ledge was small, four steps deep and maybe a dozen wide, and the five of them huddled closely together. That would help them keep warm, but it also made it awkward when one of them had to answer nature's call. And they found no food. No plants, insects, lichen or grubs, so their evening meal was dried sheebok skin that Rhiana had brought with her all the way from Marrakash. It was bitter and hard, but at least chewing it to pulp took time and concentration, and it was a high-energy food.

When full darkness fell and Rhiana made sure they were all tied in tightly, the cold really began to take effect. Nomi had Beko on one side of her and Ramin on the other, and they all pressed in close to share warmth. She pitied Noon and Rhiana at either end.

Things cried out in the darkness, some of them from the plains far below, others from the open air before the cliffs. Shadows appeared high above and drifted across the land, and smaller shapes darted in and seemed to attack or feed from them. The sounds of hunter and hunted echoed from the rock, and Nomi closed her eyes to shut it out.

'I have a story,' Ramin said at last, and Nomi could have hugged him.

Ramin told his tale of sea caves, smugglers and water serpents, and his voice was strong enough to take her far away for a while.

They hardly slept, and next morning as the clouds to the east lightened, they were keen to move.

They took the same formation as before, and Nomi was sure her fingers and toes were so stiff and bruised that they would fail her. But she quickly found a rhythm, working with Ramin ahead of her and Beko behind, and the climb proceeded well. Physically it was the hardest thing Nomi had ever done, and she discovered depths of determination she never knew she had. But mentally, though it was a challenge climbing so steadily and painfully towards the unknown, excitement won out. By midday of that second day, they had started to work as a true team, and by the time light began to fade again, Nomi realised she had actually enjoyed the climb.

Some of what they saw underlined that this was a unique place. There were spiders that lived on the cliffs, legs growing up from the top of their torso and down from their abdomen. They moved quickly across the rocky surface, and they seemed unconcerned at these human invaders, watching with what could only be curiosity as the clumsy climbers went by. There were also a few insects that had adapted to vertical living, building small homes from spit and dust that clung solidly to the rock.

That evening there was no wide ledge. Though they had passed a crevasse in the cliff earlier that afternoon, it had been too early to stop. So Rhiana passed down the spare rope she carried over one shoulder, and one by one they fixed extra crampons into the rock and tied themselves in. Nomi still held herself up to begin with, finding it difficult to trust the rope cradle. But as weariness stiffened her limbs she eased down, and by the time darkness fell she was sitting fully in the rigged harness.

She had been able to look down and behind her that day; they were so high that there were no real details visible on the ground below. The sense of vast space behind her and the solidity of the end of Noreela before her was still staggering, but the scale had changed.

Looking down now was like staring into nothing.

'How far do you think to the clouds?' Beko asked. He was tied in ten steps below and to the side of her, giving her room to do whatever she might need to during the night.

'We've gone well today,' Nomi said. 'Maybe we'll reach there tomorrow?'

'We won't be able to see so far then,' he said.

'No.'

'We won't know how high to go. Don't even know for sure whether there's a top at all. Maybe we'll find climbers tied in like we are, dead from old age.'

This defeatist voice did not sound like Beko. '*I'm* sure it ends,' she said. 'And so was Ramus.'

Later that night Noon called out from above and directed their attention to the east. Clear in the night, far along the cliff and lower than them, Nomi saw the diffused glow of a fire.

Ramus, she thought. *Brave Ramus. Mad Ramus.* She *was* scared of him, but as things became more remarkable – and Noreela felt further and further behind – she found herself hoping that they would meet again.

❊   ❊   ❊

Next morning, Rhiana woke them all from troubled, uncertain rest. She had woken early and climbed on alone, and now she was a hundred steps above Noon. 'Eggs!' she called down. 'Eggs for breakfast, and a ledge to cook them on!'

They climbed, and by the time they reached Rhiana she had started a small fire on the ledge and boiled three huge, blue eggs. Nomi was startled by their size and worried that the parents would return, but the Serians seemed unconcerned.

They shared an egg between two and it was the most filling, satisfying breakfast Nomi could remember. Up here in the fresh, cool air, much of Noreela laid out behind her as she ate, she felt the familiar thrill of exhilaration drive through her again.

I wonder if Ramus is breakfasting as well as this, she thought, and she sent a good-natured thought his way.

'They were miles away, and much lower,' Rhiana said unprompted. She dropped the eggshell she had been licking and the strengthening breeze plucked it away. 'We'll reach the clouds before them.' She looked up and the others followed her gaze. Sometimes the constant cloud cover seemed close enough to touch, other times it was too far away to discern anything but a uniform grey.

'Feel like I could just let go and fall into them,' Ramin said.

'A favour, Ramin,' Beko said. 'Don't try.'

The bald Serian raised an eyebrow and looked past Nomi at Beko. 'Captain, surely you'd catch me if I fell?'

'Depends on my mood,' Beko said. 'I've had no meat for more than a day, and my stomach gets...cranky.'

'Beko's cranky stomach,' Rhiana said, quietly shaking her head as if it was something they'd all had to deal with before.

Another gust of wind whispered across the cliff face from the west. They leant into it, and an instant of panic seized Nomi – cool, dark and deep, the fear of falling and the greater fear of climbing some more – but she squeezed her eyes shut and willed it away.

'We're doing well,' Rhiana said, and Nomi silently thanked her with a glance.

'So let's carry on!' Noon said. 'Maybe if this thing does have a top, there are people there. And if there are people, there will be daughters, widows, wives.' He laughed out loud and released his harness.

We are *doing well,* Nomi thought. *There's a breeze, but it's not yet a gale. The nights are cool, but not too cold. There's no meat, but we found eggs. And those clouds...we may even reach them by this afternoon.*

They climbed on. The weather remained stable, interrupted by occasional gusts of wind that came and went without warning. They made the climb challenging but exciting. Nobody complained. The cliff offered numerous handholds and narrow ledges, and Nomi fell into an exhausted rhythm.

They heard it before they saw it.

They were climbing with quiet concentration. Nomi had already spotted the rent in the cliff face directly above Ramin – Rhiana had climbed past it, and Noon hung a dozen steps along the cliff – and when the low growl sounded, that was the first place she looked.

There was nothing to see. But the sound came again, like a rumbling stomach. She glanced around, wondering whether thunder was rolling in from the distance.

When she looked up again, Rhiana was gesturing to Noon

and Ramin. She put her finger to her lips, leant back, and took a small crossbow from her belt.

'What is it?' Beko whispered below her.

'Hole in the cliff.'

'Cave?'

Nomi shrugged. 'It's coming from there. I think Rhiana—'

The noise came again, this time a definite growl.

Nomi heard Beko climbing, pulling himself up the cliff face to reach her level. She looked up at Ramin where he hung suspended a few steps below the wound in the rock face. He was motionless and silent, head bent back so that he could look up, one hand grasping the long, curved knife he had taken from his belt.

Rhiana was above and to the right of the hole, trusting her ropes completely as she leant back into space. She held the crossbow in her left hand, its aim sure and unwavering.

'Ramin!' Nomi whispered. 'Move back down.'

Ramin shook his head slowly, gently, and Nomi wondered what he could see or sense up there.

Beko drew level with her. 'Take this,' he said, offering her a knife similar to the one Ramin bore.

'I don't—'

Beko scowled at her and drew his own sword, careful not to scrape it against the stone.

They waited, Ramin just below the hole, Rhiana and Noon above and to the right, Nomi and Beko lower down to the left, and listened to the growls growing in volume and frequency. Nomi splayed one hand against the rock, feeling for any sign of movement.

And then something came out of the cliff. A long snout, covered with scales and spiked with thick black hairs, sniffling and twitching at the air. It was at least as long as Ramin was tall, Nomi guessed, and the two clawed hands that appeared around the edges of the hole were the size of her head.

Nobody fired, nobody spoke; everyone became as still as stone.

The creature snorted as it came further from the hole, displaying at least two more sets of clawed hands on long, muscled legs. The large head and mouth came next, and as it paused Nomi was sure she saw the hint of wings either side of its pale pink torso.

Its snout shifted again and the head moved slowly from side to side. Its mouth opened, and Nomi saw teeth.

Ramin moved. Perhaps his foot slipped, or maybe he pressed his legs and locked one knee against the cliff face, slipping him sideways. He hurriedly regained his balance, just in time for the animal to lash out and down with two long limbs and clasp him in its claws.

Ramin screamed. He swung his knife, missed, and the creature's limbs spasmed as it tore his arm off at the shoulder.

Nomi felt the Serian's blood patter down on her upturned face, and as she went to scream, Beko's hand clapped across her mouth, splitting her lip.

Ramin's feet slipped and he hung face-first against the cliff, held in place by one vicious claw buried in his shoulder. The thing was eating his arm.

Something whistled and the creature jerked, screeching in pain. It emerged more fully from the hole, even more limbs uncurling to fix it across the entrance, and turned to face Rhiana.

She had already reloaded her crossbow, and she sent a bolt into the animal's head.

Noon was scampering across the cliff, sword swinging in one hand, but the thing lashed out. The frayed ends of a slashed rope whipped at the air.

Ramin, still shouting, blood pulsing from his tattered shoulder, drew back his right arm and threw a knife at the thing's pink underbelly. It bounced off and fell away, and the animal turned back to the tall Serian.

'Piss on you!' he shouted, spittle and blood darkening the stone before him. He reached for another knife.

The thing's wings twitched. They were huge and leathery, laid back across its body like those of a massive beetle, and when they moved it sounded like metal on metal. It was preparing to take flight.

Rhiana fired a bolt into the thing's back, pinning one of its wings to its body. It screeched, drowning Ramin's cries with its own.

Beko threw a knife at its snout and it pierced, drawing blood but falling when the thing shook its head.

'Ramin!' Rhiana shouted. 'Cut your rope!'

'Hold on!' Beko said to Nomi. He slammed a crampon into a small crack before them and took some slack from the rope above Nomi, tying it tight.

Ramin strained on his ropes and cursed. Blood had soaked his clothing now, and Nomi knew that he would bleed to death if they could not get to him soon.

'Noon!' Rhiana shouted. 'Cut the rope!'

The line between Noon and Rhiana was slashed, and he had wrapped the frayed end around a small rocky spur to his right. But he had not yet tied a knot. He was holding his own weight against the cliff, sweat standing out on his face. Yet still he reached out again, hand going low, the knife tantalisingly close to the taut rope that held Ramin in place.

'Piss!' Rhiana shouted. She drew her sword and slashed the rope that tied her to the cliff.

'No!' Beko shouted.

Rhiana held herself in place, muscles taut on her right arm. Then her left foot turned out into space, her body slowly followed, and Nomi sensed her gathering her strength.

'Rhiana, don't—'

But she did. She leapt along the cliff face, judging the arc of her plunge perfectly. Three beats after letting go she had fallen fifteen steps and landed across the creature's back.

Its one good wing slid open and Rhiana sliced it off. It flipped away, whooping at the air as though delighted at its freedom. The animal shook. Rhiana stuck her sword into its back and held on with both hands. It shivered and screeched, then turned back to Ramin. Its long limbs reached, claws opening, and Nomi shouted, 'No!' But her words held no power. One set of claws sank into Ramin's good shoulder, the other crunched sickeningly into his neck and left cheek, and the animal roared as it ripped off the Serian's head.

It fell between Nomi and Beko, tongue lolling, tattered neck spewing blood.

Nomi closed her eyes and felt the whole world sway.

There was a moment of stunned silence, broken only by the sound of the creature suckling blood and flesh from Ramin's open neck.

Then Rhiana screamed, an exhalation of pure rage, and drew two short knives from her belt. She hacked at the animal's neck, holding on with her legs as she raised the weapons again and again, and as it went to roll over completely, she fell away into the hole from which it had emerged.

The animal was bleeding profusely now, dark red blood pouring down the cliff face just to Nomi's right. More sounds of fighting and fury came from the hole, and then the creature let out a hideous, fading wail before growing still.

Ramin hung dead below the hole, one foot tapping gently against the cliff as his leg spasmed.

'Rhiana?' Beko called.

Her hand appeared at the edge of the hole, and it was covered in blood.

'*Rhiana!*'

The hand was followed by an arm, and then Rhiana's face. She was looking down at Ramin. Her eyes were wide, stark white against the blood smeared across her skin.

The sense of shock was almost unbearable, unreal.

'Is it dead?' Nomi said.

Rhiana tore her gaze from Ramin's butchered corpse at last and looked directly down at the Voyager. *Does she blame me?* Nomi wondered. *Is this all my fault? First Konrad, now Ramin, and do I attract death simply because I once gave it away?*

'It's dead,' she said.

'What the piss is it?' Noon said. His voice was strained, muscles still tensed from holding on to the slashed rope.

'Never seen anything like it,' Beko said. 'Like a bat with scales.'

'Eight legs,' Rhiana said. 'If it had taken flight, we'd have been finished. We have to cut him down.'

'Stay here,' Beko said, leaning closer to Nomi to whisper the words. He made his way slowly up beside Nomi and then across the cliff face above her, pausing as he arrived close enough to Ramin to touch the dead Serian's body.

Rhiana tugged the dead thing back from the edge of its hole, making sure it could not tumble out and take Nomi and Beko with it.

'This doesn't feel right,' Beko said.

Rhiana lowered herself from the hole, found a footing and carefully descended the few steps to Beko. 'There's no choice,' she said softly. Nomi was shocked to see that the Serian was crying.

Nomi turned away. She did not want to see their grief. She did not want to see them cut Ramin free, though she heard Beko's grunt as the corpse fell away, and she caught movement from the corner of her eye as he tumbled down, down the way they had come. Most of all, she wanted to look away from the second death her voyage had caused.

CHAPTER SIXTEEN

Climbing the chimney was easy. It was a massive fault in the cliff face, varying in width from a few steps to dozens. Its walls were rough and textured, providing many handholds and footrests, and for a long time Ramus and Lulah did not need to use the equipment they had scavenged from the camp site. The rope was heavy across Ramus's shoulder, the gear clanking where he had strung it around his waist on a leather belt. His hands burnt, his feet ached, but he was ecstatic with their progress. It also helped, he believed, that climbing the chimney meant that they could not see the whole expanse of the cliff around them. It was a long way up and down, but their views were often blocked by protruding rocks. The scale of the Divide was shattering, but here they could concentrate.

There were places where water ran down from far above, and they drank and filled their water skins. It tasted pure and fresh. Lulah found a species of insect grub that lived in shallow cracks in the rock walls, and though they looked disgusting they tasted sweet and nutty, and Ramus could tell that the grubs were full of energy. They both filled their pockets with the things.

Even light was not too much of a problem in the chimney. When its opening was wide enough light filtered in to make their going easy, but when it was narrow they found that some of the rocks possessed something of a glow themselves. Lulah said it was crystal specks buried in the rock's surface, and that such stone fetched a high price back in Mancoseria. Ramus did not care. It lit their way, and that was priceless.

They heard occasional noises from the rear of the chimney, issuing from the darkness where the fault penetrated the cliff. Whispers and sighs, squeals and grunts, and Lulah attributed them to the wind. Ramus was not so sure, but nothing threatened them, and nothing emerged. Whatever lay within the cliff preferred to maintain its mystery as it watched them climb.

Towards the end of that first full day, it became apparent that the chimney was fading out. The walls were closing in, the darkness of the crevasse was no longer so deep, and the slice of Noreela that had been visible through the cliff opening grew narrow. They decided to find somewhere to stay for the night before venturing out onto the cliff face proper the following morning.

'How far do you think we've come?' Ramus asked.

Lulah was chewing on another grub, and she nodded at the opening before them. 'It's a long way down,' she said.

Ramus saw light fading from the wedge of Noreela before them. Grasslands, that was all he could see, and even the texture of hills and valleys was uncertain from up here. *We must have come a long way,* he thought. *I wonder whether Nomi has started climbing at all?*

Lulah clambered up a steep scree slope, moved around for

a while and returned with an armful of twigs and dried moss. 'The chimney even gives us a fire,' she said, grinning. Ramus thought it was the first time she had smiled in days.

'Good,' he said. 'These grubs are fine, but I'd prefer their guts hot and cooked.'

Next morning they emerged out onto the cliff face for the first time, and the whole view of Noreela was opened to them. They hung there for a while, trying to take everything in, but it was a sight neither of them could have prepared for. Distance was only swallowed by haze.

'On the clearest day, we could see for ever,' Lulah said, and Ramus nodded.

Whoever or whatever lives up there, they have Noreela set out before them, he thought.

'We should tie on,' Lulah said. 'You climbed well yesterday, and we've come too far for one of us to slip away because of a stupid mistake.'

Ramus raised his eyebrows and tried not to show the pain he was suffering. Every time he blinked it was like a pulse of fire behind his eyes. 'You're sure?' he asked.

Lulah was already shrugging the coil of rope from her shoulder, knotting one end and threading the other through the hoops on her belt. 'We need to do things the right way,' she said.

While Lulah tied them together, Ramus looked first east, then west, wondering whether he would see the shifting silhouettes of Nomi and her group. But it was a foolish thought. The Divide dwarfed Noreela itself, and anyone or anything crawling upon it would be lost.

Lulah went first, and to begin with the going was relatively easy. Ramus shut out the sense of space by concentrating on his hands and feet. Though he had never feared heights, he did fear loss of control, and the farther they went the more he knew the cliff had them. He was trapped in every moment, and the only way to defy the cliff would be to fall.

The Sleeping God guides me in, he thought. The standing stones had led them to the chimney – an easy climb, food, water, shelter – and now even this exposed face provided them with adequate ledges and cracks to climb with relative ease. If he thought of the god and the cliff together, they had both stolen control. Perhaps illness was numbing his fear.

Around midday, Lulah halted above him and let Ramus draw level. She was panting and sweating. She nodded at the cliff just to Ramus's left and he saw the rusted remains of a set of old crampons.

'We're not the first,' she said.

'I never thought we were.' But Ramus looked away from Lulah so that she could not see his face. It was foolish, but he no longer felt quite so special.

'I wonder how far they made it?' Lulah said.

'Maybe we'll see.'

And later, they did. The body first, way above them, difficult to make out but definitely apart from the cliff. As they drew closer, they could see the shape swaying in the breeze, and closer still they could make out what it was. A climber, hanging from a frayed length of rope that looked as though it could give out at any moment. His or her hair flipped in the breeze, straining to loose itself from the tight leathery scalp. They drew level, a dozen steps across the cliff from the dead climber, and paused.

'Must have been climbing alone,' Lulah said. 'Anyone else would have cut them free and let them fall.'

'What a way to die,' Ramus said. The body was bent backwards almost in half, dried out by the sun and wind. Flakes of skin drifted from it with every gust. The clothing was nondescript and the person carried no weapons, so it was difficult to make out who it was, or where they may have come from.

'I promise if you fall, I'll cut you loose,' Lulah said.

Ramus turned to her to give sarcastic thanks, but she was already grinning at him. 'What, you won't cook and eat me?' he asked.

She acted mock-offended. 'Not *all* Serians are cannibals.'

They moved on, strangely buoyed up by the fact that they had progressed farther than this climber. It marked a changing point of sorts – the going became harder, but they were more confident than before.

Two camps at the base of the Divide, the easy climb up the chimney, this dead climber... Ramus began to wonder just how many the Sleeping God had guided in this way. And why. Those words from the old texts returned again, talk of a Fallen God, and the thought filtered quickly away, swallowed by that thing that sat next to the sickness in his mind, and nothing came back, nothing answered. The silence was heavy.

'The greatest voyage,' he whispered. *Greatest Voyager,* he thought.

He hid his pain well. It thumped behind his eyes, stronger with the pounding of his heart, but in a way it was welcome. It made the ache of his limbs, the pull of his shoulders, the dozens of cuts and scrapes on his hands and fingers, seem trifling. He left evidence of himself on the cliff below, and that seemed only right.

They spent that second night in the lowest of a series of

caves. They'd been cautious, fearing creatures that would cause them harm. Lulah went first, slipping over the ledge and into the cave, disappearing for almost too long. She appeared again with an uncertain smile. 'Safe,' she said, and as Ramus hauled himself up into the shadows, he wondered on what basis she had judged that.

The uneven cave floor was white with bones. Many of them were crushed, as if something of immense weight had settled upon them. There were hundreds of small animal skeletons, a few larger creatures – wolves, perhaps, or other wild dogs – and towards the rear of the cave Lulah found three humanoid skeletons. Humanoid, because the skulls obviously belonged to men or woman…but the limbs were far too long. The back was stretched. The hips were narrow.

'They've been distorted by whatever lay on them,' Lulah said.

Ramus nodded, but they both knew that was not the truth.

Lulah's 'safe' pronouncement was based on the fact that these were all skeletons, and none of them had a scrap of meat left upon them. Whatever had nested here had left long ago. But Ramus felt far from safe. Even after Lulah lit a fire he could not sleep, and he lay awake all night listening to flying things crying in the darkness, smelling the musty odours of the long-dead, and waiting for the shadow of something huge to obscure the cave entrance.

Soon after setting off the next morning, Ramus slipped. He shouted first – he could feel it happening – and scrabbled at the sheer cliff face as he slid down. His toe caught against a stone lip and his upper body leant out, and then he fell away from the cliff with a jerk.

Lulah was ready. She grunted as the rope between them tautened with a snap. The grunt turned into a groan, which turned into a roar as Ramus felt for purchase. His fingers slipped into a fissure and his feet found a crack, and he took his own weight.

Lulah eased up above him, breathing hard. He looked up and saw her legs shaking with the effort she had just expended.

'Sorry,' he said.

She looked down and shook her head, unable to speak.

After a while they started climbing again. Ramus was sure that they would make it to the cloud level today, and already the rock before them was damper than before, even beneath the constant breath of the wind. *We should have been swept from here by now by the gales,* he thought. But though there were occasional strong gusts that forced them to hold tight, the winds they had been expecting this high up were absent. Ramus did not know why, and he did not dwell on the fact. He simply gave thanks.

He slipped again before noon. One moment he was holding on well, the next his feet went from beneath him and his sore fingers scraped away from the handholds. It surprised him this time and Lulah cried out when the rope pulled at her waist. Ramus hung in space, spinning slowly, head and arms back, and he thought he probably looked not much different from the corpse they had passed way below. The pain in his head that had knocked him from the cliff consumed the whole of him for a beat, forcing blood rapidly around his body and staggering his heart. He thought he cried out, but he could say nothing. The sound was only in his mind.

The agony receded as quickly as it had come, leaving him weak and uncertain. A voice came in from the distance, louder, louder, and it was telling him to wake up.

Nomi, in one of her nightmares?

Ramus looked up and saw Lulah straining above him, her mouth opening and closing as the distant voice grew closer and found itself.

'Pissing wake up, Ramus, or I swear by whatever god you choose I'll cut this fucking rope!'

Ramus lifted his hands to hold the rope. They moved very slowly. He looked down, found footholds and then pulled himself flat against the cliff.

'What the piss was that?' Lulah shouted.

'Slipped,' Ramus said.

'Slipped? You were gone there, Ramus! I thought you'd passed out.'

'No, slipped, that's all.' He pressed his face to the cool stone and shivered as the breeze kissed his sweaty body. He needed a drink but he dared not unstrap the water skin from around his neck. Not right now. The sickness in his head, the cruel betrayer, might choose that moment to punch him again.

'I need you to stay with me,' Lulah said. 'I'm here under your pay, Ramus, but I'll not kill myself for you. Not like this.'

He looked up at last and nodded, seeing past her anger to the fear. He could *smell* fear in the sweaty aroma that drifted down from her and rose from his own body. They had both almost died then, and not quickly. If they fell, missed the ledges, drifted out past the rocky projections, it would take a long time for them to strike the ground.

'Maybe we should stop and rest when we can,' he said.

'Yes.'

They remained there for a while, gathering their composure and letting their beating hearts settle a little before moving on.

Later the pain came again, and he slipped for a third time, and when he regained his hand and footholds he really believed Lulah was going to cut the rope. If she did, they would no longer be climbing together, and if and when he slipped for a fourth time, he would fall out of Noreela for ever.

Lulah found a small ledge where they could spend the rest of that day and the night, and for a long time she did not speak. Ramus drifted off to sleep, exhaustion taking him down past the terror that had him in its clasp. He thought he may visit Nomi's own nightmares, but when he woke up there was nothing but pain. The sickness grew worse, a traitor to his body, and he began to wonder whether he would live to see the top of the Divide at all.

After Ramin's death, it took them the rest of that afternoon to reach the cloud cover. And it was the worst afternoon of Nomi's life.

The cave from which the creature had emerged was the first of several. They came across the next one soon after Ramin tumbled away, and this time the creature inside came out long before they reached it. Growling, wings whisking like metal sails, it perched on the lip of the fissure and wailed down at them. Beko again climbed up beside Nomi, and Noon and Rhiana put distance between them so that it could not take them both at the same time. Rhiana fired an arrow up, but the distance was too great; it bounced from the huge creature's underside and clattered from the rock face. Rhiana tried to catch it but missed.

The thing tipped forward, leaning out into space until it could unfurl its wings and launch into the air. It drifted away from the Divide, wings making great thumping sounds at the sky, legs hanging below it like a giant wasp, snout sniffing at the air.

Rhiana had reached a narrow ledge and she managed to turn, facing away from the cliff and held in place by a single crampon.

As the creature drifted in at them, Beko moved sideways so that he was pressed against Nomi. He curled one arm around her and pushed her firmly against the cliff.

'Shouldn't you be shooting at that thing?' she asked.

'We're hired to protect you.' She heard little affection in his voice, and she wondered yet again whether they were resenting her now, thinking she'd lost control.

Noon fired crossbow bolts out into space, every one of them finding their target. A few ricocheted from the creature's hide or its scaled snout, but others struck home and lodged there, eliciting screeches that bounced from the cliff face and seemed to make it shake. The animal came on, angling for Noon, aiming for what it perceived as its greatest risk. That was where the Serians' deception worked.

Above Noon and twenty steps to the side, Rhiana loosed her arrow only when she was sure of her aim. It struck the flying thing behind its wide head and went deep. The animal's legs tensed out and down, its wings forked upward and its head pulled back and turned, trying to dislodge the arrow.

Noon stepped from the cliff as the stricken animal headed for him.

It struck the rock with the sound of wet breaking things, and it was already dead when it fell away.

The rope connecting Noon and Rhiana tensed and swung him to the west, and the falling animal caught him a glancing blow with one of its flailing legs. He reached for a rocky outcropping and held on, the rope sagging again, and he grinned down at Nomi.

'Piece of piss!' he said.

And that time, it was. But there were more. They climbed, and each time they saw the shadow of a cave above them they tried to shift sideways to avoid it. And each time that happened, the snout of a monster would appear silhouetted against the underside of the clouds, its claws hauling it to the edge of its home, and when the time was right it would fall into space, wings unfurling, legs trailing, swooping up and out in readiness to scream in and pluck them from the cliff.

The creatures' dumbness saved them. They attacked one at a time, and if others were watching, they seemed to learn nothing. Twice more Noon played bait, and then Rhiana would finish them with an expertly placed arrow behind the head. One time Noon had to swing to avoid the plummeting animal, the other it was Nomi and Beko who were almost swept from the cliff by the falling corpse.

Others came. Noon and Rhiana swapped roles, and between each attack they climbed as hard and fast as they could. Nomi had taken it to mind that once in the cover of clouds, the attacks would end, but the dark idea lingered that these things would only use the clouds for cover. If that happened, they were all finished.

And to add to their problems, smaller flying things started buzzing them. To begin with, Nomi thought they may have been the young of those larger monsters, but these looked very different, and in some ways more disturbing because of that. They had light wings and furred bodies, and their fleshy legs looked almost like thin, human arms. They never attacked, but they flew in close enough to keep everyone on edge between encounters with the larger creatures.

Nomi was utterly exhausted, traumatised at seeing Ramin slaughtered by the animal and then cut away by his comrades, and the fear of being trapped haunted her between each attack. She felt sick, and a headache pounded at her skull – altitude sickness, Beko said. The weight of the emptiness above Noreela was heavier than the Great Divide, and it pulled at her, making her woozy.

They climbed, fought off the flying things, and at last Nomi believed that dusk was falling. They would be trapped out here on the cliff in the dark. Somewhere far below, Ramin waited to welcome them into his broken embrace.

'We're almost there,' Beko said below her. 'Nomi?'

She turned and looked down, trying to concentrate her vision so that she saw only his face and not beyond. 'Where?' she asked.

'The clouds. We're almost there.'

She looked up and saw that he was right. Rhiana was climbing ahead, leaning back to scan the cliffs above her, but also eager to reach the clouds.

It started raining. It was a fine, cool mist, and as long as they kept climbing Nomi knew it would refresh them. She opened her mouth and relished the chill on her tongue.

'One more cave!' Rhiana called down.

No, Nomi thought. *No more.* She had lost count of how many things Noon and Rhiana had taken down between them. There were few arrows and crossbow bolts left.

They all waited where they were, Noon loading his crossbow, while Rhiana edged closer to the opening. She was almost out of sight in the misty haze, just a shadow moving across the dark dampness of the cliff, and Nomi blinked several times as she saw the Serian reach the cave.

'Nothing!' Rhiana called. Her voice floated down, softened by the cloud.

Noon grinned at Nomi and she smiled back, but even that took strength she no longer had.

'Nothing in here!' Rhiana shouted, louder this time. 'Only water, and grubs to eat, and somewhere dry for the night.'

Nomi rested her forehead against the cliff. *We'll beat you,* she thought, hoping the Divide could hear her. *We'll find your secrets yet.*

Lulah stood on the edge of the ledge, rope-free, and Ramus felt queasy just watching her. A gust of wind could send her plummeting for ever.

'Do you think you're strong enough?' she asked at last.

'I think so, yes.'

'If you fall again, Ramus, I'll do my best to hold on to you. But if you fall and I don't think I *can* hold you, I'll not let you pull me from this cliff.'

It was cold, but it had to be said, and Ramus appreciated that. 'I wouldn't want you to die for me,' he said.

Lulah nodded. 'You know I'm afraid of you?'

'Afraid of what I'm learning from those pages, more like.'

'No,' she said. 'I'm afraid of *you*. Those words you used on Konrad...they were a weapon. It takes a person to use a weapon, and it's that person that scares me.'

Ramus did not know what to say. He had the sudden urge to share everything with this woman he barely knew, but how would that sound? Could he really tell her that the god that *might* be atop this Divide *might* be fallen?

He thought not. Even he did not really know what that meant. A myth within a myth…

'We should go,' Lulah said.

On that third day, they passed a ledge where a dead body lay sprawled. It was to the west and difficult to see, but from that distance it seemed to Ramus that it was too tall for a human, arms and legs too long. One limb trailed over the edge of the ledge and hung down, and he could make out the separate sticks of its lengthy fingers. It wore clothing of some sort, and that's what troubled Ramus the most. If it was not human and it wore clothing, then what was it?

He wanted to investigate, but Lulah refused. 'We go up or down,' she said. 'Not sideways. Besides, something killed who or whatever that is.' So they climbed on and left the corpse where it lay.

Nausea came and went, and the pain in his head, and Ramus thought it was his illness until he saw Lulah rubbing at her own temples. The impact of how high they were hit him then. They were climbing out of the world.

To the west, they saw things drifting out from the cliff and back again, too far away to be identified. Ramus hoped they remained at that distance, and saw Lulah casting nervous glances their way for the rest of the morning.

As he climbed, Ramus whispered those new words to himself, and when they paused in a fissure at noon, he took out the parchment pages and ran his fingers over them, reciting the words he had learnt in his head, trying to read those he had not. He wrote in his journal and Lulah sat apart from him, back turned, obviously not eager to see the pages for herself. Ramus could understand. They frightened him as well.

They reached the clouds. They were cool, and though the rock face became wet and slippery, Ramus welcomed this new step on their climb. *Through the clouds,* he thought, *and everything will change.* Noreela would be out of sight, the sun above them, and perhaps they would be able to see the top of the Divide. Either that, or they would find that it truly had no top.

They climbed slowly, pausing frequently to adjust to the altitude. The nausea remained. It took most of an afternoon to climb through the clouds.

When they emerged above the mist and looked up, and saw at last where the Great Divide ended high above them, Ramus felt a thrill of discovery that threatened to swipe him from the cliff. He held on tight and Lulah looked back down at him, smiling. There was a tear in her eye, because they had found something remarkable.

And the thing in his mind – that alien presence nestled next to the illness that would kill him – swallowed his pain, and gave him the strength to climb.

Part Three

WHERE SLEEPING GODS LIE
VOYAGER – THE SCHEME OF THINGS – DESCENT

———◆———

'To the discovered, the discoverer can be a god.'
Sordon Perlenni, the First Voyager

CHAPTER SEVENTEEN

Nomi wanted to complete the ascent herself; it was something about pride. Rhiana and Noon stood on top of the cliff, looking down at her and Beko, but unable to stop glancing back over their shoulders every few beats. Their eyes were wide and amazed, their hands reached down, and Nomi did not want to know. *Don't tell me,* she thought. *I want to see it for myself.*

Beko was climbing beside her now, and she had the impression that he had slowed his pace to climb with her. She was exhausted. With the end so close, it felt as though her body was giving up on her at last. Her chest wheezed as she gasped in thin air, her arms and legs shook uncontrollably, nausea seemed to leach strength from her muscles, but she did not want anyone's help. If Beko reached out for her she would have to tell him that. She was sure he would understand.

She climbed until there was no longer blank stone in front of her face. Instead she saw Rhiana's scratched and bruised legs and, beyond them, a world that should not exist.

Rhiana reached down to grab her arms but Nomi shook her head. 'No! I'll do it. We've come so far...' The Serian stepped back, still keeping a good hold on the climbing rope, and Nomi hauled herself from the cliff face and onto the ground above.

Grass grew right to the cliff's edge, and it was a deep, dark green, lush beneath her face. There were small white and yellow flowers pressing against her cheek, and she inhaled their scent. They were similar to the meadow daisies of Noreela, but not exactly alike. Up here, she guessed that nothing would be *exactly* like anything else.

She raised herself on her arms and Rhiana stepped aside to let her see.

The plateau was rolling tundra, with a few stark trees growing here and there and frequent, heavy clumps of a thick gorse. She was not exactly sure what she had expected – a ridge, perhaps, falling rapidly away to whatever lay south of the Great Divide – but what she saw was so similar to much of the Noreelan landscape that she felt a moment of disappointment. But only a moment. Because as she stood on shaking legs, accepting Rhiana's steadying hand at last, she was struck by two things. First, the few trees she saw were of a species she had never seen before; spidery yet strong, hardy growths that would bend easily to the winds that must howl across this place. And secondly, this was somewhere new. Whether it resembled Noreela or not, this was *somewhere else entirely*.

She had discovered the top of the Great Divide.

Nomi closed her eyes and swayed, feeling Rhiana's hand tighten around her wrist. She breathed deeply of the scant air and smelt scents she had never smelt before, looked up at the sun blazing down on a land no one had ever seen and returned from to tell the tale.

'We're here,' she croaked. Climbing through the clouds had made her chest heavy, one of many discomforts that marked what they had done. 'We're all here.'

'Not all,' Beko said. 'Ramin would have been amazed. Even he would have found no jokes to make about this.'

'I look south and see nothing,' Noon said. 'I thought there may be...I don't know. *Something*.'

'There *is* something,' Nomi said. 'Grass, trees, plants. Low hills. That sky, a deeper blue than I've ever seen. A few clouds, even so high. A whole new world.'

'But farther south?' Noon said. He shook his head, perhaps unable to comprehend what he was seeing and what it meant. 'What's at the other edge of the plateau?'

'I don't know,' Nomi said. 'Not yet. A fall into another land, perhaps?'

'Maybe there's just another Great Divide.' Beko stood behind Nomi, his heat touching her like he had not touched her for days. As if reading her thoughts he placed his hands on her arms, gentle enough to make her believe he meant it.

'That's just chilling, thank you,' Rhiana said.

Beko laughed. It had the taint of madness to it, but they all took it up and enjoyed the venting of emotion, amazed that they had made it, traumatised by the climb. Nomi felt sick and exhausted, and it was only now that she appreciated how weary the others looked. And they had been fighting as well as climbing.

Her laughter turned to tears, and the Serians did not notice because they also wept.

❖   ❖   ❖

Her body needed nothing more than rest, but Nomi could not allow that. Rhiana guessed they had climbed almost three miles, and the other Serians agreed, and Nomi found it incredible that such a short distance could separate two worlds.

They followed the line of the cliff to the west to begin with, finding no signs that anyone else had ever climbed this far. The first time they saw animal life, the Serians tensed, bearing their weapons against what was revealed as a herd of heavily horned goats. The animals scampered out of a gulley a hundred steps to the south and wandered towards them, fearless and calm. Even when they started walking again, the goats simply watched them go.

There were birds up here, all of the species strange to them. They wittered and whistled, sang and called, and for a while Nomi and the others were buzzed by a playful flock of small ochre birds. One of them landed on Beko's shoulder, another alighted on Rhiana's head, and after eating seeds from Nomi's palm they disappeared as quickly as they had arrived. She plucked the seeds from a plant she did not know: stout green stem, wide white flowers, a bright red central seed pod.

I wish Ramus were here with me, she thought, and she felt a sudden pressure behind her eyes. How useless to let it go the way it had! How foolish, how *stupid!* They had let their closeness drive wedges between them – irrational jealousies and unforgivable betrayals destroying such a special, unique relationship. They had started this voyage together and they should still be together, here and now, to witness the wonders of this new land. There were much greater things than her and Ramus, if only the two of them had acknowledged that.

But I killed him. She thought of the agony of the sickness she had passed on. Hardly the gift of a friend.

'I wonder if Lulah and Ramus made it up,' Beko said.

'I was thinking the same.' Nomi looked past him to the east, the lush greenness atop the plateau to her right, the soft sea of cloud cover stretching toward the horizon on her left. 'If he did, he'd have gone inland. I'm sure there's plenty to explore.'

'Look!' Rhiana said.

Nomi followed where she was pointing, and at first she saw nothing. A few goats on a small, distant slope, green grass spotted with purple and pink plants, sprays of white flowers here and there among the grass, trees...

At least, some trees. But what she had taken to be a tree a couple of hundred steps away suddenly resolved itself into something else. Tall, spiked with branches, it had far too many straight edges.

'Someone made that,' Rhiana said.

They stared in silence for a beat, all of them thinking the same but leaving it to Nomi to say. 'We're not alone.'

We're not alone. Those words hung heavy in the air as the four of them stared at whatever the shape may be.

Nomi moved first. She slipped away from Beko's hand as he tried to hold her back, and ran. She heard the footfalls of the Serians following, and by the time she reached the shape, her legs were shaking again, and her body was telling her that there really was no energy left. She fell to her knees, leg muscles cramping, and looked up at what they had found.

It had been a tree, once. But its branches had been removed, its bark hacked away, trunk carved straight, and into the pale wood were impressed a series of faces and symbols. The faces were long and oval, eyes painted black. And, projecting from the carving at various heights, were long, thick sticks. Things hung from these false branches, and it took Nomi a moment to make out what they were.

Foetuses. Mummified somehow, but the curled shape of arms, legs and head was unmistakable. They had been painted along with the structure, elaborately decorated with heavy dyes that held the elements back.

'Piss on me,' Rhiana said quietly.

'They're not real,' Beko said.

Nomi shook her head. 'They are.'

'They look wrong,' Noon said. 'Like they were stretched when they were born. Look at their heads. And their arms: too long.'

'These are unborn,' Nomi said. 'Not fully formed.' She tried not to think of where they had come from, how they had been removed from their mothers.

Rhiana stepped forward and reached out for one of the lowest hanging things.

'No!' Beko said. 'We don't know anything about this place. We can't just storm in and do our own thing.'

'I just wanted to—' Rhiana said, but Nomi cut in.

'Beko's right. We have to be careful. We need to respect whoever did this.'

'Or whatever,' Noon said. 'It's monstrous!'

'We don't know anything about them, or what this is about, or why they did it,' Nomi said. The responsibility of what they were doing struck her then, and she could say no more.

'We should move on,' Beko said for her. 'Maybe this is something holy for whoever lives up here. We should find the lie of the land. But we have to be careful.'

Rhiana chuckled. 'I'm down to two arrows, Noon is out of

crossbow bolts, and I don't think I could lift my sword in both hands if I had to. How careful do you think we can be?'

'Careful enough to show respect,' Beko said. 'There's nothing to say we're facing a fight.'

Nomi let Beko hold her up this time, and they walked away leaning against each other. Noon and Rhiana went ahead, glancing back several times at the gruesome foetus-tree, and Nomi saw true exhaustion in their features for the first time. *We need to rest,* she thought, *or we'll be making mistakes.* But as they walked, she felt her sense of wonder extend to Beko – the idea that they were seeing things never before seen by Noreelan eyes. With such discoveries to make, sleep was the last thing she wanted.

It felt like for ever since the sun had touched their skins. They walked towards where it was setting, and Nomi relished the warmth and thought of that high, dark cliff which the sun barely kissed. It soothed her cooled bones and calmed cramped muscles.

They followed the line of the cliff for a while, and her vision was still split into land and cloud. It reminded her of those parchment pages, and the line on each sheet which Ramus had said described the Great Divide. She was on the other side now; the side where words and images were drawn, away from the blankness beyond the cliff wall.

When the bizarre tree was out of sight behind them they turned south and headed for what Nomi thought of as inland. They passed several more trees, but these were still growing and bearing natural fruits. She had never seen anything like them: spindly branches, silvery bark, small husky fruits with spiked skins to protect them from birds and other predators.

Their route took them into a natural hollow in the side of a hill and here they decided to camp. Beko, Rhiana and Noon gathered a few steps from Nomi and talked in hushed tones, looking around and never once glancing her way.

When Beko came back to her, his face was grim.

'What's wrong?' Nomi asked.

'Worried,' he said, and he sat beside her without elaborating.

'Well?' she asked after a pause.

'It's a new world,' Beko said. There was fear in his voice now instead of wonder. 'We're spending our first night out in the open, we're all beyond exhaustion, and we have no idea who or what is out there. And that tree...'

'It doesn't mean they're dangerous.'

Beko glared at her.

Nomi shrugged. 'Could have been stillborn. A religious thing, a superstition.'

Beko drew a short knife and a sharpening stone and began to work, meticulous and slow. 'I can't help remembering the bodies we saw down on the cliff.'

'They could have fallen.'

'Or maybe some were pushed.'

He continued sharpening his weapons, and Nomi found the sound soporific. She leant her head against Beko's shoulder, and he nestled down a little to make her more comfortable.

'What about us?' she asked, half asleep and less afraid of his answer.

'When this is over,' he said. 'When it feels safe. When we know more about this place...' He said some more, but his voice faded into words and phrases she did not understand, and sleep welcomed her down.

*   *   *

If she had nightmares she did not remember them. She had gone to sleep expecting her rest to be unsettled, waking when the night sounds of this place began, dreaming of the climb they had finished and the fall they had avoided. But when she woke it was daylight again. Her joints were stiff and her muscles ached, and Beko was crouched beside her with his hand pressed to her mouth.

'Be still,' he said. 'And quiet. That most of all.'

Nomi nodded and he took his hand away.

Behind Beko she could see Noon and Rhiana crouched at the lip of the hollow where they had made camp. They were looking east, their outlines silhouetted against the rising sun. Noon had his sword drawn, and Rhiana was holding her bow strung with one of her remaining arrows. They were very still, very quiet, and their tension was palpable.

In the distance, she heard something screech. Another voice answered, a cry followed by a series of harsh rattles and cracks.

Beko had turned away and Nomi touched his leg. When he looked, she raised her eyebrows. *What?*

He leant in close and whispered in her ear. 'Things out on the grassland. We've seen four but I think there may be more. Big. Fast.' But Nomi knew he had not told her everything. She sat up and crawled towards Noon and Rhiana, Beko by her side.

He held her shoulder just before she reached them and whispered again. 'They're strange. Like people, only different. Best to warn you.'

Nomi nodded, not quite sure what he meant. Once beside Rhiana, she pulled herself up the small incline and peered over the top. At first she could see nothing moving save shifting shadows thrown by bushes rustling in the breeze. The wind took her breath away for a beat – a cool gust that seemed to usher in the rising sun. It brought smells she did not recognise from places she had yet to visit.

She heard that cry again, followed by the same clicks and rattles as before. If there was language in there it was strange, and unrelated to anything she had ever heard. Then she saw the first shape. It emerged from the landscape two hundred steps away; tall, stooped, long legs marching it delicately but speedily across the grassland, long arms hanging down and ending in wide hands. Its head stood atop a short thin neck, and grey hair hung down in tied bunches around its face. It was too far away to make out for sure, but from what Nomi could see it looked almost human. And it wore clothing.

She gasped. 'What the piss is that?'

'There are several of them out there,' Rhiana said. 'Just wandering around. I've been watching them since sunup. Not sure if they're looking for food or just walking the night from their bodies. When they meet up, they communicate with those strange clicks, and they touch each other as well. I'd say they're half as tall again as me, but they're hunched down. And they're all wearing clothing of some sort, though most of it looks like rags tied on with string. Nothing too elaborate. I don't think you've found a new fashion for Long Marrakash.'

Nomi looked sidelong at the Serian but she was not smiling. 'Do you think they're dangerous?' she asked.

Rhiana shrugged. 'No way of knowing, so for now I assume yes.'

'They must be the ones who made that tree,' Noon said.

'Maybe,' Beko said. He had moved up beside Nomi. 'Maybe not.'

They watched the creatures for a while. Several of them gathered together and seemed to sit and talk. They were never quite still; their heads swayed, bodies shifted as though waving in the wind. As the sun left the horizon, something seemed to alarm them, and they stood as one and ran quickly into the distance. In a few beats they were out of sight, their clicking calls still just reaching the Voyagers where they lay.

'They were definitely human,' Beko said.

Nomi frowned. *Almost,* she thought. *Or maybe they had been once.* Something about them bothered her, and it was not only their exaggerated appearance – longer legs, taller bodies. The way they had sat together talking, bodies shifting to the breeze, grey hair tied in elaborate-looking braids, their clothing rough and ragged but also cut in very particular ways...

'What do you think?' Rhiana asked. She stared at Nomi, obviously expecting an answer.

'I'm not sure,' she said. 'I had no real idea of what to expect up here.'

Rhiana grunted, nodded and went back to their camp.

'So what now?' Beko asked.

Nomi smiled. 'Now we explore.'

Rhiana killed a creature that looked like a cross between a rabbit and a sheebok. Its chunky back legs were still shaking as she dragged it back into their camp, and they only stopped when she gutted and skinned it. They debated briefly about the merits of starting a fire, but hunger overcame caution. Half an hour later they were picking slices of cooked meat from a stick propped over the fire, and it tasted incredible. Soft, moist, sweet, the smoke gave it a tang that negated the need for any herbs or spice. They ate in contented silence.

Rhiana extinguished the fire and buried the ashes, and they left the remains of the creature for scavengers.

They headed south. The plains rose and fell in gentle undulations as far as they could see, and maybe twenty miles in the hazy distance they saw the darker smudge of thickly forested slopes. The trees seemed to be various shades of red, and clouds hid the tops of whatever hills or mountains they skirted.

As they walked, Nomi thought of the Sleeping God. Without the parchment pages – and without Ramus's ability with languages – there was no way for her to tell where the mythical god was supposed to be. This plateau was huge. Twenty miles deep at least, and if it truly ran from east coast to west, several hundred miles wide. But they had seen firelight on the cliff that first night, and assuming it was Ramus and Lulah, they were climbing only miles apart. That gave her confidence. If Ramus had found a reason to climb in this particular place, then she could find it as well.

But as they walked south, a whole new aim presented itself in her mind. They were not only on top of the Great Divide, but also heading towards whatever might lay beyond. The joy of discovery was clear in her mind, a very sharp aim that had been temporarily appeased upon reaching the head of the Divide, but which now bit harder than ever before. South there were hills or mountains, and beyond those…who knew? More mountains? Another new world?

She knew that at some point she would have to return to Long Marrakash, but such a return could wait.

'Shouldn't you be recording this somehow?' Beko asked as they walked.

'Can you draw, Captain?' Nomi asked, smiling.

'Badly.'

'Can you write?'

'Barely.'

'Badly and barely are about my limits as well. But I can see, feel and smell. And that's good enough for me.'

'But what will they say when we go back? What about the Guild?'

Nomi was silent for a while, thinking about what she wanted to say and what it really meant. It felt good and pure, but there was also an aspect of separation which she had not yet vocalised to anyone. 'I'm doing this for me,' she said. 'Voyaging…it's about fame or fortune, or perhaps both. For me, the Ventgorian trips were about fortune, and I've made that. But now we've found this place, I realise how superficial that really is. I've never known the true heart of voyaging, not like…'

'Ramus,' Beko finished.

'I only hope he's all right,' she said quietly. She looked east, her view across the landscape soon blocked by trees and the contours of this high place. The air smelt fresher and sweeter up here, the sky was a deeper blue and the sun was warmer on her skin than she had experienced for a long time. Ramus would have loved such differences. They would tell him that he was somewhere else, and Nomi prayed to whatever gods would listen that he was feeling and seeing them right now.

By midday they had barely travelled two miles. The terrain was easy, but there was so much to see that they paused every hundred steps to examine something new.

They found snakes that carried hundreds of young on their backs. The serpents hissed and reared up when anyone drew near, but from a distance they seemed placid and calm. They ranged from yellow through to a deep brown, and their young waved infantile heads at the air, smelling every new scent. They saw fat, bulbous fungi that popped audibly when they were touched, releasing a mist of spores into the breeze. Noon worried about infection, disease and poison, but Nomi shrugged and carried on. If they were to contract a disease and die up here, it would happen however careful they were.

Around the base of one large rocky mound, they saw hundreds of stones beginning to move. They ground and rumbled together, and it was only when the explorers approached closer that they saw legs protruding from the stones' undersides. There were small pincers hidden away too, flashing out when flies or bees came close and snapping them back inside the stony shells as the creatures ate.

They moved on from one wonder to the next. Amazing new sights – animals or plants that resembled those they had known from Noreela but which displayed marked differences – and several new things they could not understand at all. They found a tall metal pipe protruding from the ground, ragged with splits and rusted tears, and they did not know what it was for. Several parallel trenches in the ground, thirty steps long, contained watery sand, tinged green by some sort of moss and smelling of rotting fruit. More pipes crossed these trenches, pierced with regularly spaced holes and knotted together in complex joins. 'Something up here builds,' Beko said, but Nomi was more amazed at the extracted, melted and moulded metals.

She welcomed mysteries such as these, because to understand everything would be to equate this place to Noreela. It was *not* Noreela. They had travelled beyond the world they knew, and there was still some way to go.

❊   ❊   ❊

They found the statue early that afternoon, about four miles in from the edge of the Divide. They had spent some time exploring a network of steaming pools and streams, and as they mounted a slope, they saw the shape outlined on top of the next small hill. It took an hour to reach, but long before they gathered around it and stared with a mixture of awe and disappointment, Nomi recognised what it was.

Carved from the bole of an old tree, the man gazed at them with black-painted eyes. It was obvious that the carving was quite old; the wood had cracked, parts of it were rotten, and any sharp features had been smoothed by sunlight and weather. But there were signs that whoever had carved this image still visited. Garlands of dried flowers were gathered around its base like discarded clothes, and suspended from one wooden shoulder was a more recent floral tribute, still moist with decay.

'Who is it?' Noon said.

'Not me,' Beko said.

'But he's like us.' Nomi stepped forward, reached up and touched the wooden face. 'Not like the things we saw. He's Noreelan.'

'Maybe there are human tribes up here as well,' Rhiana said.

Nomi stared into the dark eyes. The Serian was right, there could well be humans up here. Someone had written those parchment pages after all. The humanoid figures they had seen that morning could well be capable of doing so, but there had been something wild about them that gave her doubts. Maybe they couldn't do it now, but what about in the past? A bird flitted by above them, and a shadow at the corner of the statue's mouth twitched.

Nomi blinked. She looked back at the others, then again at the statue.

'What?' Beko said.

Nomi shook her head. 'Foolish.'

'What's foolish?'

She shrugged. 'Feel like I know this face.' She was hoping they would laugh to diffuse her nervousness, but they looked more serious than ever.

'So what about the Sleeping God?' Beko asked. They had left the carving behind, though Nomi could still see it if she looked back. She was glad that its eyes stared northward.

'That would be amazing,' she said. 'But even if it does exist, there's more to this place than that.'

'I agree,' Beko said. 'Let's leave the myths alone. For all we know, this is a land as large as Noreela.'

Nomi looked to the hills in the distance and the red-tinged trees. 'It could be,' she said. 'That's what drives me.'

'Scares the piss out of me,' Beko said, but she heard the excitement in his voice, and she was so glad that he was there.

Nomi reached out for his hand. When she turned to speak again, Beko's face exploded and he went down.

She would never remember what she was about to say.

His eye was ruptured. *Look at me,* Nomi wanted to say, but he could not, because his other eye was already swelled shut from the bruising. His cheek and temple were wet with clear fluids and blood, and his left brow looked soft and sunken. He foamed at the mouth. Nomi wiped it away but he kept foaming, starting to shake now, and she could only wince as he squeezed her hand.

Something screeched and clicked, and she recognised those sounds instantly.

They emerged from a clump of bushes to their left, four of them rising on those long, thick legs until Nomi thought they would never stop. They were almost twice her height. They had the faces of people, though their faces were long and oval. And even their bodies, though elongated and impossibly tall, looked human.

But their viciousness and rage were unnatural. They spat and clicked as they came, spinning leather pouches loaded with heavy stones above their heads. One of them released another stone and Noon fell aside just in time. The creatures were fifty steps away.

Rhiana knelt, drew her bow, and fired. An arrow found a home in the lead creature's face and it went down, its screech pained, and painful to hear. The others paused as if amazed, standing like statues as their companion held the arrow with one large hand and scratched at the ground with its other hand and feet.

One of them clicked, the others answered, and they turned their attention back to the Voyagers.

Rhiana fired her last arrow. A creature turned impossibly quickly and the arrow bit through its arm, tip stabbing through its clothes and into its side, drawing a gush of bright red blood.

Rhiana threw her bow aside and drew her sword in one hand, knife in the other.

Noon had found his feet and was also bearing his sword. He swapped a brief glance with Nomi and she saw his fear.

The second shot creature lifted its arm and bit through the arrow's shaft, tugging the split timber through the hole in its wrist and hissing at the pain. It threw the weapon aside. The three started advancing again, more warily now, spreading out and crouching down in predatory stances.

Nomi was amazed at how human they looked, and how wild they obviously were. Their grey hair was tied in intricate braids, and their clothing was not as ragged as she'd first assumed. Some of it bore dyed designs.

Some of these designs reminded her of the images on Ten's parchments.

'Beko?' Nomi said. She looked down at the Serian captain – her lover – and he did not respond. He shook and foamed, blood leaking from his shattered eye socket. She was sure she could see his pulse through the softened patch of skull above his eye.

'How is he?' Rhiana asked without turning around.

'Bad.'

'Draw his sword.'

Nomi complied without question. Rhiana and Noon were no longer able to protect her when they had to fight for themselves. She drew the sword, surprised at its weight, and crouched before the stricken Serian, facing the advancing creatures, ready to lash out should they come near.

Oh, for Ramus's cursed words right now, she thought.

The tall creature on the left darted for Noon. He feinted with his sword then flipped out his left hand, launching two throwing stars at its face. One missed, the other sliced across its cheek and ricocheted away. The thing screeched but kept coming, and the spinning pouch went from being a slingshot to a club. It battered at Noon's head and he rolled to one side, striking with his sword and catching the thing across one knee.

The two other creatures launched their slings at Rhiana. She ducked one stone but another hit her on the foot, the impact flipping her over sideways.

Beko, still blinded but obviously not deaf, drew a knife from his belt. Nomi touched his shoulder and squeezed. He could not even sit up.

One creature snapped up another rock and loaded its sling again, swinging it at Rhiana, while the other darted in with hands outstretched. She rolled and avoided the rock, slashing up and around and catching the creature across the underside of the hand. It screamed, and three fingers flopped down, dangling by shreds of skin. Rhiana stood, and the thing backed away.

Noon screamed. His enemy had one of its big hands wrapped around his face, arm extended to keep his sword away from its body. The Serian swung, but the thing caught his arm and twisted, crushing his hand and forcing him to drop the weapon. It uttered something that may have been a laugh, and Noon's other hand thrust up, the spike of a throwing star protruding between his fingers. It struck the creature's underarm and blood misted the air. Noon drew his hand back to stab again, but before he connected, the thing kicked out with one long leg, heel connecting with Noon's chest.

Nomi heard the appalling crunch of bones, and the Serian flew back several steps before falling into the short grass. She wanted to shout at him to pick up his sword, to watch out, but then she saw the blood bubbles at his mouth and the dreadful wound in his chest, and she knew that he was dead.

'No,' she said, because everything was falling apart. They had overcome the greatest obstacle in Noreela, for this? To be slaughtered by these *things*? 'No!' she shouted, standing and hefting the sword.

While Noon's bleeding enemy bent low to sniff at his body, the other two again went for Rhiana. She ducked below one heavy fist and stabbed at the thing's gut, but its reach was too long. The other one struck at her with its ruined hand, screeching as its bloody stumps raked Rhiana across the side of the head, her own involuntary grunt of pain adding to the noise.

Nomi needed to help, but she could not leave Beko's side. Not while he was like this.

The thing that had killed Noon turned to look at her.

She stood and hefted the sword, and suddenly its weight was a comfort. It would give momentum to a swing and power to a thrust, and she stood astride Beko, ready to fight.

Rhiana shouted in rage. One of her attackers had entangled its fingers in her weapon belt, and as she swung her sword the other grabbed her arm and twisted. Her shout turned to a scream, but even above that Nomi could hear the bones breaking and her arm crunching from its socket.

The things kicked Rhiana to the ground and stood back as she tried to sit up. She managed to turn and look at Nomi, then her skin grew shockingly pale and she passed out.

'Piss on you,' Nomi said. 'All of you.'

The three of them advanced slowly. They knew they had won so they were taking their time, and Nomi wondered whether they would play with her before delivering the final blow.

'Like your dress,' she said to one of the things. Maybe it was female, maybe not; she really could not tell. It blinked at her, and for a beat she wondered if it understood. But they came on without pause. There was no sense of hope in their expressions, and absolutely nothing human in their eyes.

They struck the sword from her hands and a heavy fist hit her in the chest, driving her away from Beko. One of them stepped over the shivering Serian and kicked Nomi, sending her rolling even further away. Then it squatted beside her. She could smell it, rank and sweet. It panted and spat as it stared at her. She tried not to meet its gaze.

The other two prodded and sniffed at Beko. Obviously satisfied that he was not a threat, they too squatted, and then the three things began to click in that strange language Nomi had heard earlier.

She blinked slowly, trying not to see the way Beko's chest was moving slower and slower. Blood still pulsed from his eyes and depressed skull. His left hand shook, still holding the small knife he had drawn. They had not even bothered to disarm him.

The clicking stopped and the creature squatting beside her suddenly reached out, forced both arms above her head with one hand and squeezed her breasts with the other. She cried out, cursing herself for showing the pain. It blinked at her, mouth working as if chewing the air. Then it bent low and sniffed at her chest, stomach and groin. She struggled, trying to kick out, but it had already let go and moved back. It clicked a few times, staring at her for a beat more before turning around.

One of the other things was performing the same strange examination on Rhiana. She spat and cursed, kicked and writhed, but the thing merely flicked her flapping arm and she screamed and fainted away again.

None of them examined Beko.

Each of the creatures picked up one of the surviving explorers, slung them over a shoulder and started walking.

❋   ❋   ❋

Their captors did not tire. They marched northward, their long legs covering the ground faster than a human could run. If Nomi turned left, she could see Beko, bouncing on the shoulder of the thing carrying him, dripping blood. The other way, and Rhiana hissed and groaned as her dislocated and snapped arm banged against her bearer's back.

It was not long before Nomi could see the blankness of cloud cover beyond the edge of the Great Divide.

The things paused then, and the one carrying Beko dropped him heavily to the ground, cupped its hands around its mouth, and bellowed. Nomi cringed against the noise.

'Beko,' she said, and the creature holding her pinched her leg so hard that she felt the skin rip. She bit her lower lip, breaking the skin there as well but holding in her scream.

She looked at Rhiana. The battered Serian was staring at her, and her expression was shocking, because it lacked any trace of hope. Nomi wondered whether she looked the same. She shook her head, but Rhiana closed her eyes.

A call came from the distance and their three captors clicked and clacked. One of them coughed what could have been a chuckle, and Nomi's fear was suddenly heightened. These were far more than the wild things she had taken them for.

She heard something approaching from the distance. When she saw movement, she was confused to begin with, but then the clicking sounds came in closer, and scores of the things were pouring over a small hill to the east. They spread out and advanced, and as they came she viewed them upside down. They were similarly attired as her captors and wore their hair in the same manner.

What is this? she thought. *A sacrifice? A meal?*

'Rhiana,' she said, 'we can't just let this—' The thing squeezed her leg again, fingers sliding into the gash it had already made. Nomi screamed. 'Piss on you, shit on you, fuck fuck fuck! Rhiana, we can't just be still and quit!' The thing moved its hand up her leg to the knee and started squeezing there, but one of its companions clicked quietly and it stopped.

The other creatures arrived and formed a rough half-circle about the captives. There were fifty of them, maybe more. They seemed excited, fidgeting and shouldering each other out of the way, but then they fell silent, eyes darting from one prisoner to the next.

Beko groaned. The thing picked him up again, holding him before it like a babe in arms. It muttered that strange language, and coughs of laughter rumbled through the crowd.

Then it started walking towards the cliff.

'No,' Nomi said. The thing holding her turned to let her see. This time it seemed unconcerned at her talking. 'Beko!' she called. 'Beko, *fight*!' But all the fight had bled from him.

The creature reached the edge of the cliff and threw him. Hanging upside down, the grass above Nomi and the sky below, it looked as though he rose into the ground.

She did not scream or shout, rage or cry. It was useless. She closed her eyes and thought of Beko falling, and with every heartbeat she hoped that he was dead already. *Three miles,* they had said. *We climbed three miles.*

By the time they did the same to Rhiana, Nomi found it in herself to cry.

CHAPTER EIGHTEEN

With a whole new world before him, Ramus could only rest. His muscles would allow little else. His body betrayed him, and when he closed his eyes he felt a moment of vertigo, so profound that he thought he'd walked through his exhaustion and tumbled back over the cliff. When he opened his eyes again he was spreadeagled on his front, hands grabbing on to the world.

Something eased the pain. It was inside his head, separate from the illness, and bleeding its agony. Perhaps it was simply elation.

Lulah sat beside him. She was looking away, and he saw several small flies crawling in her beaded hair. He waved at them and she turned, glaring. The stud in her eyepatch caught the sun.

'We made it,' he said.

Lulah nodded, her expression softening. 'You look ready to drop dead.'

'You don't look much better.'

She began massaging the muscles in his calves and thighs as she scanned their surroundings. 'We should find somewhere more sheltered to rest,' she said. 'We're high, the air's thin. Hopefully we'll adjust.'

'Rest? No rest. Get me on my feet.'

'Ramus—'

'I need to see,' he said. 'Just a little, maybe. But I need to walk. This is a new place, Lulah. Somewhere unknown. Do you know what that means to a Voyager?'

She actually looked a little hurt. 'Of course I do.'

Ramus nodded and held out his hand. Lulah helped him up, and she was still holding his arm as they walked away from the cliff.

Didn't you guide me here? Ramus thought. *Isn't this the place you wanted me to climb?* But as ever, his silent entreaties went unanswered.

They walked south, and to begin with Ramus thought they could reach the edge of the plateau and see the other side. But as the breeze grew stronger and whisked away the haze, he saw the first signs of wooded slopes far to the south. This was more than a narrow ridge or a plateau.

His initial idea that he would have to collapse and rest before moving on soon evaporated. His muscles burnt, but walking prevented them from cramping. It felt good being able to move without worrying about the wind sweeping him from the cliff face, fingers failing or ledges crumbling beneath his weight. Below him now was the solid immensity of this new place, not the astounding nothingness of the drop.

There were trees and plants he did not know, insects and birds that defied categorising, and by the time they'd walked a mile in from the cliff, Ramus was convinced that this was a place totally separate from Noreela. For all he knew, it went on for hundreds of miles to the south, and if he kept walking he might find new civilisations and societies, all believing that they existed alone, and all existing with the same introverted outlook as the majority of Noreelans.

What will this do? he wondered. *This could change everything.*

But much as there was plenty to explore, there was only one thing he had come up here to find.

Didn't you guide me here? he thought, again and again. He issued pleas to the Sleeping God, inviting it into his mind, but its only response was silence.

'Maybe it's dead,' Ramus muttered, and Lulah turned from where she had walked on ahead.

'No,' she said, misunderstanding. 'The whole place is alive. Look!' She pointed at several huge butterflies that had lifted off a hundred steps away, their wings easily as wide as a man's reach, bodies thick as an arm. Lines of bright yellow ants marched past Ramus's feet, a beetle the size of his thumb fought with several tiny serpents, and something scurried through the undergrowth, squealing and whistling as it disappeared.

And then in the distance he saw the first square edge, a corner of stone peering above a slight rise in the ground. 'There,' he said pointing. 'There...' His voice failed him, and he was not sure whether it was the altitude or shock that took it away.

From the top of the slope, it was obvious that this place was dead.

It had once been a large settlement, and even from his slightly elevated position, Ramus could not make out its extremes. No building was more than a single storey high. They were built mostly of carved square stones, though he could see the remains of a few timber buildings intermingled here and there. Roofs had rotted and fallen in, walls had collapsed, and plants obviously held dominion here once more. Walls were covered in swathes of a small-leafed creeper, its stems twisting between stones and forcing cracks through walls. Taller shrubs and trees grew around the village, many of them erupting through buildings, pushing down walls, and taking the homes for themselves.

'Too late,' Lulah said, but too late for what she did not say.

'This doesn't look that old,' Ramus said. 'There are places like this in Cantrassa, abandoned when the farming land grew sterile. Maybe whoever was here moved on.'

'Maybe.' Lulah walked down the slope, shrugging the bow from her shoulder. She did not walk like someone who had recently climbed a three-mile cliff.

Ramus followed. He was very conscious of the roll of parchment pages in his backpack, the figures and writing displayed there, and what that writing could do. He scanned the abandoned streets for signs of people, but there was nothing.

Animals lived in the village, and they seemed unconcerned by the new visitors. Birds continued to sing, ground-dwellers called and barked, and even as Lulah and Ramus approached the first building, there did not seem to be a hint of panic in the sounds.

'Wait here,' Lulah said. She strung an arrow and walked slowly into the village. Grasses swished about her legs, creeping plants tried to trip her, but she stepped lightly and never took her eyes from the buildings. Ramus noticed for the first time just how tall the main doorways into the buildings were.

He waited nervously. This place was no longer lived in, but that did not mean there was no one or nothing here. Perhaps they were being watched even now.

Lulah drew level with the first building. She paused there for a long time, like a person turned to stone. Then she glanced over her shoulder and nodded to Ramus.

By the time he joined her, she had moved to the front wall of the first building and was peering inside through an opening in the wall. If there had ever been a window shutter of some sort, it had long since vanished. Ramus looked in as well. The ceiling was holed, and it let in enough light for them to see one wall swathed in metal pipes. They were as thick as a finger and curved around each other, tied into junctions here and there that reminded Ramus of the rope charm he had bought for Nomi. Most of them were rusted, and a couple had ruptured and spewed blood-coloured dust down the wall.

'Dead place,' Lulah said.

Ramus did not like her choice of words, but they felt right. Part of the building's roof lay in a tangle of timber beams and rotten thatch. Any furnishings had vanished, and the floor was carpeted in a mass of creeping plants. If he went inside the undergrowth would reach his knees at least, and he was not sure he could fight his way through. There was no sign of any decoration, no carvings on the walls. Only those pipes.

'What do you think they were for?' he asked.

Lulah shrugged as she stepped back. 'More there,' she said, pointing up. There were pipes passing across the spaces between buildings as well, many of them bowed over time. Others were propped and remained a dozen steps up, way out of reach. Spaced along the pipes were small boxy structures, with spiked wheels the size of a human hand attached to them.

'That one looks different.' Lulah headed deeper into the village, past several more ruined buildings to one that was wider and slightly taller, and Ramus followed. The structure retained a heavy pair of doors, though they hung askew and their bottoms were shredded by rot.

What are we looking for? Ramus thought. He would give anything just for a sign.

When they came to the larger building, Lulah again went first. There were several steps leading up to the main doors, their dulled edge hidden by plant growth but obvious nonetheless. They looked too tall to Ramus, but perhaps that was an illusion.

Lulah peered inside, then shouldered one door aside and entered. Ramus lost sight of her. He waited nervously, looking around, watching for any movements that should not be there, any shadows lurking beside buildings. There was nothing, and yet he felt watched.

'Here,' Lulah said from the doorway. She did not look concerned, yet there was a strange expression on her face.

'What?'

'See.' She disappeared back inside and Ramus entered the building.

Perhaps it had once been a place of worship. It had that air, that almost reverential way in which walls met and windows glared. Even below the carpet of plants, Ramus could see a row of stone seats, all facing toward the back wall of the building which was curtained with a bright red-flowering plant. The other walls were somehow bare of plant growth, and on closer inspection he knew why. There were shapes carved into their surfaces, and these seemed sharper and more recent. He squinted against sunlight leaking in through the shattered roof, and then he made out what one spread of shapes went to make up: a face. It was long, bearded, and the eyes were stained black, but it was definitely a human visage. He looked around the walls and saw other places where this face was carved or scraped – a mix of large and small images. All of them seemed to represent the same person. Black eyes, heavy beard, mournful mouth. The representations were not expertly drawn, but Ramus had the sudden, chilling idea that he knew this person.

He blinked slowly and shook his head.

'What is it?' Lulah asked.

'Strange face.'

'Looks human to me.'

'I'm sure he is.' Ramus looked again, trying to ally the face with a memory, but nothing came. *Of course not,* he thought. *We're the first here.* But that suddenly seemed less than certain.

Lulah walked between the stone seats and approached the spray of red flowers. As she touched one thick stem and lifted it aside, a swarm of flies erupted from the plants, weaving and flexing through the air like one organism. They circled Lulah's head without landing, then came to Ramus. He felt the breeze of thousands of wings, but not one of them touched his skin. When they exited the open roof he could not shake the sense that he had been examined.

'Here,' Lulah said. 'This one's *definitely* not human.' She lifted aside some of the heavy stems to reveal an intricate design on the wall, colours still vivid, shape stark.

Ramus caught his breath. *There it is.* It was more a series of diverse shapes than a single discernible form, but he knew straight away what it was meant to represent. The swirls and curves, the spirals and twists, as though illustrating limbs curled in on themselves, back twisted around a sleeping form. An endlessly sleeping form.

He saw the stumps of wings, and thought, *Fallen,* but a throb of pain behind his eyes drove that idea down.

'Your god,' Lulah said quietly.

Ramus glanced at her, but he did not see the disrespect he heard. Maybe it had been fear. Her eye was wide, and her dark skin seemed to have paled.

'That's it,' Ramus said. 'But...'

'But where are its worshippers? My thoughts exactly.' She let the plants fall back into place, wiping her hands as if to rid them of something distasteful. 'Maybe it's already woken up.'

'No,' Ramus said. But it was a plea more than a statement.

'Shall we move on?' Lulah said.

'I don't know,' Ramus said. 'I'm not sure I can. Not now, not if I'm here too late. A whole new world, yes, but if that Sleeping God is awake...'

But he realised that if it *was* awake, then they had nothing to fear. This place had been abandoned for a long time, and whoever had once worshipped here was long gone. Perhaps the god had also vanished.

'I don't like the thought of resting here,' the Serian said.

'South,' Ramus said. 'Maybe it went that way.'

Lulah shrugged because she had nothing to say.

'Deeper into exile,' he continued. 'Fallen...' He felt the pain behind his eyes readying again, threatening like a raised fist, and that presence in his head seemed to expand larger than was possible.

'Come on,' Lulah said. 'We'll go through the village and camp on its outskirts. I want to spend tonight on open ground, where we can see anything closing in.'

They went back out into the ruined settlement, moving from building to building and pausing only if they saw something new. The structures were basic but remarkable, lined and joined as they were with sprays of pipes and tubes, metal junctions and thicker columns that entered the ground at regular intervals. Lulah tried to shake one such column, but it did not budge. To be so solid, it must have been buried deep.

Toward the centre of the village, they found a small square. Unlike the buildings, it was not clogged with rampant plant growth, but there was a patch of trees that seemed to wave and lean even though there was no breeze. Mist hung around their roots, and when they drew closer, Ramus saw several small holes in the hard ground from which steam issued in short, weak puffs. Whatever forces existed beneath and between the trees' root systems set them shifting with power.

Lulah went close to one of the steam holes, knelt down and reached out with her sword. Moisture beaded on the blade and she drew back quickly. 'Hot,' she said.

'Nomi should feel at home here,' Ramus said. 'If they even made it up.' He saw Lulah's face darken at that, and he almost apologised. They were her friends he was talking about, after all.

'They'll have made it,' Lulah said. 'We should move on.' She sheathed her sword and walked away from the gently moving trees.

They saw more likenesses of the bearded man, though not

every carving or etching was the same. When formed in rock, many of the images had weathered, showing that they had been there for some time. Those formed in wood – plaques on the sides of ruined buildings, carved into the trunks of trees – the elements had aged, drying the timber until some images were split in many places. In some of the older impressions, he seemed unbearded, leaner, as though they followed his years.

'I know that face,' Ramus said.

Lulah shook her head. 'If it's a god of theirs, I doubt that.'

'Is it a god?' Ramus asked. 'We saw what they worshipped. And I hope it still sleeps. But this…? Him…?'

Most of the buildings they saw were open, with doors missing, roofs caved in and windows absent or almost decayed to nothing. But as they came within sight of the far edge of the village – there were woods beyond, over a bridge crossing a small stream – they saw a building that seemed relatively intact. The door was off its hinges but leant against its frame, allowing only a small gap for animal and plant ingress. The thatched roof was heavily bowed but whole, and the windows had been covered with rough boards nailed across from the outside.

Ramus could not resist the mystery of such a place.

'We should go,' Lulah said. 'We need to find a place to rest for the night. You're exhausted, Ramus, I can see it in your eyes. And your illness…'

Ramus nodded, but then looked at the small building again. 'One more look,' he said.

That face, he thought. *By all the gods, I know that face, and the next time I see it carved or formed somewhere, I'll stare until I give it a name.*

They approached the leaning door and Lulah lifted it to one

side. It fell with a crash and Ramus held his breath, glancing around the village. They had come all the way through without seeing anything larger than a small bird, yet still he felt as though they were intruding somewhere sacred.

'After you,' Lulah said. She pointed at the doorway and Ramus entered.

It was not as dark as he had expected. A window in the far wall had been stripped of boards, and the blank opening let in a stream of light. The inside comprised of one large space, and it was a landscape of humped shapes, all of them covered with a thick layer of moss. Plants grew here and there, but they were the wide-leafed, short-stemmed plants of dark places.

Ramus reached out for the first bulky shape, scraped moss from its surface and leant over to see what was revealed. It was a large wooden box, about the size of the coffins some of the Cantrassan peoples used to bury their dead. He wondered whether they would at last see the builders of this place, or at least their time-withered remains.

'What's in there?' Lulah asked.

'Put your sword to the lid and we'll see.'

Lulah probed beneath the lid with her blade and heaved. It came off with a screech of metal leaving wood, and flipped over onto another box.

A cloud of dust wafted from within, and Ramus gasped. He knew that smell, that texture to his mouth and nose, because he worked with this so much. Old parchment.

'Let the light in,' Ramus said, and Lulah stepped aside.

The box was filled with rolls of parchment. Forty or fifty of them, neatly stacked side by side. A few at one end of the box were slumped into a decayed mess where moisture had penetrated, but the others were still strong and whole. Ramus

reached out and touched one, almost afraid that it was some
sort of hallucination brought on by his illness. *Is Nomi seeing
this right now,* he wondered, *and I'm just dreaming it?* But the
parchment was rough, dry and brittle beneath his touch, and
when he brought his hand to his face he smelt the scent of
ages.

'Three pages,' he sighed. 'Three pages brought us so far.
And now, look. Look at this.' He lifted out one roll and knelt,
turning into the light from the open doorway. He unrolled
carefully, wincing as he heard the crackle of the outer page
splitting, but the inner sheets seemed to unfurl with little
complaint.

'What does it say?' Lulah asked sharply. 'What's it about?'

Ramus did not know. Some of the language he could
recognise from the pages in his backpack, but much of what
was symbolised there was a mystery to him. And that made
him smile.

'I don't know,' he said. 'Perhaps it's the history of a new
world.'

'A new world that died,' Lulah said. She leant over the box
and looked inside, sniffing lightly at the dusty, age-rich scent.

'Maybe,' Ramus said. 'But like I said, there are ruined
places in Noreela as well. People move on.'

'Usually for a reason.'

A reason, Ramus thought, and he scanned the page before
him for anything that could represent a Sleeping God. There
was nothing immediately evident, and he lifted that sheet to
see the one beneath.

'We should go,' Lulah said.

'But—'

'You'll have time to read your books, but not before we

know this place is safe. We have no idea—'

The sound came from far away but it was different from any they had heard before. A clicking, throaty noise, obviously made by something larger.

Lulah glanced at Ramus then went for the door, low and quiet. She pressed herself to the wall and scanned the street outside.

Ramus let go of the parchment and it rolled back into its original shape. *So much here,* he thought, but looking at Lulah tensed by the door, braided hair swinging gently as she squatted there tense and ready, he knew that she was right. There was much to see and know, but safety must be their first concern.

If the Sleeping God really was close, perhaps here he would find directions for how and where to find it. Or perhaps it had been found already.

The noise came again, this time from further away. Lulah backed away from the door until she was beside Ramus.

'I can't see anything,' she said. 'But I thought I heard something big moving through the village.'

'How big?'

She looked at him, her one eye twinkling. 'How should I know?'

Ramus picked up the parchment and held it to his chest. Lulah glanced at it then away again, and when she returned to the door, he followed.

They waited for a while and, when the noise did not return, Lulah led the way out into the street once more. Ramus helped her lean the door back against the doorway, to protect what lay inside as much as to leave things as they had found them. Then they headed cautiously south, and within a hundred steps they reached the stream. The timber bridge was strong, though the decking had rotted through here and there, and as they left the village behind Ramus felt a sense of relief.

There was a whole new civilisation here! The implications on Noreela were only just impressing themselves upon Ramus, feeling their way through his shock and tiredness, and his fear for what may be sleeping. *Another reason to never go back,* he thought.

The carved human face glared at him from the wall of the final building, and he wondered whether the decision to reveal or hide what they had found – and may yet find – was even his to make.

Beyond the village there was a path leading into the forest. Lulah said it could have been an animal trail, but her nervousness was obvious as they followed it in between the trees.

They found the first stone man a mile south of the village. From a distance it looked like a natural rock formation beside the path, but as they drew closer Ramus made out the features that could not hide what this was. His right arm had broken off, the break smoothed over time, and his solid face had been assaulted by the weather so that the features were blurred and indistinct. But it was obviously a man upon whom those words Ramus knew had been used, because around his feet they found the remnants of clothing, a rusted knife and a charm on a cracked leather thong.

Ramus picked up the charm, his eyes never leaving the man's vague face.

Lulah stood back, eye wide and hand closed around the handle of her sword. 'Is this what Konrad became?' she said.

Ramus felt the dead Serian's fingers hanging against his

chest, a guilty weight. 'Maybe,' he said. 'They're words I learnt, but I don't really know how to wield them.'

'Someone here does.'

Ramus turned from the petrified man, weighing the charm in his hand. It was a piece of hardwood, hewn into a horn or tusk and holed through the heavy end for the leather cord. Words had been carved into it, but he could not make them out. He was not even sure whether he knew the language. But he knew the intent.

'This is Noreelan,' he said, and his heart sank as he vocalised his thoughts. 'I've seen charms like this for sale in Long Marrakash, imported from Pengulfin Landing. Carved from the wood of the wellburr tree, because it's the hardest wood they have. Heavy.' He could not stop staring at the charm. *Someone was here before us,* he thought. *And if one, perhaps many. What's the chance of us coming across the only other person who has ever climbed the cliff?*

'Those bodies we saw,' Lulah said. 'On the way up. Maybe they didn't fall at all. Maybe they were thrown.'

Ramus looked up at her without really understanding what she was saying. His mind was on the Sleeping God, and if that meant the god knew how close he was and what he was thinking, so be it. *Fallen,* he thought, ignoring the throb of pain behind his eyes. *If you fell, how far up do you have to rise?* And now that he knew others had been here before him, it was not the fact that discovery no longer tasted so sweet that troubled him so much. It was the god, and only the god.

But Ramus's fascination was wearing down his caution. Always something more to discover, something more to explore...and he remembered the warning on the first page of his journal: *Never wake the fallen.*

The agony punched at him then, a pain like he had never felt before pulsing in his head and driving him to the ground. He passed out before he struck.

His whole being is restrained by something, hanging above a vast abyss, crushed beneath an uncompromising sky, harried all around by dangers he cannot see, feel or smell but which he senses with every nerve ending, every fibre of his dying body. He is no longer awake, yet he is aware of death more than he ever has been before. *Am I really seeing this from Nomi?* he thinks, and he tries to open his eyes. All he can see is a blur. It could be blinding light or crushing darkness, he cannot tell. He is not falling, but he knows that he is no longer in Noreela...and suddenly he feels a breeze on his skin and other things there, touching and probing. Still his vision is a blank but he begins to smell, something animal and raw, and he can hear a clicking noise that sounds so much like communication.

He will never get used to living Nomi's nightmares. But whereas before they had given him some measure of sick satisfaction, now he is as terrified as her.

For a while, after seeing them kill Noon and throw Beko and Rhiana from the edge of the cliff, Nomi went away. It was easy to do. She was exhausted from the climb, both physically and mentally, and closing her eyes seemed to give that exhaustion free reign to work over her body and through her thoughts. Her muscles relaxed, burning but no longer cramping with resentment at what she had put them through. Her hands were cool, fingertips boiling points of pain at the ends of sore digits. The wound on her leg where the thing had dug in its fingers was agony. Her bladder relaxed and she pissed, but as the warmth turned to cold in the strengthening breeze, she did not care.

She tried to project herself out and down, away from the awful place they had climbed into and back to the Noreela she was only just starting to know. But attempting that was no escape, because way below were broken bodies, one of whom she had perhaps loved. So she went inward instead of without, and deep inside there were many matters to settle. She briefly met Timal, but that innocent, beautiful young man was no part of what her life had become. He did not have the eyes to face reality, and Nomi could find nothing to say to him. He faded and Ramus was there, holding his head and accusing Nomi with his glare. *I'm sorry,* she said, but even the horrible illness she had passed on to him seemed irrelevant. *The scheme of things,* she thought, and the Ramus she dreamt of lowered his hand, smiled and nodded, understanding that there was far too much between them to let momentary weaknesses drive them apart.

She thought of Beko, but it was the sight of his shattered body that answered. His memory would come back to her, she knew. If she survived this, which was doubtful, she would think of him again.

Nomi stayed away for as long as she could, but she did not know how long that was.

When they started prodding her stomach and between her legs, she came back.

'Piss on you!' she hissed. The thing stood back and looked up at her. Then it crackled something low in its throat and turned away.

There were maybe a dozen of the tall creatures before her.

They sat in pairs or alone, intermittent growls and clicks the only sign of their communication. They seemed confused and sometimes amazed, as though revelation after revelation were coming to them.

'Why don't you throw me, too?' she shouted. 'I'm tired of hanging around.' They'd tied her to a rough wooden frame, its four corners buried in the ground and various cross posts supporting her feet, behind and shoulders. Her arms were stretched to either side and tied tightly, as were her legs. She could hardly move. *Hanging here waiting to die,* she thought, and she giggled.

The cliff was maybe twenty steps behind her.

Nomi felt wretched and alone, and she could not hold down the terror. It was selfish, and painful, but fear of what was to come sickened her.

Another of the things stood and strode across to her, scratching at her chest through shirt and jacket. It came closer, sniffing, and she jerked her body, hoping to strike it in the face. But it was too fast, backing just beyond her reach.

Its hand darted forward and touched her stomach, and when she struggled again it turned around and stalked back to its resting place.

What are they doing? Nomi had no idea why she was still alive while all the others were dead. The things had been vicious and merciless in their attack, and their execution of Beko and Rhiana. Why keep her? Why tie her up here like this? When she looked around at the wooden frame she could see that it was not new. Grass grew long around the feet, and a variety of plants sprouted beneath her where birds had roosted and shit out seeds.

Whatever the reason, it could not be good.

At that moment, as if from nowhere, a face leapt out at Nomi from the hallowed halls of the Guild of Voyagers. A memory that confused her for a beat because she did not know why it had manifested here, and now. But then she understood. The face was that of Sordon Perlenni, the First Voyager who had disappeared over a hundred and thirty years before.

It was his face that graced the wooden statue.

Oh, by all the gods, Nomi thought, *Sordon Perlenni, what did you do?*

Another creature appeared, carrying a cloth bag slung from one elbow and a broken jug in the other hand. It came straight to Nomi and offered the jug up to her mouth. She looked into it suspiciously for a beat, smelt only water, and then decided that little mattered anyway. If they chose to poison her now, so be it. She drank, swallowing the water and almost groaning at the fresh taste.

The thing pulled the jug away and opened the bag.

'You expect me to eat that?' she said, a laugh slipping into a sob. It held a small dead creature in its hand. Its flesh was purple and red – evidently recently skinned – and its head and limbs had been torn off. Try as she might Nomi could not identify it, but perhaps that was a blessing.

The creature pressed the skinned corpse against Nomi's mouth. She pursed her lips and clamped her jaw shut, trying to turn her head. But it grasped her chin in its other hand, forcing her to face forward while it worked the meat against her lips. She tasted its blood, rich and basic. She could smell it, and she could not prevent her stomach from rumbling, hunger rearing its head. She found it hard to breathe.

No one was coming to help her. She knew that, but the

realisation suddenly hit her hard. The Serians had been guarding her all the way from Long Marrakash. Konrad had died doing her bidding, Ramin was killed protecting her and now the others were dead as well, and their deaths made everything pointless.

When Nomi opened her mouth to gasp in a breath, the creature pressed the meat between her teeth. She bit down, groaning as she did so, shaking her head to tear a small chunk of raw flesh away.

The thing stepped back. It watched her, eyes never wavering. She could see no hint of emotion anywhere in its expression. Its face was as blank as a sheebok's, and that was what disturbed her most about these things. It was not the long legs and arms, the spindly necks or the scraps of clothes they wore. It was the lifelessness in such human eyes.

She started chewing. The thing clicked and growled, and a few of the other observers did the same. They seemed pleased.

The meat did not taste too bad, and Nomi swallowed quickly. Her feeder came forward again. *The quicker I eat, the quicker this is over,* she thought.

She closed her eyes and bit, trying to find her way inward once again.

The sun went down and she could not sleep. They had left her clothed, but the garments were scant protection against the cool breeze that came from the east. She only hoped it did not turn into a gale. If they really were three miles above Noreela, she could freeze to death should the weather decide to roar.

Two creatures remained close by. They sat motionless thirty steps from her, one of them nodding its head and seeming to doze. She supposed they were guarding her, though the idea of escape seemed very foolish right now. The idea of dying, however...that felt like her future.

When night established itself fully and she heard things calling in the dark, she thought perhaps they had been left behind to protect her.

She dozed between gusts of wind, tensing and relaxing her muscles to try and encourage some warmth into her limbs. Her shoulders and shins hurt more than the rest of her, because even though she was tied to the frame still they took some of her weight. She wondered how long she could survive up here. She was not sure how long she *wanted* to survive.

When the shape emerged from the darkness, she thought she was dreaming. It started as a shadow shifting against shadows, no secrecy in its movements, and nothing particularly threatening. Nomi squinted, looking to the left and right of the shape, but she could see no more.

There was little against which she could judge, but she was sure it was no taller than her. *Beko!* she thought, but that was a foolish idea. That was tiredness talking, and a nightmare awaiting her in true sleep.

'Ramus?' she said. Her guardians looked up but did not respond.

The shadow moved closer. Its pace was slow, as if its owner bore wounds.

One of the things sat up abruptly and turned around, but when it saw the shape it uttered a few clicks and slouched back down.

One of them, she thought. *That's all. One of them come to poke and prod at me some more. Or maybe it's a child of theirs, come to mock this new pet.*

As the shape passed the seated guards and came close, Nomi saw that it was a man. For a beat the truth did not register, *could* not, because it was too incredible. And when at last the man stood before her, Nomi stared down in wonder.

He opened his mouth and uttered a series of clicks, similar to the things that had captured her. It sounded awkward coming from his mouth.

It's him, Nomi thought, and perhaps this was still a dream.

'Who…is…Ramus?' the man asked. His voice grated with lack of use.

'It's you,' Nomi said. 'Sordon Perlenni.'

The old man's eyes went wide. His beard was long and white, his hair matched, and his melancholia was as heavy as the land beneath them, as dark as the shadows. 'That is an old, old name,' he said.

Nomi shook her head. 'Sleeping,' she said. 'Dreaming. Nightmare.'

'Soon,' the First Voyager said, and his voice carried more sadness than she could bear. Asleep or not, Nomi Hyden began to cry.

They did not seem to mind when the old man sat on the timber frame beside her. He sighed as he settled, leaning his tall walking stick beside him.

'Tears,' he said. 'I shed so many when I came here. None for a long time. None for…many years.'

'Your voice,' Nomi said.

Sordon nodded. 'Rarely used. Forgive my hoarseness.' He did not look at her as he spoke, as though afraid to show her something, or to see something reflected in her eyes.

'They'll just let you sit here with me?'

'The Sentinels? Of course.'

'Sentinels...' Nomi said. 'Guarding the Sleeping God?'

Sordon glanced at her, then away one more. *I surprised him,* she thought. *He didn't think I'd know, and...he's Sordon Perlenni! He shouldn't even be here, he should be dead. He's almost two hundred years old!*

'You should be—'

'Are you a Voyager?' he asked.

'Yes. You don't see the band on my arm?'

He looked but seemed confused. 'Band?'

'Guild of Voyagers,' Nomi said.

Sordon smiled behind his heavy beard. 'So, they have a guild now.'

'You're the first,' Nomi said. 'You started the Age of Expansion. You should be dead! Maybe *I* am.'

'No,' he said. 'You're not.' He shook his head sadly. 'I'm sorry about your friends.'

'How do you know?'

'The Sentinels told me.'

'Told you? Why? You walk among them, you talk to them, but...?' Nomi realised she had so many questions that she could not find a place to begin. She felt tears threatening again but she swallowed them down. 'Will you release me?' she asked.

Sordon looked directly at her for the first time. He glanced at the ropes binding her arms and legs, and she thought he looked briefly at her stomach. 'No,' he said.

'What are they going to do to me?'

'When your child has grown, they'll tear it from you and hang it from a foetus tree.'

'Child?' Nomi shook her head and closed her eyes, and the tears came then whether she fought them or not. 'I'm not pregnant.'

Sordon sighed. 'If you weren't, you'd be at the bottom of the Divide with your friends.'

'Sordon...'

'You cry,' he said. 'You rage. And when you've finished, I'll ask you once again who Ramus is. And then I'll tell you how I doomed this world.'

'He fell,' Nomi said. 'He was a Voyager as well, my friend, and he fell. One of those bird things knocked him from the cliff and his rope didn't hold.'

'You thought *I* was Ramus.'

'I thought I was dreaming.' Nomi's head was dipped and she looked down at her feet, not trusting her lying eyes. She guessed by his silence that he did not believe her, but she was not about to tell him the truth. Not yet. Not until he did the same for her.

He suddenly moved in close until she felt his old breath against her ear. 'It cannot be woken,' he said. 'It's fallen, and if it rises again... I will not permit it. And though the Sentinels are vastly weaker than they were before I came, they will not allow it either.'

'Fallen?'

'The Sleeping God fell. It went mad, rampaged, and the other gods fought to put it down. And it *cannot be woken.*'

'I'm the last of my group,' Nomi said, shocked, confused. 'Not much chance of me fighting my way from here to wake it, I think.' And at the same time she thought, *Does Ramus know? Did he know all along?*

'Maybe,' Sordon said. 'Maybe you are the last one.' But suspicion was obvious in his voice.

'So tell me,' she said.

Sordon Perlenni chuckled. 'Guild of Voyagers,' he said. 'Do they have their own building?'

'Yes. A big one.'

'And is my likeness hanging there?'

Nomi nodded. 'It's how I knew who you were, when I saw the statue of you.'

'The statue,' Sordon said. 'Which one? There are many. So many that I've never bothered to count. Statues and pictures, carvings and paintings. Of me.'

'Why?'

'To those discovered, the discoverer is sometimes a god.'

'But they're animals. They look human in some ways, but they seem wild.'

'They are, now. But not always.' Sordon shook his head again. 'What's the point? I could tell you, but nothing can absolve my guilt. And you, hanging there, can do little to help me.'

'Then cut me down!'

Sordon shook his head again. 'They would be upon you before you hit the ground. They're fast and strong, and more intelligent than you think. They used to be so much better, until I came.'

'Tell me anyway,' she said. *Whatever I can learn could help me,* she thought. *Any details, any clues as to how I could escape.* Because now that Sordon was here and she knew that Ramus had not yet been caught, she suddenly found determination again, and a survival instinct that had been made lazy by being looked after. She wanted to live.

Sordon Perlenni, the First Voyager of Noreela, settled back against the timber cross bracings of Nomi's sacrificial rack and looked up at the star-speckled sky.

❋   ❋   ❋

'I had been to the Divide before, when I was thirty, twelve years into my exploring. My porters were strong and determined, there was plenty of food and water, and we had not encountered any marauders for a hundred miles. So we kept riding. And when we saw the Divide in the distance we stopped, turned around and fled. Such a massive barrier. So final. My porters were scared – they were from the south of Cantrassa, a wild place then as now, I suspect – and they had their myths, gods and superstitions.   They believed that if we ventured too close to the Great Divide, it would fall and swallow us up, and then rise again that much higher. One of them believed it was built from the wraiths of all those who had died in Noreela's history, and that it was forever striving to grow.

'For me, I feared it was the end. If I continued walking south I would go as far as I could go, and that would be all of Noreela for me. Not that I'd seen all of it. No one can see all of Noreela, and that I'm still confident of, even now. There's more to the land than simply seeing, and travelling, and more to know than can be learnt in a hundred lifetimes. But I was still young then, and as well as the fear there was an idea that perhaps I could save it for later.

'So over the following years I explored the land, east to the sea, west to the sea and much of what lay in between. But as time passed, the Divide called to me, luring me back into its shadow. And at last, alone, I heeded the call.

'After a year studying many books back in Long Marrakash, I came down here with the idea that it may not be the end, but the beginning. If each wraith taken into the Divide made it grow, then it must have limits. I didn't believe that it was built on the deaths of Noreela, of course, but such thinking helped me come to a decision: that I *must* climb. And climb I did, without equipment, without weapons, with no idea of how far I would be climbing or what I'd meet on the way.'

'You came alone?' Nomi said in wonder. 'No ropes?'

'I had my shoes,' Sordon said. 'Good grip. And I had gloves that preserved my fingertips, and a belt looped three times around my waist, that I used on several occasions to tie myself around a suitable rock. I don't need to tell you about the difficulties of the climb, I'm sure. Or the things that inhabit the cliffs.'

Nomi nodded.

'I climbed in almost the same place as you. That was the silent influence of the Fallen God, though back then I did not know its nature or form. And when I reached the top and stood here in amazement, the Sentinels emerged from their settlements and converged on me. This was a very different place back then, and the Sentinels were very different as well. They looked much the same as they do now – a strange race, for sure – but they were far more...civilised.

'Word spread, and more Sentinels came from all along the Divide. I was nervous but not afraid, because they exuded an air of wonder. They were *amazed*. It was obvious to me then that I was the first to reach the top of the Divide, though perhaps not the first to try.' He looked into the distance, as though the past still existed there. 'You know, there were tens of thousands of them back then, their society as diverse as Noreela's. They walked tall and with grace, and were dressed in fine clothes, and carried their young in slings across their chests. They had art and writing, music and strange technologies I couldn't begin to understand, and still don't now. They worked with water and steam, air and fire, and they could do miraculous things. They taught their young to read. They could have taught us so much.'

'How could they change so quickly?' Nomi asked.

Sordon shook his head, sighing. 'They took me in. Fed me, gave me water, tended my aches and wounds. And then a shaman came, one of their spiritual leaders, and he collapsed at my feet. Perhaps it was intentional. Maybe he had it planned, but he passed out as though he were dead, and woke again after seven days. When he came to he seemed mad. I could hear him from my rooms, shouting and raging and crying, and they left me alone for a while as they cared for him.

'When they returned to me, it was with a reverence that hadn't been there before. The Sentinels that tended me were quiet and would not look me in the eye. They shivered and wept when they bathed me, and when I ate they would watch as though I were changing food into charms. I suppose I took advantage, and much as I wished to be up and about exploring this new world, my exhaustion held me down. I had broken toes on the climb without even noticing, and two of my ribs were cracked from a fall. So I soaked up their attentions and ate all the good food they brought. They brought drink as well, a fluid so light that it was almost a gas. I drank and breathed it at the same time and it gave me such dreams! They would be there when I emerged from sleep, kneeling around my bed with an expectant look on their faces. Whatever I said they would try to repeat, but their voices could not manage my language. However, I soon began to speak theirs.

'I should have realised I was becoming their god. I did

know, I think, though even now I can't be sure. I was vain and filled with self-importance, trying to imagine the glory I could take back to Noreela when I eventually left this place.' Sordon laughed, such a natural sound that it lifted Nomi's spirits for a moment.

'But you never left,' she said. 'And they changed.'

'Of course. Time went on, I practised their language and remained here to learn of their culture, their world. I was an explorer, after all.'

'You *are* an explorer.'

'No, I *was*. I'm not sure what I am now. A fool? Destroyer of worlds? Maybe. Certainly not a god. Nowhere near that.'

'And the Sleeping God?' Nomi asked.

'I told you, it's a fallen thing!' Sordon whispered. 'Curse it to oblivion, it's a foul thing that they were put here to guard.'

'Who put them here?'

'The Sleeping Gods, of course. It's a myth only to be found in the most obscure of texts, hidden in the darkest past, and the gods intended it that way. All the legends tell of their benevolence toward the land, but this one raged and rampaged and destroyed so much that they had made. They buried it up here. What stories there must be from that time! A time when gods walked the land! A time when they went to *war*! But they are stories none of us will ever know, because it was a time before Noreela. Perhaps before time itself. It was the gods' time to leave the land, and sleep in readiness for an occasion that might warrant their return. So they took Noreela's early tribes and brought them here, gave them language and knowledge and the will to learn, and left them with one simple purpose: protect the Fallen God and let no one or nothing near it. And in the Sentinels' minds back then as now, the prayer: *The sleeper cannot be woken.* That is their mantra and their meaning. Though they've lost their way, it is still central to their existence.'

'A Fallen God,' Nomi said. 'I can't imagine.'

'It's beyond imagining.' Sordon sighed. 'I know little more about them than you. Myths and legends, but we're so much closer up here.'

'How close?'

Sordon turned to look at her, his old eyes bearing the dreadful weight of his years. 'Who is Ramus?' he asked.

'Ramus is dead,' she whispered. But she feared that her thoughts revealed her.

A Sentinel came to them, gave Nomi a drink and bowed its head before Sordon. He took a drink and handed the jug back to the Sentinel, saying something in their strange tongue. The creature turned away before looking up.

'They'll not look me in the eye,' Sordon said. 'None of them talk to me anymore. I wander around, and sometimes they'll leave food and drink. Sometimes I have to find it myself. The only time they interact with me is if I go south. Two miles, three, once I think I even managed four miles before they came and turned me back.'

'Then that must be where the Fallen God sleeps!'

'No,' he said, but he glanced sidelong at Nomi and shook his head. 'I think there are dangers south of here, that's all. As I was once their god, they still find it in their mad hearts to protect me.'

'What sort of dangers?'

'I no longer care.' Sordon rose as if to leave.

'Wait! Don't leave, not now. Not yet.'

'I can't release you, Voyager.'

'You haven't even asked my name.'

He looked at her blankly for a beat, then offered what may have been a smile. 'And why would I wish to know your name?'

The question confused Nomi, and she could think of no reason. 'Sit with me,' she said. 'I want to hear more. I'm a Voyager, like you, and though I'm tied up here I can travel in my mind. I can *learn*.'

'Learn,' he said. 'You don't seem like the learning type.'

'Then why tell me?'

Sordon shrugged. 'Because you're here.' He started walking away.

When Nomi shouted after him, the Sentinels stood and approached, ignoring Sordon when they passed him, clicking and growling angrily. 'How did you ruin them?' she shouted. 'How did you change them so much?'

Sordon paused, Nomi fell silent and the Sentinels stopped, sitting slowly to the ground and staring up at her.

The old man leant on his walking stick and stared at her, his gaze travelling farther across the space beyond the cliffs. 'They made me a god when I rose up from the mythical lands of their past. But then reality intruded, as it must. I learnt their language and I told them far too much – where I was from, what it was like – and they realised what they had lost. Perhaps in a way, they believed that Noreela had been taken from them. I took their offerings, their women, and eventually they saw me for what I was: a mocker of their beliefs, a charlatan. And it drove them mad.' He trailed off, looking up at the sky as though he could see his sad reflection there. 'Oh, but even *my* ego is not that large. They had the seed of madness in them, ready to be fertilised, ready to grow. I was merely the catalyst.' Then he turned and walked away.

Nomi watched him leave, leaning heavily on his walking stick. She did not call to him again. He would be back, and he would tell her more.

Ramus, she thought, *you seek a Fallen God.* For once she wished that she would sleep and nightmare about such a thing, and then maybe Ramus would know.

Or perhaps he knew already.

Her friends were dead, Noreela's First Voyager had come to her, she was pregnant and she would be the Sentinels' prisoner until her baby was large enough for them to rip from her womb and hang from their foetus tree, for whatever twisted reasons they had. Cold and uncomfortable though she was, the sudden wretchedness of her existence encouraged Nomi into a deep, dark sleep.

She thought she was in a nightmare. Dawn burnt the eastern horizon, blazing across the clouds and singeing the horizon. The subtle warmth of the sun felt good on her chilled body, but it could not match the heat in her shoulders and hips. Waking seemed to allow the agony access to her mind, and it melted in and scorched away any dregs of dreams.

Nomi shifted left to right as far as she could, testing her bonds. There was very little give. She had pissed herself again, but there was no pride left to lose. She leant her head back and closed her eyes, craving sleep to take her away once more.

'They'll be here soon,' a voice said from behind her, and her first thought was, *Ramus!* But this time she did not speak his name. And when she heard the hoarseness of that voice she was glad.

'Come to tease me again?' she asked.

'Tease?' He sounded genuinely shocked. She heard the *tap tap* of his walking stick as he came around in front of the frame, and when he looked up at her, Sordon Perlenni's face was aghast. 'I don't tease. I would never tease. I'm talking to you, that's all, and I thought you *wanted* to know.'

Nomi began to laugh. It felt good. She let the laughter overrun her, then after a few beats it faded as quickly as it had come. 'What possible good can it do me?' she said. 'I'm stuck up here and they're going to kill me, eventually, so why the fuck do you think I really want to know anything?'

Sordon smiled. 'Well, I said you weren't the learning type. Even when I was starting my exploring, there were others around me whose interests were personal gain. Not knowledge. Not *discovery*.'

'You expect me to give a piss now?' Nomi said.

'Yes.' The word was quiet, but Sordon gave it such weight.

Nomi blinked and looked away toward the sunrise. *Ramus could be out there somewhere,* she thought. *I hope he is. And I hope he finds what he's looking for.*

'So tell me,' she said. And curse him, the old man was right. There was so much she still wanted to know, despite the fate that awaited her.

'What more do you want to know?' He sat in the grass before her, groaning as his old bones creaked and ground.

'So much,' Nomi said. 'But first, what do you mean by "they'll be here soon"?'

'You'll die if you keep hanging there. The Sentinels will come and take you somewhere safer.'

'Where?'

Sordon shrugged. 'I don't know. Perhaps where they keep

the Sentinel women when they fall pregnant.'

'They do this to themselves?'

Sordon sighed. 'Only since I arrived. As I told you, the focus of their worship passed across me for a while, but they found me wanting. The Sentinels were blessed by the Sleeping Gods, made pure, and my own impurities corrupted them. Such corruption sent them into a spiral that ended where you see them now. They returned to their one constant – the Fallen God, the doom hanging over them, which they called the Great Unborn. But their perception had been tainted. So now, in their eyes, if something is born it becomes unclean and corrupt, and that's why there are no young Sentinels anymore. They're wiping themselves out.'

Nomi closed her eyes, but she saw something bloody and slick being pierced, strung up and hung on that foetus tree. And it belonged to her. 'No,' she moaned, shaking her head against the wooden support behind her.

'Perhaps they've sought such release for generations,' Sordon said. 'I try to comfort myself with that idea – that they're not mad, but regressed to how they were when the Sleeping Gods gave them such responsibility. But it's no real comfort. What happened to them is my fault.'

'So throw yourself from the cliff!'

'I can't,' he said.

'How are you so old?'

'I don't know. Maybe the food they eat, the drinks they make. The steam from the ground…I don't know.'

Steam? Nomi wondered. But every time this old man spoke it made things worse, expanding her nightmare and driving her deeper into a despair she already believed had found its deepest parts. She wanted to hear no more. She hated him,

Noreela's First Voyager and one of its heroes, sitting before
her feeling sorry for himself yet refusing to cut her down. She
hated him.

'Go away,' she said.

'No.'

'Leave me alone.'

'No. I believe I'll stay. Until they come, at least.'

'Why?'

'Because talking to you is making me feel better.'

She opened her eyes, and the bastard was smiling. 'My
name is—'

'It won't change anything,' Sordon said. 'I'm far too old to
care.'

She had to hang there and listen. She shouted at first, trying
to drown out his hoarse voice with her own, but he
pummelled her legs with his walking stick until she fell
silent.

He told her that he knew others would eventually come,
lured by the Fallen God, and they had. But the Sentinels had
always caught them. At first they killed them up here, but as
they regressed, so the Sentinels started throwing them back
down. Even as the guardians of the Fallen God were changing
– venting their knowledge, reverting to a far older state – so,
ironically, their purpose became more entrenched in their
minds than ever. They fought several long, terrible wars,
projecting their confusion and chaos into violent
confrontation, and their numbers reduced.

'I don't care!' Nomi shouted, and Sordon probed the
wound in her leg. She screamed, she cried. He cleaned it
afterwards, conscious of infection, and chewed a herb and

root before pressing it into the flesh. Her screams seemed to draw him on.

He told her how the Sentinels that won the wars started slaughtering the unborn. They feared the sleeper, and when they moved out of their villages and returned to the land, the trees bearing the mummified foetuses became their shrines.

'Leave me,' Nomi said, appealing to his pity. But he only had pity for himself. He cried as he spoke but did not look at her, and Nomi knew that Sordon Perlenni was seeing only his own desolate past.

He said more and she heard it all, but by the time the Sentinels came to take her down, her mind was far away, and much of what he had said was forgotten. She was glad. She was suffering her own terrible fate, and next to that his miserable utterances were nothing.

They put her in a pit. It stank, faeces and piss staining the walls, and in one corner a pile of dried, bloody matter attracted flies and crawling things. Nomi cried but they took no notice, throwing food down at her until she caught something. She hated doing so, but she ate. And when they lowered a water jug down to her, she drank.

The old man refused to let her go. She suspected that he would also refuse to kill her, should she ask.

But there was always Ramus.

CHAPTER NINETEEN

Something touched his face. He felt it from a distance, deep down in sleep or unconsciousness, and it was cool and slick like a living thing's tongue. It moved across his closed eyes and up to his forehead, leaving a chill trail where it passed. He tried to lift his hand to feel what touched him, but he could not find his arms. *Perhaps I'm still suspended there,* he thought, even though he was sure that had been Nomi's nightmare rather than his own. *Perhaps I'm still being held up and examined, probed, prodded by things I don't want to understand.* The sensation faded and he tried to rouse himself. It was not easy. The pain was still thumping in his head, central to everything he sensed. If he went back under he could escape that pain, but if he rose up to face it...

'Ramus,' a voice said.

'Nomi,' he whispered.

He opened his eyes and felt that coolness on his forehead again. A shadow moved above him, blurred in his vision. It could have been immediately before his eyes or five miles away.

'Ramus,' the voice said again, and this time he heard relief. 'I'll get you something to drink.'

Nomi, he wanted to say, but his mouth was dry and this time it came out as a gasp. Water trickled onto his tongue and he swallowed greedily. The cold thing touched him one more time and he managed to raise a hand, grabbing the arm of whoever touched him.

'It's night,' she said. It was Lulah. Ramus felt a momentary flush of disappointment, but then she said more that shamed him. 'I can hear things moving around in the forest, but you're safe here. Understand, Ramus? You're safe with me.'

Safe, he thought. *Can she really mean that? Does she know something I don't?*

He thought of the Fallen God, and wondered whether Lulah had found its dried, forgotten corpse.

The Serian gathered some nuts and fleshy grubs from beneath a fallen tree. Neither of them knew whether they were safe to eat, but Lulah said she'd eaten similar things many times before in Noreela. Ramus was too hungry to question her, and too tired to care. The nuts tasted earthy, and the grubs burst sour in his mouth. As he chewed quickly to merge the tastes, he rested one hand against the charms on his chest.

'We need to move on,' he said.

'I thought you'd died.' Lulah sat close by him, her weapons drawn and laid before her.

'Everything hitting home,' he said. 'I'm exhausted.'

'And that,' she said. She touched his head with the damp cloth one more time, but this was not a soothing gesture.

'Yes,' he said. 'Worse now that I'm tired.'

'I can't protect you if you keep collapsing like that.' She

peeled another husk and popped the nut into her mouth.

Ramus could not answer. 'So we should move on,' he said instead. 'Explore some more.'

'We need to go back down,' Lulah said.

'But—'

'Not now. Not immediately. But you need to accept that we can't stay up here indefinitely.'

Why? he thought. But he nodded, sitting up gingerly and accepting that he should tell her what she needed to hear.

'So when?' she asked.

'I don't know. Not today. Not tomorrow. There's so much to see, and I didn't climb so far just to turn around and leave again.'

Lulah nodded. 'Perhaps after the god,' she said.

Nomi's in pain, Ramus thought, vague sensations from his dream returning in fleeting glimpses.

After more food he stood, doing his best to ignore the dizziness that threatened to tip him over. Lulah could see, he knew, but he did not look at her. He concentrated very hard and, after a few steps, found his rhythm. His muscles still ached but he welcomed that. Pain confirmed that he was awake, here and now, not hanging and suffering like Nomi.

Perhaps he should go to help. But he did not know where she was or what was happening to her. And there was something larger on his mind than the doom she had visited upon him, and her own pains he knew as a result. Something drawing him on, calming his illness or prodding it depending on the way his own thoughts went.

He thought of going farther south, and the pain lessened.

He thought of helping Nomi, and dizziness threatened him once more.

'Into the trees,' Ramus said. 'It looks like an old path, though it's overgrown. We'll follow.'

'You think it might be that way?'

He looked at the trail through the forest, and in the distance he saw the hint of something grey and solid standing among the trees. 'Something is.'

It was another stone man. He stood upright but his head was missing. Ramus searched through the knee-high ferns surrounding the petrified figure but could find no sign. There were no clothes or other belongings scattered around either, and many pieces of the body were snapped off or worn away by the elements. It was disconcerting looking at this statue that had once apparently been a living, breathing person. He wondered whether, if he broke it in half, he would be able to identify the insides.

Lulah found another twenty steps away. This one had fallen before being turned, arms stretched out as if to ward off some terrible fate. It was equally worn by wind and rain, features long since eroded to a shadow.

They followed the obvious path through the forest. Here and there were stumps of trees that had been cut down long ago, almost hidden by the ferns and other plants that had sprung from the ground now that the tree canopies above were gone. There was no sign of the fallen trees. Perhaps they had been used for building back in the ruined village they had just passed through, though there was more to this path than simple harvesting. It led somewhere, and if the cleared trees were not proof enough of that, the stone bodies certainly were.

Ramus felt events pressing in on him. On their long journey

down here from Long Marrakash there had been trials and pressures, but now he sensed his past drawing to a close, and his future stretching out before him like this long-hidden trail through the forest. The present struck him harder than it ever had before.

'Another,' Lulah said. She stepped beneath the tree cover and approached a moss-clad mass.

Ramus stood beside the path and watched as she scraped away some of the moss with her sword. The shape was almost subsumed beneath the plant growth, but one arm protruded, fist closed around something long since stolen away. Two fingers had broken off, and Ramus thought of the digits he had tied on a leather thong around his neck. Konrad. What charms did he hope to gain from that dead Serian's pieces?

'Two of them,' Lulah said, surprised. She lifted a curtain of creepers aside to let Ramus see.

The taller of the two figures was worn and cracked by the plant growth, but the shorter shape – both arms slung around their protector, face pressed into his or her shoulder – had retained their features. Delicate, sharp and terrified, their face was damp and crawled with tiny golden insects.

He shook his head in wonder, then shuddered in terror as he remembered those words again. Mutter them now, with Lulah this close, and she would turn to stone. *I have the power of a god,* he thought, and he expected to be struck down for such presumptuousness.

'We should leave,' the Serian said. She held her sword and her eye flickered from here to there, scanning the path and trying to pierce the shadows on either side. 'Back to the village, there's that place of books for you to examine. You'll learn a lot more about this place by reading its history than wandering its forgotten paths. And we can take them.'

'Maybe,' he said. 'But reading isn't seeing, touching or tasting.'

'It'll tell you more than—'

'You'd rather read about humping, or do it?'

Lulah glared at him for a beat, then looked away.

Ramus led the way this time, wincing now and then against the pain in his skull. Every heartbeat of pain reminded him of Nomi. He tried hating her, but it seemed that only certain emotions could travel from one world to the next, and hatred was not one of them.

And every time the agony throbbed in, there was something else there to instantly calm it again: a presence illuminated by the pain, like a shape in the darkness lit by lightning flashes.

The forest followed gentle slopes down into a valley. The air became heavy and warm, and to begin with it was a pleasant relief from the cool breeze that had bitten through their clothes since reaching the plateau. Ramus felt sweat dribble down his sides, sticking his shirt to his back, and Lulah's face was beaded with moisture. But the further they went down into the valley, the warmer it became. They stripped off their outer layers, afraid that they would dehydrate and use their water too quickly. And when they came to the tree line and the bulk of the valley was laid out before them, they had to pause to take everything in.

Here was another ruined village, but the destruction wrought upon this place was much greater. Barely a wall was left standing. It was spread across the floor of the valley, several small streams bisecting the destroyed settlement, spanned here and there by intricate timber bridges suspended from stone columns. The bridges, strangely, remained untouched by whatever had swept through this place.

Even from this distance, Ramus could see that there were more stone people scattered around the village. Some stood or lay in the fields outside, often piled here and there as if many of them had died together. Others were in the village itself, vague humps between shattered buildings, standing against piles of rubble or broken down into fragments.

He could also see that these dead stone things were not human.

'What is this?' Lulah asked.

'War, perhaps,' Ramus said. He recognised the tall, long-limbed shapes from some of the images of the parchment pages still in his backpack. They made surreal sculptures in death, ragged, stick-like things that threw strange shadows across the grass around their feet. Some of the limbs were missing, sliced or snapped away either before or after their turning from flesh to stone, but the detail in their faces seemed remarkable.

'These are more recent,' Lulah said. 'This is something else. Nothing to do with those behind us in the forest.'

'They were human, for a start.' Ramus led the way. He was frightened, but also utterly fascinated. *Here they are,* he thought, *the people of the plateau. A new civilisation.* It was a pity that they were dead.

Lulah did not want to go close to any of the things, but Ramus paused to examine each statue he passed. They were all tall, lithe and well muscled, their proportions seemingly exaggerated in every way. Longer limbs, larger hands, even their heads were slightly larger than humans, bearing faces that were remarkably familiar. But there was something about their frozen expressions that troubled Ramus, and the more stone bodies he looked at, the worse his confusion became.

It took Lulah to give him the answer. As they came to the first ruined building, she looked down at a stone body sprawled at her feet. 'They look like animals,' she said. And Ramus knew that she was right. However humanoid they appeared – however much he had been unconsciously attributing them with humanity – their faces held little to support that. They had all died snarling, expressions twisted into fighting shapes. There was little here that he truly recognised.

'We should go,' Ramus said. 'Look.' He pointed past the ruins, and further down the valley a cloud hung low in the air, slow graceful swirls the only sign of active air currents. And though it drifted, still it was fed from below.

'What's that?' Lulah asked.

'Perhaps nothing,' Ramus said. 'Or perhaps it's what this place was built to protect.'

Lulah led the way. Past the village the land took a sudden dip, a shale slope leading down to a lower portion of the valley floor. The streams feeding through the village rumbled down the slope in two waterfalls, throwing mist and small rainbows into the air. Behind them, a scene of conflict and death. Before them, beauty. Ramus commented upon it, and Lulah nodded and smiled. 'You'll often find both together,' she said. 'Sometimes I believe the land has to provide balance.'

'Which land? This one, or our own?'

Lulah looked confused. 'Surely they're the same? There's a cliff between us, but this place is higher, that's all. It's still Noreela.'

Ramus could think of no reply.

Steam rose from the ground. It came up from between

rocks, bleeding from the soil and wafting higher until the slight breeze caught it and strung it out. As Ramus and Lulah went further, they found larger vents, gushing steam in a gentle, almost constant flow. The steam smelt strange. It touched the back of his nose and slicked into his throat, soothing his tongue and inspiring flashes of imagery that could not have been memories. He closed his eyes to see more, but the steam did not give itself away so easily.

'What is it?' Lulah said.

'I don't know,' Ramus said.

'It feels like I'm dreaming, but I know I'm awake.'

'We both are. We're here. Maybe there's a gas here, giving us waking hallucinations.'

'It's like being swayed,' Lulah said, 'but without taking anything to get there.'

Ramus did not feel swayed. He felt more in control of his body and mind than he had since reaching the top of the cliff, but the warm, moisture-laden air he breathed was heavy with something else.

'Perhaps the god is very close,' he whispered. His voice was no louder than the steam, and he was not sure whether Lulah heard.

There were other things here, the remains of some sort of technology. Metallic legs strutted either side of the vents, and rusted arms spanned through the steam, bearing the remnants of other, more intricate things. There was little vegetation, most of it smothered by the steam, and as they walked their boots crunched on loose, stony soil. Ramus took shallow breaths and exhaled harshly, as if to purge himself of the things circulating at the periphery of his consciousness. This was like that place he and Lulah had come across in the forests of southern Noreela, except that these bad memories were not their own.

'Leave us alone,' he said. But if the Sleeping God was close by, why should it leave them alone? Why, when Ramus sought to find it?

'Another body,' Lulah said. She sounded glad to have something to say. 'There, over by that outcrop, standing with one hand against the rock. But...'

'But it's not all there,' Ramus said. They approached together. The stone body was deformed, containing hollows and gaps as though only part of the body had turned and the rest had decayed to nothing. He leant in closer and saw the hint of bone protruding around the thing's chest, grey stone at its base, gradually changing to white at its snapped tip.

'Another,' Lulah said. 'And another.'

The bodies here were all partial. Solid stone giving way to something with a more sandy texture, and then stone tendrils and spikes fading altogether. Bone was visible here and there, and on one of the bodies there was still a sheath of leathery skin around the unchanged skull.

'Would those words do this?' Lulah asked.

'I don't know. I know nothing.' Ramus touched one of the bodies and a thread of stone linking one exposed rib to the next crumbled between his fingers.

'Whatever these things are, I hope there are no living ones close by.' Lulah hefted her sword in one hand, a short knife in the other.

The atmosphere here was hot with steam, heavy with moisture and thick with thoughts neither of them could explain. Ramus's breath wheezed with the effort of breathing the saturated air, and every now and then he saw shapes that implied movement, direction and purpose. But when he blinked, the shapes resolved into nothing more than steam wisps. Lulah must have been seeing the same thing because she walked ahead of him, constantly dipping down into a defensive stance when a fresh breath of warm air passed by.

They passed several more stone things, none of them Noreelan. It was as if no Noreelan had ever been allowed to reach this place. *Perhaps I really am the first person here,* Ramus thought, but the idea did not thrill him as much as it should.

Another gush of warm air, more dancing shapes. And this time Ramus felt something through his feet, as though the ground itself rumbled to the scent of the breeze.

'What was that?' Lulah whispered.

'I don't know.' If Nomi were here with him she could tell him of the Ventgorian Steam Plains, how the ground acted there, what the sounds were and the smells, the feels and tastes, and perhaps she would even know the cause of those brief, haunting visions which plagued him.

A cloud of steam a hundred steps to his right swirled and dissolved around a shadow. Ramus blinked, expecting the shape to fade away into the air, but when he looked again, it was still there. It moved slowly, long arms and legs shifting up and down as though to mimic the shape of steam.

'Lulah,' Ramus whispered.

The Serian had already seen it. She crouched down before Ramus, wielding her sword and knife. The shape advanced. It was the same as the solidified creatures they had seen, only this one was whole. A rapid clicking noise came from its mouth, a chuckle or words in an unknown tongue, and Ramus was about to step forward and try to communicate with it when three more emerged from the steam around them.

They had been stalked, and now was the attack.

There was more movement underfoot as a sheet of steam hushed from the ground to their left.

And Ramus thought, *Heartbeat*.

His own heart thundered in his chest. He wanted to help, but he could not. He clasped the charms that hung around his neck – animal bone, holed stone, Konrad's fingers – but he had never been a true charm breather either, and they felt like nothing more than cheap trinkets.

Lulah sidestepped the first thing's charge and lashed out, catching it across the back of its thin legs and sending a splash of blood through the air. It howled and fell, hooting as it reached around to the wounds.

The Serian rushed back to Ramus but the other things were already there, grabbing for his legs and arms. A closed fist bashed the side of his head and his vision swam. He vomited, and blood ran warmly from his nose and mouth. He felt strong hands squeeze around his arms and legs and suddenly he was held aloft, carried between the two things as they ran quickly back up the gentle incline.

'Ramus!' Lulah shouted. He heard her but he could not twist his head to see, and he could not tell precisely what happened next. Footsteps pounded at the gravelly ground, something swished at the air – an arrow or crossbow bolt – and he heard a cry that definitely was not human.

A pause, more footsteps and then another cry. This one *was* human, and he recognised Lulah's tone as it lowered into a hoarse curse. Metal struck stone, something grunted, and then that same human shriek erupted again. This time it was cut off suddenly. Something metal clattered to the ground, closely followed by something of flesh and bone.

'Lulah!' Ramus shouted, and the thing holding his knees squeezed hard. He shrieked with pain and the creature holding his arms did the same, crunching fingers into biceps and bones until he felt they would burst and shatter. He bit his lip, shaking his head at the pain ebbing and flowing across his body like drifts of steam. He managed to swallow his scream, and the things carried him away.

The air grew cooler and lighter, and glancing to the side he could see the outskirts of the ruined village they had just passed through. The things skirted around, apparently not wishing to take the more direct route.

Just as one of them smacked the side of his head to make him look up at the sky once more, he glimpsed one of the grotesque stone statues.

And he wondered what exactly had become of Konrad.

I can do this, he thought. *I have the words. I have the knowledge. Whether it's the voice of the god or words these things speak or once spoke...*

He started muttering and the thing squeezed his legs once more. But they slowed down, and one creature clicked and hooted to the other in what could have been surprise.

Gritting his teeth against the expected pain, Ramus closed his eyes and spoke those words all the way through. He said them loud, projecting his voice as far as he could, and when the hands crushed into his knees once more, his voice rose into a shout...but still those words flowed.

They dropped him. He managed to get one arm out to break his fall but still it knocked the breath from him. He looked up, expecting to see them fall upon him with bared teeth and clawed hands.

One of them had gone to its knees and raised its hands to its ears. They never arrived. He only saw from the back, but he could hear the crackle of crunching stone, and the thing's skin turned from pale pink to grey, hair hardening and snapping from its scalp. The creature whined slightly, trying to shout through flesh becoming less and less responsive, and its fingers closed in like the legs of a dying spider. One of them snapped off and bounced from its shoulder.

Ramus rolled onto his stomach and looked behind him. The other thing was there on its knees, hands down by its sides. Its body beneath the ragged clothes was cool, grey and hard, and he was sure it must be dead. But then its eyes grew wider in a look of delayed shock, and the grey tide flowed up from its neck and painted its head as stone. Hair stopped swaying in the breeze, three of the thing's teeth shattered and its eyes lost their depth.

Ramus took in a deep breath and stood. *I did it.* He grimaced against the pain in his knees and arms, closed his eyes when his head throbbed agonisingly several times. *Not now, don't strike me down now, after I did that.* He breathed deeply, started back toward the village, and the pain in his head faded to an ache.

He started running, his muscles finding strength from somewhere, and his compacted knees, creaking at every step, carried him as faithfully as ever.

As he entered the ruined village one of the things came into view from behind a line of stark dead trees. Ramus shouted the words. It turned to flee, eyes going wide in shock, and he did not even stop to see it turn. As he dashed by he heard a sharp crack as something ruptured.

Ramus tried to ignore the effects of the steam breaths. He felt the movement beneath his feet again, heard the hissing of venting steam and tried to steer himself to the spot where the creatures had fallen upon them. He felt so dreadfully alone, and the power he had in those words removed him even further from the world. He barely knew himself anymore.

He saw one of the creatures before him, kneeling forward with blood dripping from its cleaved skull. Lulah's short knife was jammed into its throat. It was dead, but still he gave it a wide berth.

He thought of calling her name, but he did not know how many more were out there.

The Serian appeared from behind a low shrub. She must have been squatting but she rose quickly to her full height, swinging the sword in an arc that would slice off the top of Ramus's skull.

He started to mutter those words. He could not help himself. They came from within him, yet he was theirs too, wielded by them instead of wielding them himself. As Lulah's eyes went wide and she let go of her sword, Ramus bit his tongue. Blood gushed into his mouth.

'Piss on me, Ramus, I almost took off your fucking head.'

He smiled a bloody smile, and Lulah smiled back. 'And I nearly turned you to stone.'

Lulah dashed across to where she had dropped a knife, and only then did Ramus notice her left hand, mangled and flipping.

'What happened?'

She glanced down at her hand, then away again quickly. 'Bastard bit me as I was cutting its throat.'

Her hand was ruined. Three fingers were gone, and the rest of it was a distorted mess. 'We have to sort that out,' Ramus said.

'Not yet. We go. Away from here, away from this pissing steam, and when we find somewhere—'

They both heard the hoots and clicks of the things closing in. There were too many voices to count, and Lulah's face fell. 'Ramus, I don't think I—'

'Run,' he said. He nodded deeper into the valley. 'That way. They're coming from both sides, so we leave. Don't stop running. You need to be far enough away so that you can't hear my voice.'

'Ramus—'

'It's our only hope!'

'No. *You* could go, I could stay and hold them off.'

'Achieving what?'

Lulah winced as her hand banged against her leg. 'It's why I'm here.'

Ramus snorted. 'Then you don't get paid. Run now, Lulah. No more time.' Already he could see the steam parting to his left as something came through, and behind him he heard the harsh footsteps of things running across the loose ground. Lulah ran, and Ramus turned around.

He had no idea what power he wielded, where it came from or what it was supposed to protect. But this was as basic as it came: kill, or die.

So he killed. He waited until the last moment, then spoke words that took a few beats to utter, listening to the sounds of pursuit change to screeches of surprise and pain. Things fell to the ground behind him, some of the impacts fleshy but most hard, and in the distance he heard the tone of their calling change as those nearby fell silent.

The mist no longer drifted; it *boiled*. Upset by the creatures running through its lazy streams, it swirled and danced, added to by several loud gushes from vents behind and to Ramus's left. Something came at him and he said those words again, louder this time, and hoped Lulah was far enough away to avoid their effect. The thing skidded past him and struck another changed creature, both of them tumbling to the ground and shattering. Stunned by what he had done he fell silent, almost forgetting that they were still coming at him.

The air sang with violence, the ground shook with its effects, and though blood did not flow, Ramus smelt the stink of battle. It was not a smell he liked. Yet deep down there was enjoyment; he wielded words of such power that they could change the physical in a way no one had ever dreamt.

Something pattered across his scalp and he held out his hand, catching several small flies whose fine wings were already crumbled away.

When at last he heard no more hooting or crackling, no more footsteps closing in, and the steam around him rose relatively calmly once more, Ramus sighed and slumped to the ground. He felt exhausted, but elated. His muscles twitched with cramps and sang with the need to be flexed again.

He stood slowly and surveyed the grey carnage around him. Nothing moved save the mist. It was time to find Lulah.

As he left the steam clouds behind and hurried through clear, cool air once more, he heard more of those things hooting and bellowing behind him. The noise was much louder than before, more urgent and filled with a sense of dread that turned him cold.

Let them come, he thought.

But when he passed through a clump of trees, emerged on the other side and saw what stood before him, he knew that they would not stop pursuing until he was dead.

CHAPTER TWENTY

She tried to think of Beko. If what Sordon Perlenni said was true, and the Sentinels had kept her alive because she was with child, then Beko was the father. So as Nomi huddled in the corner of her pit trying to ignore the various discomforts, she tried to remember the big Serian captain, his surprising smile, his love of free poetry, the scarred face that gave away his profession. But the only way she could think of him was dead. He grinned up at her through a rent in his skull, arms and legs angled out around him where he lay on a ledge halfway down the Great Divide. She shook her head and he was there again, broken across the lower slopes of the Divide. Animals picked at him, taking away the tastiest morsels to leave his bones to be picked clean by insects and ants. She still recognised his hair.

She tried for a long time, keeping her eyes closed so that she did not have to see the Sentinels that passed across the timber grate ceiling of her cell. When she did look at them, they were animals. She could think of them in no other way. They may have built a great civilisation up here, existed for unknown hundreds or thousands of years to guard or protect the Sleeping God, and they did have human features. But they grunted and stank, bickered and spat. They stared into space with vapid eyes, and whatever they saw excited nothing in them. Theirs was a history she would have once loved to discover and unearth. But not now. Now they were just another animal, ready to rip her unborn child from her womb and hang it from a tree.

She sobbed and leant back against the cool ground. Beko fell, and he smiled as she fell with him. For now, that was the best she could do.

They gave her more food, dropping it through the grille above her. She caught what she could, and what she missed she kicked into the far corner where the bloodied mess lay. The pit floor stank, and she would not risk eating something that had touched it. Some of what they brought smelt and tasted foul, but there was a small orange fruit that was both rich and meaty in its taste, and several of those filled her to satisfaction. They brought meat as well. Nomi was thankful that it was dead when they dropped it, but none of it was cooked, and she was unsure whether her stomach would accept such basic fare again. If she had been able to identify the flesh, she would perhaps have taken the risk, but it came in small, stringy slabs, heavily laced with fat and still displaying clumsy cutting marks where it had been skinned or shelled. Try as she might she could not cleanse the blood from her skin. If it stained her like this on the outside, she did not trust it to eat.

The water they gave her tasted fresh, clear and clean. She sometimes used it to wash, and when they saw her doing that they would fetch more. The thought came briefly that she was an object of fascination rather than a prisoner, but then she remembered what they were going to do.

When none of the Sentinels watched from above, she touched her stomach. She felt nothing, sensed nothing, yet she was becoming fiercely protective of whatever might be inside her. She closed her eyes and saw Beko's smile as he fell, hoping that given time she would remember how it was to be alone with him.

She cried. She hated that, hated the weakness, but she felt so painfully alone and forgotten that she could not hold back the tears. They were not only tears of self-pity, though there was an element of that. She cried also for the friends she had lost, and the lovers, and the friend whom she loved more than anyone. She thought of Ramus constantly, trying to imagine him falling or broken at the bottom of the Great Divide. Those images would not come. What she saw was Ramus wandering these new landscapes, avoiding the Sentinels and exploring farther inland, dodging sentries, making his way deeper than even the Sentinels had gone. She tried not to see the agony in his eyes as the sickness ground him down. And when she imagined him writhing amongst strange grasses and plants she could not identify, dying of the sickness she had sent to him, she screamed the image away.

Perhaps he's closer than I think. She took a bite of one of the orange fruits and it was rotten on the inside. She threw it away, gagging. A Sentinel stood on the grille above her and stared down, blocking out most of the light, and when it saw the discarded fruit it reached beyond the pit and dropped in some more. Nomi let them fall to the ground. If they were not corrupted as they fell, they were when they struck.

'I'm sorry, Ramus,' she said. She realised it was the very first time she had thought those words, let alone uttered them.

Her second morning in the pit, Nomi was woken by the sound of Sentinels calling in the distance. She kept her eyes closed in an effort to hang on to her dreams, but Beko fell away from her and his smile faded as the ground pulled him down. *If he hits the ground in my dreams, he'll really die,* she thought, but she opened her eyes because he was already dead.

There were no Sentinels above her. She could see deep blue sky through the heavy timber grating, with a few wispy clouds moving slowly from left to right. She inhaled but smelt only the pit, and she tried to recall the taste of unspoilt fruit to drive her sickness down. Her skin was gritty with dust and dirt. She desperately needed to wash, and she hoped they would bring her a jug of water soon.

The Sentinels' call came in again, a hooting and bellowing the likes of which she had not heard before. It was so distant that she could have been mistaken, and she stood, opened her mouth and exhaled slowly, striving to hear more.

Next time the call came it was closer. Then closer still, the same collection of rising and falling notes as though one call was echoing in from the distance.

All around the pit, in whatever settlement they had brought her to, Sentinels started crying out. She heard them dashing here and there in apparent panic, and a few growls and snarls as the creatures collided. A shadow fell over her pit and quickly passed, and Nomi recognised the willowy waving of a creature's long limbs.

'Hello!' she called. She was suddenly afraid that if they left, she would remain down here unfed and unwatered for an unknown length of time. They were looking after her now, but though they thought her pregnant she did not seem special to them. The pit proved that. The pit, and that stinking bloody mass in the far corner that she had doggedly refused to examine. 'Hey, ugly pissers! Where's my food? Where's my fucking water?'

Sordon's words came back to her, his unwanted descriptions of wars the Sentinels had fought against each other. Perhaps this was another such battle, starting because she had arrived with something else unborn for them to worship.

Nomi paced the small pit, five steps one way, five the other. She heard Sentinels calling again in the distance, and the silence above and around her suggested they had just left.

'Hello!' she shouted again. 'Food! Water!'

'They can't hear you.' Sordon Perlenni said. She could not yet see him but she knew that he was close, perhaps sitting a few steps away from the pit and listening to her growing panic.

'What's happening?' Nomi asked.

Sordon started chuckling, then laughing, but there was nothing of humour there at all. He sounded mad. He tried to talk but his laughter increased, and it eventually turned into loud, extended sobbing.

'Sordon!' Nomi called. She jumped and held on to the timber grating, trying to pull herself up. But her arms were still weakened from the climb. 'What is it? Why have they gone?'

'The god,' he said at last, stuttering the words between sobs. 'The Fallen God. Someone is going for it.'

'It's close?' she asked, feeling a thrill of fear.

'Not so far away,' he said. 'Is it your Ramus?'

'Ramus died. He—'

'I'm here to let you out,' he said. 'Listen to me, Nomi. If he's close—'

'I can't trust you,' she said. 'You left me hanging there on that rack. Used me to assuage your own sick guilt.'

His head appeared above the edge of the pit for the first time, and in his old man's eyes Nomi saw such terror that she slumped to her knees, trying to draw as far away from him as possible.

'This is much more than either of us!' he hissed. 'This is about the whole of Noreela, *all* of it – the Noreela you know, and here, and whatever may lie beyond. The god...can you possibly *imagine*? Can you even *attempt* to think of what that thing is, when the power of all the Sleeping Gods combined could only manage to put it down to sleep? Something that can't be killed. Something so wrong...' He trailed off and looked past her at the floor of her pit, and deeper still. She wondered what he saw.

'Is it buried?' she asked.

'Of course. A cave. An abyss, deeper than anyone knows.'

'You've been in?'

'*No one* has been in. No human, no Sentinel, no one and no thing since it was put down. But now the Sentinels panic, and if they panic like this, it's because someone has approached closer than ever before.'

'Ramus,' Nomi said.

Sordon stared at her, sober and serious. 'Can you stop him? I'm here to let you out, but can you stop him from doing whatever it is he intends?'

'I don't think so,' she said. 'He can turn people to stone.'

Sordon Perlenni had started working at the ties locking the grating, but now he stopped and stared down at her. 'He knows that?'

'He does. He's used it.'

Sordon frowned, his old man's face wrinkling even more.

'We found parchment pages on a body at the base of the Divide. Ramus...he's an academic. He must have translated the words.'

Sordon nodded, his face suddenly slack and eyes dark. He was fumbling at the ropes holding the grating down, his breath coming faster. 'An old Sentinel weapon,' he said. 'They had many, once, bestowed upon their ancestors by the Sleeping Gods. So much to protect them other than just tooth and claw. I'm not sure any of them can even speak it anymore, but if your Ramus knows the curse...'

'You'll have to tell me the way.'

Sordon nodded, gasped and lifted the cover from the pit.

Nomi jumped and held on to the pit's lip, struggling to haul herself out. Sordon did not help. He could not, because he seemed to suddenly be his true age, sitting aside like a dying thing bleeding its last into the ground, face sagging, breath light. But his eyes were still strong, and filled with reflections of calamity.

'You must stop him,' Sordon said. 'The sleeper cannot be woken.'

He told her the way. Without a backward glance Nomi left Sordon Perlenni, the First Voyager, sitting beside the pit that would have become the site of her violent death.

In a way, perhaps Ramus really had saved her.

❊   ❊   ❊

Fear gave her speed; that, and the sudden sense of a freedom she had least expected. She quickly left the Sentinels' settlement, a collection of ragged hut-like structures that barely formed a village, and found their path through the long grass easy to follow. There must have been many of them on the move to leave this much damaged vegetation behind.

Three of them had killed Beko, Noon and Rhiana. Even if Ramus did wield the curse against them, surely this many Sentinels would kill him in the end?

Yet as she ran, Nomi's intentions were far from clear. If he really was going down for the Fallen God, who was she to stop him? Perhaps she would join him, Voyagers together, as they should have been all the way through this journey. She had met Sordon Perlenni and he was mad, and could she really let his exhortations steer Ramus – and perhaps her as well – from the greatest discovery in history?

A Sleeping God...they were the stuff of legend. Who was to say it had fallen? Sordon? Perhaps everything he had told her was a lie.

Nomi snorted as she ran, enjoying the feel of her heart galloping and sweat forming on her forehead and upper lip.

Yet the Sentinels were here for something. She had seen evidence of what they had once been, and there was no denying that some event in their history had driven them back towards their animalistic origins. *What could make them regress like that?* she wondered. *Just one man and the stories he brought?*

There was so much to know, explore and discover, but as she ran she sensed that her time here was drawing to a close. Things were about to change.

The Sentinels' trail lost itself in a small forest but she ran straight on, hoping to pick it up again once the trees ended. Soon she could run no longer and she slowed to a brisk walk, pausing to take a drink from one of the many streams flowing between the trees. A low mist hung off to her left, and she saw steam rising from the ground around several huge trees. It seemed to curl around their trunks and caress the bark, and the trees were dark from continuous soaking. Nomi could feel its clamminess from here.

Sordon had mentioned steam from the ground, his tone one of wonder.

Nomi started running again. She reached the edge of the forest and paused for a breath, leaning on her knees and looking ahead at the sprawling plains before her. Here and there were clumps of stark, bare trees, leaves small and sharp as protection against the winds that must thunder across this landscape on occasion. Between two such wooded areas, she saw a wide trail of trampled grass and undergrowth.

Something shouted to her right, its call echoing across the hills. Nomi fell to her stomach in the grass and peered over the swaying stems, fearing that she had been seen. There were a score of Sentinels loping along the ridge of a distant hill. They bellowed as they went, cupping their large hands around their mouths and repeating the panicked cries she had heard from her pit. An answering cry came from the other direction and Nomi looked that way, but she could see nothing.

She had to go. There was no way she could match their speed, even if she was not already exhausted from the long voyage and climb. But Ramus was somewhere ahead of her, and his presence suddenly seemed to be drawing her on. He was all she knew up here now that everyone else was dead.

'Wait for me,' she whispered. Standing, stretching a cramp from her right calf, Nomi hurried after the pale figures even now disappearing into the distance.

It was the most intricate, ornate, staggeringly beautiful building Ramus had ever seen, and Lulah knelt before it. The Serian had dropped her sword – he could see the glint of blood on its wide blade from where he stood – and she was slumped in disbelief or supplication. Ramus could not tell which, though he would have believed either.

'Lulah,' he said, and somehow he walked to her.

She pointed at the building, unable to speak. There were temples in Long Marrakash and elsewhere, tombs for the Old Chieftains of Cantrassa, watchtowers on the western shores of the Pavissia Steppes, cliff dwellings carved into the sheer extremes of Pengulfin Heights and statues to the Sleeping Gods dotted across the entirety of northern Noreela, but none of them could compare to this. None had the grace and impact, the architectural force, or the sense of something threatening and altogether alien that this building exuded from every squared stone, feature or carved decoration. It took his breath away, and by the time he reached Lulah, he was glad to sink to his knees beside her.

'No human could have built this,' she whispered.

'No,' Ramus said. 'No human.' The building was pyramidal, its sides steep and its pinnacle taller than any building he had ever seen. Great steps the height of a man had been formed into its sides, and there must have been a hundred of them. He wondered what they had been meant for. Even the things that pursued them were not tall enough to use them. Precious metals were cast into the walls in many places, designed into arcane symbols that made the etchings on the parchment look childlike in comparison. Some of these symbols actually seemed to stand from the building, projecting themselves beyond the walls and into space, yet the stone sculptures that protruded here and there seemed even more solid. Sentinel faces, and the images of things Ramus had never imagined, stared out from the two walls of the building they could see.

Around its base was a wide open area where nothing grew. Its surface had a black sheen, like glass, and – though dusty – Ramus could still brush away the dirt and see the cool perfection of the ground. It felt warm. He leant forward and pressed his face to it, shielding his eyes with the crazy idea that he would be able to see deeper. He could not, and for that he was partially glad.

'All my life...' Lulah began, voice catching in her throat.

'All your life?'

'The Sleeping Gods. I've followed and honoured them. Not something good for a Serian. Those on Mancoseria...we follow more grounded gods. The life moon, the death moon...gods that make a difference *today*.'

'You should have told me,' Ramus said. The weight of charms about his neck suddenly felt so foolish. He took them off as she spoke, not caring now whether Lulah saw Konrad's petrified fingers.

'I wanted a god that would make a difference tomorrow. Being betrayed, let down...that's only natural, isn't it? So I've pretended all my life to follow the death moon, but every time I spoke in its direction I had my eyes closed, and it was the Sleeping Gods to whom I paid homage. I wanted a god that would wake one day and make everything right again. And the chance of *finding* one...*waking* one...'

He threw the charms aside and they shattered, skittering dust and sharp-edged stones across the smooth ground. Lulah watched them go then looked back at Ramus.

'This one may not be what you seek,' he muttered, pain thudding in behind his eyes and cooling again. A warning?

'And who are we to say?' Lulah said, suddenly scathing. 'Me, a one-eyed warrior. And you...?'

'What of me?'

Lulah looked back to the building, but not before Ramus saw the glitter of tears. 'Is it in there now?' she asked.

Ramus stood and walked a few steps across the smooth ground, and the building seemed to leap suddenly closer. 'Maybe,' he said. 'But perhaps this is just a way in.'

'We need to decide.'

He glanced back at Lulah and heard the sounds in the distance. *More of them!* He nodded down at her sword. 'You took some?'

'One. And only because it seemed to be wounded, or old. Slow. More than one of those things comes at me, I don't think I'll get away.' She looked at her ruined left hand, then raised her eyebrows as if to ask the same of him.

'Those words work on them,' he said. He looked back at the looming building, eyeing the large steps and the way its top seemed to flatten out. 'They sound a long way off. Help me find a door, maybe we can get in before—'

'I won't end up like that,' Lulah said.

'Like what?'

'Turned to stone. I'll die fighting.'

Ramus could not decide whether that was suspicion in her

eye, or fear. 'I'd never hurt you like that.'

She nodded once, unconvinced.

They went together to the base of the building, always keeping one ear on the sounds of those creatures approaching from the north and west. Ramus had suspected there would be no entrance at ground level, and he was right. As he looked up at what seemed this close to be sheer walls, he began to fear that there would be no entrance anywhere. Why should there? If the gods had put this here, would they leave an easy route inside?

'We need to climb,' he said.

'I thought we'd had enough of that.' Lulah sheathed her sword and reached up to the lip of the first step. She touched the stone gingerly, paused, then pulled herself up. Squatting a man's height above him, she reached back down.

'I'll do it myself,' he said. Something was happening. Something was wrong. His was not the only consciousness in his mind, and his were not the only thoughts. It was similar to the feeling he'd had by those steam vents, but there the invaders into his mind had been memories from elsewhere. Here, they had the immediacy of thought.

'What is it?' Lulah asked.

'Nothing...'

'We're trapping ourselves here, you know.' She stood above him and looked down, a warrior viewing things from aspects he had not even considered. He thought about going onward, and she looked back at their flanks. 'If those things come close enough we'll never get down. And if they choose to climb as well...we could hold them off, for a while. Maybe. But they don't seem inclined to give up.'

'There's an entrance up there,' Ramus said.

'You're sure?'

'Something tells me it's there.' He looked past Lulah up the side of the incredible building, carvings and steps silhouetted against the sky and casting their shadows across his face. *And that something is drawing me in,* he thought. *It has been for a long time. Guiding me. Resting in my mind until the time's close, and then...*

And then, he did not know.

Lulah looked out past Ramus. 'Well,' she said, 'it's no longer our choice. Come on, you go first.' She held out her hand.

Ramus heard the calls of those things as they emerged from the woods behind them, the clicks and hoots, and then the *slap slap* of their feet on the smooth glassy surface.

This time, he accepted the Serian's help.

The steps were the height of his eyes. He had to place his forearms flat on the next step, heave himself up, swing a leg and roll. After doing it four times he was exhausted, and he guessed there were a hundred more to go until they reached the top. He went on – heaving, lifting, rolling – and the exhaustion in his bones, the pains in his muscles, the throbbing in his head, urged him on. They marked what he had been through to get here and he welcomed them, because they gave him the impetus to climb. He could not believe that he had come so far to be stopped now. *I'm coming for you,* he thought, and nothing answered. Not in words, at least. But something else climbed with him, settled in a dark corner of his mind that he felt would open up to him soon. It waited there and exuded a dream of freedom. For a beat he lay back on a step and looked up at the sun, and it was as if he were seeing it for the very first time.

Never wake, he had read in his journal and on the parchment. And at the thought of those words, the thing in his mind touched the cancer and threatened to squeeze.

'Keep going,' Lulah said, rolling gracefully onto the step beside him. 'We have a chance.' Ramus glanced to his right and down. There were maybe twenty of those tall, gangly creatures down there, all of them holding back from the building. They clicked and grumbled, heads twitching left and right as if looking for a way around, and sometimes they looked up at Ramus and Lulah. They seemed angry when they saw them – their hands clawed, mouths open in grotesque growls – but something prevented them from advancing.

'Maybe they can't come,' Ramus said.

'We can hope.'

As Ramus stood to climb the next huge step, one of the things screeched. He could not help looking, and he saw a creature stalk forward, reach out and touch the cool grey stone of the building's edge. It jerked its hand back as if stung, then reached out again, slower this time, stepping aside so that the others could see its hand pressed flat against the stone.

'Not good,' Lulah said. She unshouldered her bow, held it in her ruined left hand, drew one of her few remaining arrows and fired at the creature. The arrow pierced the side of its head, tip exiting at jaw level and sticking into its shoulder. It made no sound as it fell down dead, but every other creature on that glassy black surface roared.

Lulah looked sidelong at Ramus. 'Even worse,' she said.

As if the death of their companion spurred them on, the creatures suddenly lost their fear.

❋   ❋   ❋

Ramus climbed as fast as he could. Fear drove him, and a sense of hopelessness that it could all end like this. Lulah came with him to begin with, climbing lithely, reaching back to help him up, climbing again, helping some more. Every time he glanced at her face she was looking past him, mouth slightly open as she gasped in short, heavy breaths. *She wants to see her god,* he thought. *But we should be running from this one, not toward it.* She still carried her bow, and five arrows remained in her quiver. After that would be the throwing knives on her belt – three, maybe four of them – and then the sword. He tried not to dwell on the odds because he knew they were so bad.

And that thing still climbed with him. He felt the weight of it in his mind, and it was heavier and darker than the sickness he had assumed for years would be the end of him.

'Go on,' Lulah said.

'Keep climbing!'

'Go *on*!' She boosted him up onto the next step.

Ramus rolled, stood and looked back down. The creatures were coming, and the only reason they had not reached them yet was caution. They climbed with ease, their long arms and legs reaching spider-like over the weather-smoothed edges of the huge steps. They were stalking the two intruders. Ramus was not sure, but some of them seemed to be looking past him towards the top of the building.

Lulah strung an arrow and aimed at the nearest creature, four steps down. It jigged quickly to the left, jumped to the right, and Lulah's aim shifted to follow the movements. When the creature's head lowered and it exposed its teeth in a hiss she fired. The arrow pierced its cheek and neck and it slumped to the step, slipping slowly off to the level below.

Others passed it by without a glance.

Lulah strung another arrow. 'Haven't you gone yet?' she asked.

Ramus levered himself up, swung a leg and climbed. He moved quickly and methodically, breaking the movements down into parts and naming each part. The lean, the lift, the swing, the roll, the stand, the step, the lean... He made six steps this way before glancing back again. He was pleased that Lulah had also climbed two more steps, but now she was down to her last arrow. Another creature lay dead below them but the others came on, and some were now slipping around the building to the left and right, climbing over carvings and protuberances and disappearing from view. They would be scaling the sides he could not see.

I have those words, he thought. The presence in his mind seemed to swell as he thought of the curse. *I have them, at least.* But there was Lulah. She would know what he was thinking, and yet she fought hard to give him time to reach the top. He felt sad for her – so near and yet so far from her god – but if she turned to run as well, they would both be dead. She was being a true warrior to the last.

And what does that make me? he thought. There was a trail of bodies behind him that clouded his true name.

The next step was broken left and right with elaborate stone carving, reaching out past the edge and hanging over the steps below. There were various creatures mixed in there – faces and wings, legs and claws – and he could not identify any of them. They were all fierce.

Lulah grunted behind him. Ramus saw that she had dropped her bow and was now weighing a throwing knife in her good hand. She had already thrown one, and a creature three steps below her was clasping its chest, leaning left and right as though deciding which way to fall. She threw again, grunting with the effort, and the knife glanced off an enemy's shoulder and spun away.

Ramus went on, step after step, sweat soaking his clothing, blood running down his arms from where his fingers and forearms were scratched and scraped, passing more carvings and the cool weight of precious metals inlaid into the structure, and even through the panic his explorer's mind sprinted, trying to take in what he was seeing and find explanations for it all. There were words and symbols here, some familiar, others nothing like those on the parchments. There were images of things he did not know, and illustrations of things he was not sure he wanted to understand. *Surely this is a gateway,* he thought. *This must be a way to somewhere!* The fear came that they had somehow missed an entrance, either on the ground or one of the stepped levels they had passed below, but he could not worry about that now. With the creatures closing in and Lulah's weapons rapidly dwindling, defeatism would be the end of him.

And I always have those words...

He whispered them to the air, testing them, and a spider on the vertical face of a step fell and cracked apart.

For the first time he risked looking up. They were maybe halfway, and the steps above actually seemed to be lower than those below. He climbed, rolled, climbed again and he was right, they were lower, now rising only to his chest. He snorted a laugh and hoped that Lulah heard.

From above, a creature hissed into his face.

Something whined past his head, slashing the air and flicking his hair. He blinked in shock, and when he looked again the thing's head tilted to the side on a fountain of blood.

'Go on!' Lulah said. She was beside him now, weighing up another throwing disc. 'They're coming. Go *on*!'

Ramus climbed, stepped over the dead creature and climbed again. His vision blurred from the exertion. When he struck one of the great stone carvings he scurried to the left until he could climb again, then also had to move along the next step.

He heard the hiss of another throwing disc, and then Lulah cried out in pain.

Ramus climbed two more steps before turning to look down. The Serian came after him, creatures flowing up the bloodied steps behind her, but something was wrong. At first he could not place what it was, but then he saw a dark metallic shape lying in a splash of blood ten steps down, and he looked back at Lulah. Her face was set into a pained grimace as she tried to climb. Her right arm was missing below the elbow leaving shreds of flesh, skin and a strikingly white shattered bone. She grunted with exertion, her eye glittering with tears of agony and shock.

'Go on!' she screamed. 'I'm coming! I won't wait for you anymore!'

Ramus turned and climbed, rolled, climbed, and when he was a handful of steps from the flattened top of the building he realised what she had done.

He paused and looked back down. Lulah was ten steps below him now, holding her sword in her ruined left hand, the stump of her right arm raised high. A creature below her lifted itself toward her step and she swept the sword at it, but it had already ducked back down. Another came and she stabbed, catching its arm and eliciting a high-pitched shriek.

A third creature appeared from around the side of the building, climbed over a sculpture of a two-headed thing and ran at her. Ramus was about to shout when Lulah fell, rolled and launched a throwing knife into its face. She picked up her sword and swung again.

There were too many of them. He could see maybe ten of the monsters on the steps below her, and a few lay dead between the Serian and the ground, but there must have been others circling around the structure.

I have those words, he thought again, and they almost sprung to his lips of their own accord. He shouted the first word and ended it in a scream that shocked a flight of birds from the forest canopy below and to his left.

For a beat the creatures paused in their attack and looked up at him, clicking and hooting in shock or fear, or perhaps both.

Lulah turned and stared up at him also. Her dark skin had turned a sickly grey, blood drenched her clothing and she swayed where she stood, her eyelid drooping. The stud on her eyepatch flashed in the sun. 'I won't die like that!' she shouted into the silence.

Wait, Ramus wanted to say, but there was nothing to wait for.

Lulah turned and leapt from the step, sword raised, uttering a scream that surprised the two creatures below her into silence. She fell on them, her sword piercing a chest and slipping from her hand as she and the other creature started tumbling.

Ramus watched until he was sure she was dead. Then he drew in a huge breath, closed his eyes and screamed the words he should not know.

CHAPTER TWENTY-ONE

A distant sound faded away to nothing and Nomi's skin crawled. The breath was squeezed from her, her flesh felt suddenly too expansive for her body and her skin contracted. She fell to her knees on a carpet of pine needles and ants, and as she leant forward the ants reared up at her, preparing to fight something a million times their size with blind instinct.

She gasped at last, releasing some of the pressure, extending the sound into a drawn-out groan that seemed to bleed tension from her bones and muscles. Ants crawled on the stickiness of her leg wound and she flicked them off. The tree canopy above her grew silent. She clasped her hands to her stomach and wondered what was there, whether it was safe or dead, and for the first time she cared.

The silence was broken again by the thundering sound of rocks tumbling and rolling down a cliff. A landslide? Nomi could not feel the ground shaking, and the noise ended as suddenly as it had begun.

She stood and stumbled on, soon finding her pace again. To her left the forest was obscured by a low mist, and here and there she saw movement as though shapes were passing through. She paused and hid low several times, but the shapes never manifested into anything solid. *If it was* them, *they'd have come at me by now,* she thought, and the next time she saw movement she ignored it and hurried on.

The tree cover ended suddenly, and there was not only nature before her, but something beyond nature. The breath was knocked from her. Taller than any building she had ever seen, more intricate, terrifying in its mass and height, awe-inspiring in its ambition...

But there was something wrong.

At first she thought the building had been damaged, such was the profusion of jumbled stones around its base and littering its stepped sides. She moved closer, though every instinct told her to turn and flee, and the wildlife around her suddenly burst into life. Perhaps the birds and ground creatures had been scared, but no more. Something here had ended.

Nomi saw a head made of stone. It lay on the shiny black ground at the base of the huge building. *This is what I heard,* she thought. *These statues of Sentinels, falling. But what made them fall?*

She looked up at the steps of the building, and here and there she could make out other statues. Some of them were broken, but a few still stood tall and proud on the steps where they had been placed.

And then she saw the blood.

And scattered amongst the stone statues she made out several Sentinel bodies, only these were flesh and blood. Some missed body parts, others seemed to have been pierced by arrow or knife.

None of them moved.

'Ramus,' she whispered, because this was the place Sordon had directed her to, the gateway, the entrance, and such violence could only have been the result of Ramus's presence.

She stared at the bottom of the building and scanned upward, and when she reached the top she saw the figure pacing there. It walked around the edge of the structure's flattened summit, passing out of sight and appearing again, describing the same route over and over. Nomi shaded her eyes against the sun, trying to make out whether it had long arms and legs, or whether it was someone…

Someone she knew.

'Ramus!' she shouted.

The figure halted at the edge of the summit. Birds fell silent once again at the sound of her voice. His name echoed from the building as though it were shouting back at her, and she realised how foolish and impulsive she had been.

Ramus had just killed these Sentinels with the power of his voice.

Nomi backed away a few steps, bringing her hands up to cover her ears. But then she stopped because she was fascinated. There he was, her old friend and nemesis, standing at the gateway to the Fallen God, and this was truly the greatest voyage anyone had ever undertaken. Sordon Perlenni may have been here long before them but he had stayed, and now madness informed his every movement and thought. Surely she and Ramus could make more of this place?

'He says it's fallen!' she shouted.

Ramus may have responded, or perhaps it was her own words echoing back again. But between one blink and the next he vanished. And the only way for her to go was up.

❋   ❋   ❋

She climbed, avoiding the Sentinel bodies where she could. Most of them were broken into several chunks or completely shattered, but the ones that must have been killed before Ramus used the curse still cooled into the stone. Arrows had killed a couple, knives some more, and further up the building she found a Sentinel's head that must have tumbled down from above.

She resisted the temptation to stop and stare at the carvings, images, small faces sunk into the stone, lines of strange writing and symbols displayed all across the side of the incredible building. Their time may come, but for now there was something even more incredible to find.

She found Lulah a dozen steps from the top. The Serian's throat had been ripped out and her arm torn off, but two dead Sentinels lay with her, one of them bearing teeth marks in its own gashed throat. Blood still dribbled from the wound. Nomi paused for a moment to look into the dead warrior's pale eye, then she carefully took the last knife from Lulah's belt and continued upward.

Five steps from the top, exhausted and in pain from the leg wound that had started bleeding again, Nomi heard Sentinels calling and clicking behind and below her. When she reached the summit she looked back down, knowing what she would see.

They were already climbing. They seemed unconcerned at their dead comrades, passing by both shattered stone and bloodied flesh corpses without a glance. They had eyes only for her. And for the first time in the face of a Sentinel, even from this distance, she saw purpose.

Nomi turned around to see what Ramus had been circling when she saw him.

There was an opening on top of the building. It disappeared
into a circular staircase that led down, the stairs just as deep
as those she had recently climbed. It was covered by an
elaborate stone canopy propped on pillars, various drainage
channels carved into the floor to guide rainwater away from
the hole. The entrance was dark and forbidding. Nomi
inhaled the must of ages.

She could enter the hole, as Ramus had done, or wait here
to be slaughtered. There really was no choice. After her climb,
Nomi began her descent.

It quickly grew dark. She sat on the edge of a step and slid
down to the next one, moving fast, conscious of the Sentinels
racing up the sides of the building outside. *I could just leave
him to them,* she thought, surprised that the idea had not
come sooner. *Could have gone down the other side of the
building and hidden, let them come in after him, find him...*

But there was more to this than whatever may or may not
be hidden down here, more than exploration and discovery.
There was Ramus and her.

As the huge circular staircase curved around to the left the
light from above faded away, leaving her in complete
darkness. She felt her way to the edge of the next step and
slipped out into the void, finding stone beneath her feet. She
repeated the process again and again, and every time she
slipped from the level surface she feared that it would be the
last step, and the next drop would be a hundred times greater.

'Ramus!' she shouted. Her voice echoed away above and
below her, but nothing answered back. *He could be too far
down,* she thought. *Or maybe he doesn't want to answer.*

Perhaps he was dead.

If he had fallen from the last step, and she fell too, she could die when she hit his remains. They would rot down here together in an eternal embrace, never having said they were sorry.

'Ramus!' she called again. 'Wait for me!'

There was no answer, so she carried on falling. After a while she realised she should have been counting the steps. There had been maybe a hundred steps up to the top of the building, and she had come down perhaps thirty. Seventy more like this until she reached ground level. Or less, if whatever this building contained was hidden away at its very heart. Or more, if it was simply the gateway to somewhere deeper and darker. An abyss, Sordon had said. It may have been a hundred steps up, but Nomi was suddenly terrified that it was a thousand back down.

She went on, and when she paused a few steps later she heard shuffling sounds from above her, and the crackling sounds of Sentinels communicating. They were descending but they sounded cautious, no longer hooting in anger, and perhaps they were coming down here for the very first time. She knew so little about them. Sordon had told her a little, venting his guilt at her whether she wanted to hear or not, and now she wished she had asked him more. He had been up here for so long...

'They're coming down, Ramus!' she shouted. 'The fallen sleeper cannot awake, and they're here to make sure of that!' Her words echoed before her and she listened for a response. Again, nothing.

The stone became slimy. Water trickled somewhere in the darkness, and Nomi's hands slipped on the slick surface. Warmth wafted from below and she paused again, breath held as she tried to make out what had just happened. Her heart hammered against her chest, blood pulsed in her ears, she heard a drip as blood from her leg fell to the step below. Another gush of warm air, and this time she breathed it in to see what it contained.

'Breath of a god,' a voice said beside her.

Nomi screamed. A hand clasped across her mouth and pressed hard, and when she struck out another hand grabbed her arm. She was pulled back onto the flat surface and pushed down, struggling, kicking at empty air.

'Nomi,' the voice spoke again, as quiet as before yet filling the darkness. 'It's me.'

Nomi stopped struggling. The hand lifted from her mouth, though she could still sense it just above her face, ready to push down again should she scream.

'Ramus,' she whispered. 'The Sentinels are coming.'

'Sentinels? That makes sense. I can hear them. Slow. They're scared. They know what's down here, and they're scared.'

'Do *you* know what's down here?' she asked.

For a beat the darkness did not answer. She sensed Ramus sit away from her, and only then did he speak. 'I'm a Voyager. I'm here to find out. We found somewhere, didn't we, Nomi? Didn't we find somewhere?'

We're not the first, she wanted to say. There was so much to tell him, but here and now was not the place.

'You're pregnant,' he said.

'How...?'

'You gave me the gift of your nightmares, remember?'

'I'm sorry,' she said, and two simple words spoken into endless darkness made her feel so much better.

Ramus snorted softly but did not reply.

'Ramus, we can't wake this thing. We know nothing about it. We don't know—'

'*I* know,' he said. 'It's here with me, and it will guide me down. Do you see?'

'No, I don't understand.'

'I mean, do you *see* Nomi? *I* see. I see you huddled there, staring into a darkness deeper than you've ever imagined, wondering whether the next step will drop you into an abyss. But the Sleeping God gives me sight, and I can see the way.'

'It's a Fallen God, Ramus.'

'And who judges what falls and what does not?'

Nomi did not understand the question and could offer no answer. 'Are you going to kill me?' she asked.

Ramus laughed then, a soft sound that whispered away below them. She wondered what his laughter found down there, and whether it was ready.

'No,' he said. 'You've said you're sorry. And I think, really, you gave me more than you could know.'

Nomi leant forward, reaching for where she thought Ramus sat. She touched clothing and held on, pulling him closer, laying her hand on his face and trying not to let go. 'Ramus, you don't know what's in your head.'

'I *do* know,' he said. '*It* is in my head, and it got there through the sickness it knows so well. Mind-worms, you told me, Nomi? I think you were lied to. I think you breathed something of a Sleeping God, back there in Ventgoria.'

'No...'

'Yes! Maybe the final breath of an old god dying. Maybe something more.'

'But if you wake the Fallen God...have you thought about

that? Have you really thought about what it might do?'

'No,' he said. He laughed again. 'If you could only see your face. No, Nomi, I haven't thought about it. I don't need to. I don't care. This is what I was born for. This is the greatest voyage ever.'

'It's *doing* this to you! This isn't you Ramus, this is—'

'Did you untie your charm?'

Nomi blinked, surprised at the question. She remembered the rope charm sinking quickly into the pool, and her fear that had sent it there. 'No,' she said.

Ramus was quiet for a beat. 'Then you'll never know what *I* gave *you*,' he said. And he slipped away.

Nomi shouted after him at first, then followed, almost losing control and sending herself tumbling several times. But fast though she moved, Ramus moved faster.

'It'll lie to you!' she called.

But Ramus was gone. And even if he did hear her pleas, he chose not to answer.

Nomi continued down, feeling more alone in this absolute darkness than she had ever thought possible.

The Sleeping God called him down and showed him the way. It was still there inside him, giving and taking dreams and nightmares from the cancer eating his brain. It sat beside the cancer – memory of another Sleeping God? Perhaps, perhaps not – and called it weak. Maybe it could remove it entirely, but this was not what drove Ramus. It had been a passing thought, but he considered it no more. He was used to the idea of dying, but now the god gave him the chance to achieve something before he went away. *Have you really thought about what it might do?* Nomi had asked. He had, and it did not matter. The Sleeping Gods were myth and legend, just like all the other gods worshipped in Noreela and perhaps beyond. Myth and legend.

As a Voyager, it had always been his one aim in life to find the truth. This greatest truth would make him the greatest Voyager.

He could see every step, every sigil carved into the wall of the giant staircase, every thin stalactite hanging from the ceiling and glimmering wetly in the complete darkness. He could see them because the god gave him sight beyond light. And it called him down.

Nomi shouted after him for a while, and then she started descending again. It would take her a long time. Ramus saw the way and he slipped down, down, not needing to count the steps because the god would let him know when he was nearing the bottom.

He came to a step whose edge had cracked and fallen away. He had to move in close to the central column to bypass the break, easing himself carefully down to the step below, only a foot's width of stone beneath his feet this close to the centre. Nomi could fall here, he knew, and for an instant there was a flicker of something within him. Concern? Grief, already? But then the god whispered words he could not hear or understand, and their tones drew Ramus on.

Nomi had called those things Sentinels. Perhaps they had been, once, but that must have been in some distant past. The ruined village spoke of their fall, and the remains of unknown technologies were testament to where they had once been, and where they were now. But there were two questions which rang in his mind. Had the Sleeping God brought them here to defend itself? Or had someone or something else placed them here, to guard the Sleeping God?

Perhaps even hours ago, Ramus would have found the answer to that question of utmost importance. But now the god smiled at his querying mind, lulled him with whispered appeasements, and he felt its breath on his skin once more.

The breath of a Sleeping God, he thought, and the pungent clammy breeze became sweet and comforting.

After a while, he came to the bottom of the large spiral staircase. He waited on the final step and listened, and from far above came the faint sounds of someone else descending. He could not make out whether it was one person or many. Perhaps Nomi was still ahead of the Sentinels, perhaps not.

The staircase opened out into a huge cavern. There was true light down here, emanating from great swathes of moss growing across the floor, up walls and onto the ceiling of the cave. In a far corner, a thousand specks of lights danced in the air, describing complex patterns that repeated again and again. Flies perhaps, or something else entirely. Here and there, the floor was taken with shallow pools of water, reflecting the wondrous stalactites that hung down from the ceiling and creating landscapes of fantastic cities that never were, but may one day be.

The cave was utterly silent but for Ramus's laboured breathing. He held his breath for a moment to take in the unspoilt wonder of this place.

Across the cave, in the shadows where floor and walls met in a drift of fallen rock, a darker shadow indicated the beginning of a tunnel. From that tunnel, illuminated from below by a splash of moss, came a faint waft of steam.

Where are you? Ramus thought.

The ground beneath his feet thumped, a gentle but definite movement, and the steam swirled as though disturbed from within.

Ramus walked across the cave. The flitting spots of light suddenly darted across the cave toward him and he hurried on, but they could move much faster. They gathered around him, never near enough for his waving arms to knock them aside, and this close he could hear the hum of tiny wings. As he walked so they moved, and he crossed the cave contained within a sphere of light. He could make out a curious synchronicity to their movements; some flitted this way, some the other way, and whole groups of light-flies seemed to be describing the same patterns in the air again and again. The movement resulted in regular, angled light drawings all around him, morphing every few beats into something equally as complex and wonderful. It was almost as if they acted with one mind.

Ramus reached the far edge of the cave and stood before the tunnel entrance. The air was warmer and damper here, and a wisp of steam caressed his face like the touch of a forgotten lover. Within, the presence in his mind smiled.

He entered the tunnel. The light-flies spread out a little, creating a larger, weaker area of illumination that moved with him. The tunnel was almost perfectly circular, the walls smooth except in a few places where stone had crumbled. In these places fleshy, gnarled plants peered through, like the impossibly deep roots of trees long-since vanished from the surface. Ramus wondered what he would find growing were he to excavate and pursue the course of these roots. The light gave the effect of the tunnel moving past him, rather than him moving through the tunnel. The walls flowed by, the floor whispered past his feet, and he was being carried closer.

The shape in his mind grew slightly and made itself known once more, swallowing down the discomfort of his illness and sheltering him from the pain. *Yes, now I am sure,* he thought.

The tunnel curved to the left and dipped down. He passed through places where moisture hung heavy in the air, and steam drifted in veils that seemed too dense to float. He felt these veils break around him, his senses expanded beyond the realities and potentials of his own life, and another thump transferred through the ground and into his feet.

He knew that he was below and far away from that building now, though he could not tell which direction he was taking. If the tunnel took him far enough north it would end at the Great Divide, but he thought that unlikely. This was a place very definitely of this new world.

Ramus lost track of time. The flies hummed around him, drawing light shapes in the air and illuminating his path, and when he stopped they stopped as well. He did so intermittently, listening for signs of pursuit. Nomi would come after him, her worry about what may be down here hiding the true reason for her descent: fascination. She wanted to see the god as much as he, and if he had suddenly turned around on that massive staircase and gone to leave, she would have continued down. They both wanted to be the first.

But he heard nothing behind him. If Nomi still came, she was keeping incredibly quiet. If the Sentinels had caught up with her...

The tunnel became warmer, more clammy, and he passed through thicker clouds of mist. Sometimes it seemed to touch and alter his perception of things, other times it simply dampened his clothes and beaded on his skin.

When the tunnel before him grew wider and taller, its walls splashed with light from beyond, the light-flies left.

He emerged into another cavern, much larger than the first. This one was home to a lake, its shores illuminated by the same curious moss, its surface reflecting the stunning array of stalactites that hung from the high ceiling. Perspective was difficult to make out with no real point of reference, but Ramus thought some of the hanging gallery of stalactites were the width of several men and fifty steps long. Their colours were a mixture of deep purples to a milky white, and all shades in between. Many seemed to strive to touch their reflections, though none broke water, and the only part of the high ceiling bare of them was directly above the island at the lake's centre.

Stone cones broke the water's surface here and there, a couple close to the shore and many more farther out. Steam rose gently from some and gushed from others. It condensed on the ceiling high above and sprinkled the cavern with intermittent rain. Some of the rain fell onto the island and gave that place a glimmering sheen.

The surface of the water broke here and there, agitated by shapes Ramus could not quite make out. They did not surface for long. He also saw skimming things, leaving lines of expanding ripples in their wakes. They were small and many-legged, though none were still long enough for him to properly make out. They seemed to avoid the water close to the island, and the spit of land stood in a spread of calm. It almost looked as though it floated in a sea of darkness.

The island…

There was a building there, made from the same stone as that tall, pyramidal structure above ground. This one was much simpler and more functional. A square, each side perhaps twenty steps in length, the flat roof twenty steps above ground.

'Is that you?' Ramus asked. The thing in his mind shifted, sending ripples through his thoughts like shock waves through a deep lake.

The walls of the building looked uneven, and though Ramus squinted he could not make out why. Rough stone? Carvings? He would have to cross the lake to find out. There were also eight or nine heavy, thick tubes protruding from the building, a couple of them curving out and dipping into the lake, the rest twisting and rising through the cavern and disappearing into the walls or ceiling. They looked to be made from stone, but he was certain that they pulsed.

'Are you in there?' The building suddenly drew all his senses, made itself the centre of his world, and the astonishing cavern and its flora and fauna faded away to the memory of a dream. There was Ramus and the building, and inside that building slept a god.

'I'll wake you,' Ramus said. His voice left him, and beats later it came back from the walls and ceiling of the cavern as a continuous whisper, an endless promise.

'Ramus,' a voice said.

Ramus blinked several times before remembering he could turn around. His muscles obeyed slowly, and he saw Nomi standing at the entrance to the tunnel. Steam flowed and twisted and made a wraith of her. It was only the blood on her face and the way she stood that confirmed to him that she was truly still alive.

※　※　※

Ramus looked as though he had never seen her before. Nomi tried to stand up straighter, not sure why she wanted to hide her injuries from him. She certainly did not expect pity. For some reason, she felt the need to seem strong.

'Ramus,' she said again. She looked past him into the cavern, saw the lake and the island and what was built thereon, and she knew they had found it. 'We have to go back.'

'You can't go back,' Ramus said, and she was not sure what he meant. He would not allow it? Or she would not?

I can, she wanted to say, but then she looked at the building again and realised how close they were to something remarkable. *No one ever meets their gods,* she thought.

'I'm going out there,' he said, pointing behind him without taking his eyes from Nomi's. 'I'm going to see what we've found, and I'll go inside and touch it, and...' His gaze shifted slightly to the side, his attention suddenly elsewhere. Somewhere far beyond here, or deeper inside.

'No one ever meets their gods,' Nomi said. 'Don't you wonder why?'

Ramus frowned and looked back at her, and she thought she had got through to him at last. But then he smiled. 'Because they never give themselves the chance.'

Nomi still held Lulah's knife. She took a painful step forward, wincing at the pain in her leg. Something was broken in there, she could feel it like a white-hot dagger slicing into her shin every time she moved. She'd slid down onto one of the stairs, found a chunk of it missing and fallen down three more. She was amazed she had not cracked her skull or broken her back.

'Did you fall?' he asked, and the question carried so much weight.

'Who are you asking?' Nomi said. 'You're looking at me, but are you asking something else?'

And then she heard the noises behind her. Feet shuffling across stone, whispers, the soft crackles of Sentinels. They may well be terrified, but that could only make them even more dangerous than before.

'It's fooled you,' she said. 'And the Sentinels are coming.'

'Then you can't go back.' Ramus held out his hand. 'Come with me.'

Nomi took a few more painful steps forward until she and Ramus were almost in touching distance. He lowered his hand but smiled, his offer standing.

'Out there?' she said. She looked over his shoulder, across the surface of the lake past steam cones and stone pipes, and things rippling the surface. 'Out there to that?'

'There's nowhere else to go.'

'Why are you asking me? One whisper and you could turn me to stone.'

Ramus frowned again as if listening to voices she could not hear. 'What we did to each other was in another world.'

The echoes of the Sentinels' approach passed them and muttered around the great cavern.

Nomi dropped the knife and held out her hand.

They would drown before they reached the island, or the things breaking the water's surface would kill them, or the Sentinels would arrive and take them down before they had a chance to move. Ramus had those words, but perhaps he would be too scared to use them in here, too fearful that the cavern's acoustics would distort them into something else over which he had no control. He seemed alternately fearful and ecstatic, and Nomi could not help feeling that he was now much more than he had ever been.

The dying Voyager walked around the edge of the cavern, climbing over fallen rocks, leaping dark crevasses, ducking beneath an overhanging gallery of stalactites whose ends looked unnaturally sharp in the weak light. The moss grew thick around the shores of the lake, exuding a low illumination and providing a soft carpet on which they could walk.

Nomi's leg screamed with every step, and she bit her lip to stop from crying out. Blood was already drying into a stiff scab across the side of her head and cheek, and every time she worked her jaw she felt the wound reopen and fresh blood flowing. *I'm badly hurt,* she thought, but it was a vague idea, as though this, too, mattered only in another world.

Nomi looked to her left at the island and the building that stood there. It seemed incongruous down here, its square edges the only unnatural things in sight. *How do we get out there?* she thought.

She was about to ask Ramus the same question when she heard the Sentinels arrive.

They emerged from the mouth of the tunnel and started hooting mournfully at the sight of the island. They pressed themselves against the wall of the cavern, as though trying to force themselves back through the stone, and for a moment they looked nowhere else. The enormity of what they were seeing seemed to steal their purpose.

Nomi was looking at one particular Sentinel when it turned its head and stared at her. Its mouth fell open, its long arm rose and it bellowed in rage.

'This way,' Ramus said. He walked directly toward the water.

'They're coming,' Nomi said.

'They won't follow.' Ramus stepped out into the lake. Ripples spread from his feet, slow and shallow as though the water were something thicker. He walked out several more steps and did not sink.

'How are you doing that?' Nomi asked, aghast. *What magic is this? What curse?*

'Follow me,' Ramus said. 'I know the way.'

The Sentinels were scampering around the edge of the cavern now, leaping over stones she and Ramus had climbed, loping across beds of luminous moss and throwing sparks behind. She had no choice.

Stepping out onto the water, Nomi prepared for the plunge. She knew that something had him – this was not the Ramus she knew, not really – and there was a potential about this place that seemed to seed itself in the air she breathed. It may well carry him, but it would send her down.

She did not sink. Her foot met something solid, and though she felt the coolness of subterranean water seeping into her worn boots, she also felt safe. She looked down and followed Ramus's footsteps, aiming for the centres of the rippling traces he had left behind. Even now, the splashes were fading. She hurried to catch up, trying to ignore the pain, because he strode quickly, never once doubting where his next step would take him.

The stepping stones were as black as the water around and above them. There was no way to see them without already knowing they were there. Nomi paused for a beat and glanced back, and already all traces of their passing had rippled away to smoothness.

The Sentinels were almost level with her now, twenty steps

away but separated by waters unknown.

This is where they follow, she thought. *They'll try for us, they have to, and some will find the way.*

The first Sentinel stepped out and sank up to its knee. It howled and withdrew, shaking water from its leg, and another shoved past it and tried again. This one found the first two stones before slipping and splashing heavily into the lake, arms flailing and bubbles rising as its head went under.

A shape rose and submerged, and when the Sentinel surfaced it was screeching, holding up its arm to display its chewed hand.

Nomi turned back to Ramus and had to hurry, just able to follow his steps before the waters smoothed over. She caught up with him, keeping pace for a while before looking back. They were still on the shore, the stricken Sentinel nursing its gnawed hand, the others striding back and forth but not actually touching the water.

'They won't come,' Ramus said.

'They will.' She thought of everything Sordon had told her, all his guilt wrapped up in the Sentinels' pure, perpetual purpose. 'All they know is keeping this thing down.'

Ramus paused and looked back at her, and his eyes were sparkling, shimmering like reflections in water. 'We're almost there,' he whispered.

The building was close now, not more than twenty steps away, and it seemed larger than it had appeared from the shore. The wall facing them was adorned with intricate symbols and lettering, and Nomi guessed the others were the same, and perhaps the roof as well. She could feel a steady vibration in the air, and sometimes the structure's walls seemed blurred as if it were moving, though the water lapping gently at the island's shore seemed undisturbed.

'There's something wrong,' Nomi said, not quite sure how to explain what she felt.

'It's amazing!' Ramus said. 'This is a treasure. Everything we've ever lived for, Nomi!' The Sentinels roared behind them. They were trying to cross the stepping stones again, but now they were moving in pairs. Every time one of them fell into the water, the one following on behind would continue, and another would leave the shore and hurry with uncanny precision across the stones they had already passed. At this rate, Nomi knew they would be on them soon...but Ramus seemed unconcerned.

'What do you know?' she asked.

'I know it's here, inside, a Sleeping God. Doesn't that amaze you?'

'It terrifies me. It's fallen, Ramus, and—'

'How can you truly know that?' he snapped, but his eyes betrayed him.

'*You* know that,' she said. 'You've known all along.'

Ramus hissed and shook his head, taking four more steps and then stepping onto the island.

'We have no idea what's going to happen!' Nomi shouted. 'We're just people, playing with gods!' She hurried after him, ignoring every instinct that screamed at her to turn around and flee. She was a Voyager, and with that came responsibilities she could never shirk.

When she reached Ramus, she grabbed his arm, and he turned and punched her in the face.

Nomi gasped and staggered back, but did not fall. Her vision blurred. The tears were not only from the pain.

'You never had any sense of greatness,' Ramus said. 'I

always sought…' He shook his head and waved a hand at her. 'Time moves on.' He crossed the few steps to the building's wall and pressed himself to the cool stone.

Something thumped through the cavern. It was as if the surface of the lake had been used as a great drum, and its impact echoed from the walls. The Sentinels fell silent for a beat and then hooted louder, most of them advancing, a couple falling from the stepping stones and trying to swim for shore. One of them made it. The other was taken down, a brief, frothy thrashing the only sign of its demise.

Nomi darted forward and grabbed Ramus's knife, drawing it smoothly and stepping back. It felt much heavier than it should, as though it carried the fates of worlds along its blade's keen edge. She held it by her side, the thought of threatening Ramus with it ridiculous. Yet this moment stretched on – Ramus pressed against the building, Sentinels clacking as they came closer across the lake, the air beating, throbbing – and Nomi knew that it had to be broken somehow.

'Nomi,' Ramus said. He closed his eyes. Next time he spoke, it was barely a whisper. 'It's alive.'

He turned his head, keeping contact with the stone. It was not as cool as it should have been.

Nomi had taken his knife and now held it down against her leg. Blood dripped from her wounded temple, and from where he had struck her lip. She favoured her left leg. She looked terrified and determined, and she had no idea what they had found.

'It's just beyond this wall,' he said. 'Living. Trapped, but alive.' It was there in his mind, larger than ever and striving for some sort of release.

'It's not for the likes of us,' Nomi said.

'The likes of us? You put us together, Nomi?'

'Of course.' She was staring at him unwaveringly, as though to see the building he was pressed against would change her mind. 'We're both Voyagers, and both Noreelans.'

'Both murderers?'

Nomi nodded. There was not even any hesitation, and that surprised Ramus.

'This is beyond such pettiness,' he said. He relinquished contact with the wall and started walking towards the building's corner. He trailed his right hand along the stone, feeling the dips and ridges of ancient carvings and inscriptions that he would never know. Whether they had been placed here as celebration or warning, he no longer cared. Time moved on, death racing birth, and sometimes a change was required.

'Ramus!'

He spun around, expecting to see Nomi coming at him with the knife. But she had her back to him now, knife held out towards the Sentinel that had just leapt from the final stepping stone and onto the shore.

For a beat, he almost went back. Two of them against the Sentinel would perhaps stand a chance. And he even took a step, reaching into the sheath on the back of his belt where he kept a spare knife. But the thing in his head sent a shadow across his mind, erasing the idea of rescue, stripping aside his last few moments' thoughts, and turning him once again onto his previous course of action. He felt no regrets or confusion, because he had made up his own mind. He acted of his own free will. That thing in his mind, holding back the pain of the sickness Nomi had given him…it was merely helping.

Ramus turned the corner of the building and walked

carefully along the base of the wall. He searched for the handholds he needed, and two-thirds of the way along he saw them, spaced unevenly up the wall in the body of an intricate carving. The image showed a creature he did not know, and he used its feet, knees, hips, wings, shoulders and horns to climb to the top.

He heard Nomi's scream, and shook his head to clear the sound.

The Sentinel did not pause to consider its actions; it simply stepped onto the island and came at her.

Nomi brandished the knife and stumbled back, struggling to keep her footing on the uneven ground. She could not help remembering Noon and the others fighting these things, and how the Serians had been quickly beaten. *So is this it?* she thought. *Killed by something inhuman in the belly of the Great Divide?*

Any hope that Ramus would come to her aid had vanished. He had asked her to come with him, but only to share in his discovery. Not because he cared. He had said they were past pettiness, and to Ramus perhaps everything that had been between them – the bad *and* the good – was all part of that.

The Sentinel clicked as it came, its almost-human face twisted with hatred...and fear. She could see that in its eyes and stance, and it was the first time she had seen anything in a Sentinel's expression other than sheer blankness.

Nomi fell aside and the creature's clawed hand cut through the air above her. She rolled until she felt the solidity of the building against her back, then stood, one hand holding the knife out, the other pressing against the wall.

The Sentinel turned and faced her, eyes growing wider.

Nomi felt something beneath her hand. The rock was warm, like the flesh of a living thing, and it *throbbed*. But she did not step away.

Another Sentinel gained the shore and approached from her left.

There was something watching her. Not with eyes, not with thoughts, but with a presence that lessened her humanity. She was a speck of dirt beneath an ant's foot, a fly crawling on a sheebok's hide. She gasped with the weight of insignificance and fell to her knees, and the lake erupted.

Nomi screamed.

Two things surged from the lake and struck the Sentinels, driving the creatures across the rocky shore and striking the building either side of Nomi. The Voyager scrabbled away on hands and knees, slipping on slick rock and falling onto her back. She could already hear the sounds of the Sentinels being torn apart, and her new aspect meant that she could not help but see.

The things looked like the crabs which fishermen in Long Marrakash hauled from the river mouth, except a hundred times larger. Bodies as long and wide as a human's, legs thick as her thighs, pincers wide enough to envelop her head, they thrashed and slashed at the Sentinels, spreading blood and shreds of flesh across the wall. It only took a few beats and then the crab creatures backed away, claws still snapping at the air. Their several eyes rose on stalks and surveyed what they had done. Then they backed away to the water, passing either side of Nomi, one of them actually brushing her hand with a stubbled leg. They submerged as quickly as they had appeared, leaving barely a ripple.

One of the Sentinels shifted and Nomi gasped, but it was only its bloodied torso slipping down the wall.

Carvings and symbols glittered with spilt blood. Nomi closed her eyes but she could smell the carnage, and when she managed to gasp in a fresh breath, she could taste blood and death on the air.

'Protecting you,' Ramus said from somewhere above her. His voice was casual and surprised, as though he had fully expected to find her dead.

'Piss on you,' Nomi said. Her throat hurt as she gasped in another breath, her chest heavy and tight. 'I don't want it to protect me.'

Ramus blinked, then looked up and behind her. 'More Sentinels coming,' he said. 'They won't be put off. Wait down there, see if it'll help you again.'

'Or?' Nomi said.

'Around the corner. You can climb. Footholds and handholds in the carvings, and we've had enough practice at that.'

'You left me to die,' she said, but the words held little power.

Ramus turned his back on her but remained standing on the edge of the roof, staring down at something at his feet.

'What's up there, Ramus?'

He did not answer. He was perfectly motionless, as if waiting for something to happen.

Nomi heard more Sentinels closing in on the island, undeterred by the fate of their cousins. Without even looking to see how close they were, she stood and hurried around the corner of the building.

The stone was warm, she thought. *Like something alive.*

She started to climb, pushing against the grating agony in her leg, suddenly convinced that Ramus would no longer be there when she reached the roof.

The only way in, he thought. *It has to be. But I can't open it yet.*

The Sleeping God had saved Nomi from the Sentinels, and there had to be a reason for that. The shadow in his mind bade him wait.

There was movement to his left. Nomi made the roof and stood, swaying slightly, wiping blood from her mouth. She still carried his knife but seemed to have forgotten about it. She glanced across the rooftop, the smooth stone with the circular mark at its centre, the places where the thick tubes joined like fluid limbs sprouting from a solid body. When she had taken it all in, she looked at him at last.

'It's so close,' he said. 'You and I, we can see it.'

'I don't want to see it,' Nomi said, but her voice betrayed her. Either she had given up hope of avoiding what must happen, or she was submitting to her true desires. The result would be the same.

Ramus wasted no time. He stepped to the centre of the roof and knelt beside the circular shape. He plunged his fingers into the groove and pulled them around, dislodging a thick drift of loose dust as he went. 'Help me,' he said.

'No.' Nomi knelt at the edge of the roof and watched.

Ramus dug out the whole circle, then drew his spare knife and began working at the crack with that.

'It can't be this simple,' Nomi said.

'Of course it can. It *wants* us in.'

'But whatever put it in there didn't. Can't you see that?'

Ramus shook his head. *It doesn't matter now,* he thought. *I'm so close. Nothing matters now but this.*

The stone beneath his knees was suddenly almost too hot to touch, and he rose into a crouch. A tendril of steam escaped the circular crack he'd cleared, hanging in the air like a condensed breath.

Ramus gasped again as his head pulsed with white-hot pain, and the presence there expanded quickly to smother it, casting it down and showing him the way.

'Ramus?' Nomi said, but her voice seemed very far away.

He put his knife into the groove and levered, and the circular stone slab rose easily. 'That side,' he said. 'Do the same. Push, lever.'

'No.'

'Nomi.' He saw her indecision, but also the knowledge that she could not turn back now. 'Please.'

She knelt opposite him, gasping at the pain from her damaged leg. When she probed with her own knife the stone slab seemed to rise almost of its own accord, and Ramus pushed at its revealed edge, sliding it onto the surface of the smooth roof.

Behind and below, the Sentinels hooted and clacked as more of them reached the shore of the island. No more crab things came, but they would if they were needed. Events were flowing now, histories being forged, and whatever his intrusion had awoken in the Sleeping God must surely be growing with every beat.

As if in response, another heavy throb sang through the cave, shaking the building beneath them and echoing from the oily surface of the water.

'What *is* that?' Nomi asked, but Ramus was sure she knew already.

Heartbeat, he thought.

Steam rose from the hole. A smell as well, like time gone off or life long forgotten.

Ramus sat back, wanting to see into the hole more than anything he'd ever wanted in his life. Yet he was also more terrified than he had ever been. The thing in his mind opened up into a grin, and a flash of agony coursed through his cancer as if to remind him of mortality.

'You should go first,' Nomi said.

Ramus locked eyes with her and leant forward, falling towards his future.

CHAPTER TWENTY-TWO

Ramus had spent a long time trying to imagine a Sleeping God, but he knew now that they were unimaginable.

He fell, struck a warm, leathery membrane and slid down its side. He hit one of the fleshy pipes that came through the ceiling and penetrated the huge sac at the building's centre, turning upside down and striking the soft floor on his shoulder. Pushing with his feet, pulling with his hands, he was soon pressed back into a corner of the room, staring at what sat before him.

It did not move, yet he knew that it was more than alive. The age of this thing hung in the air, a miasma of smells and sensations that he could not escape even if he closed his eyes. Its surface was hard and tensed, testament to the pressures within.

'I'm here,' Ramus whispered. His whole life had led to this.

There was more steam in here, but not as much as he had expected, and the open roof allowed some of it to vent to the outside. The walls and floor were warm, and not made of stone. The strange pipes strung across the cavern outside ended here, piercing the leathery surface and pinned there with stitching of shiny metallic clips. What metal they were made from, he did not know. Who had fixed them there, what had handled those clips and why, all were mysteries to him. But Ramus knew that his time of mystery was drawing to a close. Everything was about to change.

Nomi lowered herself through the hole. She was straining on her arms, looking down at what lay beneath her and sweating as she struggled not to step on it. But there was no alternative. She slipped, crying out as she fell, rolled and struck the floor across the room from Ramus. Out of sight, she spoke.

'What do we do, Ramus? What now?'

'Now it wakes,' he said.

Nomi stood in the far corner of the building, and he could see that she was terrified. Her eyes were wide, the left one surrounded with a dark sheen of fresh blood, and she stared directly at him. *How?* her eyes asked. Ramus smiled because he could see excitement there as well.

'It wakes,' he said, 'but I'm not sure how.'

'You've come all this way...?'

'I don't think it was ever truly asleep,' he said. 'Its body may be, but not its mind. That's alive. Dreaming of escape perhaps, or locked in nightmares about *never* being freed, but it's always active. Always waiting.'

'Waiting for someone like you?'

He nodded. 'Someone like me.'

'I hear them,' Nomi said, and Ramus heard them too. Clicking, hooting, the Sentinels were climbing the sides of the building, using their long legs and arms to haul themselves up onto the roof. They sounded wilder than ever, but Ramus thought it was probably fear. They made noise because silence would allow them to think.

'Cut the sac,' Ramus said. 'Put your knife in, Nomi, and let what's inside out.'

'It can't be that easy. After so long?'

'We can only try.' And the more Ramus thought about it, the simpler it became. The thing was trapped in there somehow, unable to break free of its own accord, but if someone willing to do the freeing came here, then why *should* it be difficult? This place was hidden from the rest of the land, protected by the Sentinels because of how simple it would be to wake.

'Nothing should sleep for ever,' Ramus said, and he placed the tip of his knife against the hard, leathery sac.

Shapes appeared at the circular hole above the centre of the room. Sentinels. They stared down with wide eyes and mouths hanging open, and for once they uttered nothing. They were looking at the thing with dreadful awe.

Ramus leant on his knife and pushed it through.

Age hissed out from the fresh wound. He held his breath, but he felt the warm exhalation against his neck and chest.

Words from the parchments came back to him, strange phrases other than the stone-curse he had used so much. The shadow in his mind seemed to filter them and make one phrase outstanding, and Ramus spoke it. He felt power throbbing out through the knife and into his hands.

The Sentinels screamed. They sounded like children being slaughtered, and they carried on screaming as they scrabbled away across the roof and fell to the ground outside. Others took up their scream – a wailing lament that filled the room and raised the hairs on Ramus's neck and arms.

He pushed harder and tugged at the knife, cutting upward. He muttered that phrase again, but this time it felt redundant, its purpose already achieved.

More air hissed out, and it had a brownish tinge.

'Nomi?' he said.

'I can't,' she said. She had backed into the corner and held the knife up before her, shaking as if she did not know which way to aim the blade; outward, or inward. 'What have we done?'

'Found a god,' Ramus said, but his voice sounded distant and insignificant now, and nothing he could say would match the grandness of this moment. So he fell silent as he worked the knife upwards, widening the cut and trying to see inside. It was too dark, and the air emerging was joined by a waft of steam that scorched his face, dried his eyes. He winced and stepped back. He still held the knife, aimed at another part of the sac, ready to start another cut...but it was not needed.

The sac shivered all across its surface. Dust shimmered into the damp air. The pipes protruding from the sac shook, and the junctions where they met the roof and walls cracked and poured dust and grit. Ramus saw for the first time that they were partly transparent, and something seemed to boil and roll within, like clouds driven into a frenzy by a terrible storm.

Shadows reached into the pipes. These shapes had defined edges, sharp against the tumult, and they bent and pressed against the fleshy sides, stretching them to the point of breaking.

The Sentinels screeched, Nomi shouted something, but Ramus did not understand. Language seemed superfluous against something so powerful and elemental.

The first pipe broke. Something gushed from it, a heavy

fluid that barely splashed when it touched the ground. Gases rose and twisted in the air, forming shapes that seemed to move of their own volition. A black, shiny thing protruded from the rent in the pipe. Its sharp end opened like a giant claw. It clicked shut again, and in that brief, violent sound Ramus heard laughter and weeping.

The Sentinels had fallen silent.

Another pipe ruptured, and another, and the chamber floor was covered with the slick, hot fluid. Vapours danced before Ramus's eyes and within, seemingly working their way into his mind and flirting with memories, toying with identity. He felt threatened and courted, and when he raised the knife it burnt his palm and fell into the fluid at his feet.

The things withdrew back into the sac, and for a while it was silent and motionless. The shapes trembling in the air dispersed into shapeless drifts, waving here and there with the effects of their combined exhalations.

I'm still breathing, Ramus thought. He remembered Ten, their journey south and the climb, and history flooded back in, returning his self. The presence was no longer in his mind with hands wrapped around his illness, ready to squeeze and coerce.

He looked away from the sac for a beat and Nomi was looking at him. She no longer seemed shocked, terrified or surprised. Her eyes now were full of blame.

'They've gone,' he said, nodding up at the roof.

Nomi shook her head, but she seemed unwilling or unable to talk.

I know, he thought. *Not gone. Just waiting. They know things have changed, and their purpose is dead.* He wondered whether the Sentinels would be murderous or suicidal.

The sac started to move. The gash where he had sliced it puckered open, fleshy lips parting, fluid flowing, vapours dancing once again.

And Ramus bore witness to a great rebirth.

A shadow rose. Nomi could hear the sound of ripping, see the dark things emerging from the sac, scratching at the stone wall behind Ramus and the ceiling above. They were similar to the claws on those crab-things outside but more complex, their shiny surface home to thousands of stiff hairs, joints silvery and almost metallic in appearance. Where they touched the walls, they carved deep scratches, and symbols began to take shape. The walls shook. The ceiling rattled, actually lifting up and down on the wall behind Ramus so that Nomi caught brief glimpses of the outside.

The ground shook, sending heavy ripples through the fluid that now covered the floor.

Ramus! she wanted to shout, but her voice had left her.

The thing rose before her old friend, colleague and enemy, and she could no longer see his eyes.

She looked up at the circular entrance hole. No faces there now, but she could see things falling from the cave's ceiling and hear the heavy splashes. Stone cracked, steam hissed and roared somewhere far off. The wall she was leaning against shook and she pushed herself away, but that did not lessen the vibration that seemed to move the air itself.

The Sleeping God was awake, the Fallen God had risen, and as it emerged from its place of rest or prison she could hear, above the sounds of the building and the cave beyond slowly destroying themselves, the creaks of its joints snapping back into use. It was vaguely reminiscent of the Sentinels' communication, and she wondered whether the god was speaking to them.

It heaved itself suddenly from the sack, reared up, and placed several black limbs against the stone ceiling. It lifted and threw, and as it spun into the darkness, the stone slab cracked in two.

Nomi looked up, amazed, exposed. To her left, she could see where one of the fleshy pipes spanned the cavern, and molten rock now gushed from where it entered the cave wall. It sprayed down and out, and though she could not see where it struck the lake, she *could* see the clouds of steam rising up. The hissing was almost unbearable. She looked around, searching for where the other strange pipes had led...

...and then she was no longer alone.

She felt its gaze upon her, piercing her skin and becoming a part of her, melting into her mind and casting Nomi aside. She sighed and slid down against the wall, but something closed around her chest and beneath her arms and held her there. Her head dipped and she saw the black flesh of the Fallen God. Each hair on that skin twitched and waved as if smelling or tasting, and something rippled beneath like a bag of snakes.

When she looked up, she stared into its face. *You are fallen,* she thought, because though she had never seen anything like it, its expressions were more human than she could have ever believed. Its six eyes exuded a sense of release. Its mouth hung open, dry lips cracking up and out in a triumphant grin. When its voice came, it shook the world, and it uttered dark promises she could never understand.

It lifted her and held her suspended above the roofless structure. She looked around at the storm – molten rock spewed from the places where pipes had once hung, the lake was a chaos of waves and violent steam columns, rocks cracked and tumbled from the walls and roof – and then she turned and looked for the Sentinels.

They were still there. A few stood below and to her left, still on the shores of the small island. Others had turned to flee. A couple made it to the far shore; several were washed away by waves. Whether they drowned or were killed by the things living there, Nomi could not tell. She looked back down at the Sentinels that had remained. None of them had eyes for her. She and her unborn child were meaningless to them now, because their charge had arisen. She realised that they were talking, clicks and groans that she could barely hear above the chaos of destruction from around the cave. They seemed suddenly very determined and calm. Her skin crawled. Her breath came short and hard, and at first she thought the Fallen God was squeezing her tightly. But the claws around her were loose, suspending rather than holding her.

It rose, Ramus clasped in another of its several hands. Limbs writhed above and around it, more forced against the ground below, and it turned its great triangular head to look at the Sentinels.

One limb snapped forward and sliced a Sentinel in two. The others stood their ground, and when the god drew its limb back it had turned from black to grey. But the god laughed – a terrible sound that made Nomi scream for the first time since it had emerged – and shook its arm. It shifted back to black.

They're trying, she thought. *Doing their best to remember the words they were given to guard against its release. But they've changed too much.*

The remaining Sentinels stepped forward, striving to form

their mouths into shapes more used to uttering cries and hoots than complex sounds.

The god kicked over the wall of its prison. Stone tumbled and killed two Sentinels, and the others stepped aside. It reached down and picked one up, casting it across the lake where something rose and snatched it from the surface. The remaining Sentinel stood its ground, brave and determined to the last, trying to utter lost words. The Fallen God picked it up and threw it hard, aiming for the closest gushing torrent of lava falling from the wall of the cavern. The creature disappeared in a flash.

'Ramus!' Nomi shouted, projecting her voice past the terror of what had happened. 'Those words!' Whether he heard her she was not sure, because he was hanging limp in the god's hand and staring up at its face. Its head turned this way and that, eyes turning individually as if revelling in sensory input. A falling rock struck its back and shattered. Another bounced from its head and caused a huge splash as the lake swallowed it up. 'Ramus!'

The god turned its attention to her again, then looked across at Ramus in another hand.

And now what? Nomi thought. *The water? The lava? Its mouth?* She closed her eyes and wished a quick end.

She felt herself moved through the air and then she was still again, and when she opened her eyes Ramus was a hand's breadth away from her. He stared at her, and she could not read his expression. Perhaps he was gone.

'Can you feel the power?' he asked, voice flat.

She nodded.

'No one should,' he said. 'No one, not now, not ever. This is more than Noreela can take. What have I...?'

'I tried to...' Nomi whispered.

Ramus closed his eyes and lowered his head.

The god pulled them apart again, then close together. It was as if it was testing to see whether they would punch or kiss. They did neither.

'Ramus,' Nomi said the last time they were close enough to talk. 'You have to say those words. They're the language of the Sleeping Gods, and now you're the only one that—'

'You want me to *destroy* it?' he asked, aghast. And he glanced into the eyes of the Fallen God, which in turn examined them.

Yes, Nomi thought as it pulled them apart. *Of course.*

It strode out across the lake and entered the tunnel. The ground shook around them, the air was on fire with the sounds of destruction, their way was lit by molten rock flowing across their path or visible through cracks in the walls, the earth quaked, and Nomi thought, *Yes, Ramus, destroy it.* But when she spoke, she could not even hear herself. And she knew that, even if the tumult did die down for a moment, Ramus was far beyond listening.

His god carried him up, sprinting up the staircase it had taken Ramus so long to descend. The ground below them was in turmoil, and in the tunnel the god had walked through streams of lava, nudged aside cave-ins and ground on through an avalanche of dust, diamonds and bones from some hidden opening. It held Ramus and Nomi close to its chest and used its body to protect them from danger. Ramus pressed his face to its slick, dark skin. It was surprisingly soft. He thought he heard its heartbeat, but it may have been earthquakes thumping through its feet.

It emerged into daylight at the top of the tall pyramid, shouldering its way through the opening and knocking aside the stone canopy. It stood there for a while, relaxing its arms so that Nomi and Ramus swung by its side. Ramus stretched down with his feet but could not quite reach the floor. And then it sighed. It was long and loud, like steam escaping a pierced chamber. It slumped slightly, relaxing, revelling in daylight for the first time in aeons. Then it turned its huge head to the north.

Ramus looked past the god's stomach at Nomi. She hung limp in its grasp, hair falling across her face. He could not tell whether she was awake, or even if she was alive. Perhaps a rock had struck her...

But no, the god was protecting them. Saving them, because they had saved it. Ramus wondered what came next.

A great explosion thundered in the south, rumbling through the air and following through the ground. The god staggered atop the pyramid and turned, allowing Ramus to see what had caused the noise. In the distance, over the heads of trees being consumed by fires from below, he saw the range of hills pluming flames and venting clouds of boiling smoke. Fireballs rose and rained down across the landscape, beautiful from this far away yet more destructive than anything Ramus had ever seen before.

The god made another noise, a long way from a sigh.

It turned north again, descended the building in several huge leaps and ran into the trees. Birds scattered before it or fell dead from the sky in shock. Other animals fled through the undergrowth or turned on each other. It paid scant attention to its surroundings, but when it stormed through the ruined village and emerged on the other side, a lone Sentinel stood ahead, stricken dumb and motionless with shock.

The god snapped it up in another limb and carried on running.

The Sentinel started clicking and calling, and Ramus saw fleeting grey shapes slicking across the god's pincers, but only briefly. It grumbled what could have been a laugh, snapped a tree with one kick and crushed the Sentinel down onto the jagged stump. It was the last Sentinel Ramus saw.

You have to say those words, Nomi had said. *They're the language of the Sleeping Gods.* He looked up at the thing carrying them – its massive head, six eyes, sturdy legs and the stumps of long-lost wings on its back – and shook his head.

'They won't work,' he said. He looked across at Nomi once more and she was looking at him. It was difficult to tell with the constant movement, but he thought she was crying.

Ramus was surprised to find his own cheeks damp with tears.

The Fallen God stood on the edge of the Great Divide and gazed down upon Noreela. The constant cloud cover was still there, but in the distance the hazy horizon showed a smudge of dark green, and closer by a slab of cliff had fallen away, forging a hole through the cloud that was still billowing. Far down, the ground. The Noreela this Fallen God had perhaps once known, before being sent down by its kin.

Nomi had no idea what it was about to do. It stood there for a long time, while all around it the tumult continued. The destruction was growing worse. The sky to the south was a furnace of towering clouds lit from within by unimaginable fires. From the east came a long, enduring grinding sound, seeming to shake the air in that direction so that it became blurred and indistinct. The noise went on and on, and Nomi hoped that Sordon Perlenni was already dead. Whatever he had turned into – whatever he had caused – she could not wish more suffering upon him.

Several miles to the west, another huge slice of cliff parted from the Divide and began to fall away. It seemed to take for ever, lowering down first as though the trees and bushes on its surface wanted to become a part of the ground below. Several hundred steps below the level of the plateau, it tilted out, crumbling and breaking as it tumbled eventually into the soft cloud cover and disappeared.

Flocks of birds poured past above them, all heading north. The sky had grown dark, lightning sparked here and there, and Nomi saw a thousand birds turned to ash. They drifted down, caught in thermals from Noreela below and held aloft for a final flight.

'What have you done?' a voice said, and she thought Ramus had come to his senses. *Yes*, she thought. *Accept it and make it better.* But Ramus was looking at her, and his mouth did not move as that voice spoke again. 'What have *I* done?'

She looked around, trying to see past the thing holding her, and she spied a swish of white hair behind them. 'Sordon,' she muttered. He came closer, staring up at the Fallen God with nothing but dread in his eyes. He was shaking his head slowly, grasping on to his walking stick with both hands, blood matting his beard from some injury. He did not look at Nomi or Ramus, only at the god. His mouth hung open, but he could say no more.

The god turned around.

It will know him, Nomi thought. *It will recognise him.* With one flick of a limb it had the First Voyager in its grasp, lifting him, twisting him this way and that as it examined him. And then it turned back towards Noreela and threw.

Nomi saw him fall.

'That was Sordon Perlenni,' Ramus said. He sounded as though nothing could surprise him ever again.

The god shifted forward, feet so close to the edge of the cliff that Nomi could look directly down. She saw the old man swallowed by the clouds. *This is it,* she thought. *Whatever it's about to do, this is it.*

'Drop me before you leap!' she shouted. 'I want to die my own death.'

Hold me with you, Ramus thought. He looked out and down, anticipating the rush of air as he and his god fell together. *And hold me tight. I want to be there when you return to Noreela.*

Nomi looked at Ramus and he looked at her, and she saw his right eye turn red as something gave out in his brain, blood gushing, pain twisting his face as the Fallen God rose onto its long legs and roared.

Kang Kang!

It relaxed again, breathing harshly, staring out and down with each of its six eyes. And then, having told Noreela its name for the first time in aeons, it turned its back on that land and fled south.

CHAPTER TWENTY-THREE

Nomi bore witness to the extinction of a world.

She was certain that Ramus was dead. That was the end of her world and the people she cared for, and to mirror that misery she watched the plateau they had found atop the Great Divide – bountiful, brutal, rich and mysterious – destroy itself. Those fleshy pipes that had pinned the Fallen God in place in that deep cavern must have been the final fail-safe. But there was something wrong, and Nomi was becoming more and more aware of this with every mile the thing ran, every obstacle it overcame.

A boiling river, heated from below and breathing steam from several bubbling parts, was no barrier. The Fallen God strode into the water and waded across, holding Nomi and Ramus high. Nomi gasped for air and felt her throat scorching and her lungs filling with fluid, but at the other side of the lake the thing ran on.

A hill exploded and sent a landslide against the god. It stood its ground and the rocks and dust parted around its legs and hips. When the cascade was over, it hauled itself out and continued its journey southward.

A deep ravine, which the Fallen God vaulted.

A river of molten rock which it walked across, leaping from one floating boulder to the next with an agility that belied its size.

It should have been destroyed, but it forged on. A score of times Nomi should have died, but somehow she survived. Protected by the god. Saved, for some special purpose.

Nomi had no desire to know what that purpose would be. But try as she did, she could not use the knife she still clasped on herself.

This is the final voyage, she thought. And there was some obstinate pleasure in knowing that, even after all his years up here and his century and a half of being so revered in Noreela, Sordon Perlenni had never seen anything like this.

The Fallen God finally stopped running and sat on top of a hill. To the south, a new volcano vented the land's molten guts, and everywhere earthquakes cracked the ground. Dust and smoke filled the air, and night fell before the sun went down.

It set Nomi and Ramus on the ground. There was nowhere to run, and it did not seem to be watching, but it took a long time for Nomi to find the courage to move. She crawled eventually to Ramus, enjoying the feel of cool, damp grass beneath her as the world around them sank into chaos.

Even when she reached out and touched him she was sure that he was dead. Yet he was warm, and when she lay down beside him and hugged him close, he mumbled something in his sleep. She did not catch the words. She thought perhaps he was speaking another language.

❊   ❊   ❊

When Ramus woke up, his god stood before him. He had been touched. He was blind in his right eye but the pain seemed to be gone from his head, the weight that had been growing behind his eyes for years now absent. It left a hole which Ramus thought he might fall into, but as he sat up and blinked, he realised that he felt better than he had for a long time.

He leant over to pay homage to the god, but it kicked him across the ground.

'Ramus,' Nomi said. Her voice came from above, and Ramus looked that way. Though it was still dark, there was enough light from fires and the volcano by which to see, and he made out Nomi's shadow grasped in the god's hand.

'Is this your nightmare?' he asked.

'No nightmare,' she said. 'Real.'

Ramus touched his head again, amazed that he felt so different.

The god turned and began to walk away.

'Wait!' Ramus shouted.

It went south, striding across the summit of the hill and heading down its far side to the burning forests beyond.

'Ramus!' Nomi screamed.

'Wait!' he shouted again, running after his god. 'Don't leave me here, not like this. Not *alone*!'

Nomi screamed again, and he could see her hands stretching out as though he could jump up and hold them, pull her back to him, rescue her from the thing they had awoken.

He ran, but even walking, the god outpaced him. Nomi's voice faded into the background chaos of the falling land. The god's shadow shifted left and right, and it was briefly silhouetted against a fire reaching hundreds of steps into the sky. Ramus stopped running. He thought he saw Nomi still in one of its hands, her hair flying and arms still outstretched.

'Wait,' he said weakly. 'No. Don't leave me. Don't *go*. Not without *me*.' He sank to his knees and watched his god disappear into fire.

Later – he did not know how much later – he rolled from his back onto his stomach and looked to the north. Something drew his attention that way, though he was not sure what. It was certainly not one of his senses, assaulted as they were by the destruction all around. Perhaps it was the new void inside his mind – that cured, hollowed place which left him feeling so lessened.

He saw three shapes drifting from north to south. He could not fully discern their forms, because they flew very high, above the clouds of smoke and steam, floating on distant air currents as yet untouched by chaos. His eyes stung from smoke and he wiped them, but his vision was no clearer.

They drew closer, and Ramus felt a sudden sense of history gathering around him; dreadful, powerful, endless, and way beyond the understanding of a simple human. He tried to avert his eyes. But he could not.

One of the shapes flew directly over him, high up, impossibly large, unknowable, distorted in his vision by the heat and smoke of the plateau's destruction. The other two drifted past to the east.

And in that moment, Ramus felt greatness passing him by.

He was certain that he would die there on that hillside. But when he did not die, he started walking north towards Noreela. He expected death at any moment, but it stayed away. *Three miles down,* he thought. *The cliff was three miles high, so it's three miles down. On the flat, I could walk that in a short morning between dawn and noon.*

It took more than a morning. Daylight and night-time were confused now, as the sky was blotted out by great sheens of dust, gas clouds rolled across the altered and still-changing landscape, and the sun seemed to have hidden itself away. After what he judged to be the first day of his new voyage, spent walking through tunnels exposed to the sky and across grassy plains now hidden below ground, Ramus began to think the god had left him with something. After the second day, during which he descended a sheer cliff into a new valley of sharp rocks, venting steam pits and boiling lava pools, he became more confident of his survival. Rain fell and he gathered water from rock pools, and here and there he found strange animals killed in the chaos and ate their flesh raw. If it poisoned him, so be it.

Sometimes he sat and wrote in his journal, aided by volcanic glows and arcing streams of lightning. He tried to tell everything that had happened. He drew pictures. But he knew that reading these words in the stark light of day would paint them a very different colour.

It was a place filled with spirits. He saw them from the corner of his eye, whispering things trying to form words that would not work. When he looked he saw only shadows or veils of steam, but he knew the spirits dwelt within. They watched him pass and they were many, and he sensed age emanating from them, as though each fleeting wraith was a lost memory of the fallen thing he had awoken, cast adrift and floating in search of somewhere else.

He did not know their language, but he was confident that they would make a home of this new place.

❋   ❋   ❋

Ramus went down, and every step should have been his last. The land was in turmoil and no natural features remained steady for long. Yet he missed landslides, dodged eruptions and found his way around new ravines and pits that seemed bottomless.

All the way down he mourned Nomi and tried to understand what they had done. And he wondered whether there would be a Noreela for him to return to.

Ramus Rheel, Voyager, should have died. Yet he lived. After four days walking, climbing, and descending into pits and ravines that should have been his grave, the land about him began to level out. Dust clogged the air and he coughed up thick wads of black phlegm. Tiredness beat him down but he ignored it, knowing that if he did stop to rest perhaps death would catch up with him. For a man who had lived life for so long knowing that he was dying, his determination to survive was a fire in his chest.

Sometimes, he dwelt on why the god wished him to survive, for it was clear to Ramus that was the case. The risen thing had blessed him to escape the changed and still-changing landscape of the Great Divide. But his was not the place to question a god.

After another day's travel, Ramus suddenly realised that there was dusty grass beneath his feet. The sun was still blocked out but he could see its smudge above him, tracking him through the clouds of steam and smoke as if eager to shine upon him once more. He walked on, voyaging across Noreela, and when he found one of the standing stones he had used to navigate south he sat down at last. When sleep claimed him, he had the first of Nomi's nightmares.

❈   ❈   ❈

She is in a world she cannot see. She is awake in a nightmare, and though she has been screaming, no one listens; no one cares. The Fallen God carries her tight against its chest as it strides through a land without edges or definition, a place where even the sky and ground are blurred into one. *It's here to make a whole new world,* Nomi thinks, and she does not want to be a part of it. The blurring passes by as the god moves ever-southward, leaving behind Noreela and whatever has become of the Great Divide, and heading into lands beyond comprehension or understanding. Sometimes there is a vague, terrible sense of pursuit, and for a while Kang Kang moves faster. And she wonders whether the god can see what she cannot, or if it is only imagining what will be.

She cries herself to sleep and cries herself awake, because she carries a new life in her womb. She knows that her own future is shattered. But perhaps whatever she gives birth to will be remade as a part of this new, unknown place.

There is no comfort in that at all. So Nomi screams, cries herself to sleep, cries herself awake.

Ramus could not travel that next day. His exertions caught up with him and he sheltered against the standing stone, putting it between him and what had become, and was still becoming, of the Great Divide. The ground still shook and cracked, the air stank of volcanic gases and dust, but Ramus sat there for the whole day and tried not to see Nomi's dreams again. He had not wanted them before, and he wanted them even less now, and he felt more cursed than ever because he was convinced the god had taken his illness away.

Later that day, the first travellers came by. They were wanderers, come this far south to feed their natural curiosity.

They eyed Ramus suspiciously for a while, and then the leader of the small group drew his sword and came forward. But when he saw Ramus's bloody eye, he put away his weapon and squatted by his side.

'What happened?' he asked in broken Noreelan, nodding towards the south.

And Ramus knew at last why the Fallen God had spared him. Because like any corrupt thing, it had its pride, and its ego, and it wanted its story told.

Ramus closed his eyes and fought hard against the words balancing on his lips.

'Kang Kang,' he spat, and then he groaned and thought, *I will not tell your tale. There might be a thousand more "what happened"s, but I will not tell.*

'Kang Kang?'

Ramus's eyes went wide and he sat up straight. 'I will not tell your story!'

The wanderer stood and backed away, evidently less certain now of his appraisal of this man.

'I *will* not!' Ramus shouted again. The Fallen God could become infamous, or it could fade away in time.

'Kang Kang!' one of the wanderer's children shouted, and she and her little brother started singing that terrible name, back and forth as though they could make their own stories, given time.

'No!' Ramus roared. *If I tell it they will* follow, *they will* search, *and however far it has gone, one day it might be found again.* And he whispered, 'I am the greatest Voyager.'

He pulled the small knife he had kept, grasped his tongue in his left hand and with one hard slice, took it off.

The wanderers were kinder than most. They did their best to stop the bleeding and tend him as a fever took hold. It burnt through him, scorching his skin and branding his mind with memories he did not want. When he woke from the fever there was a weight in his head once again, a familiar pain growing hotter and heavier, and his right eye was bleeding. He nodded his thanks and went on his way.

The wanderers watched him go. Ramus knew that they wondered about the story he could not tell.

He passed the standing stones and entered the forests, and here he set a fire. It was easy to burn his journal; it was incomplete and inaccurate, and as he tore out the pages and fed them to the flames he smiled at some of the foolishness written there. The parchment pages, old and new, should be next...but he held them in his hands for a while.

These were the last of their kind. Everything else was gone, swallowed in the turmoil of the fallen Great Divide. Blood and saliva dripped from his ruined mouth onto the uppermost page, staining the image of the god that Ramus had always known was fallen, and he closed his eyes.

He dropped the parchment pages onto the fire. When he looked again the only part left was the drawing of the god, dampened by his blood and spit. But soon even that burnt away to nothing.

At night, Nomi's nightmares came. And during the days when he walked north, away from the Great Divide and Kang Kang, away from Nomi, Ramus held on to the hope that they would not last for ever.